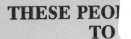

Then, suddenly, the invaders were *there*. Toller closed his throttle and allowed his fighter to coast while he snatched an arrow from one of his quivers. The oil-soaked wad at its tip caught fire as he thrust it into the hooded igniter cup. He nocked the arrow and drew the bow, feeling heat from the warhead blowing back on his face, and fired at the balloon of the nearest enemy ship. The vast convexity of the balloon was an absurdly easy target.

Toller's arrow needled into it and clung like a spiteful mosquito, spreading its venom fire; and already he was plunging down past the gondola and its doomed occupants. As he passed there came a spattering of flat reports, and splinters erupted from the wooden engine cowling scant inches from his left knee.

He was shocked by the speed with which the Landers had brought their muskets into action. *These people know how to fight!*

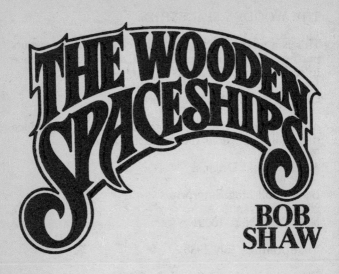

THE WOODEN SPACESHIPS

BOB SHAW

BAEN BOOKS

THE WOODEN SPACESHIPS

Copyright © 1988 by Bob Shaw

A Baen Books Original

Baen Publishing Enterprises
260 Fifth Avenue
New York, N.Y. 10001

First printing, July 1988

First paperback printing, July, 1989

ISBN: 0-671-69830-3

Library of Congress Cataloging-in-Publication Data

Shaw, Bob.
  The wooden spaceships.

  I. Title.
PR6069.H364W66   1988   823'.914   88-3512
ISBN 0-671-65419-5 (hardcover edition)

Cover Art by Alan Gutierrez

Printed in the United States of America

Distributed by
SIMON & SCHUSTER
1230 Avenue of the Americas
New York, N.Y. 10020

To M.E., with thanks

Contents

PART I

Gathering Shadows

Chapter 1

Lord Toller Maraquine took the bright sword out of the presentation case and held it in such a way that the foreday sun flamed along the blade. As before, he was captivated by its lucent beauty. In contrast to the black weapons traditionally used by his people it seemed to have an ethereal quality, akin to sunlight striking through fine mist, but Toller knew there was nothing unearthly about its powers. Even in its simplest, unmodified form the sword would have been the best killing instrument in history—and he had taken its development a step further.

He pressed a catch which was concealed by the ornamentation of the haft and a curved section sprang open to reveal a tubular cavity. The space was filled by a thin-walled glass vial containing a yellowish fluid. He made sure the vial was intact, then clicked its cover back into place. Reluctant to put the sword away, he tested its feel and balance for a few seconds and impulsively swept it into the first readiness position. At that moment his black-haired solewife, using her uncanny ability to materialise at precisely the wrong time, opened the door and entered the room.

"I beg your pardon—I had presumed you were alone." Gesalla gave him a smile of sweet insincerity and glanced all about her. "Where is your opponent, by the way? Have you cut him into pieces so small that they can't be seen, or was he invisible to begin with?"

Toller sighed and lowered the sword. "Sarcasm doesn't become you."

"And playing warriors doesn't become *you*." Gesalla crossed the floor to him, moving lightly and silently, and put her arms around his neck. "What age are you now, Toller? Fifty-three! When are you going to put notions of fighting and killing behind you?"

3

"As soon as all men become saints—and that may not be for a year or two yet."

"Who's being sarcastic now?"

"It must be infectious," Toller said, smiling down at Gesalla, deriving a pleasure from merely looking at her which had scarcely diminished in the long course of their marriage. Their twenty-three years on Overland, many of them hard years, had not materially altered her looks or thickened her gracile form. One of the few discernible changes in Gesalla's appearance was the single strip of silver which might have been applied to her hair by a skilled beautician. She still adopted a long and flowing style of dress in subdued colours, although Overland's burgeoning textiles industry was as yet unable to produce the gauzy materials she had favoured on the old world.

"At what time is your appointment with the King?" Gesalla said, stepping back and examining his clothing with a critical eye. It was sometimes a source of contention between them that, in spite of his elevation to the peerage, he insisted on dressing like a commoner, usually in an open-necked shirt and plain breeches.

"At the ninth hour," he replied. "I should leave soon."

"And you're going in that garb?"

"Why not?"

"It is hardly appropriate for an audience with the King," Gesalla said. "Chakkell may take it as a discourtesy."

"Let him take it any way he pleases." Toller scowled as he laid the sword in its leather case and fastened the lid. "Sometimes I think I've had my fill of royals and all their ways."

He saw the fleeting expression of concern on Gesalla's face and was immediately sorry he had made the remark. Tucking the presentation case under his arm, he smiled again to indicate that he was actually in a cheerful and reasonable mood. He took Gesalla's slim hand in his own and walked with her to the front entrance of the house. It was a single-storey structure, as were most dwellings on Overland, and had few architectural adornments, but the fact that it was stone-built and boasted ten spacious rooms marked it as the home of a nobleman. Masons and carpenters were still at a premium twenty-three years after the Great Migration, and the majority of the population had to make do with comparatively flimsy shelter.

Toller's personal sword was hanging in its belted scabbard in the entrance hall. He reached for the weapon and then, out of consideration for Gesalla, turned away from it with a dismissive gesture and opened the door. The precinct beyond glowed so fiercely in the sun that its walls and pavement seemed to be light sources in their own right.

"I haven't seen Cassyll today," Toller said as heat billowed in past him. "Where is he?"

"He rose early and went straight to the mine."

Toller nodded his approval. "He works hard."

"A trait inherited from me," Gesalla said. "You'll return before littlenight?"

"Yes—I have no wish to prolong my business with Chakkell." Toller went to his bluehorn, which was waiting patiently by a spear-shaped ornamental shrub. He strapped the leather case across the beast's broad haunches, got into the saddle and waved goodbye to Gesalla. She responded with a single slow nod, her face unexpectedly grave.

"Look, I'm merely going on an errand to the palace," Toller said. "Why must you look so troubled?"

"I don't know—perhaps I have a premonition." Gesalla almost smiled. "Perhaps you have been too quiet for too long."

"But that makes me sound like an overgrown child," Toller protested.

Gesalla opened her mouth to reply, changed her mind and disappeared into the house. Slightly disconcerted, Toller urged the bluehorn forward. At the precinct's wooden gate the well-trained animal nuzzled the lock actuating plate, a device Cassyll had designed, and in a few seconds they were out in the vivid grasslands of the countryside.

The road—a strip of gravel and pebbles confined by twin lines of rocks—ran due east to intersect the highway leading to Prad, Overland's principal city. The full acreage of Toller's estate was being cultivated by tenant farmers and therefore showed different shades of green in strips, but beyond his boundaries the hills had their natural uniformity of colour, a rich verdancy which flowed to the horizon. There were no clouds or haze to soften the sun's rays. The sky was a dome of timeless purity, with only a sprinkling of the brightest stars and an occasional meteor showing up against the overall brilliance. And directly above, gravitationally fixed in place, was the huge disk of the Old World, looming but not threatening—a reminder of the most momentous episode in all of Kolcorron's history.

It was the kind of foreday on which Toller would normally have felt at peace with himself and the rest of the universe, but the uneasiness caused by Gesalla's sombre mood had not yet faded from his mind. Could it be that she had a genuine prescience, intimations of forthcoming upheavals in their lives? Or, as was more likely, did she know him better than he knew himself and was able to interpret signals he was not even aware of giving?

There was no denying that of late he had been in the grip of a strange restlessness. The work he had done for the King in exploring and claiming Overland's single continent had brought him honours and possessions; he was married to the only woman he had ever loved and had a son of whom he was proud—and yet, incredibly, life had begun to seem flat. The prospect of continuing on this pleasant and undemanding course until he silted up with old age and died filled him with a sense of suffocation. Feeling like a betrayer, he had done his utmost to conceal his state of mind from Gesalla, but he had never yet managed to deceive her for long about anything. . . .

Far ahead of him Toller saw a small group of soldiers moving north on the highway. He paid them little heed for several minutes until it came to him that their progress towards Prad was unusually slow for a mounted party. In the mood to welcome any distraction, he took his small telescope out of his pouch and trained it on the distant group. The reason for their tardiness was immediately obvious—four men on bluehorns were escorting a man on foot who was almost certainly their prisoner.

Toller closed the telescope and put it away, frowning as he contemplated the fact that crime was virtually unknown on Overland. There was too much work to be done, few people had anything worth stealing, and the sparseness of the population made it difficult for wrongdoers to hide.

His curiosity now aroused, Toller increased his speed and reached the intersection with the highway shortly ahead of the slow-moving group. He brought his steed to a halt and studied the approaching men. Green gauntlet emblems on the breasts of the riders told him they were private soldiers in the employ of Baron Panvarl. The lightly built man stumbling along at the centre of a square formed by the four bluehorns was about thirty and was dressed like an ordinary farmer. His wrists were bound in front of him and lines of dried blood reaching down from his matted black hair showed that he had been roughly handled.

Toller had already decided that he had no liking for the soldiers when he saw the prisoner's eyes lock on him and widen in recognition, an event which in turn stimulated Toller's memory. He had failed to identify the man right away because of his dishevelled appearance, but now he knew him to be Oaslit Spennel, a fruit farmer whose plot was some four miles to the south. Spennel occasionally supplied berries for the Maraquine household, and his reputation was that of a quiet, industrious man of good character. Toller's initial dislike for the soldiers hardened into straightforward antagonism.

"Good foreday, Oaslit," he called out, advancing his bluehorn to block the road. "It surprises me to find you in such dubious company."

Spennel held out his bound wrists. "I have been placed under false arrest, my. . . ."

"Silence, dung-eater!" The sergeant leading the company made a threatening gesture at Spennel, then turned baleful eyes on Toller. He was a barrel-chested man, somewhat old for his rank, with coarse features and the glowering expression of one who had seen a great deal of life without benefiting from the experience. His gaze zigzagged over Toller, who watched impassively, knowing that the sergeant was trying to relate the plainness of his garb to the fact that he rode a bluehorn which sported the finest quality tack.

"Get out of the way," the sergeant said finally.

Toller shook his head. "I demand to hear the nature of the charges against this man."

"You demand a great deal—" The sergeant glanced at his three companions and they responded with grins. "—for one who ventures abroad unarmed."

"I have no need of weapons in these parts," Toller said. "I am Lord Toller Maraquine—perhaps you have heard of me."

"Everybody has heard of the Kingslayer," the sergeant muttered, augmenting the disrespect in his tone by delaying the correct form of address. "My lord."

Toller smiled as he memorised the sergeant's face. "What are the charges against your prisoner?"

"The swine is guilty of treason—and will face the executioner today in Prad."

Toller dismounted, moving slowly to give himself time to assimilate the news, and went to Spennel. "What's this I hear, Oaslit?"

"It's all lies, my lord." Spennel spoke quickly in a low, frightened monotone. "I swear to you I am totally without blame. I offered no insult to the baron."

"Do you mean Panvarl? How does he come into this?"

Spennel looked nervously at the soldiers before replying. "My farm adjoins the baron's estate, my lord. The spring which waters my trees drains down on to his land and. . . ." Spennel's voice faded and he shook his head, momentarily unable to continue.

"Go on, man," Toller said. "I can't help you unless I know the whole story."

Spennel swallowed audibly. "The water lies in a basin and makes the land swampy at a place where the baron likes to exercise his bluehorns. Two days ago he came to my house and ordered me to block the spring off with boulders and cement. I told him I needed the water for my livelihood and offered to channel it away from his land. He became angry and told me to begin blocking the spring without further delay. I told him there was little point in doing so, because the water would find another way to the surface . . . and it was . . . it was then that he accused me of insulting him. He rode off vowing that he would obtain a

8

warrant from the King for my . . . for my arrest and execution on a charge of treason."

"All this over a patch of muddy ground!" Toller pinched his lower lip in bafflement. "Panvarl must be losing his reason."

Spennel managed a lop-sided travesty of a smile. "Hardly, my lord. Other farmers have forfeited their land to him."

"So that's the way of it," Toller said in a low hard voice, feeling a return of the disillusionment which at times had almost made him a recluse. There had been a period immediately following the arrival of mankind on Overland when he had genuinely believed that the race had made a new start. Those had been the heady years of the exploration and settlement of the green continent which girdled the planet, when it had seemed that all men could be equal and that their old wasteful ways would be abandoned. He had clung to his hopes even when the realities of the situation had begun to become obtrusive, but eventually he had reached the point of having to ask himself if the journey between the worlds had been an exercise in futility. . . .

"Have no fear," he said to Spennel. "You're not going to die on account of Panvarl. You have my word on that."

"Thank you, thank you, thank you. . . ." Spennel glanced again at the soldiers and lowered his voice to a whisper. "My lord, is it in your power to free me now?"

Toller had to shake his head. "For me to go against the King's warrant would prejudice your case even further. Besides, it is more in accord with our purpose if you continue to Prad on foot—that way I can be there well ahead of you and will have ample time in which to speak to the King."

"Thank you again, my lord, from the bottom of my. . . ." Spennel paused, looking oddly ashamed of himself, like a merchant pressing for an advantage which even he conceded was unfair. "If anything *should* befall me, my lord, would you be so . . . would you inform my wife and daughter, and see to their . . . ?"

"Nothing untoward is going to happen to you," Toller said, almost sharply. "Now be at your ease as far as is possible and leave the rest of this sorry business to me."

He turned, walked casually to his bluehorn and hoisted himself into the saddle, feeling some concern over the fact that Spennel, regardless of the guarantees he had been given, still half-expected to die. It was a sign of the times, an indication that not only was he no longer in favour with the King, but that his fall from favour had been widely noted. Personally he cared little about such things, but it would be serious indeed if he found himself unable to help a man in Spennel's predicament.

He nudged his bluehorn closer to the sergeant and said, "What is your name?"

"What concern is that of yours?" the sergeant countered. "My lord."

To his surprise Toller experienced that flickering of redness at the edges of his vision which had always accompanied the most reckless rages of his youth. He leaned forward, stabbing with his eyes, and saw the challenging expression fade from the other man's face.

"I will ask you but one more time, sergeant," he said. "What is your name?"

The sergeant hesitated only briefly. "Gnapperl."

Toller gave him a broad smile. "Very well, Gnapperl—now we know each other and can all be good friends together. I am on my way to Prad for a private audience with the King, and the first thing I will do is ensure that Oaslit Spennel receives a full pardon for his imaginary crime. For the present I am placing him under my personal protection, and—I dislike mentioning this now that we have become good friends—if any misfortune were to befall him *you* would soon be overtaken by an even greater misfortune. I trust my meaning is clear. . . ."

The sergeant responded with a malevolent stare, his lips twitching as he debated making a reply. Toller gave him a nod of mock politeness, brought his mount around and put it into a fast canter. It was about four miles to Kolcorron's major city, and he could expect to be there at least an hour ahead of Gnapperl and his squad. Toller glanced up at the vastness of the sister planet, poised directly above him and occupying a large arc of the sky, and knew by the width of its sunlit crescent that he would be in good time for his appointment. Even with Spennel's release to

10

be negotiated he could still complete his mission and reach home again before the sun vanished behind the Old World—provided that the King was in a reasonable frame of mind.

The best approach, he decided, would be to play on Chakkell's antipathy towards the idea of his noblemen extending their territories. When the new state of Kolcorron had been founded, Chakkell—the first non-hereditary ruler in history —had sought to protect his position by severely limiting the size of aristocrats' domains. There had been some resentment, especially among those related to the old royal family, but Chakkell had dealt with it firmly and, in some cases, bloodily. Toller had been too busy to pay much attention.

Those early years now had a dreamlike quality in his memory. He could no longer readily visualise that wavering line of sky-ships, a stack a hundred miles high, drifting down from the zenith after the interplanetary crossing. Most of the craft had been dismantled soon after the landing, the balloon fabric going to make tents for the settlers, or in some cases being restitched to create envelopes for airships. On a whim of Chakkell's a number of the skyships had been preserved intact to form the basis of museums, but Toller had not viewed any of them in a long time. The inert, mould-encrusted reality of the ships was incompatible with the inspirational dynamism of that high point in his life.

On surmounting a fold in the land he saw the city of Prad in the distance, its centre cradled in the bend of a wide river. The city presented a strange appearance to his eye because, unlike Ro-Atabri where he had grown up, its origins lay in an abstraction, an architectural strategy. A cluster of tall buildings marked the core, oddly circumscribed and highly visible amid the green horizontals of the landscape, while the rest had only an attenuated existence. Patterns of future avenues and plazas were sketched on the terrain, sometimes with lines of timber dwellings, but for the most part with nothing more than posts and white-painted boulders. Here and there in the suburbs a stone-built official structure brought the plan a step closer to reality, each building suggestive of a lonely outpost under siege from armies of grass and scrub. In many areas nothing moved but the bubble-like ptertha, gently bounding across the open ground or nuzzling their way along fences.

Toller followed the straight highway into the city, a place he rarely visited. He passed increasing numbers of men, women and children who were on foot, and in the central section found a bustling atmosphere reminiscent of a market town on the Old World. The public buildings were in the traditional Kolcorronian style—featuring overlapping diamond patterns in vari-coloured masonry and brick—which had been modified to suit local conditions. Deep red sandstone should have been used to dress all corners and edges, but no useful sources had yet been found on Overland and the builders had substituted brown granite. Most of the shops and hostelries had been deliberately made to resemble their Old World counterparts, and in some areas Toller found it almost possible to imagine himself back in Ro-Atabri.

Nevertheless, the rawness and lack of finish of many structures reinforced his opinion that King Chakkell had tried to do too much too soon. Only twelve thousand people had successfully completed the journey to Overland, and although they were multiplying rapidly the population of the entire planet was less than fifty thousand. Many of those were very young and—as a result of Chakkell's determination to create a world state—were scattered in small communities all around the globe. Even Prad, the so-called capital city, housed less than eight thousand, making it a village uncomfortably glorified with the trappings of government.

As he neared the north side Toller began to catch glimpses of the royal palace on the far bank of the river. It was a rectangular building, architecturally incomplete, waiting for the wings and towers which even the impatient Chakkell had to entrust to future generations. The white and rose-coloured marble with which it was clad gleamed through ranks of immature trees. Within a few minutes Toller was crossing the single ornate bridge which spanned the river. He approached the brakka wood gates of the palace itself, where the chief of the guard recognised him and signalled that he should pass through unimpeded.

In the forecourt of the palace there were about twenty

phaetons and as many saddled bluehorns, an indication that this was a busy foreday for the King. It occurred to Toller that he might not get to see Chakkell at his appointed hour, and he felt a sudden stirring of anxiety on Spennel's behalf. The threat he had issued to the sergeant would cease to be effective in the presence of an executioner and high officials carrying death warrants. Toller dismounted, unstrapped the presentation case and hurried to the arched main entrance. He was admitted by the outer guards quickly enough, but—as he had feared—was stopped at the carved door of the audience chamber by two black-armoured ostiaries.

"I'm sorry, my lord," one of them said. "You are required to wait here until the King bids you enter."

Toller glanced at the other people, some of whom were wearing the sword-and-plume insignia of royal messengers, who were standing about the corridor in groups of two or three. "But my appointment is for the ninth hour."

"Others have been in attendance since the seventh hour, my lord."

Toller's anxiety increased sharply. He paced a circle on the mosaic floor while he came to a decision and then, making a show of seeming relaxed and untroubled, returned to the guards. When he engaged them in smalltalk they looked gratified, but not unduly so—their control of that particular doorway had enhanced their standing with many petitioners. Toller conversed with them for several minutes and was just beginning to have difficulty in dredging up suitable trivia when footsteps sounded on the far side of the double door.

Each ostiary swung upon a leaf and a small group of men dressed in commissioner's robes emerged, nodding in evident satisfaction at the outcome of their meeting with the King. A white-haired man who looked like a district administrator stepped forward, obviously expecting to be ushered into Chakkell's presence.

"My apologies," Toller murmured, moving ahead of him. The startled ostiaries tried to bar the way, but even in his early fifties Toller retained much of the speed and casual power which had distinguished him as a young soldier, and he thrust the two men aside with ease. A second later he was striding through the high-ceilinged room towards the dais upon which Chakkell was seated. Chakkell raised his head, alerted by the clattering of the ostiaries' armour as they came in pursuit of Toller, and his expression changed to one of anger.

"Maraquine!" he snapped, heaving himself to his feet. "What is the meaning of this intrusion?"

"It's a matter of life or death, Majesty!" Toller allowed the guards to seize him by the arms, but resisted their attempts to draw him back to the door. "An innocent man's life is at stake, and I beg you to consider the matter without delay. Also, I suggest that you order your doorkeepers to withdraw—they would be of little value were I obliged to separate their hands from their wrists."

His words caused the guards to redouble their efforts to move him, but Chakkell pointed a finger at them and slowly veered it to indicate the door. The guards released Toller immediately, bowed and backed away. Chakkell remained on his feet, eyes locked with Toller's until they were alone in the large room, then he sat down heavily and clapped a hand to his forehead.

"I can scarcely credit this, Maraquine," he said. "You *still* haven't changed, have you? I had hoped that my depriving you of your Burnor estates would have taught you to curb that damned insolence of yours, but I see I was too optimistic."

"I had no use for. . . . " Toller paused, realising he was taking the wrong road to his objective. He eyed the King soberly as he tried to gauge how much damage he had already done to Spennel's prospects. Chakkell was now sixty-five; his sun-browned scalp was almost devoid of hair and he was burdened with fat, but he had lost none of his mental vigour. He was still a hard, intolerant man—and he had lost little, if any, of the ruthlessness which had eventually gained him the throne.

"Go on!" Chakkell drew his eyebrows together to form a continuous bar. "You had no use for what?"

"It was of little consequence, Majesty," Toller said. "I apologise most sincerely for forcing my way into your presence, but I repeat that this is a matter of an innocent man's life, and there is no time to spare."

"What innocent man? Why do you trouble me with this?" While Toller was describing the events of the foreday Chakkell toyed with the blue jewel he wore on his breast, and at the end of the account he produced a calmly incredulous smile. "How do you *know* that your lowly friend didn't insult Panvarl?"

"He swore it to me."

Chakkell continued to smile. "So it's the word of some miserable farmer against that of a nobleman of this realm?"

"The farmer is personally known to me," Toller said urgently. "I vouch for his honesty."

"But what would induce Panvarl to lie over a matter of such little import?"

"Land." Toller gave the word time to register. "Panvarl is displacing farmers from his borders and absorbing their holdings into his own demesne. His intentions are fairly obvious, and—I would have thought—not to your liking."

Chakkell leaned back in his gilded chair, his smile broadening. "I get your drift, my dear Toller, but if Panvarl is content to proceed by gobbling up smallholdings one by one it will be a thousand years before his descendants can pose any threat to the monarchy of the day. You will forgive me if I continue to address myself to more urgent problems."

"But. . . ." Toller experienced premonitions of failure as he saw what was behind Chakkell's use of his given name and sudden accession of good humour. He was to be punished for past and present misdeeds—by the death of another man. The notion escalated Toller's uneasiness into a chilly panic.

"Majesty," he said, "I must appeal to your sense of justice. One of your loyal subjects, a man who has no means to defend himself, is being deprived of his property and life."

"But it *is* justice," Chakkell replied comfortably. "He should have given some thought to the consequences before he offered insult to Panvarl, and thus indirectly to me. In my opinion the baron behaved very correctly—he would have been within his rights had he struck the clod down on the spot instead of seeking a warrant."

"That was to give his criminal activities the semblance of legality."

"Be careful, Maraquine!' The genial expression had departed the King's swarthy face. "You are in danger of going too far."

"I apologise, Majesty," Toller said, and in his desperation decided to put the issue on a personal footing. "My only intention is to save an innocent man's life—and to that end may I remind you of a certain favour you owe me."

"Favour? *Favour?*"

Toller nodded. "Yes, Majesty. I refer to the occasion when I preserved not only your own life but those of Queen Daseene and your three children. I have never brought the matter up before, but the time has. . . ."

"Enough!" Chakkell's shout of incredulity echoed in the rafters. "I grant you that, while in the process of saving your own skin, you incidentally delivered my family, but that was more than twenty years ago! And as for never referring to the matter —you have used it over and over again when you wished to pry some concession out of me. Looking back through the years, it seems to have been your sole topic of conversation! No, Maraquine, you have traded on that one for far too long."

"But all the same, Majesty, four royal lives for the price of one ord—"

"Silence! You are to plague me no longer on that point. Why are you here anyway?" Chakkell snatched a handful of papers from a stand beside his chair and riffled through them. "I see. You claim to be bringing me a special gift. What is it?"

Recognising that for the moment it would be unwise to press the King further, Toller opened the leather case and displayed its contents. "A *very* special gift, Majesty."

"A metal sword." Chakkell gave an exaggerated sigh. "Maraquine, these monomanias of yours become increasingly tiresome. I thought we had settled once and for all that iron is inferior to brakka for weaponry."

"But this blade is made of steel." Toller withdrew the sword and was about to pass it to the King when a new idea occurred to him. "We have learned that ore smelted in the upper part of a furnace produces a much harder metal, one which can then be tempered to form the perfect blade." Setting the case on the

16

floor, Toller adopted a fighting stance with the sword in the first readiness position.

Chakkell shifted in his chair, looking uneasy. "You know the protocol about carrying weapons in the palace, Maraquine. I have half a mind to summon the guard and let them deal with you."

"That would provide a welcome opportunity for me to demonstrate the value of the gift," Toller said, smiling. "With this in my hand I can defeat the best swordsman in your army."

"Now you're being ridiculous. Go home with your shiny toy and allow me to attend to more important matters."

"I meant what I said." Toller introduced a degree of hardness into his voice. "The best swordsman in your army."

Chakkell responded to Toller's new note of challenge by narrowing his eyes. "The years appear to have weakened your mind as much as your body. You have heard of Karkarand, I presume. Have you any conception of what he could do to a man of your age?"

"He will be powerless against me—as long as I have this sword." Toller lowered the weapon to his side. "So confident am I that I am prepared to wager my sole remaining estate on the outcome of a duel with Karkarand. I know you are partial to a gamble, Majesty, so what say you? My entire estate against the life of one farmer."

"So that's it!" Chakkell shook his head. "I am not disposed to. . . ."

"We can make it to the death if you like."

Chakkell leapt to his feet. "You arrogant *fool*, Maraquine! This time you will receive what you have so assiduously courted since the day we met. It will give me the greatest pleasure to see daylight being let into that thick skull of yours."

"Thank you, Majesty," Toller said drily. "In the meantime . . . a stay of execution?"

"That will not be necessary—the issue will be settled forthwith." Chakkell raised a hand and a stoop-shouldered secretary, who must have been watching from a spyhole, scurried into the room through a small doorway.

"Majesty?" he said, bowing so vigorously as to suggest

17

to Toller that he had acquired his posture through years of deference.

"Two things," Chakkell said. "Inform those who wait in the corridor that I am departing on other business, but they may take consolation from the fact that my absence will be brief. *Extremely* brief! Secondly, tell the house commander that I require Karkarand to be on the parade ground three minutes from now. He is to be armed and prepared to carry out a dissection."

"Yes, Majesty." The secretary bowed again and, after casting one lingering and speculative look at Toller, loped away towards the double door. He was moving with the eager gait of one for whom a dull day had suddenly shown promise of memorable entertainment. Toller watched him depart and, having been granted time for thought, began to wonder if he had overstepped the bounds of reason in his championing of Spennel.

"What's this, Maraquine?" Chakkell said, his former joviality returning. "Second thoughts?" Without waiting for a reply he crooked his finger and led the way out of the audience chamber by means of a curtained private exit.

As he walked along a panelled corridor in the King's wake Toller suddenly glimpsed a mind-picture of Gesalla at the moment of their parting, her grey eyes deeply troubled, and his misgivings increased. Had some intuitive power enabled her to *know* that he was setting out to court danger? The meeting with Spennel and his captors had been pure coincidence, of course, but Toller lived in a society where violent death was not uncommon, and in previous years he had been unperturbed by reports of summary and unjust executions. Could it be that, in his mood of destructive discontent, he would have sought out a way —even without the chance encounter on the road to Prad—to place himself in a position of peril?

If he had been unconsciously trying to put himself in danger he had been spectacularly successful. He had never set eyes on Karkarand, but he knew the man to be a rare phenomenon—a gifted sword fighter, unhampered by any trace of morality or regard for human life, with a physique so powerful that he was rumoured to have dispatched a bluehorn with a single blow of his fist. For a middle-aged man, regardless of how well he was armed, to pit himself against such a killing machine was an act of recklessness bordering on the suicidal. And, as the ultimate flourish of idiocy, he had wagered the estate which supported his family on the outcome of the duel!

Forgive me, Gesalla, Toller thought, mentally cringing from his solewife's level gaze. *If I survive this episode I'll be the model of prudence until the day I die. I promise to be what you want me to be.*

King Chakkell reached a door which led to the outside and, in a complete reversal of protocol, pulled it open and gestured for Toller to precede him into the parade ground beyond. Some remnant of a sense of propriety caused Toller to hesitate, then he noticed Chakkell's smile and understood the symbolism of his action—he was happy to suspend the normal rules of conduct for the privilege of ushering an old adversary out of the world of the living.

"What ails you, Toller?" he said, jovial once more. "At this point any other man would be having second thoughts—are you, perhaps, having first thoughts? And regrets?"

"On the contrary," Toller replied, returning the smile, "I'm looking forward to some gentle exercise."

He set the presentation case down on the gravelled surface of enclosed ground and took out the sword. There was comfort to be gained from the balanced weight of it, the sheer *rightness* of the way it took to his hand, and his anxiety began to abate. He glanced up at the vast disk of the Old World and saw that the ninth hour was just beginning, which meant he could still reach home before littlenight.

"Is that a blood channel?" Chakkell said, looking closely at the steel sword for the first time and noticing the groove which extended down from the haft. "You don't go in to the hilt with a blade that long, do you?"

"New materials, new designs." Toller, who had no wish for the weapon's secret to be revealed prematurely, turned away and scanned the line of low military quarters and stores which bounded the parade ground. "Where is this swordsman of yours, Majesty? I trust he moves with greater alacrity when in combat."

19

"That you will soon discover," Chakkell said comfortably.

At that moment a door opened in the farthest wall and a man in line soldier's uniform emerged. Other soldiers appeared behind him and spread out sideways to merge with the thin line of spectators who were noiselessly materialising on the ground's perimeter. The word had spread quickly, Toller realised, attracting those who anticipated seeing a dash of crimson added to the dull monochrome of the palatial day. He returned his attention to the soldier who had come out first and was now walking towards him and the King.

Karkarand was not quite as tall as Toller had expected, but he had a tremendous breadth of torso and columnar legs of such power that he progressed with a springy gait in spite of the massiveness of his build. His arms were so packed with muscle that, unable to hang vertically at his side, they projected laterally at an angle, adding a touch of monstrousness to his already intimidating appearance. Karkarand's face was very broad, yet narrower than the trunk of his neck, its features blurred by a reddish stubble. His eyes, which were fixed on Toller, were so pale and bright that they seemed to fluoresce in the shadow of his brakka helmet.

Toller immediately understood that he had made a serious mistake in issuing his challenge to the King. Before him was a creature, less a human being than an engine of war, who had no real need of artificial weapons to supplement the destructive forces nature had built into his grotesque frame. Even if successfully disarmed by an opponent he would be capable of pressing the engagement through to a lethal conclusion. Toller instinctively tightened his grip on his sword and, choosing to wait no longer, depressed a stud on its haft. He felt the glass vial within shatter and release its charge of yellow fluid.

"Majesty," Karkarand said in a surprisingly melodious voice as he approached and saluted the King.

"Good foreday, Karkarand." Chakkell's tone was equally light, almost conversational. "Lord Toller Maraquine—of whom you will doubtless have heard—appears to have become enamoured with death. Be a good fellow and cater to his wishes at once."

"Yes, Majesty." Karkarand saluted again and in a continuation of the movement drew his battle sword. In place of standard regimental markings the blackness of the brakka wood blade was relieved by crimson enamel inlays in the shape of blood droplets—a sign that its owner was a personal favourite of the King. Karkarand unhurriedly turned to face Toller, his expression one of calmness and mild curiosity, and raised his sword. Chakkell moved several paces back.

Toller's heart began to pound as he made himself ready, speculating as to what form Karkarand's attack would take. He had half-expected a sudden onslaught which would have been designed to end the duel in a second or so, but his opponent was playing a different game. Moving slowly forward, Karkarand lifted his sword high and brought it down in the kind of simple direct stroke that might have been used by a small child at play. Surprised by the other man's lack of finesse, Toller automatically parried the blow—and nearly gasped aloud as the incredible shock of it raced back through his blade, twisting and loosening the haft in his fingers, causing a geysering of pain in his hand.

The sword had almost been struck from his grasp by Karkarand's first blow!

He tightened numb fingers on the still-reverberating haft just in time to counter an exact repetition of the first stroke. This time he was better prepared for the devastating power of it and his sword remained secure in his grip, but the pain was more intense than before, surging back into his wrist. Karkarand kept moving forward at his deliberate pace, repeating the downward blow without any variation, and now Toller understood his opponent's strategy. This was to be death by contempt. Karkarand had indeed heard of Lord Toller Maraquine, and he was determined to enhance his own reputation by simply walking through the Kingslayer like an automaton, annihilating him in a demonstration of sheer strength. *No special skill was required*, was to be the message to the onlookers and the rest of the world. *The great Toller Maraquine was easy meat for the first real warrior he ever encountered.*

Toller leapt back well clear of Karkarand to gain some respite from the punishing contacts with the black sword and to give himself time in which to think. He could see now that Karkarand's weapon was thicker and heavier than an ordinary battle sword—more suitable for formal executions than prolonged combat—and only one possessed of superhuman strength could use it effectively in a duel. The heart of the problem, however, lay in the odd fighting style which had been adopted by Karkarand. An unrelenting series of vertical strokes was probably the best technique, albeit chosen unwittingly, for countering the secret additional power of Toller's steel sword. If he wanted to survive—and thereby prove his point—he would have to force a radical change in the style of combat.

Hardening his resolve, Toller waited until Karkarand's sword was again raised above his head, then he went in fast and blocked the coming downstroke by locking the two blades together at the hilt. The move took Karkarand by surprise because it could only have been completed successfully by an opponent of greater physical strength—and such was manifestly not the case. Karkarand blinked, and then with a snort of gratification bore downwards with all the power of his massive right arm. Toller was able to resist for only a few seconds before being obliged to yield, and as his opponent's drive gained momentum he was actually forced into an undignified backwards scramble which almost ended in a fall.

The onlookers, who had advanced to form a circle, raised some ironic applause—a sound in which Toller detected a note of anticipation. He played up to it by bowing towards Chakkell, who responded with an impatient signal to continue with the duel. Toller wheeled quickly on his opponent, now feeling satisfied and relieved, knowing that the upper sections of the two blades had been in contact long enough for Karkarand's weapon to have been liberally smeared with yellow fluid.

"Enough of this play-acting, Kingslayer," Karkarand growled as he drove forward with yet another of the swishing, murderous vertical strokes.

Instead of fending it off to the right, Toller—using smallsword technique—swept his blade over and around the blow, and concluded the movement by striking across the line of it. Karkarand's sword snapped just below the hilt and the black blade tumbled away across the gravel. Running a few paces towards the ruined weapon, Karkarand emitted a cry of anguished surprise which was amplified by the stillness which had descended over the crowd.

"What have you done, Maraquine?" King Chakkell bellowed, his paunch surging as he strode forward. "What trickery is this?"

"No trickery! See for yourself, Majesty," Toller called out, his attention only partially centred on the King. The duel would have been ended or suspended had the normal Kolcorronian rules been in force, but he had assessed Karkarand as a man to whom behavioural codes meant nothing, who would always go for the kill using any means at his disposal. Toller faced the King for only an instant, judging the time available to him, then spun with his sword held level in a glittering horizontal sweep. Karkarand, who had been running at him with the organic club of his fist upraised, slid to a halt with the point of Toller's sword in his midriff. A crimson stain spread quickly in the coarse grey weave of his tunic, but he held his ground, breathing heavily, and even seemed to be pressing forward regardless of the metal which was penetrating his flesh.

"Make your choice, ogre," Toller said gently. "Life or death."

Karkarand stared at him wordlessly, still without backing off, eyes reduced to pale venomous slits in the vertically compressed face, and Toller found himself making ready for an action which had become foreign to his nature.

"Use your brains, Karkarand," Chakkell said, reaching the scene of the confrontation. "You would be of little use to me with a severed spine. Return to your duties immediately—this matter may be concluded another day."

"Majesty." Karkarand stepped backwards and saluted the King without once allowing his gaze to stray from Toller's face. He turned and marched away towards his quarters, the ring of spectators hastily parting to let him through. Chakkell, who had been happy to indulge his subjects as long as he had believed Toller would be slain, made a dismissive gesture and the crowd rapidly dispersed. Within seconds Toller and Chakkell were alone in a sunlit arena.

"Now, Maraquine!" Chakkell extended his hand. "The weapon!"

"Of course, Majesty." Toller opened the compartment in the haft, revealing the shattered vial bathed in yellow ooze, and a pungent smell—reminiscent of the stench of whitefern—permeated the warm air. Holding the sword by the lower part of the blade, Toller passed it over to Chakkell for inspection.

Chakkell wrinkled his nose in distaste. "This is brakka slime!"

"A refinement of it. In this form it is easier to remove from one's skin."

"The form is of no account." Chakkell looked down and nudged the discarded handle of Karkarand's sword with his foot. The black wood of the blade stump was visibly seething and frothing under the action of the destructive fluid. "I still say you resorted to trickery."

"And I maintain there was no trickery," Toller countered. "When a superior new weapon becomes available only a fool stubbornly clings to the old—that has always been a precept in military logic. And from this day forward weapons fashioned from brakka wood are obsolete." He paused to glance up at the looming convexity of the Old World. "They belong up there—with the past."

Chakkell returned the steel sword and broodily paced a circle before again locking eyes with Toller. "I don't understand you, Maraquine. Why have you gone to such lengths? Why have you taken such pains?"

"The felling of brakka trees has to stop—and the sooner the better."

"The same old tune! And what if I suppress all details of your new toy?"

"It's already too late for that," Toller said, turning a thumb towards the line of military quarters. "Many soldiers saw the steel sword survive the worst shocks that Karkarand could inflict, and they also saw what happened to his blade. It is beyond the power of any ruler to restrict that kind of knowledge. Soldiers will always talk, Majesty. They will feel uneasy, and resentful, if required to go into battle armed with weapons they know to be inferior. If in future there were to be an insurrection

24

—perish the thought!—the traitor leading it would ensure that his soldiers were equipped with steel swords of this new pattern. That being the case, a hundred of his men could rout a thous—"

"Stop!" Chakkell clapped his hands to his temples and stood that way for a moment, breathing noisily. "Deliver twelve examples of your damned sword to Gagron of the Military Council. I will speak to him in the meantime."

"Thank you, Majesty," Toller said, taking care to sound gratified rather than triumphant. "And now, about the reprieve for the farmer?"

There was a stirring in the brown depths of Chakkell's eyes. "You can't have everything, Maraquine. You overcame Karkarand by deceit—so your wager is lost. You should be grateful that I am not claiming the stipulated payment."

"But I made my terms clear," Toller said, appalled by the new development. "I said I could defeat the best swordsman in your army as long as I held *this sword* in my hand."

"Now you're beginning to sound like a cheap Kailian lawyer," Chakkell said, his smile stealing back by degrees. "Remember you're supposed to be a man of honour."

"There is only one here whose honour is in question."

The words he had spoken—his own sentence of death—quickly leached away into the surrounding stillness, and yet it seemed to Toller that he could hear them still being chanted, slow-fading in the passageways of his mind. *I must have planned to die*, he told himself. *But why did my body proceed with the scheme on its own? Why did it make the fatal move so quickly? Did it know my mind to be an irresolute and untrustworthy accomplice? Does every suicide recriminate with himself as he contemplates the empty poison bottle?*

Bemused and numb—stone-faced because the last thing he could do was to show any sign of regret—Toller waited for the King's inevitable reaction. There was no point in trying to apologise or make amends—in Kolcorronian society death was the mandatory punishment for insulting the ruler—and there was nothing Toller could do now but try to shut out visions of Gesalla's face as she heard how he had engineered his own demise. . . .

"In a way, it has always been something of a game between us," Chakkell said, looking reproachful rather than angry. "Time after time I have allowed you to get away with things for which I would have had any other man flayed; and even on this foreday—had your bout with Karkarand taken its natural course —I believe I would have stayed his sword at the end rather than see you die. And it was all because of our private little jest, Toller. Our secret game. Do you understand that?"

Toller shook his head. "It is entirely too deep for the likes of me."

"You know exactly what I'm saying. And you know also that the game ended a moment ago when you broke all the rules. You have left me with no alternative but to. . . ."

Chakkell's words were lost to Toller as, looking over the King's shoulder, he saw an army officer come running from a doorway in the north wall of the palace. Chakkell must have given a secret signal, Toller decided, his heart lurching as he tightened his grip on the steel sword. For one pounding instant he considered making the King his hostage and bargaining his way to the open countryside and freedom, but the obdurate side of his nature came to the fore. He had no relish for the idea of being hunted down and trapped like a bedraggled animal—and, besides, the act of threatening Chakkell would rebound on his own family. It would be better by far to accept that he had entered the last hour of his life, and to depart it with what remained of his dignity and honour.

Toller stepped clear of Chakkell and was raising his sword when it came to him that the orange-crested captain was hardly behaving like an arresting officer. He was not accompanied by any of the palace guard, his face was agitated and he was carrying binoculars in place of a drawn sword. Far behind him other soldiers and court officials were reappearing at the edges of the parade ground, their faces turned to the southern sky.

". . . if you make no attempt to resist," Chakkell was saying. "Otherwise, I will have no recourse but to. . . ." He broke off, alerted by the sound of approaching footsteps, and wheeled to face the running officer.

"Majesty!" the captain called out. "I bear a sunwriter message from Airmarshal Yeapard. It is of the utmost urgency." The captain slid to a halt, saluted and waited for permission to continue.

"Get on with it," Chakkell said irritably.

"A skyship has been sighted south of the city, Majesty."

"Skyship? Skyship?" Chakkell scowled at the captain. "What is Yeapard talking about?"

"I have no more information, Majesty," the captain replied, nervoulsy proferring the leather-bound binoculars. "The airmarshal said you might wish to use these."

Chakkell snatched the glasses and aimed them at the sky. Toller dropped his sword and reached into his pouch for his telescope, narrowing his eyes as he picked out an object shining in the south, about midway between the horizon and the disk of the sister world. With practised speed he trained the telescope, centring the object in a circle of blue brilliance. The magnified image produced in him a rush of emotion powerful enough to displace all thoughts of his imminent death.

He saw the pear-shaped balloon—impressively huge even at a distance of miles—and the rectangular gondola slung beneath it. He saw the jet exhaust cone projecting downwards from the gondola, and even discerned the near-invisible lines of the acceleration struts which linked the upper and lower components of the airborne craft. And it was the sight of the struts—unique to the ships designed more than twenty years earlier for the Migration—which confirmed what he had intuitively known from the start, adding to his inner turmoil.

"I can't find anything," Chakkell grumbled, slewing the binoculars too rapidly. "How can there be a skyship anyway? I haven't authorised any rebuilding."

"I think that is the point of the airmarshal's message," Toller said, keeping his voice level. "We have visitors from the Old World."

Chapter 2

The thirty-plus wagons of the First Birthright expedition had travelled too far.

Their timbers were warped and shredded, little remained of the original paintwork, and breakdowns had become so frequent that progress was rarely as much as ten miles a day. In spite of adequate grazing along the route, the bluehorns which provided the expedition's motive power were slouched and scrawny, weakened by water-borne diseases and parasitical attacks.

Bartan Drumme, pathfinder for the venture, was at the reins of the leading wagon as the train straggled up to the crest of a low ridge. Ahead of him had unfolded a vista of strangely coloured marshland—off-whites and sickly lime greens predominating—which was dotted with drooping, asymmetrical trees and twisted spires of black rock. The sight would have been un-appealing to the average traveller, but for one who was supposed to be leading a group of hopefuls to an agricultural paradise it was deeply depressing.

Bartan groaned aloud as he weighed various factors in his mind and concluded that it would take at least five days for the party to reach the horizontal band of blue-green hills which marked the far edge of the swampy basin. Jop Trinchil, who had conceived and organised the expedition, had been growing more and more disillusioned with him of late, and this new misfortune was not going to improve the relationship. Now that Bartan thought of it, he realised he would be lucky if any of the other farmers in the group continued to have dealings with him. As it was, they only spoke to him when necessary, and he had an uneasy feeling that even the loyalty of his betrothed, Sondeweere, was becoming strained by his lack of success.

Deciding it would be best to face the communal anger square-ly, he brought his wagon to a halt, applied the brake and leapt down on to the grass. He was a tall, black-haired man in his mid-twenties, slim-built and agile, with a round boyish face. It was that face—smooth, humorous, clever-looking—which had led to some of his previous difficulties with the farmers, most of whom were inclined to distrust men not cast in their own mould. Aware that he already had enough problems to cope with in the next few minutes, Bartan did his utmost to look competent and unruffled while he signalled for the train to halt.

As he had anticipated, there was no need for him to call a meeting—within seconds of glimpsing the dismal terrain ahead, the farmers and their families had quit their wagons and were converging on him. Each of them appeared to be shouting something different, creating a confusion of sound, but Bartan guessed that their scorn was about equally divided between his ability as a pathfinder and this latest in a series of infertile, unworkable tracts of land. Even small children were staring at him with open contempt.

"Well now, Drumme—what fanciful tale have you for us this time?" demanded Jop Trinchil, arms folded across the pudgy billows of his chest. He was grey-haired and plump, but he carried his excess weight with ease and had hands which looked like natural farming implements. In a straight fight it was likely that he would be able to dispose of Bartan without even getting out of breath.

"Tale? Tale?" Bartan, playing for time, chose to sound indignant. "I don't trade in tales."

"No? What was it when you told me you were familiar with this territory?"

"I told you I had flown over the region several times with my father, but that was a long time ago—and there is a limit to what one can see and remember." The final word of the sentence was out before Bartan could check it, and he cursed himself for having given the older man another opportunity to use his favourite so-called witticism.

"I'm surprised you even remember," Trinchil said heavily, glancing about him to solicit laughs, "to point your spout away from yourself when you piss."

And I'm surprised you even remember where your spout is, Bartan thought, keeping the riposte to himself with difficulty as those around him, especially the children, burst into immoderate laughter. Jop Trinchil was Sondeweere's legal guardian, with the power to forbid her to marry, and reacted so badly each time he was bested in a verbal duel that she had made Bartan vow never to score over him again.

"I see no profit in going any farther west," a blond young farmer called Raderan put in. "I vote we turn north."

Another said, "I agree—if the bluehorns last long enough we're going to end up arriving back where we started, but from the other direction."

Bartan shook his head. "If we go north we'll only drive into New Kail, which is already well settled, and you will be obliged to split up and take inferior plots. I thought the whole purpose of the expedition was to claim prime land for yourselves and your families, and to live as a community."

"That *was* the purpose, but we made the mistake of not hiring a professional guide," Trinchil said. "We made the mistake of hiring *you*."

The truth contained in the accusation had a greater effect on Bartan than the vehement manner in which it was delivered. Having met and fallen in love with Sondeweere he had been devastated to learn that she was leaving the Ro-Amass vicinity with the expedition, and in his determination to be accepted by Trinchil and the others he had exaggerated his knowledge of this part of the continent. In his ardour he had half-convinced himself that he could recall the broad geographical features of a vast area, but as the wagons had groped their way west the inadequacies of his memory and handful of sketch maps had become more and more apparent.

Now he was reaping the reward for his manipulation of himself and others, and something in Trinchil's manner was making him fear that the reward might contain an element of physical pain. Alarmed, Bartan shaded his eyes from the sun and studied the shimmering marshland again, hoping to pick out some feature which would have a stimulative effect on his memory. Almost at once he noticed a kink in the horizontal line which was the area's far boundary, a kink which might indicate a narrow extension of the marsh in a river-bed. How would that look from the air? A thin white finger pointing west? Was he deceiving himself again or was there just such an image buried in some recess of his mind? And was it linked to an even fainter vision of lush, rolling grasslands traversed by clear streams?

Deciding to take the final gamble, Bartan produced a loud peal of laughter, using all his vocal skills to make it sound totally natural and unforced. Trinchil's silver-stubbled jaw sagged in surprise and the discontented babble from the rest of the group abruptly ceased.

"I see nothing amusing in our situation," Trinchil said. "And even less in yours," he added ominously.

"I'm sorry, I'm sorry." Bartan giggled and knuckled his eyes, the picture of a man fighting to control genuine merriment. "It was cruel of me, but you know I can't resist my little jokes—and I just *had* to see your face when you thought the whole venture had come to naught. I do apologise, most sincerely."

"Have you lost your reason?" Trinchil said, hands clenching into huge leathery clubs. "Explain yourself at once."

"Gladly." Bartan made a theatrical gesture which took in the whole of the marshy basin. "You will all be delighted to hear that yonder dish of mildewed porridge is the very landmark for which I have been aiming since the outset. At the other side of it, just beyond those hills, you will find an abundance of the finest agricultural land you have ever seen, stretching for league upon league in every direction, as far as the eye can see. My friends, we are almost at journey's end. Soon our days of toil and tribulation will be over, and we will be able to lay claim to the. . . ."

"That's enough of your wind," Trinchil shouted, raising his hands to damp the rising note of excitement among some of the onlookers. "We have suffered this kind of rhetoric from you too many times in the past—why should we believe you this time?"

"I still say we should turn north," Raderan said, stepping forward. "And if we're going to do that it would be best to do it from here rather than waste time circling that swamp on the say-so of a fool."

"Fool is too kindly a word for him," said Raderan's hulking gradewife, Firenda. After a moment's thought she suggested what she considered a more appropriate description, bringing a gasp from several of the other women, and an even more ecstatic howl of laughter from the children.

"It is well that you are protected by your skirts, madam," Bartan protested, privately doubting his ability to stand up to the giantess for more than a few seconds, and to his dismay she immediately began to fumble with the knot of her waistcord.

"If it is only my shift that deters you," she grated, "we can soon. . . ."

"Leave this to me, woman!" Trinchil had drawn himself up to his full height and was conspicuously asserting his authority. "We are all reasonable people here, and it behoves us to settle our disputes through the exercise of reason. You would agree with that, wouldn't you, Mister Drumme?"

"Wholeheartedly," Bartan said, his relief tempered by a suspicion that Trinchil's intentions towards him had not suddenly become charitable. Beyond the circle of people he saw the yellow-haired figure of Sondeweere part the canopy of a wagon and begin to descend to the ground. He guessed she had hung back, knowing he was in fresh trouble and not wishing to increase his discomfiture with her presence. She was wearing a sleeveless green blouse and close-fitting trews of a darker shade. The garments were quite standard for young women in farming communities, but it was evident to Bartan that she wore them with a special flair which distinguished her from all the others, and which signified equally rare qualities of mind. Even with his present difficult situation to occupy his thoughts, he was able to take a keen pleasure in the graceful, languorous movement of her hips as she climbed down the side of the wagon.

"That being the case, *Mister* Drumme," Trinchil said, moving towards Bartan's wagon, "I think the time has come to rouse your sleeping passenger and make her start paying her way."

This was the moment Bartan had been hoping to avert since the beginning of the expedition. "Ah . . . It would occasion a lot of hard work."

"Not as much hard work as crossing those hills and perhaps finding a swamp or desert on the other side."

"Yes, but. . . ."

"But what?" Trinchil tugged at the wagon's stained canvas cover. "You *have* got an airship in here, and you *can* fly it, can't you? If it transpired that you had turned my niece's head with a pack of lies I would be very angry. More angry than you have ever seen me. More angry than you can even *imagine*."

Bartan glanced at Sondeweere, who was just reaching the edge of the group, and was taken aback to see that she was gazing at him with an expression which was frankly questioning, not to say doubtful. "Of course, my airship is in there," he said hurriedly. "Well, it's more of an air*boat* than an airship, but I can assure you that I am an excellent pilot."

"Ship, boat or coracle—we're listening to no more of your excuses." Trinchil began unfastening the cover and other men willingly went forward to help him.

Not daring to object, Bartan watched the operation in a mood of increasing gloom. The airboat was the only object of any value he had inherited from his father, a man whose passion for flying had gradually impoverished and eventually killed him. Its airworthiness was extremely dubious, but Bartan had concealed that fact when presenting the case for his being allowed to join the expedition. An aerial scout could be of great value to the commune, he had argued, and Trinchil had reluctantly assigned wagon-space to the craft. There had been several occasions during the journey when reconnaissance from the air would indeed have been worth the trouble of sending the boat aloft, and each time Bartan had tested his ingenuity to the limit by devising plausible reasons for remaining on the ground. Now, however, it looked as though the day of reckoning had finally arrived.

"See how eagerly they scrabble," he said, taking up a position beside Sondeweere. "It's like a sport to them! Anyone would think they doubted my ability as a pilot."

"That will be soon put to the test." Sondeweere spoke with less warmth than Bartan would have liked. "I only hope you're better as a pilot than as a guide."

"Sondy!"

"Well," she said unrepentantly, "you must admit you've made a fine pig's arse of everything so far."

Bartan gazed down at her in wounded bafflement. Sondweere's face was possibly the most beautiful he had ever seen—with large, wide-spaced blue eyes, perfect nose and well-delineated voluptuous lips—and his every instinct informed him she had an inner loveliness to match. But now and then she would make an utterance which, taken at its face value, indicated that she was quite as coarse as some of the slovens with whom circumstances of birth had forced her to associate. Was this a matter of deliberate policy on her part? Was she, in her own way, warning him that the agricultural life he was about to embrace was not for milksops? His thoughts were abruptly diverted to more practical matters by the sight of a farmer aboard the wagon picking up a green-painted box and preparing to drop it to the ground.

"Careful!" Bartan shouted, darting forward. "You have crystals in there!"

The farmer shrugged, unimpressed, and lowered the box into Bartan's hands.

"Let me have the purple one too," Bartan said. When he had received the second box he tucked one under each arm and carried them to a safe resting place on a flat-topped boulder. The green pikon and purple halvell crystals—both extracted from the soil by the root systems of brakka trees—were not really dangerous unless allowed to mingle inside a sealed container. But they were expensive and difficult to obtain outside the largest communities, and Bartan was very solicitous with the small quantities remaining to him. Accepting that he was now virtually committed to making a flight in spite of the hazards involved, he began to supervise the unpacking and assembly of the airboat.

Although the little gondola was extremely light he had no worries about its strength, and the jet engine—being made of brakka wood—was practically indestructible. Bartan's main concern was with the gasbag. The varnished linen of the envelope had been in doubtful condition when he had packed it, and the long period of stowage in the back of the wagon was likely to have caused further deterioration. He inspected the material and the stitching of the panels and load tapes as the gasbag was being rolled out to its full length on the ground, and what he found added to his misgivings about the proposed flight. The linen had a papery feel to it and there were numerous loose ends of thread wavering on the tapes.

This is madness, Bartan thought. *I'm not going to get myself killed for anybody.*

He was choosing between the alternatives of facing up to Trinchil and simply refusing to fly, or of surreptitiously disabling the boat by putting a hole in the envelope, when he noticed that a change was coming over the other members of the group. The men were asking questions about the construction and operation of the craft, and were listening to his replies with interest. Even the unruliest children had become more respectful in their manner. It slowly dawned on Bartan that the settlers and their families had never been close to a flying machine before, and a sense of wonder was stirring to life inside them. The boat and its strange mechanisms, seen for the first time, were proof that he really was a flier. Within minutes his status had improved from that of mistrusted novice farmer, a liability to the commune, to that of a man possessing arcane knowledge, rare skills and a godlike ability to walk the clouds. His new eminence was very gratifying—and it was a pity it was destined to be so brief.

"How long would it take to reach the hills with a device like this?" Trinchil said, with no trace of his usual condescension.

"Thirty minutes or so."

Trinchil whistled. "It is truly wondrous. Are you not afraid?"

"Not in the least," Bartan said, regretting that he could no longer delay making his position clear. "You see, I have absolutely no intention of trying to fly this. . . ."

"Bartan!" Sondeweere arrived at his side in a swirling of yellow tresses and put an arm around his waist. "I'm so *proud* of you."

He did his best to smile. "There's something I ought. . . ."

"I want to whisper." She drew his head down, at the same time applying her body to his in such a way that he felt the warm pressure of her breasts against his ribs and her pubis nuzzling into his thigh. "I'm sorry I was rude to you," she breathed in his ear. "I was worried about us, you see, and Uncle Jop was getting

35

into such a dark mood. I couldn't *bear* it if anything got in the way of our marriage, but now everything is all right again. Show them all how wonderful you are, Bartan—just for me."

"I. . . ." Bartan's voice faded as he became aware that Trinchil was staring at him with an inquisitive expression.

"You were about to say something." There seemed to be a rekindling of the old animosity in Trinchil's eyes. "Something about not flying."

"Not flying?" Bartan felt Sondeweere's hand slide down his back and come to rest on his buttocks. "No, no, *no*! I was going to say I'd be in no danger because I have no intention of trying to fly too fast, or of performing any injudicious aerobatics. Aviation is a business with me, you know. Strictly a business."

"I'm glad to hear it," Trinchil said. "I'd be the last man in the world to tell another how to conduct his business, but may I offer you a pertinent piece of advice?"

"Please do," Bartan replied, wondering why he found the older man's grin less than reassuring.

Trinchil clamped an enormous hand on each of Bartan's shoulders and gave him a mock-playful shake. "If, by any chance, you *fail* to find good land beyond those hills—keep on flying in a straight line and be sure to put as many leagues as you can between the two of us."

The boat was handling well and—had he not been fearful of a sudden and catastrophic failure of the gasbag—the experience of being airborne again might have produced an equivalent lift in Bartan's spirits.

Enigmatic though it had seemed to the farmers, the engine designed and built by his father had only three basic controls. A throttle fed pikon and halvell into a combustion chamber, and the hot miglign gas thus generated was exhausted through an aft-facing jet pipe to propel the boat. The pipe could be swivelled laterally by means of a tiller to give some directional control; and when required another lever diverted gas upwards into the envelope to create and maintain buoyancy. As miglign was lighter than air, even when cool, the assemblage was compact and efficient.

Bartan took the boat to a height of fifty feet and sailed it in a circle around the wagons, partly to please Sondeweere, mainly to check that the extra strain of turning would not be too much for the attachment gussets. Relieved at finding the craft still airworthy for the time being at least, he gave a stately wave to the watching farmers and set a course to the west. It was just past noon, with the sun very close to the zenith, so he was riding in the protective shadow of the gasbag and could view his surroundings with unusual clarity. The marshlands stretched out ahead of him like pastel-tinted snow, in contrast to which the distant hills seemed almost black. Apart from the occasional flash of an extra-bright meteor there was little to be seen in the sky. Its brilliance was overpainting all but the brightest stars, and even the Tree—the most important constellation in the southern heavens—was barely visible to his left.

After a few minutes of uneventful flight Bartan began to cease worrying about his safety. The intermittent sound of his jet was fading quickly in the pervasive stillness, and he had little to do but hold his course, now and then pumping the pneumatic reservoir which force-fed crystals to the engine. He might have been able to enjoy the sortie had it not been for Jop Trinchil's parting words, and once again he found himself regretting that he had never been able to persuade Sondeweere to leave the Birthright group.

He had been only two years old at the time of the Migration and had no real memories of the event, but his father had told him much about it and had given him a good understanding of the historical background. When the ptertha plague had forced King Prad to build an evacuation fleet capable of flying to Overland from the sister world, Land, there had been strong opposition from the Church. The basic tenet of the Alternist religion had been that after death the soul flew to Overland, was reincarnated as a baby, lived out another life and returned to Land in the same way, part of an eternal and immutable process of exchange. The proposal to have a thousand ships physically undertake the voyage to Overland had been an affront to the Lord Prelate of the day, and the riots he led had threatened the whole enterprise, but the Migration had been accomplished despite adverse conditions.

When Overland was found to have no human inhabitants, no counterpart to Land's civilisation, religious conviction had largely ceased to exist among the colonists. The fact that it had not disappeared entirely was, according to Bartan's father, a triumph of stubborn irrationality. *All right, we were mistaken*, was the argument advanced by the remnants of the devout. *But that was only because our minds were too puny to appreciate the grandeur of the plan devised by the Great Permanence. We know that after death the soul migrates to another world, and so inadequate was our vision that we presumed that other world to be Overland. We now realise that the departing soul's actual destination is Farland. The High Path is much longer than we realised, brethren.*

Farland was roughly twice as distant from the sun as the Land-Overland pair. It would be many centuries before ships from Overland would be able to undertake that kind of journey, Vlodern Drumme had concluded—passing his natural cynicism to his son—so the high priests had made a good choice. Their jobs were safe for a long time to come. . . .

He had been wrong on that point, as it had transpired. In designing Overland's infant society, King Chakkell—an old enemy of the Church—had made certain it contained no vestiges of a state religion. Satisfied with having abolished the clergy as a profession, the King had occupied himself with other matters, careless of the fact that his edicts had created a vacuum to be filled by a new kind of preacher, of whom Jop Trinchil was a good example.

Trinchil had embraced religion late in life. At the age of forty he had willingly taken part in the interworld migration, with no qualms about desecrating the High Path, and for the most part his life on Overland had been one of unremitting hard work on a smallholding in the Ro-Amass region. On nearing his sixties Trinchil had become disillusioned with the normal pattern of agricultural life and had decided to be a lay preacher. Unlettered, uncouth in word and manner, inclined to violence, he nevertheless had a raw force of personality which he was soon exerting over a small congregation, whose donations hand-somely supplemented the rewards of his own physical toil.

Finally, he had conceived the idea of leading a flock of the faithful to a part of Overland where they could practise their religion without interference—especially from busybodies who might report Trinchil's illegal activities to the prefect in Ro-Amass.

It was during the preparations for the Birthright Expedition that Trinchil's and Bartan Drumme's paths had intersected. Bartan had been earning a reasonable, if irregular, income by selling cheap jewelry of his own design and manufacture. Normally his commercial judgment was sound, but for a brief period he had allowed himself to become infatuated with the appearance of the newly discovered soft metals, gold and silver. As a result he had been left with a batch of trinkets he found almost impossible to sell in his normal markets, where there was a conservative preference for traditional materials such as glass, ceramics, soapstone and brakka. Refusing to be discouraged, he had started touring the rural areas around Ro-Amass in search of less discerning customers, and had met Sondeweere Trinchil.

Her yellow hair had bedazzled him more than gold had done, and within minutes he was hopelessly in love and dreaming of taking Sondeweere back to the city as his solewife. She had responded favourably to his overtures, obviously pleased by the prospect of marrying a man whose appearance and manner contrasted so sharply with those of the average young farmer. There had been, however, two major obstacles to Bartan's plans. Sondeweere's desire for novelty stopped short of any interest in changing her way of life—she was adamant that she would never live anywhere but on a farm. Bartan's reaction had been to discover within himself a hitherto dormant passion for agriculture and an ambition to work his own plot of land, but the second problem had been far less amenable to a quick solution.

Jop Trinchil and he had taken an immediate dislike to each other. There had been no need for a conflict of interests, or even for a word to be spoken—the mutual antagonism had sprung into existence, deep-rooted and permanent, on the very instant of their first meeting. Trinchil had decided at once that Bartan would be an abject failure as husband and father; and Bartan had known, without having to be told, that Trinchil's only interest in religion was as a means of lining his pocket.

Bartan had to admit that Trinchil was genuinely fond of his niece, and although he seized every opportunity to complain about Bartan's shortcomings he had not forbidden the marriage. That had been the situation up to the present, but Bartan had a feeling that his future was in the balance, and his state of mind had not been improved by Sondeweere's behaviour at the impromptu meeting. She had acted as though her love was beginning to waver, as though she could turn away from him if he failed to make good his latest promise.

The thought caused Bartan to concentrate his gaze on the irregularity at the far edge of the swampy basin. Now that he was closer and higher he was almost certain that it indeed represented an extension of the marsh into an arroyo, in which case the chances that he actually was recalling an aerial view were somewhat improved. Wishing his memory was more trustworthy, he fed several bursts of hot miglign into the gasbag which swayed above him, and slowly he gained the height he would need for crossing the hills. The spires of rock rearing up from the pale surface shrank to the semblance of black candles.

In a short time the boat was scudding over the marsh's ill-defined boundary and Bartan was able to confirm that a narrow finger of it ran due west for about two miles. With increasing confidence and excitement he followed the course of the ancient waterway. As grassy contours rose up beneath the boat he saw groups of deer-like animals, disturbed by the sound of the jet, make swerving runs, with white hindquarters beaconing their alarm. Frightened birds occasionally erupted from trees like wind-borne swirls of petals.

Bartan kept his eyes on the slopes ahead. They seemed to form a barrier which was being raised higher and higher to block his view, then he was crossing a ridge and with dramatic suddenness the horizon receded, fleeing into the distance before him. The intervening space was revealed as a complex vista of savannahs, gentle hills, lakes and occasional strips of woodland.

Bartan gave a whoop of glee as he saw that the territory,

spilling out in front of him like a rich man's hoard, was a homesteader's dream translated into reality. His first impulse was to turn the airboat and head back to Trinchil and the others with the good news, but the hillside was shelving away beneath him now in a silent invitation to fly onwards. He decided it would do no harm to spend a few extra minutes in getting a closer and more detailed view of the nearer tracts, and perhaps to locate a stream which would afford a good preliminary stopping place. It would help impress on the farmers that he was a competent and practical man.

Allowing the boat to lose altitude naturally through the cooling of the gasbag, Bartan continued sailing west, sometimes laughing aloud with sheer pleasure, sometimes sighing in relief over the nearness of his escape from humiliation and expulsion. The clarity of the air defeated perspective, stacking geographical features on top of each other as in a meticulously executed drawing, allowing him to pick out details of rock formations and vegetation at ranges he would normally have considered impossible. Thus it was that—although he was a good five miles from the white speck on the hillside when he first noticed it—identification was immediate.

He was looking at a farmhouse!

His pang of disappointment seemed to darken the sky and chill the air, drawing an involuntary moan of protest from his lips. Bartan knew that King Chakkell's first major decision on ascending the throne had been to establish Kolcorron as a single world state. To that end, a fleet of large airships had been employed to disperse the newly arrived migrants around the globe. Those seedling communities had served as nodal points for vigorous expansion, but it had been Bartan's understanding that this southerly part of the continent was as yet untouched. To help maintain the impetus of growth, farmers moving into new territories were entitled to claim much larger plots than were granted in comparatively settled areas—a consideration which had motivated Jop Trinchil—and now it seemed that the self-same factor could thwart Trinchil's ambitions. Bartan's own plans could be similarly affected unless it transpired that settlement of the region had only just begun, in which case there might

41

be ample land for new families. Definite information had to be obtained before he returned to the expedition.

Encouraged by the flickering of hope, Bartan altered his course slightly to north of west, aiming directly for the minuscule white rectangle of the farmhouse. In a short time he was within a mile of the house and could discern drably coloured sheds around it. He was preparing to shed buoyancy for a landing when he began to notice something wrong with the general aspect of the place. There were no people, animals or vehicles in sight, and the ground slipping beneath the prow of his boat did not look well tended. Faint variations in coloration showed that crops had once been planted in the familiar six-strip pattern, but the edges of the sections were blurred and there seemed to have been an invasion of native grasses which showed as an overall green haze.

The realisation that the farm had been abandoned took Bartan by surprise. It was possible that there had been some kind of epidemic, or that the owners had been tyros who had become discouraged and had returned to urban life—but surely someone else would have been glad to take over a unit in which all the gruelling basic work had already been done.

His curiosity aroused, Bartan shut off the jet and floated his craft down on to the level ground which surrounded the house and its outbuildings. The slightness of the breeze enabled him to make an accurate landing within yards of a patch of wryberry vines. As soon as he stepped out of the boat the craft as a whole became lighter than air and tried to drift away, but he held it down by one of the skids until he had thrown a tether around the nearest vine. The boat gently rose to the full extent of the rope and came to rest, wallowing a little in weak air currents.

Bartan walked towards the farm buildings, becoming further intrigued with the mystery of the place as he noticed a dust-covered plough lying on its side. Other smaller implements could be seen here and there. They were made of brakka, but some had rivets of iron, a metal which was becoming generally available, and from the degree of rusting he guessed the tools had been lying around untouched for at least a year. He frowned as he estimated the practical value of the abandoned equipment. It was as though the owners of the farm had simply walked away from their livelihood—or had been spirited away by some unknown means.

The notion was a strange one to come to Bartan while he was standing in the full flood of the aftday sun, especially as he had never had anything but scorn for credulous people who heeded stories of the supernatural. Suddenly, however, he was uneasily conscious of the fact that his kind had been on Overland for only twenty-four years, and that much on the planet remained unknown to them. In the past the knowledge that he was a newcomer on a largely unexplored world had always exhilarated Bartan, but now he felt strangely chastened by it.

Don't start acting like a child, he told himself. *What is there to be afraid of?*

He turned towards the farmhouse itself. It was well constructed of sawn timbers caulked with oakum, and the whitewashing showed that somebody had taken pride in it. Bartan frowned again as he saw that yellow curtains still hung in the windows, glowing in the shade of the wide eaves. It would have been the work of only a moment to snatch them down, something he would have expected any home-lover to do, no matter how hasty the departure.

Is it possible they haven't departed? Could a whole family still be in there? Dead of some disease? Or . . . or murdered?

"Neighbours would have been around before now," he said aloud to block the flow of questions. "Even in a place as remote as this, neighbours would have been around before now. And they would have taken all the tools—farmers don't let much go to waste." Comforted by the simple logic, he walked quickly to the single-storey farmhouse, unlatched the green front door and pushed it open.

His eyes were attuned to the fierce sunlight, therefore it was several seconds before they adapted to the shade of the eaves and the comparative dimness within the house, several seconds before he clearly saw the nameless beast which was waiting for him to enter.

He sobbed, leapt backwards and fell, mind's eye brimming with the dreadful vision . . . the dark, slow-heaving pyramid of

43

the body, upright and tall as a man . . . the sagging, dissolving face, with wounds in place of eyes . . . the single slim tentacle, gently groping forward. . . .

Bartan jarred down onto his backside and hands, rolled over in the dust and was in the act of surging up and away from the house in a fear-boosted sprint when the picture behind his eyes shifted and changed. Instead of a nightmarish monster he saw miscellaneous items of old clothing suspended from a hook on a wall. There was a dark cloak, a torn jacket, a hat, and a stained apron with one string being wafted by the abrupt opening of the door.

He slowly got to his feet and brushed the dust from his body, all the while staring at the dark rectangle of the doorway. It was obvious what had caused the momentary illusion, and he felt a tingle of shame over his reaction, but in spite of that he was now oddly reluctant to enter the house.

What made me want to go in there in the first place? he thought. *It's somebody else's property. Nothing to do with me. . . .*

He turned and had taken one pace towards his boat when a new thought obtruded. What he was actually doing was running away from the farmhouse because he had become unaccountably fearful, and if he allowed that to happen he would be even less of a man than Trinchil had supposed. Muttering unhappily to himself, Bartan spun on his heel and marched into the house.

A quick inspection of the musty rooms established that the worst of his fears had been groundless—there were no human remains. All the major items of furniture had been removed, but he found extra evidence that the occupants had departed in great haste. Mats had been left in two of the rooms and there was a ceramic jar full of salt in a niche in the stone fireplace. Farming people simply did not abandon items like that in normal circumstances, Bartan knew, and he was unable to rid himself of a suspicion that something sinister had occurred on the lonely farm in the not-too-distant past.

Relieved at having no further cause to remain in the uneasy atmosphere, he went outside—brushing past the slow-stirring garments hanging by the door—and walked straight to the airboat. It had lost some buoyancy as the gasbag cooled and now was resting lightly on its skids. Bartan unfastened the tether, seated himself in the gondola and took the boat aloft. It was still only a short time past noon and after a moment's thought he decided to continue flying west, following the line of a faint track into the lush green landscape. Much of the terrain consisted of drumlins—small hog-backed hills, oval in plan because of ancient glaciation—so regularly arranged that they reminded him of giant eggs in a basket. *There's the natural name for this fertile region*, he thought. *The Basket of Eggs!*

Within a short time he saw another farm agreeably positioned on the slopes of one of the rounded hills. He banked and flew towards it, and this time—in his state of alertness—he was quicker to realise that the place was not being worked. On arriving overhead he circled the farm once at low altitude to confirm his findings. No tools or equipment were visible and the farmhouse appeared to have been completely stripped, evidence that the evacuation had been more leisurely and ordered, but why had it taken place at all?

Deeply puzzled, Bartan continued with the flight, changing to a zigzag search pattern which slowed his progress to the west. In the hour that followed he discovered eight more farms, all in ideal agricultural land, all totally deserted. The sections in the region were far too large to be worked by single families, and the people who claimed them did so with the intention of laying down fortunes for their descendants. As the population of Overland increased the pioneers would be able to sell or sublet land to later generations. It was a prize not to be yielded lightly—and yet *something* had induced many hard-headed farmers to pack up their belongings and move on.

Eventually Bartan began to pick out the glint of sunlight on a sizable river and decided on it as a natural limit to the day's sortie. At the northern end of one of his sweeps he detected a hazy column of smoke arising from a point which seemed to be close to the river. It was the first sign of human habitation he had seen in more than ten days, and was made even more intriguing by the prospect of getting information about the empty land he had been crossing. He set a course for the smoke trace, flying as fast as he dared in view of the gasbag's untrustworthy condition, and soon began to realise that what he was approaching was not another farm, but a small township.

It was situated on a Y-shaped fork created by a tributary joining the main river. As the airboat brought him closer, Bartan saw that it consisted of about forty buildings, some of which were large enough to be warehouses. White squares and triangles of sails indicated the river was navigable to the southern ocean. The place was obviously a trading centre, with the potential to become important and prosperous, and its presence made the enigma of the abandoned farms all the more baffling.

Long before Bartan had reached the edge of the township the roar of his jet had attracted attention on the ground. Two men came galloping out on bluehorns to meet him, waving vigorously, and then kept pace with the boat as he guided it down into an open patch near a bridge which spanned the lesser river. Men and women were issuing from the surrounding buildings to form a ring of spectators. Several youths, needing no appeal, willingly grabbed the skids and held the craft until Bartan had tethered it to a convenient sapling.

A red-faced man with prematurely white hair approached Bartan, obviously in the role of spokesman. In spite of being slightly below average height he had an air of assurance and, unusually in such a community, was wearing a smallsword.

"I am Majin Karrodall, reeve of the township of New Minnett," he said in friendly tones. "We don't see many aircraft in these parts."

"I'm scouting for a party of claimants," Bartan replied to the unspoken question. "My name is Bartan Drumme, and I would be grateful for some water to drink. I have flown much farther than I intended today and it is thirsty work."

"You're welcome to all the water you want, but if you would prefer it you can have good brown ale. What do you say?"

"I say good brown ale." Bartan, who had not tasted an alcoholic beverage since joining the expedition, grinned to show his appreciation of the offer. There was a murmur of approval from those watching and the men began a general movement towards an open-fronted barn-like building which appeared to double as a meeting place and tavern. In a short time Bartan was seated at a long table in the company of Karrodall and about ten other men, most of whom had been introduced to him as storekeepers or riverboat crew. From the tone of the amiable banter going on around him Bartan guessed that impromptu gatherings like this were not infrequent events, and that his arrival had been seized on as a convenient excuse. A substantial two-handled jar was placed before him and when he sipped from it he found the ale to be cool, strong and not too sweet for his taste. Comforted by the welcome and the unexpected hospitality, he proceeded to quench his thirst and to answer questions about himself, the airboat and the objectives of Trinchil's expedition.

"I fear this is not the kind of news you wish to hear," Karrodall said, "but I think you will be obliged to turn north. The lands to the west of here are curtailed by the mountains, and to the south by the ocean—and the prime tracts have all been claimed and registered. It isn't much better if you head north into New Kail, I admit, but I have heard that there are one or two quiet little valleys still untouched on the other side of the Barrier range."

"I've seen those valleys," a plump man called Otler put in. "The only way you can stand upright is by growing one leg longer than the other."

The remark occasioned some laughter, and Bartan waited until it had subsided. "I have just flown over some excellent farming land to the east of the river. I realise, of course, that we are too late to claim it—but why are the farms not being worked?"

"It'll *never* be too late to claim that cursed place," Otler muttered, staring down into his drink.

Bartan was immediately intrigued. "What do you . . . ?"

"Pay him no heed," Karrodall said quickly. "It was the ale talking."

Otler sat up straight, with an offended expression on his round face. "I'm not drunk! Are you suggesting that I'm drunk? I'm not drunk!"

"He's drunk," Karrodall assured Bartan.

"Nevertheless, I'd like to know what he meant." Bartan knew he was displeasing the reeve by pursuing the point, but Otler's

47

strange comment was reverberating in his mind. "This is a matter of considerable importance to me."

"You might as well tell what he wants to know, Majin," another man said. "He'll be able to find out for himself."

Karrodall sighed and shot Otler a venomous glance, and when he spoke his voice had lost its former briskness. "The land to which you refer is known to us as the Haunt. And while it is true that all claims to it have been allowed to lapse, that information is of no value to you. Your people will never settle there."

"Why not?"

"Why do you think we call it the Haunt? It is a place of evil, my friend. All who go there are . . . troubled."

"By ghosts? By wraiths?" Bartan made no attempt to hide his incredulity and joy. "Are you saying that there are only hob-goblins to dispute the ownership of that land?"

Karrodall's face was solemn, the eyes intent. "I'm saying that you would be ill-advised to try settling there."

"Thank you for the advice." Bartan drained his ale, set the jar down with a flourish and stood up. "And thank you for the hospitality, gentlemen—I will repay it soon."

He left the table and went out into the aftday sunshine, eager to get aloft and return to the expedition with his good news.

Chapter 3

The skyship was being borne eastwards on the lightest of breezes, but the ground over which it was drifting was uneven and covered with scrub, which meant that the mounted soldiers had some difficulty in keeping pace with their alien quarry.

Colonel Mandle Gartasian, riding at the head of the column, kept his gaze firmly fixed on the ship and for the most part trusted his bluehorn to find its way around obstacles. The sight of the vast balloon and its room-sized gondola was activating bleak memories, causing a degree of pain he had not experienced since his first years on Overland, and yet he was unable to look elsewhere.

He was a tall man, with the powerful build typical of the Kolcorronian military caste, and showed few signs of his fifty years. Apart from a dusting of grey in his cropped black hair and a deepening of the lines on his square face, he looked much as he had done at the time of the hasty evacuation of Ro-Atabri. He had been an idealistic young lieutenant then, and had unhesitatingly taken his place on one of the first military ships to depart the doomed city. Thousands of times since that day he had cursed the naive trust in his senior officers which had led him to take off ahead of his wife and infant son.

Ronoda and the boy had been assigned places on a civilian ship, and he had left them in the belief that the army was in full control of the situation, that the embarkation schedules would be maintained, and that the separation would last just for the duration of the flight. Only when his binoculars revealed the growing chaos far below had he felt the first pangs of fear, and by then it had been much too late. . . .

"Look, sir!" The words came from Lieutenant Keero, who was riding at Gartasian's side. "I think they're preparing to land!"

Gartasian nodded. "I believe you're right. Now, remember to

keep your men from crowding in on the ship after it touches down. Nobody is to go closer than two hundred paces, even if the ship appears to have landing difficulties. We don't know what the crew's intentions are—and they may have powerful weaponry."

"I understand, sir. I can hardly believe this is happening. Can they really have flown all the way from Land?" Keero was infringing field discipline by making inessential remarks, but it was explained by the excitement on his pink-cheeked face. Gartasian, normally strict on such points, decided the lapse was excusable in the unique circumstances.

"There can be no doubt that they have come from the Old World," he said. "The first question we have to ask is . . . *why?* Why after all these years? And *who?* Are we dealing with a small group who managed to survive the ptertha attacks, and finally succeeded in making an escape? Or . . . ?" Gartasian left the question unspoken. The idea that the pterthacosis plague might have abated—sparing enough of the population to rebuild an organised society—was too far-fetched for words. It certainly was not the kind of fanciful speculation to be voiced before a junior officer, especially as concealed within it were the seeds of a far wilder notion. Was there the remotest possibility that Ronoda and Hallie were still alive? And had all his years of guilt and remorse been a self-indulgent waste? With sufficient vision, enterprise and courage could he have instigated a return flight to Land?

The torrent of questions, a distillation of fantastic wish-fulfilment dreams, was the last thing Gartasian needed if he were to function well as the commander of a military operation. He gave himself a mental shake and forced his mind to concentrate on the palpable realities of the situation. It had been more than a minute since he had heard the hollow, echoing roar of the skyship's burner as it discharged hot gas into the balloon—an indication that the crew had selected a suitable landing site. The gondola was now a mere twenty feet above the ground, and at its sides he could see the silhouettes of several men who appeared to be working with rail-mounted cannon. He was beginning to wonder if two hundred paces was a good enough margin of safety for his own force when the cannon fired in a downwards direction. Four harpoon-like anchors speared into the ground, each trailing a line, and at once crewmen began hauling the lines in, thereby drawing the gondola into a controlled touchdown. The balloon above it remained inflated, swaying ponderously.

"We have learned one thing," Gartasian said to his lieutenant. "Our visitors never had any intention of staying for long—otherwise they would have vented their balloon."

His only answer was a hurried salute as Keero wheeled away with a sergeant beside him to deploy the soldiers in a circle around the skyship. Gartasian took a pair of binoculars out of his saddle pouch and trained them on the gondola.

He could see the heads of the four crewmen as they went about the work of securing the ship, but something else in the magnified image attracted his attention. The gondola was of basically the same design as those used in the Migration, and yet had no anti-ptertha cannon on the sides. In spite of the weight penalty imposed by such weapons, they had been deemed necessary for the passage through Land's lower atmosphere, and Gartasian found their absence intriguing. Could it really be a sign that the ptertha—the airborne globes whose poison had all but annihilated Kolcorron—had ceased their onslaught on humanity? Gartasian's heart lurched as he again considered the possibilities. A civilisation which embraced two worlds . . . a mass return to Land for those who were discontent on Overland . . . miraculous reunions with loved ones who were believed to be long-dead. . . .

"You fool!" Gartasian made the whispered accusation as he put the binoculars away. "What new folly is this? Are you so excellent a commander that you can afford to handicap yourself with winedreams?"

As he made ready to ride forward he reminded himself of two pertinent facts—his advancement in the army had been hindered by the ambivalence springing from his guilt; and fate had now given him an unparalleled opportunity to compensate by placing him close to the landing site of the enigmatic skyship. The sunwriter message from Prad had said that King Chakkell was on his way with all possible speed, and that in the meantime

Colonel Gartasian was empowered to deal with the situation and take any steps he considered necessary. A good showing on this occasion could yield incalculable benefits in the future.

"Remain here," he said to Lieutenant Keero, who was just returning to his starting point. He nudged his bluehorn into a walk which he deliberately kept slow, demonstrating to the visitors that his intentions were not hostile. As he neared the ship he was uneasily aware that his cuirass, moulded from boiled leather, would provide little protection if he were to be fired upon, but he remained upright in the saddle, presenting the appearance of one who was satisfied with his ability to deal with the situation.

Those aboard the ship, observing his approach, ceased their activities and came to stand at the near side of the gondola. Gartasian looked for an identifiable commander, but the crew all seemed to be of an age—not much more than twenty—and were wearing identical brown shirts and jerkins. The only visible insignia were small circles of different colours sewn to the lapels of the jerkins, but the variations had no significance for Gartasian.

He was surprised to note that the men were sufficiently alike to have been mistaken for brothers—each with a narrow forehead, close-set eyes and narrow jutting jaw. As he entered the shadow of the balloon he saw, with a sudden sense of disquiet, that the four had dark jaundiced complexions and a peculiar metallic sheen to their skins. It was an appearance which would have suggested a recent brush with some cruel disease, except that the men also exuded that unconscious arrogance which can arise from being superbly fit. They regarded Gartasian with expressions which to him seemed both amused and contemptuous.

"I am Colonel Gartasian," he said, halting his bluehorn a few yards from the gondola. "On behalf of King Chakkell, the planetary ruler, I welcome you to Overland. We were greatly surprised by the sight of your ship, and many questions clamour in our minds."

"Keep your questions and your welcome to yourself." The man on the right, tallest of the four, spoke in oddly accented

Kolcorronian. "My name is Orracolde, and I am the commander here, but I also have the honour of being a royal courier. I come to this world with a message from King Rassamarden."

Gartasian was shocked by the speaker's immediate and overt hostility, but he decided to control his temper. "I have never heard of a King Rassamarden."

"That is hardly surprising under the circumstances," Orracolde said, smiling disdainfully. "Now, I expected that Prad would be dead by this time, but how did Chakkell become King? What of Prad's son, Leddravohr? And Pouche?"

"They too are dead," Gartasian said stiffly, realising that the deliberate challenge in Orracolde's manner would have to be taken up for the sake of honour. "And for your further enlightenment, I intend that this meeting will henceforth be conducted along different lines. I will provide the questions, and you the answers."

"And what if I decide otherwise, *old* warrior?"

"My men have your ship surrounded."

"That fact had not escaped my attention," Orracolde said. "But unless their flea-infested mounts can soar like eagles they pose my ship no threat. We can be airborne in an instant." He turned away from the rail and a second later the skyship's burner discharged a burst of hot gas into the balloon which loomed overhead, maintaining its buoyancy. Gartasian's bluehorn, startled by the echoing blast, half-reared and he had to act quickly to bring it under control, much to the amusement of the four onlookers. It came to him that for the present the visitors were in a greatly superior position, and that unless he devised a better method of dealing with them he could be humiliated. He glanced at the sparse circle of mounted soldiers, now seeming so distant, and chose new tactics.

"Neither of us has anything to gain by quarrelling," he said reasonably. "The message you spoke of can be relayed to the King through me, or—if you would prefer it—you can wait until his Majesty arrives in person."

Orracolde tilted his head. "How long will that take?"

"The King is already on his way and could be here within the hour."

"Giving you ample time in which to draw up long-range cannon!" Orracolde scanned the brush-covered terrain as though expecting to find evidence of troop movements.

"But we have no reason to bear you ill will," Gartasian protested, dismayed by the other man's irrationality. What kind of envoy was this? And what kind of a ruler would entrust such a man with diplomatic responsibility?

"Do not take me for a fool, *old* warrior—I will deliver King Rassamarden's message without delay." Orracolde stooped, momentarily disappearing behind the gondola's side, and when he came into view again he was removing a yellowish scroll from a leather tube.

Gartasian had time in which to find his thoughts seizing on a triviality. Orracolde derogated him with every sentence he spoke, but he uttered the word "old" with a particular venom, as though it was one of the most insulting in his vocabulary. It was a minor mystery compared to the other puzzling aspects of what was happening, even though Gartasian had never considered himself as being old, and he resolutely pushed it aside as he saw Orracolde unroll a square sheet of heavy paper.

"I am an instrument of King Rassamarden, and the following message must be regarded as issuing directly from his lips," Orracolde said.

"I, King Rassamarden, am the rightful sovereign of all men and women born on the planet of Land, and of all their offspring, wherever they may be. In consequence, all new territories on the planet of Overland are considered to have been occupied on my behalf. I therefore proclaim myself sole ruler of Land and Overland. Be it known that I intend to exact all tributes which are rightfully mine."

Orracolde lowered the paper and stared solemnly at Gartasian, awaiting his response.

Gartasian gaped at him for a few seconds, then began to laugh. The sheer preposterousness of what he had heard, combined with the pompous style of the delivery, had abruptly translated the entire scene into farce. Release of the tension which had been growing inside him fuelled his mirth, and he had genuine difficulty in bringing his breathing back under control.

"Have you lost your reason, *old* man?" Orracolde leaned over the rail, bronzed face thrust forward, like a snake spitting venom. "I see nothing to laugh at."

"Only because you can't see yourself," Gartasian said. "I don't know which was the greater fool—Rassamarden for issuing that ridiculous message; or you for undertaking such a long and hazardous journey to deliver it."

"Your punishment for insulting the King will be death."

"I tremble."

Orracolde's mouth twitched. "I will remember you, Gartasian, but for now I have more important concerns. Littlenight will soon be upon us. When darkness falls I will take my ship aloft—rather than give you the chance to launch a sneak attack—but I will pause at a height of one thousand feet and wait for aftday. Chakkell will no doubt be with you by that time, and you will communicate his response to me by sunwriter."

"Response?"

"Yes. Either Chakkell bows the knee to King Rassamarden willingly—or he will be compelled to do so."

"You truly *are* mad—a madman speaking for a madman." Gartasian held his bluehorn steady while one of the crewmen fired another burst of gas into the balloon. "Are you talking of war between our two worlds?"

"Most certainly."

Struggling with his growing incredulity, Gartasian said, "And how would such a war be prosecuted?"

"A fleet of skyships is already under construction."

"How many?"

Orracolde produced a thin smile. "Enough."

"There could never be enough," Gartasian said calmly. "Our soldiers would be waiting for each ship as it landed."

"You don't really expect me to swallow that, *old* warrior," Orracolde said, his smile widening. "I know how thinly your population must be scattered. With informed use of wind cells we can put down almost anywhere on this planet. We could land under cover of darkness, but there will be little need for stealth, because we have weapons the like of which you have never imagined.

"And on top of everything else—" Orracolde paused to glance at his three companions, who gave approving nods as though knowing what he was about to say—"there is the natural and undeniable superiority of the New Men."

"Men are men," Gartasian said, unimpressed. "How can there be *new* men?"

"Nature saw to that. Nature and the ptertha. We have been created with total immunity to the ptertha plague."

"So that's it!" Gartasian ran his gaze over the four narrow faces which, with their inhuman metallic sheen, could almost have belonged to four statues cast from the same mould, and understanding began to flicker in his mind. "I thought that . . . perhaps . . . the ptertha might have ceased their attacks."

"The attacks continue unabated, but now they are futile."

"And what about . . . my kind? Are there any survivors?"

"None," Orracolde said, smugly triumphant. "The old have all been swept away."

Gartasian was silent for a moment, saying a final goodbye to his wife and son, then his thoughts were drawn back to the problems of the present and the need to learn all he could about the interplanetary visitors. Implicit in the few words Orracolde had already spoken was a dreadful scenario, a vision of a civilisation in its death throes. The drifting globes of the ptertha had swarmed in the skies of Land, hunting down their human quarries without mercy, driving them closer and closer to extinction, until their numbers were so. . . .

My stomach is on fire!

The burning sensation was so severe that Gartasian almost doubled over. Within seconds the heat centre beneath his chest had spread tendrils into the rest of his torso, and at the same time the air about him seemed to cool a little. Unwilling to show any sign of discomfort, he sat perfectly still in the saddle and waited for the spasm to come to an end. It continued unabated and he realised he would have to try disregarding it while he gathered precious information.

"All swept away?" he said. "*All?* But that means your entire population has been born since the Migration."

"Since the Flight. We refer to that act of cowardice and betrayal as the Flight."

"But how could the babes have survived? Without parents it would have been. . . ."

"We were born of those who had partial immunity," Orracolde cut in. "Many of them lived long enough."

Gartasian shook his head, pursuing the thought in spite of the spreading fire at the core of his being. "But many must have perished! What is your total population?"

"Do you think me a fool?" Orracolde said, a sneer appearing on his dark countenance. "I came here to learn about this world—not to throw away knowledge about my own. I have seen as much as I need to see, and as littlenight is almost here. . . ."

"Your reluctance to answer my question is answer enough! Your numbers must be small indeed—perhaps even less than ours." Gartasian gave a violent shudder as, in contrast to the heat within his body, the air seemed to press in on him with a clammy coldness. He touched his brow, found it slick with perspiration, and a shocking idea was born deep in his mind, coiling like a worm. He had not seen a case of pterthacosis since his youth on Land, but nobody of his generation could ever forget the symptoms—the burning sensation in the stomach, the copious sweating, the chest pains and the bloating of the spleen. . . .

"You grow pale, *old* warrior," Orracolde said. "What ails you?"

Gartasian held his voice steady. "Nothing ails me."

"But you sweat and shiver and. . . ." Orracolde leaned forward across the rail, his gaze hunting over Gartasian's face, and his eyes widened. There was a moment of near-telepathic communion, then Orracolde drew back and gave a whispered order to his crew. One of them stooped out of sight and the ship's burner began a continuous roar while the other two men hurriedly began releasing the anchor lines from the downward-pointing cannon.

Gartasian had a pure, clear understanding of what he had read in the other man's eyes, and in the instant of accepting his own death sentence his mind had vaulted far beyond the circum-scribed present. Earlier Orracolde had boasted of weapons outside the Overlanders' imaginings, but even he had been taken by surprise, had not sensed the dreadful truth foreshadowed by his own words. He and his crew were weapons in themselves —carriers of the ptertha plague in a form so virulent that an unprotected person had only to go near them to be smitten!

Their King, though apparently insane by Gartasian's stan-dards, had been prudent enough to send a scout ship to gauge the opposition an invading force would meet. If he received word that there could be very little effective resistance, that Overland's defenders would be annihilated by pterthacosis, his territorial ambitions would be even further inflamed.

The skyship must not be allowed to depart!

The thought spurred Gartasian into action. His men were too far away to be of any assistance, and the ship was already straining upwards, making him solely responsible for preventing the take-off. The only course open to him was to rupture the fabric of the huge balloon by hurling his sword at it. He drew the weapon, twisted in the saddle to make the throw and gasped aloud as pain erupted through his chest cavity, paralysing his upraised arm. He lowered the sword into a position from which he could try an underarm lob, suddenly aware that Orracolde was bringing an oddly shaped musket to bear on him.

Counting on the delay which always occurred while power crystals were combining in a gun's combustion chamber, Gartasian began the upward swing. The musket emitted a strangely flat *crack*. Something punched into Gartasian's left shoulder, slewing him around and causing his sword—weakly thrown—to tumble wide of its mark. He jumped down from the startled bluehorn and went for the fallen blade, but the agony in his shoulder and chest turned what should have been a high-speed dash into a series of stumbles and lurches. By the time he had retrieved the sword the gondola was a good thirty feet above ground, and the balloon carrying it was far beyond his reach.

He stood and watched helplessly, his personal catastrophe eclipsed for the moment, as the skyship rapidly gained height. Although it was centred on the misty blue disk of Land, the ship was hard to see because the sun was almost in the same line of sight, already silvering the sister world's eastern rim. Gartasian gave up trying to penetrate the dazzling rays and spokes and oily needles of light. He lowered his head and stared down at the grass, musing on the fact that the last action of his career and life had ended in abject failure, and it was only the sound of an approaching bluehorn which brought him out of the dark reverie. There were duties yet to be discharged.

"Stay back," he shouted at Lieutenant Keero. "Don't come near me!"

"Sir?" Keero slowed his mount to a walk, but kept it moving forward.

Gartasian pointed at him with his sword. "This is an order, lieutenant. Do *not* come any closer! I have the plague."

Keero halted. "Plague?"

"Pterthacosis. You've heard of it, I trust."

The upper half of Keero's face was masked by the shade of his visor, but Gartasian saw his mouth distort with shock. A moment later the sunlit hills of the western horizon blinked with prismatic colour, then abruptly dimmed as the shadow of Land came rushing over the countryside at orbital speed. As its edge swept across the scene, initiating the brief penumbral phase of little-night, the darkening sky was seen to be spanned by a huge spiral of misty radiance, its arms sparkling with brilliant stars of white, blue and yellow. The knowledge that it was the last time the spectacle of the night sky would be unfurled for him filled Gartasian with a yearning to ponder it in detail, to memorise the patterns of lesser whirlpools and comets so that he would have light to take with him into the place where there was no light. Pushing the notion aside, he addressed himself to the lieutenant, who was waiting about twenty yards away.

"Listen to me carefully, Keero," he called out. "I will be dead before littlenight is over, and you must. . . ." The fire in his lungs, aggravated by the effect of shouting, forced him to abandon the plan to transmit his precious new knowledge verbally.

"I am going to write a message for the King, and I charge you with the responsibility of ensuring that he receives it. Now, take out your dispatch book, make sure the pencil is not broken, and leave the book on the ground for me. When you have done that, rejoin your men and wait with them for the King to arrive. Tell him all that has happened here—and remind him that nobody is to approach my body for at least five days."

Drained of strength by the painfully prolonged speech, Gartasian forced himself to remain upright and militarily correct while Keero dismounted and placed his dispatch book on the ground.

The lieutenant got back into the saddle and hesitated for a moment. "Sir, I'm sorry. . . ."

"It's all right," Gartasian told him, grateful for the fleeting human contact. "Do not concern yourself about me. Just go, and take my bluehorn with you—I have no more need of him."

Keero gave an awkward salute, collected the redundant animal and rode away into the twilight. Gartasian walked to where the book lay, his legs buckling further with each step, and allowed himself to sag to the ground beside it. He had barely finished removing the pencil from its leather sleeve when the last coin-clip of the sun slid behind the curvature of Land. In spite of the reduced level of illumination he was still able to see well enough to write, thanks to Land's halo and the extravagant spangling of the rest of the heavens with fierce stars, some of them in tightly packed circular clusters.

He attempted to lean on his left arm, but jerked upright again as pain flared in the wounded shoulder. Exploring the injury with his fingers, he found that the brakka slug from the musket had spent much of its energy in gouging through the rolled leather at the edge of his cuirass. It had lodged in his flesh, but had not broken the bone. Reminding himself to include a note on how the weapon had fired without the normal delay, he sat with the book in his lap and began to write a detailed report for the benefit of those who would soon have to repel a deadly invader.

The mental discipline involved in the work helped him avoid dwelling on his fate, but his body interposed frequent reminders of the losing battle it was fighting against the ptertha poison. His stomach and lungs seemed to be filling with hot coals, agonising cramps encircled his chest and occasional bouts of shivering made his writing almost illegible in places. So rapid was the progress of the symptoms that on reaching the end of his report he was dully surprised to find himself still conscious, still with some dregs of strength.

If I move away from here, he thought, *the book can be picked up without delay, and with no risk to any man's life.*

He set the book down and marked its position by weighting it with his red-crested helmet. The effort of raising himself to his feet was much greater than he had anticipated. He was unable to prevent himself from swaying in vertiginous circles as he scanned his surroundings, which seemed to be a scene painted on slowly undulating cloth. Keero had brought all his men together and a fire had been lit to guide King Chakkell to the spot. The soldiers and their mounts formed a stationary, amorphous mass in the dimness, and there was little movement anywhere but for the near-continuous flickering of meteors against the dense fields of stars.

Gartasian guessed the men's eyes were fixed on him. He turned and walked away from them, staggering grotesquely, blood beading into the grass from the fingers of his left hand. After some twenty paces his feet were snared by bracken and he pitched forward, to lie with his face buried in rough-haired fronds.

There was no point in trying to get up again.

No point in trying to cling on to consciousness any longer.

I'm coming back to you, Ronoda and little Hallie, he thought, closing his eyes on the universe. *I'll soon be with. . . .*

Chapter 4

When Toller Maraquine heard the bolt of his cell door being drawn his principal emotion was one of relief. He had been allowed writing materials, and all through the hours of littlenight he had sat with the pad on his knees, trying to compose a letter to Gesalla and Cassyll. His intention had been to explain and apologise, but explanation had proved impossible—how was he to find any shred of reason in what he had done?—and all he had written was one bald sentence.

I am sorry.

The three words struck him as being an apt but dismal epitaph for a life that had been thrown away, and now he had a profound desire to get the last minutes of futility over and done with.

He stood up and faced the opening door, fully expecting to see an executioner accompanied by a squad of jailers. Instead, the widening rectangle revealed the paunchy form of King Chakkell, flanked by stone-faced members of his personal guard.

"Should I feel honoured?" Toller said. "Am I to be seen off by the King in person?"

Chakkell raised a leather-bound dispatch book of the type used by the Kolcorronian army. "Your astonishing good luck continues, Maraquine. Our game is on again. Come with me—I have need of you." He grasped Toller's arm with as much force as the executioner would have used and marched him into the passageway, where recently extinguished wicks still smoked and fumed in their sconces.

"You have *need* of me? Does this mean . . . ?" Paradoxically, in the moment he began to entertain hope Toller was unmanned by a pang of death-fear which cooled his brow and stilled his voice.

"It means I'm prepared to forget about your stupidity of the foreday."

"Majesty, I'm grateful . . . truly grateful," Toller managed to say. Inwardly he promised: *I'll never fail you again, Gesalla*.

"And so you should be!" Chakkell led the way out of the cell block, through a gateway whose guards sprang to attention, and into the parade ground in which, seemingly an aeon ago, Toller had faced Karkarand.

"This must concern the skyship we saw," Toller said. "Was it really from Land?"

"We will talk in private."

Toller and Chakkell, still accompanied by guards, entered the rear of the palace and went through corridors to an undistinguished doorway. Walking behind the King, Toller had detected the soupy smell of bluehorn sweat from his clothing, and the indication of hard riding intensified his interest. Chakkell dismissed his men with a wave and brought Toller into a modestly proportioned apartment in which the only furnishings were a round table and six plain chairs.

"Read that." Chakkell handed Toller the dispatch book, took a seat at the table and stared down at his clenched fists. His deeply tanned scalp was glistening with perspiration and it was obvious that he was highly agitated. Deciding it would be unwise to ask any preliminary questions, Toller sat down at the opposite side of the table and opened the book. The reading difficulties he had known as a young man had faded over the years, and it took him only a few minutes to go through the pages of pencilled script, even though the characters were wildly distorted in places. When he had finished he closed the book and set it down, suddenly aware of blood stains on the cover.

Head still lowered, Chakkell looked up from under his brows, eyes showing white crescents. "Well?"

"Is Colonel Gartasian dead?"

"Of course he's dead—and from what is written there he could be the first of many," Chakkell said. "The question is, what can be done? What can we do about these diseased upstarts?"

"Do you think this Rassamarden really intends to invade? It seems an unreasonable course for one who has an empty world at his disposal."

Chakkell pointed at the book. "You saw what Gartasian said. We are not dealing with reasonable people, Maraquine. It was Gartasian's opinion that they are all unhinged to some extent, and their ruler could be the worst of the lot."

Toller nodded. "It is often the way."

"Don't take too many liberties," Chakkell warned. "You have more skyship experience than any other man in Kolcorron, and I want your views about how we can defend ourselves."

"Well. . . ." For a few seconds Toller was distracted by an upsurge of something like joy, immediately followed by feelings of shame and remorse. What kind of a man was he? He had barely finished vowing never again to set anything above the blessed peace of a contented domestic existence, and now his heart was quickening at the thought of participating in an entirely new kind of warfare. Could it be some kind of reaction to the discovery that he was not about to be executed, that life would continue—or was he a fatally flawed human being in the pattern of the long-dead Prince Leddravohr? The latter possibility was almost too much to contemplate.

"I am waiting," Chakkell said impatiently. "Don't tell me that the crisis is of so great a magnitude as to still *your* tongue."

Toller took a deep breath and exhaled it in a sigh. "Majesty, assuming that a contest does take place, fate has dictated the terms. We cannot carry the battle to the enemy, and for obvious reasons these so-called New Men must never be permitted to set foot on our world. That leaves us but one course of action."

"Which is?"

"Exclusion! A barrier! We must wait for the ships in the weightless zone—midway between the two worlds—and destroy them as they labour up from Land. It is the only way."

Chakkell studied Toller's face, appraising his sincerity. "From what I remember of the mid-passage the air was too cold and thin to support life for any length of time."

"We need ships of a different design. The gondolas need to be larger, and totally enclosed. And sealed to retain air and heat. Perhaps we will even use firesalt to thicken the air. All that and more will be necessary if we are to remain in the weightless zone for long periods."

"Can it be done?" Chakkell said. "You seem to be talking about veritable fortresses suspended in the sky. The weight. . . ."

"On the old skyships we were able to lift twenty passengers, plus essential supplies. That is a considerable weight, and we may be able to attach two balloons to one lengthened gondola so as to double the carrying capacity."

"It's worth thinking about." Chakkell stood up and paced around the table, frowning at Toller all the while. "I believe I'm going to create a new post, especially for you," he finally said. "It shall be . . . Sky Marshal . . . with complete responsibility for the aerial defence of Overland. You will be answerable to none but me, and will have the power to draw on any resource you need—human or material—for the successful prosecution of your task."

Toller was uplifted by the prospect of having purpose and direction restored to his life, but to his own surprise he felt reluctant to let himself be borne away on the tide of Chakkell's ideas. If he could be marked down for execution in one minute and raised to an exalted office in the next, then he was nothing more than a creature of the King, a puppet without dignity or a true identity of his own.

"If I decide to accept your commission," he said, "there are certain. . . ."

"If you decide to accept! *If!*" Chakkell kicked his vacated chair aside, slammed his hands down on the table and leaned across it. "What's the matter with you, Maraquine? Would you be disloyal to your own King?"

"Only this foreday my own King sentenced me to death."

"You know I wouldn't have permitted things to go that far."

"Do I?" Toller did not hide his scepticism. "And you refused me the single favour for which I begged."

Chakkell looked genuinely baffled. "What are you talking about?"

"The life of the farmer, Spennel."

"Oh, *that!*" Chakkell briefly turned his gaze towards the ceiling, showing his exasperation. "Here's what I will do, Maraquine. The execution may well have been delayed because of all the commotion in the city. I'll send a messenger with all speed, and if your esteemed friend is still alive his life will be spared. Does that satisfy you? I hope it satisfies you, because there is nothing more I can do."

Toller nodded uncertainly, wondering if the voice of his conscience could be silenced so easily. "The messenger must leave at once."

"Done!" Chakkell turned and nodded towards a panelled wall in which Toller could discern no apertures, then dropped into a chair beside the one he had overturned. "Now we must draw up our plans. Are you able to sketch a design for the sky fortresses?"

"I think so, but I want Zavotle with me," Toller said, naming the man who had flown with him in the days of the old Skyship Experimental Squadron, and who had later been one of the four royal pilots in the Migration. "I believe he flies one of your courier ships, Majesty, so locating him should be a simple matter."

"Zavotle? Isn't that the one with the peculiar ears? Why do you choose him?"

"He is very clever, and we work well together," Toller said. "I need him."

Still in his mid-forties, Ilven Zavotle looked too young to have been in command of a royal skyship at the time of the mass flight from Land. His body had thickened only a little with the passage of the years, his hair remained dark and was still cropped, emphasising the protrusion of his tiny, in-folding ears. He had joined Toller and Chakkell within ten minutes of being summoned from the adjacent airfield, and his yellow aircaptain's uniform showed signs of having been hastily removed from a closet.

He listened intently while the threat posed by the New Men was explained to him, now and then—as had always been his habit—making notes in neat, crowded script. His manner was just as Toller had remembered it—precise and meticulous, a reassurance that there was no difficulty which could not be overcome by the orderly application of reason.

"There you have it," Chakkell said to Zavotle. "What do you think of this notion of establishing permanently manned fortresses in the weightless zone?" He had disliked the idea of having to consult a lowly captain, but had acquiesced to Toller's request and had even—an indication of how seriously he regarded the situation—invited Zavotle to be seated at the table with him. Now he was eyeing the newcomer critically, with something of the air of a schoolmaster eager to fault a pupil's performance.

Zavotle sat very straight, aware that he was on trial, and spoke firmly. "It can be done, Majesty. In fact, it *must* be done—we have no other recourse."

"I see. And what about attaching two balloons to one long gondola?"

"With respect to Lord Toller, I don't like it, Majesty," Zavotle said, glancing at Toller. "The gondola would have to be *very* long to accommodate two balloons, and I think there would be serious control problems."

"So you would advocate using one monstrous balloon?"

"No, Majesty—that would introduce an entirely new set of difficulties. No doubt they could be overcome in time, but we have no time to spare."

Chakkell looked impatient. "What then? Have you something in mind, captain, or do you content yourself with deciding what *cannot* be done?"

"I believe we should continue to use the size of balloon with which we are experienced," Zavotle said, not losing his composure. "The sky fortresses should be built in sections, taken aloft in sections—and assembled in the weightless zone."

Chakkell stared hard at Zavotle, his expression slowly changing to one of mingled astonishment and respect. "Of course! Of *course*! There is no other way to proceed."

Toller felt a pang of vicarious pride as the new concept flooded his mind, bringing with it a series of giddy images. "Good man, Ilven," he breathed. "I knew we had need of you—though my gut freezes when I think about the kind of labour involved. Even with the knowledge that he was well tethered a man would be powerfully distracted by the sight of thousands of miles of thin air below him."

"Many would be quite unable to concentrate their minds," Zavotle said, nodding, "but the work would be kept to the absolute minimum. I envisage circular sections held together by simple clamps and sealed with mastic. A fortress might be constructed of three such sections."

"Before we concern ourselves with details, I must know how many of these sky fortresses will be needed," Chakkell said. "The more I think about it the more doubts plague me about the feasibility of the entire scheme. If one neglects volume and treats the weightless zone as a flat disk midway between the worlds, there are millions of square miles to defend—and I fail to see how it can be done. Even if I had the resources of old Kolcorron at my disposal I would be unable to construct the number of fortresses required. A thousand, would you say? Five thousand?"

Zavotle looked at Toller, giving him the opportunity to reply, and Toller responded with a slight shake of his head. The objection expressed by the King seemed to him a valid one, and although he could tell by Zavotle's unperturbed expression that an answer existed he was for the moment unable to deduce it by himself.

"Majesty, we are not required to defend the entire area of the zone," Zavotle said. "The two worlds have a common atmosphere, but it is shaped like an hourglass, with a slender waist. Skyships have to remain close to the centre of that waist—in a narrow bridge of air, so to speak—and that is where we will wait for the Landers. I do not know how determined they will be to press ahead with their invasion, but when we destroy the first of their ships the others may try to pass us by at a safe distance. To do that they would need to venture so far outside the air bridge that their crews would lose consciousness and then they would asphyxiate."

"I begin to form an affection for you, Zavotle," Chakkell said, half-smiling. "So, how many fortresses would you say?"

"Not many, Majesty. Perhaps as few as ten or twelve in the initial phase, while we have the advantage of surprise; perhaps a hundred later on, if the Landers begin to introduce effective counter-measures." Zavotle again glanced at Toller, obviously trying to draw him back into the discussion. "I cannot be more precise at this stage. Much depends on the distance at which we can spot an ascending ship, but—as Lord Toller will testify—the eye becomes abnormally keen in the high air. Much will also depend on the effective range of our weaponry, but my expertise in that field is minuscule compared to Lord Toller's. Perhaps he should say. . . ."

"Continue without me for the present," Toller said comfortably, appreciating Zavotle's motives. "I find your discourse both interesting and instructive."

"Your Lord Toller," Chakkell whispered to Zavotle, "is so sure of himself that he has no fear of gifted and promising subordinates. Now, I have another and more prosaic difficulty for your consideration—one I fear you will not be able to magic away so quickly."

"Majesty?"

"It is many years since I controlled the production of the Migration fleet, but I recall very clearly that the only material light enough and strong enough for the manufacture of skyship envelopes is linen." Chakkell paused and frowned, dispelling the trace of levity which had crept into the proceedings.

"You may not be aware of this, but the flax seeds we brought from Land have not taken well in the soil of Overland. Only a few acres here and there produce a useful crop, and much of the yield has already gone into airships which are currently in service. In your considered opinion, could the material of those airship envelopes be cut up and restitched to form skyship balloons?"

"No!" Toller and Zavotle spoke simultaneously, but once again Toller—whose reply had been a reflex—was at a loss for a constructive answer. He was reminded of the fact that Chakkell was not King because of an accident of birth, that he had a phenomenally detailed knowledge of those aspects of agriculture, manufacture and trade which were the true foundation of a nation's power. And again he chose to remain silent, transferring all responsibility to Zavotle. He was both surprised and impressed when Zavotle responded with a calm smile.

"The balloons must be made from new, perfect material, Majesty," he said, "but not many will be required. The ambush strategy devised by Lord Toller is a good one, and it is fortunate for us that, in the circumstances envisaged, balloons would be an encumbrance, a serious handicap."

Chakkell's frown deepened. "We seem to be parting company, Zavotle. What are you saying?"

"Majesty, we are talking about a new kind of warfare, but some ancient principles must prevail. It is essential for us to remain out of sight of the enemy for as long as possible, until he has blundered into our trap. That being the case, balloons —which are so huge that they can be seen for many miles in the purity of a weightless zone—would become a liability. The fortresses would function more efficiently without them."

Toller began to comprehend the scheme Zavotle was proposing, and for a moment he seemed to feel the coldness of the high air seeping into his body. "You want to detach the balloons, and . . . and. . . ."

"And return them to the ground, where they will be used to carry other fortress sections aloft," Zavotle said, nodding. "I see no reason why an individual balloon should not make the return journey many times."

"That is not the issue I was going to raise," Toller said. "You're talking about leaving men up there. Stranded! With no means to check a ship's fall!"

Zavotle's face became more serene, and somehow less human. "We are discussing the weightless zone, my lord. As you yourself once said to me – how can an object fall if it has no weight?"

"I know, but. . . ." Toller retreated from the use of logic. "I don't like it."

"But I do!" Chakkell half-shouted, beaming at Zavotle in a manner which suggested that his burgeoning affection had quickly reached full flower. "I like it a lot!"

"Yes, Majesty," Toller said drily, "but you won't be up there."

"Nor will you, Maraquine," Chakkell countered. "I am appointing you my Sky Marshal because of your extensive knowledge of skyships—not because of your redundant and fading physical prowess. You will remain firmly on the ground and direct operations from here."

Toller shook his head. "That is not my way. I lead from the front. If men are required to entrust their lives to . . . to wingless birds, I would prefer to be among the first of them."

Chakkell looked exasperated, then he glanced at Zavotle and his expression became enigmatic. "Have it your own way," he said to Toller. "I am investing you with the authority to take any man in my kingdom into your service—may I assume that your friend Zavotle will be given an important advisory post?"

"That was my intention from the beginning."

"Good! I expect you both to remain at the palace until we have discussed every major aspect of the defence plan, and as that will take a considerable time it will be. . . ." Chakkell broke off as his stoop-shouldered secretary entered the room, bowing vigorously, and approached the table. "Why do you interrupt me, Pelso?"

"Apologies, Majesty," Pelso replied in a quavering voice. "My information was that you were to be informed without delay. About the execution, that is."

"Execution? Exe . . . ? Oh, yes! Go on, man."

"Majesty, I sent for the holder of the warrant."

"There was no need for that. I simply wanted to know if the chore had been completed. Oh, all right—where is your man?"

"He waits in the east corridor, Majesty."

"What good is he to me in the corridor? Bring him here, you old fool!"

Chakkell drummed on the table with his fingers as Pelso, still bowing, backed away to the door.

Toller, although he had no wish to be diverted from the discussion in hand, stared towards the doorway as the thick-chested figure of Gnapperl appeared. The sergeant, carrying his helmet under his left arm, showed no sign of nervousness over what was undoubtedly his first audience with the King. He marched to Chakkell and saluted very correctly, awaiting permission to speak, but his eyes had already met Toller's and they were malignly triumphant, beaconing their message ahead of the spoken word. Self-recrimination and sadness caused Toller to lower his gaze as he thought about the hapless farmer he had met on the road to Prad that foreday. Could it really have been such a short time ago? He had promised Spennel help, and had failed him, and adding to the poignancy of his regrets was the knowledge that Spennel had expected him to fail. How was he to defend an entire world when it had proved beyond his powers to rescue one man from . . . ?

"Majesty, the execution of the traitor Spennel was carried out in accordance with the lawful warrant," Gnapperl said in answer to Chakkell's signal.

Chakkell shrugged and turned to Toller. "I did what I could. Are you satisfied?"

"I have one or two questions for this man." Toller raised his head and locked eyes with Gnapperl. "I was hoping that the execution would have been delayed. Did the sight of the skyship occasion no disturbances in the city?"

"There were many disturbances, my lord—but I could not allow them to divert me from the course of duty." Gnapperl spoke with ingenuous pride, a way of covertly baiting Toller. "Even the executioner had gone off with the crowds to follow the skyship, and I was forced to ride hard for several miles to find him and bring him back to the city."

He was the first executioner you encountered today, Toller thought. *I am the second.* "That is most commendable, sergeant," he said aloud. "You appear to be the kind of soldier who puts his duty above all else."

"That I am, my lord."

"What is going on here, Maraquine?" Chakkell put in. "Don't tell me you have descended to feuding with common soldiers."

Toller smiled at him. "On the contrary, I hold the sergeant in such esteem that I intend to recruit him into my own service. That is permissible, isn't it?"

"I told you you can have anyone you want," Chakkell said impatiently.

"I wished the sergeant to hear it from your own lips." Toller addressed himself directly to Gnapperl who—belatedly realising he had misread the situation—was beginning to look alarmed. "There will be many dangerous tasks to perform when it comes to testing our new skyships which hang in the high air without the support of balloons, and I will have need of men who put their duty above all else. Send those who are with you back to Panvarl, with my compliments, then report to the house commander. Go!"

Gnapperl, now pale and thoughtful, saluted and left the room, followed by the bowed form of the secretary.

"You told him enough about our deliberations," Chakkell grumbled.

"The sooner the word is put about the better," Toller said. "Besides, I wanted the sergeant to have some idea of what is in store for him."

Chakkell shook his head and sighed "If you intend to have that one killed, do it quickly. I won't have you wasting your valuable time on trivia."

"Majesty, there is something in this account I fail to understand," Zavotle said, abstractedly rubbing his stomach. Throughout the exchange with the sergeant his narrow head had been bent over Colonel Gartasian's dispatch book, ears protruding like tiny clenched fists, and now he was looking puzzled.

"Does it concern the musket?"

"No, Majesty—it's to do with the Landers themselves. If these odd-looking New Men are simply the offspring of men and women who were partially immune to pterthacosis, should there not have been a sprinkling of them among our own newborn?"

"Perhaps a few were born," Chakkell said, not showing much interest. "The parents would probably have disposed of them quickly without saying much about it. Or perhaps the condition is latent. It may not manifest itself until the brats are exposed to the toxins—and the ptertha on Overland are not poisonous."

"Not yet," Toller reminded him, "but if we go on destroying brakka trees the globes will surely change."

"Something for future generations to worry about," Chakkell said, pounding the table with the gavel of his fist. "Before us is a problem which must be solved in days, instead of centuries. Do you hear me? *Days!*"

I hear you, Toller thought, and already in his mind he was ascending towards the weightless zone, that realm of thin, cold and meteor-streaked air which he had entered but twice in his lifetime and had never expected to see again.

Chapter 5

The dream had returned many times during the night, taking Bartan Drumme back to the day of his airboat flight.

He had just tethered the boat and was walking towards the whitewashed farmhouse. An inner voice was shrieking at him, warning him not to enter the house, but although he was afraid he was unable to turn back. He unlatched the green door and pushed it open—and the creature was waiting inside, gently reaching for him with its single tentacle. As had happened in reality, he sprang backwards and fell, and when he looked again the monster had been transformed into a conglomerate of old clothes hanging on a wallhook. Where the dream differed from the reality was that the apron continued to beckon him, languorously, in a manner which could not have been caused by transient air currents, and somehow that struck more fear into him than the confrontation with the monster itself. . . .

At that point Bartan had always awakened with a moan of alarm, relieved to find himself back in the normal night-time world, but each time he had recaptured sleep the dream had begun again. Consequently, he had welcomed the return of daylight, even though he had risen with a lingering tiredness in his system. He had claimed an entire section on his own behalf, as Jop Trinchil had wanted him to do, and was working himself to exhaustion every day in an effort to get the place ready for Sondeweere's arrival.

Now, as he drove his refurbished wagon towards the Phoratere section, the contrast between the sunlit ambience of the morning and the terrors of darkness was invigorating him, dispelling all traces of weariness from his limbs.

There had been rain during the night and as a result the air was soft, thick and sweet. The mere act of breathing it was subtly thrilling and evocative as though it were wafting around him

75

from out of those years in which he had been a dreamy-eyed child who perceived the future as little more than a shifting aureate glow. And what added a psychic sparkle to the surroundings was the realisation that the instinctive optimism of his boyhood had been fully justified.

Life was *good*!

Keeping the bluehorn moving at a leisurely pace, Bartan reviewed the various circumstances which were conspiring to make this a special day in a special time. There had been the news from the reeve, Majin Karrodall, that all the expedition's claims had been registered and approved in the provincial capital. The farmers, who had been happy to take over readymade buildings and cleared land, now regarded Bartan as a benefactor. Jop Trinchil had set a date, only twenty days away, for Sondeweere's wedding. And, finally, there was the prospect of the festive gathering—to celebrate the ratification of the claims—at which there would be many kinds of food and drink, and dancing far into the night.

The revel was not due to begin at a set time, but would gradually accrete during the day as family groups made their way in from outlying sections. Bartan was going exceptionally early in the hope that Sondeweere would do the same, thus giving him some extra hours in her company. He had not seen her for at least twelve days, and he was hungry for the sight of her face, the sound of her voice and the dizzying feel of her body against his own.

The thought that she might already be at the Phoratere farm prompted him to urge the bluehorn to a faster pace. He soon reached the top of a shallow dome, from which he was able to see many miles ahead, and the pastoral serenity of the view accorded with his mood. The night's rain had deepened the blue of the sky, as was evidenced by the fact that he could discern several whirlpools of light in addition to a generous sprinkling of daytime stars. Below the horizon were sweeps and swathes of grassland in which the only perceptible movements were occasional reflections from near-invisible ptertha drifting on the breeze. In the middle distance, fringed by striated fields, were the buildings of the Phorateres' farm, visible as tiny rectangles of white and grey. Harro and Ennda Phoratere had volunteered the use of their place because it was one of the most central.

Bartan began to whistle as the wagon rolled more easily on the downward slope, following the parallel ruts of the track. When he neared the main farmhouse he saw that several wagons were standing by the stable, but Trinchil's—in which Sondeweere would have travelled—was not among them. It was likely that those which had arrived so early belonged to families whose female members were helping with the preparations for the party. A long table had been set up and a number of men and women were standing near it, apparently deep in discussion. Children of various ages were at play in the vicinity, producing a cheerful hubbub of laughs and screams, but as Bartan halted near the stable he received the impression that something was troubling the adults.

"Hello, Bartan—you are early." Only one of the farmers—a ruddy-cheeked young man with spiky straw-like hair—had left the group to greet Bartan.

"Hello . . . Crain." Bartan named the man with some difficulty because the Phorateres were a large family, with several cousins of similar age and appearance. "Am I *too* early? Should I depart and return later?"

"No, it's all right. It's just that . . . something has happened. It has taken the wind out of our sails a bit."

"Something serious?"

Crain looked embarrassed. "Please go into the house. Harro needs to see you. We were on the point of sending a rider to fetch you when we saw your wagon coming over the rise." He turned and walked away before Bartan could question him any further.

Bartan walked to the farmhouse's front entrance with growing curiosity. Harro Phoratere was the head of the family—a reserved and taciturn forty-year-old who had not warmed to Bartan as much as the other members of the community. The fact that he had invited Bartan into his home was unusual in itself, a hint that something extraordinary had occurred. Bartan tapped the planked door and went inside, to find himself in a large square kitchen. Harro was standing by an inner door which probably led to a bedroom. He had a cloth pressed to his right cheek and his face was devoid of the high colouring which was a family characteristic.

"There you are, Bartan," he said in a subdued voice. "I'm glad you came early—I'm sorely in need of your help. I know I haven't shown you much cordiality in the past, but. . . ."

"Put that out of your mind," Bartan said, starting forward. "Only tell me what I can do for you."

"Speak quietly!" Harro said, putting a finger vertically to his lips. "Those wondrously fine little tools that you showed us . . . the ones you use for repairing jewellery . . . have you brought them today?"

Bartan's puzzlement increased. "Yes, I always keep some by me. They are in my wagon."

"Could you unlock this door? Even with the key still in the lock on the other side?"

Bartan examined the door. It was unusually well crafted to be in a farm dwelling, and its having a lock instead of a latch was an indication that the original builder of the house had had gentlemanly aspirations. The shape of the keyhole, however, indicated that the lock itself was of the simplest and cheapest warded pattern.

"An easy enough task," Bartan whispered. "Is your wife in that room? I hope she isn't ill."

"Ennda is in there, all right, and I fear she has gone mad. That's why I didn't break the door down. She screams when I so much as touch the handle."

Bartan remembered Ennda Phoratere as a handsome, well-made woman in her late thirties, better educated and more articulate than the other farmers' wives. She was eminently practical, with a good sense of humour, and probably the last person in the community he would have expected to fall prey to fevers of the mind.

"Why do you think she is mad?" he said.

"It started during the night. I woke up and found Ennda pressing herself against me, working herself against me. Intimately, you understand. Moaning she was, and insistent—so I obliged. To tell you the truth, I had little choice in the matter."

Harro paused and gave Bartan a hard look. "This is between *us*, you understand."

"Of course," Bartan said. He had noticed before that, while being fond of using vulgar sexual references in everyday speech, the farming people tended to be reticent about their own personal relationships.

Harro nodded. "Well, at the height of it all she . . . bit me."

"But. . . ." Bartan hesitated, wondering how much difference there could be between the urban and the rural experience of passion. "It's not uncommon for lovers to. . . ."

"Like this?" Harro said, removing the cloth from his cheek.

Bartan flinched as he saw the wound on the other man's face. There were two curving incisions in the shape of an open mouth, their ends so close that it was obvious that a substantial piece of flesh had almost been torn out of Harro's cheek. The edges of the incisions had been drawn together with a cross-stitching of black thread, but blood was still oozing in places despite a generous dusting of powdered pepperbloom, a traditional Kolcorronian coagulant. The skin surrounding the wound was darkly bruised, and it was evident that Harro would be scarred for life.

"I'm sorry," Bartan mumbled. "I had no idea."

Harro covered his cheek again. "Next thing Ennda was attacking me, beating me about the head with her fists, screaming at me to get out of the room. I was so confounded that I was out of the room before I knew what was happening. Ennda locked the door. For a while she kept screaming something . . . it sounded like, 'Not a dream, not a dream' . . . then she fell silent and has been that way for hours. Except when anyone tries the lock, that is—then she starts it again. I'm worried about her, Bartan. I must reach her in case she does some mischief to herself. She sounded so . . . so. . . ."

"Wait here!" Bartan went to the front entrance and, ignoring the questioning glances of the group by the long table, walked quickly to his wagon. He opened its toolbox and was withdrawing the roll of jeweller's instruments when Crain Phoratere arrived at his side.

"Can you do it?" Crain said. "Can you manage the door?"

"I believe so."

"Good man, Bartan! When the screaming started we ran here from the sidehouses and found him naked and covered with blood. We put some clothes on him and stitched the wound, then he cleared the house. He refuses to speak to anyone—ashamed, perhaps—and we don't know whether to let the revel continue or not. Perhaps it would be unseemly."

"We'll see how she is when we get into the bedroom," Bartan said, hurrying back to the house. "Stay close by and I'll call you if we need assistance."

"Good man, Bartan!" Crain said fervently.

In the house Bartan found Harro still waiting by the bedroom door. Bartan knelt beside him and examined the keyhole closely, satisfying himself that the lock could be successfully manipulated. He selected the instrument best suited for his purpose and looked up at Harro.

"I have to do this quickly in case she guesses what is happening," he said. "Please be ready to go in immediately."

Harro nodded. Bartan turned the key with a single twist and moved aside as Harro brushed by him and into the room beyond. In the half-light from the doorway and the shuttered window he saw Ennda Phoratere standing in the far corner, back pressed to the wall. Her black hair was in wild disarray around a face that was dehumanised by the white-corona'd eyes and the blood caked on her chin. Brownish stains dappled the upper part of her nightdress.

"Who are you?" she shrilled at Harro. "Stay away! Don't come near me!"

"Ennda!" Harro darted forward and seized his wife despite the flailings of her arms as she tried to fight him off. "Don't you know me? I only want to help you. *Please*, Ennda."

"You can't be Harro! You. . . ." She broke off, staring into his face, and pressed a hand to her mouth. "Harro? Harro?"

"You had a nightmare, but it's over. It's all over, dear one." Harro drew his wife towards the bed and made her sit down, at the same time nodding meaningfully towards the window for Bartan to take heed. Bartan went forward and opened the shutters, expanding a central sliver of brilliance into a wash of sunlight. Ennda looked all around the room, mistrustfully, before turning to her husband.

"But your *face!* Look what I did to your poor face!" She gave the most anguished sob Bartan had ever heard, lowered her head and—on seeing the bloodstains on her nightdress—began to tear at the thin cotton material.

"I'll fetch some water," Bartan said hastily, leaving the room. He saw Crain Phoratere standing just beyond the front entrance and made a pushing gesture against the air to warn him to remain outside for the time being. His glance around the kitchen located a green glass ewer and basin on a sideboard. He poured some water into the basin, gathered up a washcloth, soap and towel, taking as much time as possible over the operation, and returned to the bedroom door. Ennda's nightdress was lying on the floor and she was swaddled in a sheet taken from the bed.

"It's all right, lad," Harro said. "Come in."

Bartan entered the room and held the basin while Harro cleaned and dried blood from his wife's face. With the disappearance of the scaly disfigurement Harro showed an uplift in his spirits, reminding Bartan that some nursing procedures were as much for the benefit of the caring as the cared for. He too began to feel a sense of relief, though with a twinge of conscience over his own selfishness—his special day had been threatened, but the threat was lifting. Ennda Phoratere had had a very bad dream, with unfortunate consequences, but life was now settling back into its pleasant routine and soon he would be dancing with Sondeweere, belly to belly, thigh to thigh. . . .

"That's better," Harro said, dabbing his wife's face with the towel. "It was only a nightmare, and now we can forget all about it and. . . ."

"It wasn't a nightmare!" Her voice had a thin, wailing quality which somehow checked Bartan's rising tide of optimism. "It was *real!*"

"It can't have been real," Harro said reasonably.

"What about your face?" Ennda began to rock gently backwards and forwards. "It wasn't *like* a dream. It seemed real, and it seemed to go on for ever . . . for ever and ever. . . ."

Harro tried being jocular. "It can't have been worse than

some of the dreams I have had, especially after a supper of your suet cakes."

"I was eating your face." Ennda gave her husband a calm, dreadful smile. "I didn't just bite your cheek, Harro—I ate up all of your face, and it took hours. I bit off your lips and chewed them up. I pulled your nostrils off with my teeth and chewed them up. I gnawed the front off your eyeballs and sucked the fluid out of them. When I had finished with you, you had no face left . . . nothing at all . . . not even ears. . . .

"There was just a red skull with some hair on top. That's what I was doing to you during the night, Harro, my beloved—so do not try to tell me about your nightmares."

"It's all over now," Harro said uneasily.

"Is that what you think?" Ennda began to rock more vigorously, as though driven by an invisible engine. "There was more, you know. I haven't told you about the dark tunnel . . . crawling under the ground in the dark tunnel . . . with all the flat, scaly bodies pressing on me. . . ."

"I think it would be better if I left," Bartan said, turning towards the door with the basin.

"No, don't go, lad." Harro raised a hand to detain Bartan. "She's better with company."

". . . they had many legs—and I was the same . . . *I* had many legs . . . and a trunk . . . a tentacle . . . growing out of my throat. . . ." Ennda suddenly ceased rocking, tucked her right shoulder under her chin and extended her arm forwards. It made a gentle, boneless rippling movement which was mimicked by something in the deeps of Bartan's consciousness, making him unaccountably afraid.

"Well, I'll just put the basin away," he said, feeling like a traitor, knowing that he intended to get out of the house and leave the two unfortunates to deal with their own problems, none of which had anything to do with him. He evaded Harro's hand, walked briskly into the kitchen and set the slopping basin down on the sideboard. He turned and was on his way to the bright sanity of the front entrance when he was snared by Ennda's psychic web. She had risen to her feet, unmindful that the sheet was slipping down her torso, and could have been performing a strange new dance, her arm snaking and wafting before her.

"It began oddly," she murmured. "Very oddly indeed, and it's wrong to call it a beginning because I kept going back to the house. It was an ordinary farmhouse . . . whitewashed, green door . . . but I was afraid to go in . . . and yet I *had* to go in. . . .

"When I opened the green door there was nothing there but some old clothes hanging on a hook on the wall . . . an old hat, an old cloak, an old apron . . . I knew I should have run away at that stage, while I was still safe, but something made me go in. . . ."

Bartan halted at the bedroom door, chilled.

Ennda looked straight at him, through him. "You see, I was wrong. There weren't any old clothes. It was one of *them* . . . that tentacle reaching towards me . . . ever so gently. . . ."

Harro closed with his wife and gripped her shoulders. "Stop this, Ennda. Stop it!"

"But you don't understand." She smiled again, her arm coiling around his neck as the sheet dropped to the floor. "I wasn't being attacked, dear one . . . it was an invitation . . . an invitation to love . . . and I *wanted* it. I went into the house and I embraced the horror . . . and I was happy when I felt its pale grey penis entering me. . . ."

Ennda surged against Harro, her naked buttocks pumping and contracting. With one imploring glance towards Bartan, Harro used his weight and size to force his wife down on to the bed. Bartan stepped into the room, slammed the door behind him and threw himself down against the couple, helping to imprison Ennda's threshing limbs. Her teeth clicked as she bit the air and her pelvis drove upwards again and again, but now with diminishing power. Her eyelids were drooping wearily, peace was returning to her body. Bartan took the initiative and covered her, using the sheet that had fallen to the floor, but his mind was elsewhere, wandering in a strange continuum of doubt and confusion.

Could coincidence ever be stretched far enough to explain two people dreaming the same thing at the same time? Perhaps, if the subject were a very commonplace one, but not when . . . *And at first mine was not a dream!* Bartan's brow prickled coldly as he remembered that he had been to the house and had walked through the green door in actuality. But in reality his monster had been a delusion, and in Ennda's delusion her monster had been a reality. *The universe does not work this way*, Bartan told himself. *Something has gone wrong with the universe. . . .*

"She looks better now," Harro whispered, stroking his wife's brow. "Perhaps a couple of hours of proper sleep is all she needs. In fact, I *know* that is what she needs."

Bartan stood up, trying to anchor his thoughts in the solid present. "What of the celebration? Are you going to send everybody away?"

"I want them all to remain here. It will be best if Ennda has her friends around her when she awakes." Harro got to his feet and faced Bartan across the bed. "There's no need to talk too much about all this, is there, lad? I don't want people to think she has gone mad—especially Jop."

"I won't say anything."

"I'm grateful to you," Harro said, leaning forwards to shake Bartan's hand. "Jop has no time for all this talk of dreams and nightmares that we've had of late. He says that if people worked as hard as they ought they would be too tired to dream at night."

Bartan forced a smile. Were other members of the community having bad dreams? Was this what Reeve Karrodall had foretold? Could this be only the beginning, the beginning of something terrible, something which could drive the new wave of settlers away—as had happened to their predecessors?

"When I lay my head down at the end of the day," he said ruefully, pushing aside his memories of the night's disturbing dream, "I experience a small death. There is *nothing* until daybreak."

"Anybody who tried to start off a whole section on his own is entitled to be exhausted, more so somebody who wasn't brought up to this work."

"I get some help from the neighbours," Bartan said, eager to talk of commonplace things while he strove to come to terms with his new internal picture of the world. "And after I'm married there will be. . . ."

"I must put a bandage on my war wound," Harro interrupted,

gingerly prodding his cheek. "You go outside and say I want to know why they are all standing around with both arms the same length instead of preparing for the festivities. Tell them this is to be a day to remember."

News had come that Jop Trinchil and his family would not be arriving until near the middle of the day, so Bartan passed the time by joining in where he could with the various preparations going on around the farm. His efforts were received with good humour, but the women soon made it clear to him that he was hindering rather than helping, especially as he was abstracted and prone to error. He withdrew to a bench facing the kitchen orchard, where several men were already sunning themselves and sharing a jug of green wine.

"That's right, lad," Corad Furcher said companionably, handing Bartan a full cup. "Leave the women to get on with it by themselves." He was a middle-aged man whose yellowish hair betokened a blood relationship with the Phorateres.

"Thanks." Bartan sipped the sweet liquid. "It's all confused back there, and I did seem to be getting in the way a little."

"There's the source of the trouble, up there." Furcher made a gesture which took in the clear blue dome of the sky. "The onset of littlenight was the obvious time to begin a revel when we lived on the Old World, but here the sun goes on shining and shining and shining, and you can't regulate yourself properly. It isn't natural, you know, this living on the outside. I'm as loyal as the next man, but I still say King Chakkell was interfering with the right way of things when he scattered us all around the globe. Look at that sky! Empty! It makes me feel I'm being watched all the time."

The men farther along the bench nodded in agreement and began a discussion about the disadvantages of being on the hemisphere of Overland which was permanently turned away from the sister planet. Some of the theories they put forward about the effects of the uninterrupted day on crop growth and animal behaviour sounded highly dubious to Bartan. He found himself longing for Sondeweere's company more than ever, and in between times wrestling with the problem posed by Ennda

Phoratere's terrible nightmare. Coincidence had to be ruled out, but perhaps the key to the mystery lay in the very nature of dreams. Was it possible, as some claimed, that the mind roved out from the body during the hours of sleep? If it were, then perhaps two discarnate personalities could meet by chance and commune briefly in the darkness, influencing each other's dreams.

Bartan was reluctant to abandon his vision of a perfectly happy future, and the new idea seemed to offer its salvation. As the strong wine began to do its work he began to see the episode as rare and unpleasant but perfectly explicable, a manifestation of some of nature's complexities and subtleties. The resurgence of his optimism was aided by the sight of Ennda emerging from the main house and taking part in the seemingly endless preparations for the forthcoming party. She was a little sheepish at first, but soon she was laughing with those around her, and the message for Bartan was that the black humours of the night were dispersed and forgotten. The day would be all the more joyful in comparison.

He was unaccustomed to drinking wine, and by the time the Trinchil wagon appeared in the distance he had reached a state of lightheaded euphoria, an enhancement of the one he had known in the early part of the day. His first impulse was to go out and meet Sondeweere, but it was superseded by a playful desire to surprise her with a sudden appearance. He went to where the other farmers had parked, stationed himself between two of the tall vehicles and waited until the new arrivals had rolled to a halt close by. There were more than a dozen of the Trinchil family on the wagon, and the noise level in the area increased sharply as they spilled over its sides, the children vying with the adults in the calling out of greetings to friends. In spite of his bulk, Jop Trinchil was first to reach the ground. He strode off immediately towards the laden tables, obviously in a boisterous mood, leaving the women to supervise the unloading of infants and some small hampers.

Bartan was enchanted to see Sondeweere wearing her best dress, a pale green tailored garment with an olive filigree pattern, which complemented her fair coloration and reaffirmed his impression of her as being in a class apart from all the other women of the community. She was the last to quit the wagon, languorously rising to her feet in a kind of voluptuous slow-motion shimmy which set Bartan's heart racing.

He was about to go forward when he saw that one of Jop's sons—a precociously muscular seventeen-year-old named Glave—was waiting by the wagon with arms upraised to help Sondeweere descend. She smiled down at him and swung her legs over the side, permitting him to encircle her waist with his large hands. He took her weight easily and lowered her to the ground in a deliberate manner which brought their bodies close together. Sondeweere gave no sign of being offended. She allowed the intimate contact to continue for several seconds, all the while gazing into Glave's eyes, then shook her head slightly. Glave released her immediately, said something Bartan was unable to hear and loped away in the wake of the rest of his family.

Annoyed, Bartan left his place of concealment and approached Sondeweere. "Welcome to the party," he said, quite certain in his mind that she would be disconcerted to learn that she had been under observation.

"Bartan!" Smiling brilliantly, she ran to him, threw her arms around his waist and nuzzled against his chest. "It seems *years* since I've seen you."

"Does it?" he said, refusing to return the embrace. "Haven't you found a way to make the time pass quickly? And pleasantly at that?"

"Of course not!" Becoming aware of the rigidness of his body, she stepped back to look at him. "Bartan! What are you saying?"

"I saw you with Glave."

Sondeweere's jaw sagged for a moment before she began to laugh. "Bartan, Glave is just a boy! And he's my cousin."

"Full cousin? By blood?"

"That doesn't come into it—you have no reason to be jealous." Sondeweere raised her left hand and tapped the brakka ring on the sixth finger. "I wear this at all times, my love."

87

"That doesn't prove. . . ." Bartan's throat closed painfully, preventing him from finishing the sentence.

"Why are we behaving like strangers?" Sondeweere fixed Bartan with a soft but purposeful stare and embraced him again, this time putting her arms around his neck and drawing his face down to meet hers. He had never been to bed with her, but before the kiss was over he had a fair idea of what the experience would be like and all thoughts of rivalry, or indeed of anything, had flown from his mind. He responded hungrily until she had broken away from him.

"Labouring in the field is making you very strong," she whispered. "I see I will have to be careful with you and grow a plentiful crop of maidenfriend."

Flattered and uplifted, he said, "Don't you want to have children?"

"Lots of them, but not too soon—we have much work to do first."

"We'll have no talk of work for the remainder of the day." Bartan linked arms with Sondeweere and drew her away from the farm buildings towards the sunlit peacefulness of the open land, where crops in different stages of maturation glowed in strips which narrowed into the distance. They walked together for a good hour, enjoying each other's presence, passing the time with lovers' smalltalk and counting the meteors which occasionally scribed silver lines across the sky. Bartan would have liked to keep Sondeweere to himself until nightfall, but he gave in with good grace when she decided to return to the others for the start of the dancing.

By the time they had reached the main farmhouse Bartan was thirsty. Feeling it would be prudent not to have more wine, he joined the men clustered around the ale barrels in search of a less heady brew. He fended off the expected ribaldry about what he had been doing while absent with Sondeweere, and emerged from the group with a heavy pot of ale in his hand. Three fiddlers had begun to play in the shade of the barn and several young women—Sondeweere among them—had joined hands and were opening the first of the set dances.

Bartan looked on in a mood of utter contentment, taking small but regular sips of his drink, as some male farmers overcame their self-consciousness and gradually swelled the ranks of the dancers. He finished his ale, set the pot on a nearby table, and had taken one step towards Sondeweere when his attention was caught by a group of small children at play on a grassy patch near the kitchen orchard. All were aged about three or four and were moving in a circle, silently absorbed, performing a dance of their own to a slower rhythm than that of the adults' music. Their chins were tucked down into hunched right shoulders, and their right arms were extended in front, gently wafting and undulating like so many snakes.

The movements were strangely inhuman, strangely unappealing—and exactly simulated those with which Ennda Phoratere had acted out the obscene horrors of her nightmare.

Bartan turned away from the children, frowning, suddenly feeling isolated from the merriment and innocence of his neighbours.

PART II

The Cold Arena

Chapter 6

As they walked to the palace's principal entrance Gesalla Maraquine talked continuously about domestic trivia—a tactic which Toller found more baffling and infuriating than if she had chosen to maintain a cold silence.

He had not been able to return home in the twelve days which had elapsed since the visitation by the skyship from Land, and consequently had been pleased when Gesalla had ridden up from the estate to spend the night with him. But her stay had provided none of the comforts for which he had hoped. She had arrived in a strange mood, enigmatic and slightly distant, and on learning that he had insisted on going aloft with the first fortress had become positively acidic. Later, in bed, she had responded to his advances with a dull compliance which was more hurtful than outright rejection and which had caused him to abandon all thoughts of lovemaking. He had lain apart from her all night, physically and mentally frustrated, and when he had lapsed into sleep there had been dreams of falling—not just of ordinary falling, but of the day-long drop from the weightless zone. . . .

"Cassyll is waiting for you," Toller cut in forcibly. "It's good that you'll have his company on the ride home."

Gesalla nodded. "It's *very* good—after all, you might have decided to take him into the sky with you."

"What are you saying? The boy has no interest in flying."

"He had no interest in guns, either—until you put him to work on those cursed muskets. Now I see almost as little of him as I do of you."

"Is *that* what this is all about?" Toller stopped his wife in the busy, high-ceilinged corridor, waited until a group of officials had moved out of earshot, and said, "Why didn't you come out with it last night?"

"Would you have changed your plans?"

"No."

Gesalla looked exasperated. "Then what would have been the point in my speaking out?"

"What was the point in coming to the palace in the first place?" Toller said. "Was it to cause me pain?"

"Did you say *pain*?" Gesalla gave an incredulous laugh. "I heard about your plunge into insanity with that beast of a swordsman, Karkarand, or whatever his name is."

Toller blinked at her, thrown by the apparent change of subject. "It was the only way. . . ."

"Now you're going *up there* when there is absolutely no need for it. Toller, how do you think I feel, knowing that my husband would rather court death than go on living with me?"

Toller strove for a suitable answer, gaining time through the fact that two clerks carrying ledgers were passing close by and giving him inquisitive looks. This was the sort of situation in which Gesalla could strike a near-superstitious fear into him. Her oval face was hard, pale and beautiful, and behind those grey eyes was a mind that could far outpace his own, making it impossible for him to best her in an argument, especially an important one.

"I know there is little evidence of it thus far, but this is a time of crisis," he said slowly. "I am only doing what is required of me, and I hate it as much as. . . ." He allowed the sentence to tail off as he saw that Gesalla was shaking her head emphatically.

"Don't lie to me, Toller. Don't lie to *yourself*. You are enjoying all this."

"Nonsense!"

"Answer just one question for me—do you ever think of Leddravohr?"

Again disconcerted, Toller conjured up then drove from his mind a vision of the military prince, the man whose hatred had altered his entire life and with whom he had fought a duel to the death on the day their ships had touched down on Overland all those years ago.

"Leddravohr?" he said. "Why should I think of him?"

Gesalla produced the sweet, sweet smile which often preceded her deadliest thrusts. "Because you were a pair of sixes, you and he." She turned and walked away quickly, her straight-backed figure slipping through barriers of people with an ease he could not emulate.

Nobody can say that to me, he thought in dismay, trailing in Gesalla's wake. In spite of his efforts to overtake, she had passed through the arched entrance and was in the sunlight of the forecourt before he reached her side, and Cassyll was already bringing two bluehorns forward.

Cassyll Maraquine was as tall as his father, but the maternal component of his build was evident. His physique was of the lean and long-muscled type, giving him the capability—as Toller had learned through a number of failed challenges—of running for two or three hours at a stretch with virtually no diminution of speed. He bore a strong resemblance to his mother, with a fine-featured oval face and thoughtful grey eyes beneath a widow's peak of black hair.

"Good foreday, mother, father," he said and immediately gave all his attention to Toller. "I brought samples of the new batch of pressure spheres. Not one of them has failed or even distorted under test, so we can start producing reliable muskets right away. I have them in my saddle bag—do you want to see?"

Toller glanced at Gesalla's set countenance. "Not now, son. Not today. I'm leaving it to you and Wroble to take care of the production planning—I have other work in hand."

"Oh!" Cassyll raised his eyebrows and gazed at his father in open admiration. "So it's really true! You're going aloft with the first of the fortresses!"

"It has to be done," Toller said, wishing that Cassyll had reacted differently. He had been away from home on the King's business during much of his son's upbringing and had always considered himself blessed in that, far from showing resentment, the boy had regarded him as a glamorous adventurer and a father of whom to be proud. There had been no sense of competition with Gesalla for their son's mind, even after the boy had developed a strong interest in the new science of metallurgy, but now the triangular relationship was changing and presenting difficulties—just when Toller was least able to deal with them. The first two sky fortresses had been constructed in only a few days, far too short a time for a thorough study of the problem areas, and the forthcoming ascent was looming so large in his thoughts that all else seemed slightly unreal to him. In his heart he was already soaring up into the dangerous blue reaches of the sky, and he had become impatient with earthly matters.

"I'll speak to Wroble before nightfall," Cassyll said. "How long will you be away?"

"Perhaps seven days on this first ascent. Much depends on how smoothly the operation proceeds."

"Good luck, father." Cassyll shook Toller's hand, then held one of the bluehorns steady for Gesalla to mount it. She swung herself up into the saddle with practised grace, her divided riding skirt giving her full freedom of movement, and looked down at Toller with an expression which seemed to indicate an odd mixture of anger and sadness. The silver streak in her hair shone like a military emblem.

"Aren't you going to wish me good luck also?" he said.

"Why should I? You assured me the ascent would be perfectly safe."

"Yes, but. . . ."

"Goodbye, Toller." Gesalla wheeled the bluehorn away and rode off towards the palace gates.

Cassyll gazed after her in perplexity for a moment. "Is anything wrong, father?"

"Nothing we are unable to put right, son. Take good care of your mother." Toller watched Cassyll mount and ride after Gesalla, then turned and walked back into the palace, moving like a blind man opposed by currents of humanity. He had taken only a few paces when he heard a woman's footsteps hurrying behind him. The idea that it might be Gesalla coming back to put things right between them was irrational, but nevertheless he felt the beginnings of a surge of gladness as he halted and turned to face the person who was overtaking him. The emotion subsided in disappointment as he saw a petite, black-haired woman in her mid-twenties who was wearing the saffron uniform of an air-captain. Blue patches stitched to the shoulders of the thickly embroidered jupon showed that she had been seconded to the hastily formed Sky Service. Her face was firm-jawed and full-lipped, with unfashionably full eyebrows which seemed poised to frown.

"Lord Toller," she said, "may I have a word with you? I am Skycaptain Berise Narrinder, and I've been trying to see you for days."

"I'm sorry, captain," Toller said. "You have chosen the most inopportune time."

"My lord, this will take but a moment—and it is a matter of some importance."

The fact that the woman had not been deterred by his refusal caused him to look more closely at her, and far back in his mind there flickered the thought that she would have been highly attractive but for the anomaly of being in uniform. He was immediately angry with himself, and again wished that Queen Daseene did not have so much influence over her husband. It had been on Daseene's insistence that women had been admitted to the Air Service, and she had prevailed on Chakkell to permit female volunteers to join skyship and fortress crews.

"All right, captain," Toller said, "what is this matter of some importance?"

"I was told that it was your personal decision that no woman would take part in the first twelve ascents to the weightless zone. Is that true?"

"Yes, it's true. What of it?"

Berise's eyebrows now formed a continuous line above intent green eyes. "With the greatest respect, my lord, I wish to claim the right of protest granted to me under the Terms of Service."

"There are no Terms in wartime." Toller blinked down at her. "Leaving that aside, what have you to protest about?"

"I volunteered for flight duty and was rejected—simply because I'm a woman."

"You're in error, captain. If you were a woman with experience of piloting a ship to the weightless zone and carrying out the inversion manoeuvre you would have been accepted, or at least considered. If you were a woman with gunnery experience or with the strength to move fortress sections you would have been accepted, or at least considered. The reason that you were rejected is that you are unqualified for the work. And now may I suggest that we both resume our duties?"

Toller turned quickly and was beginning to walk away when the look of frustration he had seen in Berise's eyes struck a responsive chord within him. How many times in his youth had he too frowned and chafed when thwarted by regulations? He had an instinctive distaste for the idea of sending a woman into the front line of battle, but if he had learned one thing from Gesalla it was that courage was not an exclusively male attribute.

"Before we part, captain," he said, checking his stride, "why are you so anxious to climb to the midpoint?"

"There will never be another opportunity, my lord—and I have as much right as any man."

"How long have you been flying airships?"

"Three years, my lord." Berise was carefully observing the formalities of address, but her stern expression and heightened colour made it clear that she was angry at him, and he liked her for it. He had a natural sense of kinship with people who were unable to disguise their feelings.

"My ruling about the assembly flights is unchanged," he said, deciding to show her that the years had not robbed him of his humanity, that he could still sympathise with youth's ambitions. "But when the fortresses are in place there will be frequent supply flights, and the fortress crews themselves will be rotated on a regular basis. If you can curb your impatience, albeit briefly, you will have ample opportunity to prove your worth in the central blue."

"You are *very* kind, my lord." Berise's bow seemed deeper than was necessary, and her smile could have suggested amusement as much as gratitude.

Did I sound pompous? he thought, watching her walk away. *Is that young woman laughing at me?*

He considered the questions for a moment, then clicked his tongue in annoyance as it came to him how trivial was the subject which had diverted him from his major responsibilities.

The parade ground at the rear of the palace had been chosen as the launch site, partly because it was fully enclosed, partly because it made it easy for King Chakkell to keep a close eye on every aspect of the sky fortress project.

The fortresses were wooden cylinders—twelve yards in length and circumference and four in diameter—each of which had been built in three sections. Two prototypes had been produced in the initial war effort and the sections comprising them were lying on their sides at the western edge of the ground, looking like giant drums. The huge balloons which were to carry them into the weightless zone had already been attached and were lying on the baked clay, their mouths held open by ground crew, and hand-cranked fans were being used to inflate them with unheated air. It was a technique which had been devised at the time of the Migration to lessen the risk of damage to the linen envelopes when hot gas was fired into them from the burners.

"I still say it's madness for you to go aloft at this stage," Ilven Zavotle said as he crossed the parade ground with Toller. "And even now it isn't too late for you to appoint a deputy."

Toller shook his head and placed a hand on Zavotle's shoulder. "I appreciate your concern, Ilven, but you know it can't be done that way. The crews are terrified as it is, and if they thought I was afraid to go up there with them they would be completely useless."

"*Aren't* you afraid?"

"You and I have been in the weightless zone before, and we know how to deal with it."

"The circumstances were different," Zavotle said gloomily. "Especially for our second visit."

Toller gave him a reassuring shake. "Your system will work—I'll stake my life on that."

"Spare me the jests." Zavotle parted from Toller and went to confer with a group of his technicians who were waiting to observe the take-off. He had proved himself so valuable to the sky fortress project that soon after their first meeting Chakkell had appointed him Chief Engineer, thus making Toller redundant to a large degree and freeing him for the first ascent. As a result, Zavotle felt responsible for thrusting his friend into dangers whose extent could hardly be guessed, and he had been increasingly morose over the past few days.

Toller glanced up at the sky, to where the great disk of Land was poised at the zenith, and once again it came to him that he might die up there, midway between the two worlds. On analysing his reaction to the thought, the disturbing thing was that he felt no real fear. There was a determination to avoid being killed and to guide the mission through to a successful conclusion, but there was little of the normal human sense of dread at the possibility of having his life snuffed out. Was that because he could not envisage Toller Maraquine, the man at the centre of creation, meeting the same fate as all ordinary mortals—or had Gesalla been right about him? Was he really a war-lover, as the long-dead Prince Leddravohr had been—and did that explain the malaise which had begun to affect him in recent years?

The thought was a disquieting and depressing one, and he pushed it aside to concentrate on his immediate duties. All day there had been intense activity around the six fortress sections as supplies were loaded and secured, and last-minute adjustments were made to engines and equipment. Now the area was comparatively empty, with only the launch teams and the flight crews standing by their odd-looking ships. Some of the latter exchanged words and glances as they saw Toller approaching and knew that the 2,500-mile ascent was about to begin. The pilots were all mature men, selected because of their flying experience during the Migration; but most of the others were youngsters who had been chosen for their physical fitness, and they tended to be highly apprehensive about what was to follow. Understanding their worries, Toller put on a show of being relaxed and cheerful as he reached the row of slow-stirring balloons.

"The wind conditions are perfect, so I will not detain you," he told them, raising his voice against the clattering and whirring of the inflation fans. "I have only one thing to say. It is something you have heard many times before, but it is so important that it is worth repeating here. You must remain tethered to your ships at all times, and wear your parachutes at all times. Remember those basic rules and you will be as safe in the sky as you are on the ground.

"And now let us be about the work with which the King has entrusted us."

His closing words were far from being as inspirational as he would have liked, but a traditional speech delivered in high Kolcorronian would have seemed incongruous in the context of the strangest war in human history. In past conflicts the common man had always been emotionally involved—largely through fear of what an invading horde would do to his loved ones—but in this case most of the general populace were quite unaware of any threat. In a way it was an unreal war, a contest between rulers, where a few gladiators were thrown into the ring like tumbling dice to bring about an arbitrary decision, largely influenced by their ability to endure pain and deprivation, on the viability of a political idea. How was he to explain, justify and glorify that to a handful of hapless individuals who had been lured into the King's service, originally, by the prospect of steady pay and a soft life?

Toller went to his own ship, giving the signal for the five other pilots to do likewise. He had chosen to fly a fortress midsection because it looked less airworthy than the closed endsections and its crew needed an extra boost to their confidence. A temporary floor had been installed a short distance below one rim, and on that were the crew stations and lockers containing various supplies.

The centrally mounted burner was one which had served in the Migration and had been lying in Chakkell's stores for more than twenty years. Its main component was the trunk of a very young brakka tree which had been used in its entirety. On one side of the bulbous base was a small hopper filled with pikon, plus a valve which admitted the crystals to the combustion chamber under pneumatic pressure. On the other side a similar mechanism controlled the flow of halvell, and both valves were operated by a common lever. The passageways in the latter valve were slightly enlarged, automatically supplying the greater proportion of halvell which had proved best for sustained thrust.

Because the section was lying on its side the floor was vertical and Toller had to lie on his back in his chair to operate the burner's controls. His sword, which he had not thought to discard, made the attitude all the more awkward. He pumped up the pneumatic reservoir, then signalled to the inflation supervisor that he was ready to begin burning. The fan crew ceased cranking and pulled their cumbersome machine and its nozzle aside.

Toller advanced the control lever for about a second. There was a hissing roar as the power crystals combined, firing a burst of hot miglign gas into the balloon's gaping mouth. Satisfied with the burner's performance, he instigated a series of blasts—keeping them short to reduce the risk of heat damage to the balloon fabric—and the great envelope began to distend further and lift clear of the ground. The inflation crew raised it further by means of the four acceleration struts, which constituted the principal difference between the skyship and a craft designed for normal atmospheric flight. Now three-quarters full, the balloon sagged among the struts, the varnished linen skin pulsing and rippling like a giant lung.

As it gradually rose to the vertical position the crew holding the balloon's crown lines came walking in and attached them to the section's load points, while others gently rotated the section until its axis was perpendicular. All at once the section was ready to take to the air, held down only by the pull of the men holding its trailing ropes. The remainder of the flight crew scaled its sides on projecting rungs and took their places.

Toller nodded in satisfaction as he glanced along the line of craft and saw that the other crews had gone aboard in unison with his own. It was a departure from established Kolcorronian practice for a group of ships to take off simultaneously, but successful assembly of the fortresses in the weightless zone was going to depend on precision flying in close formation. Zavotle had decided that a mass take-off would help the pilots familiarise themselves with the technique, and also give an early indication of where problems could lie. There had been no time for trial ascents, and the crews would have to learn new skills under the tutelage of the severest and most unforgiving taskmaster of all.

Having assured himself that the other five pilots were ready to fly, Toller waved to them and fired a prolonged burst to initiate the climb. The roar of the burner was magnified in the vast echo chamber of the balloon which now blotted out most of the sky, and at the end of the blast the handlers released their lines on command from the launch supervisor. As the ship began to drift vertically upwards, with no breeze to impart a lateral component to its motion, Toller stood up and looked over the rim of the section into the slowly receding parade ground. He picked out the compact form of Ilven Zavotle, easily distinguishable because of his prematurely white hair, and waved to him. Zavotle did not respond, but Toller knew he had been seen and that Zavotle was wishing he could exchange places rather than have another man put his ideas to the test.

"Bring in the struts, sir?" The speaker was the rigger, Tipp Gotlon, a lanky gap-toothed youngster who was one of the few volunteers on the flight.

Toller nodded and Gotlon began working his way around the circular deck, drawing in the free-hanging acceleration struts by their tethers and securing them to the rim. Mechanic Millyat Essedell, a competent-looking, bow-legged man with several years of Air Service experience, was not required to do anything at this stage of the flight, but he was crouched at his equipment locker, busily sorting and checking the tools. The midsection ships had three-man crews—as compared with five in the end-sections—because they were burdened with the extra weight of the armaments the fortresses would use against invaders.

Satisfied that his companions were reliable, Toller directed all his attention into finding a burn ratio which would give a climb speed in the region of twenty-four miles an hour. He settled on a rhythm of four seconds on and twenty seconds off—well remembered from his first interplanetary crossing—and for the next ten minutes the pilots of the other ships practised keeping exactly level with him. They made a striking spectacle, being so huge and close, with every detail sharply etched in pure light, while the world gently sank into the blue haze of distance.

The ships had become Toller's only reality.

Looking down on the sketchy geometries of the city of Prad, he could feel little affinity with the place or its inhabitants. He had again become a creature of the sky, and his preoccupations were no longer those of mere land-locked beings. Affairs of state and the posturing of princes now mattered little in comparison with the condition of a rivet or the correct tensioning of a rope or even the strange ruminative sounds which a balloon would sometimes emit for no apparent reason.

By the time the practice period had ended the squadron had attained a height of two miles and Toller gave the signal for a vertical dispersion to take place. The manoeuvre was carried out quickly and without mishap, changing the tight horizontal group into a loose stepped formation which could face the onset of night with little risk of collision.

Toller had driven himself to the point of exhaustion before the take-off, sometimes getting only two hours sleep in a night, and it was during the enforced idleness of the ascent that his body claimed its due compensation. Even while operating the burner he would sometimes lapse into a torpor, counting off the rhythm by instinct, and much of his rest periods were spent in dozing and dreaming. Often when he awoke he genuinely had no idea where he was, and would gaze up at the patient, looming curvatures of the balloon in fear and confusion until he had deduced what it was and where it was taking him. At other times, especially at night when the meteors flickered continuously all around, he would not succeed in awakening fully and in his tranced condition imagined that he was on an ascent of long ago, in the company of men and women who had long since died or been turned into strangers by the processes of time, all of them voyaging into the future with varying degrees of trepidation and hope.

The changing patterns of night and day enhanced his temporal disorientation. As the ascent continued Overland's night grew shorter and its littlenight expanded, slipping towards the equilibrium which would be attained midway between the sister planets, and Toller found himself almost losing track of the sequence. The surest measure of time's passing became the ship's altimeter—a simple device consisting of nothing more than a vertical scale, from the top of which a small weight was suspended by a delicate coiled spring. At the beginning of the flight the weight had been opposite the lowest mark on the scale, but as the climb continued and the pull of Overland's gravity diminished, the weight drifted upwards in a perfect analogue of the flight, a miniature ship sailing a miniature cosmos.

Another reliable indicator of progress was the increasing coldness. On Toller's first ascent the crew had been surprised by the phenomenon and had been considerably distressed as a result, but now thickly quilted suits were available and the low temperatures were made tolerable. It was even possible, while seated close to the burner, to achieve a cosy, cocooned warmth —a condition which abetted Toller's persistent drowsiness, and in which he could spend hours staring into the darkening blue of the sky, at fierce stars scattered on overlapping whirlpools of light, at the splayed luminance of comets, and at Farland hanging in the distance like a green lantern.

One of the most important problems facing the mission was that of recognising the exact centre of the weightless zone. Toller knew that in theory there was no actual zone of weightlessness, that it was a plane of zero thickness, and that a fortress positioned as little as ten yards to one side or the other would inevitably begin the long plunge to a planetary surface. It had been assumed, however, that reality would be more forgiving than absolute equations and would allow some leeway, no matter how slight.

Toller's first job was to show that the assumption had been justified.

The six ships had switched over to jet propulsion days earlier, when the lift generated by hot air had become negligible, but now their engines were silent as they hung in a gravitational no-man's-land. Toller found it eerie that the crews could communicate well with each other simply by shouting—although their voices seemed to be absorbed quickly in the surrounding immensities, they could in fact carry for hundreds of yards. For many minutes he had been busy with the device, invented by Zavotle, which was intended to show up any significant vertical motion of his ship. It consisted of a small pan containing a mixture of chemicals and tallow which gave off thick smoke when ignited, and a bellows-like attachment with a long nozzle.

The machine made it possible to shoot out from the side of the ship tiny balls of smoke which retained their form and density for a surprisingly long time in the still air. Zavotle's idea was that the smoke, being no heavier than the surrounding atmosphere, would creat stationary markers by which the ship's motion could be gauged. Basic though the system was, it seemed to be effective. Toller had forbidden Essedell and Gotlon to move in case they tilted the circular deck, and he had been sighting the smoke puffs along the line of the handrail for long enough to convince him there was no relative displacement.

"I'd say we're holding," he shouted to Daas, pilot of the second midsection, who had been carrying out similar observations. "What say you?"

"I agree, sir." Daas, barely visible as a swaddled figure at the rail of his ship, waved to supplement his message.

Foreday had just begun and the sun was positioned "below" the six craft, close to the eastern rim of Overland. The upflung brilliance was illuminating the underside of the fortress sections, casting their shadows on the lower halves of the balloons, adding an unnatural and theatrical aspect to the scene. Toller suddenly became aware of a sense of elation as he surveyed the unearthly spectacle. He felt well-rested and strong after the brief hibernation of the ascent, ready to do battle in a new kind of arena, and within him was a peculiar sensation of such intensity that he was obliged to pause and analyse it.

There seemed to be a core of lightness which had nothing to do with the zero gravity conditions, and from that core came varicoloured rays—the metaphor was too simple, but the only one available to him—characterised by feelings of joy, optimism, luck and potency, which infused every part of his mental and physical being. The overall effect was strange and at the same time oddly familiar, and it took him several seconds to identify it and realise that he felt young. No more than that, and no less—he felt *young*!

An emotional reaction followed almost immediately.

I suppose many would think it strange for happiness to come to a man at a time like this. He relaxed his grip on the handrail slightly, allowing his feet to drift upwards from the deck, and the dreaming disk of Overland, cupped in its slim crescent of brightness, came into view beneath the ship. *This is why Gesalla compared me to Leddravohr. She senses the fulfilment I get when called upon to defend our people, but she is unable to share in it and therefore she becomes jealous. No doubt she is anxious about my safety, and that too prompts her to say things she later regrets in the privacy of the bedchamber.* . . . .

"I'm ready to go, sir." Gotlon's voice came from close behind Toller, calling him back into the practical universe. Toller brought his feet down on to the deck and turned to see that the young rigger, without awaiting the order, had donned his full personal flight kit. His lanky form was all but unrecognisable in the thick quilting of a skysuit, which included fur-lined gauntlets and boots. The lower half of his face was hidden by a woollen muffler, through which his breath emerged in white vapourings, and his form was further bulked out by a parachute pack and by the air jet unit strapped to his midriff.

"Shall I go out now, sir?" Gotlon fingered the karabiner on the tether which was keeping him close to the ship's rail. "I'm ready."

"I can see you are, but curb your impatience," Toller said. "There must be a full audience for your exploits."

As well as being ambitious, Gotlon was one of those rare individuals who were totally without fear of heights, and Toller felt lucky to have found him in the short time available. The crews of the six fortress sections had been in the weightless zone long enough to start getting used to floating in the air like ptertha, but a huge psychological barrier had yet to be surmounted.

Final assembly of the fortresses could not begin until it had been demonstrated that a man could untie himself, jump free of his ship and successfully return to it by means of his air jet. Although he had intellectual confidence in the hastily devised system, Toller was unashamedly relieved that he was not required to put it to the initial test. Once in reality, and many times since in nightmare, he had seen a man begin the 2,500-mile fall from the fringes of the central blue, at first moving so slowly that he seemed to be at rest, and then, as the gravitational yearning of the planet grew more insistent, dwindling and dwindling into the plunge which would last more than a day and end in death.

Toller's lungs were labouring in the rarefied air, and he felt a stinging coldness inside his chest as he shouted the necessary orders to the other five pilots. While all crewmen were lining up at the rails of their ships their eyes were fixed on Gotlon. He waved to them like a child attracting his friend's attention before a daring playground stunt. Toller allowed him the breach of discipline in the interests of general morale.

He scanned the five men in the nearest fortress end-section and with some difficulty, because of the all-enveloping skysuits, picked out Gnapperl, the sergeant who had been so vindictive in the matter of Oaslit Spennel's execution. Now ranked as an ordinary skyman, Gnapperl had not even tried to protest when Toller had selected him for the first mission, and had gone through his few days of training with a gloomy acceptance of his fate. It was not in Toller's nature to engineer another's death in cold blood, but Gnapperl had no way of knowing that and had become a very apprehensive and unhappy man—a state in which Toller was prepared to leave him indefinitely.

"All right," he said to Gotlon when he judged the moment to be right. "You may now part company with us—but be sure to return."

"Thank you, sir," Gotlon replied, with what Toller would have sworn was genuine pleasure and gratitude. He unclipped his line, raised himself by using his wrists until he was floating horizontally, then rolled over the rail and kicked himself clear of the side, using more force than Toller would have done. A bright blue void opened between him and the ship, and from one of the other vessels came the sound of a man quietly retching.

Gotlon slid away towards the stars, cradled in sunlight, gradually slowing as air resistance overcame his momentum, and by chance came to a halt in an upright position relative to those watching. Without pause, he twisted with an eel-like motion until he was facing away from the line of ships, and rapid movements of his right arm showed that he was pumping air into the propulsion unit. A few seconds later the hissing of the jet was faintly heard. At first it seemed to be having no effect, then it became apparent that he was indeed returning to his point of departure. His course was not perfectly true, and several times he had to glance back over his shoulder and adjust the direction of his air jet, but in a short time he was close enough to the ship to grasp the cane which Essedell was extending to him. Bracing his feet against the side, Essedell pulled on the cane and Gotlon came zooming in over the side like a man-shaped balloon.

"Well done, Gotlon!" Toller reached out casually with his right hand to arrest the weightless figure, and was surprised to find his arm painfully driven back beyond its normal traverse. The impact spun him round, still clutching Gotlon, and it was several seconds before the two men were able to stabilise themselves by gripping partitions. Toller was puzzled over what had happened, but the mystery was displaced from his thoughts by an outbreak of cheering and shouting from the crews of the other ships.

Toller had to acknowledge his own feelings of relief and reassurance. It was one thing to sit in a comfortable room in the palace and accept the pronouncements of clever men on the subject of celestial mechanics; but it was a different order of experience entirely to cast free of a ship and tread the thin air of the weightless zone, precariously balanced between two worlds, trusting one's life to little more than a set of blacksmith's bellows. But now he had seen it done! Having been performed once, the miracle was no longer a miracle. It had become part of the skyman's armoury of routine skills—and, importantly, had helped ease Toller's mind with regard to the ordeal which awaited him at the end of the mission.

He gave the order for all personnel to begin practising free flight. The period he could allow for the crews to adapt to the supremely unnatural activity was ridiculously short—but King Chakkell, with Zavotle's concurrence, had decided that time was the most vital factor in the preparations for the battle against Land. The small emergency cabinet had chosen to gear the war effort to meet the most unfavourable case: ten days for the reconnaissance ship to return to Land; two days for Rassamarden to react to the news it was carrying; and, on the assumption that part of his invasion fleet was already operational, a further five days for the vanguard of the enemy to reach the weightless zone.

Seventeen days.

By the end of that time, ran Chakkell's decree, there must be a minimum of six fortresses positioned at the midpoint and ready for combat.

Toller had been stunned by the announcement. The whole concept of fortresses had been presumptuous enough, but the notion of designing, building and deploying six of them in a mere seventeen days had struck him as being absurd in the extreme. He had, however, forgotten about Chakkell's unique combination of abilities—the ambition which had raised him to the throne, the gift for organisation with which he had once assembled a thousand-strong fleet of skyships, the ruthless determination which hurled aside or burst through every obstacle. Chakkell was an able ruler in years of peace, but he only came into his own during darker hours, and his fortresses were being built on time. It now remained to be seen whether the flesh-and-blood elements of his plan could withstand the same punishing degree of stress as those fashioned from inert matter.

Toller was highly conscious of others watching when it became his turn to push himself out from the side of the ship. He did his utmost to maintain an upright attitude with regard to the balloon and its cylindrical load, and was beginning to think he had succeeded when he realised that the great blue-and-white whorled disk of Land—which had been hidden by the balloon since the start of the ascent—appeared to be on the move above him. It drifted downwards and disappeared under his feet, to be followed by a remarkably similar apparition of Overland partaking in the same stately motion. There was no sensation of tumbling—he seemed to be the only stable object in a rolling universe in which the sun, the sister planets and the line of skyships followed each other in wavering succession—and he was grateful when the movement eventually slowed and ceased. He was also glad to discover that the experience of hanging in the blue emptiness was not as bad as he had feared. Apart from the inexplicable sensation of falling, which troubled all who entered the weightless zone, he felt reasonably secure and capable of functioning.

"Anybody who feels like grinning at my acrobatics should get it over with now," he shouted to the silently watching men. "The serious work begins in a few minutes, and there will be little cause for mirth, I can assure you."

There was appreciative laughter from the crews and renewed activity among the bulkily suited figures as they made their sorties with varying degrees of aptitude. Toller quickly realised that his own initial efforts were not as good as those of young Gotlon, but he persevered with the air jet and picked up the knack of propelling himself with fair accuracy to any point he wished to reach. The skill would have been easier to acquire had the exhaust been on his back, thus enabling him to face forward when in motion, but lack of time had forced the Air Service workshop to produce the simplest possible type of unit.

As soon as Toller was satisfied with his own competence he called the five other pilots to him for a final review of the forthcoming assembly procedure.

The conference was the strangest in which he had ever taken part, with six middle-aged men—all veterans of the Migration —hanging in a circle against a panoply of astronomical features, among which meteors continually darted like burning arrows. Three of the pilots—Daas, Hishkell and Umol—had been known to Toller since his days in the old Skyship Experimental Squadron, and he had relied upon their recommendations to a large extent when recruiting the remaining pair, Phamarge and Brinche.

"First of all, gentlemen," he said, "have we learned anything new? Anything which in your opinion affects the plan for building the fortresses?"

"Only that we should do it as fast as possible, Toller," Umol replied, using permitted familiarity. "I swear this cursed place is colder than the last time I was passing by. Look at this!" He pulled down his muffler to reveal a nose that was distinctly blue.

"The place is the same as ever, old hand," Daas told him. "Your trouble is you no longer have any fire in your balls."

"Did I say gentlemen?" Toller cut in, quelling Umol's obscene response. "*Children*, we have work to do, and nobody wants our task completed faster than I, so let us make sure we know what we are undertaking."

He spoke mildly, knowing from the little he could see of their faces that his companions were pleased with the success of the air jets and that their confidence in the project had increased accordingly. For the next few minutes he rehearsed the sequential stages of the assembly plan in detail. The first step was to rotate the six ships through ninety degrees to bring the fortress sections into their operational attitudes, with their lateral portholes facing both planets. It would then be necessary to unclamp the false decks and fire short bursts on the jets to drive the balloons, still trailing the decks, a short distance away from the circular sections. Once the sections were floating free they could then be linked with ropes, drawn together and sealed to form two cylinders with closed ends.

At that point the work force was scheduled to split into two separate groups.

Those whose duty it was to man the fortresses would go inside them and prepare for their lengthy stay in the weightless zone. Meanwhile, the six pilots—each accompanied by a rigger—would begin returning the precious balloons and engines to Overland for use in further missions. The early stages of the descent were straightforward enough and caused no forebodings among the experienced pilots. It was a matter of rotating the stripped-down craft through a further ninety degrees, and—using the engines in the thrust mode—driving them a short distance into Overland's gravitational field. The ships would be travelling upside down, something no commander liked doing, but that phase would last only a few hours, until they had regained enough weight to give them the balloonist's much-cherished pendulum stability for the descent. A final rotation through half-a-circle would normalise the ships' attitudes, putting Overland in its rightful place beneath the crews' feet, where it would remain for the rest of the journey home.

So far the flight plan and its techniques were conventional —something which any surviving pilot from the Migration could have outlined in seconds—but the strictures of the crisis situation had yet to be applied. Toller could remember, with diamond clarity, all the relevant words from that first meeting with Chakkell and Zavotle, the words which told him that the sky and he had not yet tested each other to the limit. . . .

"The descent is going to be the worst part," Toller said. "Quite apart from the cold—which will be severe—the men are going to be sitting on an open platform, with thousands of miles of empty air beneath them. Just think of it! Trip on a rope and over the edge you go! It was bad enough in the old-style gondolas, but there you at least had the sidewalls to give you some sense of security. I don't like it, Ilven—five days of that sort of thing would be a bit too much for any man. I think we. . . ." He stopped speaking, surprised, as he saw that Zavotle was nodding his head in evident agreement.

"You're absolutely right, quite apart from the fact that we simply cannot allow five days for the return," Zavotle said. "We shall need you and the other pilots back on the ground again much sooner than that, to say nothing of the balloons and engine cores."

"So . . . ?"

Zavotle gave him a calm smile. "I suppose you have heard of parachutes?"

"Of course I've heard of parachutes," Toller said impatiently. "The Air Service has been using them for at least ten years. What are you getting at?"

"The men must return by parachute."

"Wonderful idea!" Toller clapped a hand to his forehead in case his sarcasm had not been noticed. "But—correct me if I'm wrong—does a man with a parachute not descend at roughly the same speed as a skyship?"

Zavotle's smile became even more peaceful. "Only if the parachute has been opened."

"Only if. . . ." Toller walked around the small room, staring down at the floor, and returned to his chair. "Yes, I see what you mean. Obviously we can save some time if a man doesn't deploy his parachute until he is well into the fall. At what height *should* he open it?"

"How about, say, one thousand feet?"

"No!" Toller's reaction was immediate and instinctive. "You can't do that."

"Why not?"

Toller stared hard at Zavotle's face, reading the familiar features in an unfamiliar way. "You remember the first time we entered the central blue, Ilven. The accident. We both looked over the side and watched Flenn being taken away from us. He fell more than a *day!*"

"He didn't have a parachute."

"But he fell for *more than a day!*" Toller pleaded, appalled at what the intervening years had done to Zavotle. "It's too much to expect."

"What's the matter with you, Maraquine?" King Chakkell put in, his broad brown face showing exasperation. "The end result is the same whether a man falls for a day or a single minute—if he has no parachute he dies, and if he has a parachute he lives."

"Majesty, would *you* like to take that drop?"

Chakkell gazed back at Toller in simple bafflement. "Where's the relevance in your question?"

Unexpectedly, it was Zavotle who chose to reply. "Majesty, Lord Toller has practical cause for concern. We have no idea of the effects such a fall might have on a man. He might freeze to death . . . or asphyxiate . . . Or there may be ill effects of a different ilk—a pilot who was physically sound but insane would be of scant value to you." Zavotle paused, his pencil tracing a strange design on the paper before him. "I suggest that, as I was the one who proposed the scheme, I should be among those who put it to the test."

You had me fooled, you little weasel, Toller thought, listening to his former crewmate with a resurgence of his affection and respect. *And, just for that, I will ensure that you remain where you belong—right here on the ground.*

In general, there was little difference in outlook between the men who had volunteered for the mission and those who had simply been told they were taking part. Both groups understood very well that defying the King's will in a time of war would result in summary execution, and some of the volunteers had simply been making a virtue out of necessity, but confirmation of the fact that they could fly independently of the ships and come to no harm had boosted the general morale. If we have not died thus far, the reasoning had been, perhaps there is no reason for us to die at all. The outward sign of that optimism had been the shouting with which the men filled the sky as they developed their new skills and prepared for the next phase of the undertaking.

But now, Toller noticed, they had again fallen silent.

The last of the balloons had been separated from its fortress section, and—burdened with only its circular false deck and engine unit—had retreated a short distance from the centre of activity. Insubstantial though they were, the sheer hugeness of the gas-filled envelopes had made them dominant features of the aerial environment. In the mind they were vast friendly entities with the power to transport humans safely from world to world —and now, suddenly, they were withdrawing their patronage, abandoning their minuscule dependants in the hostile blue emptiness.

Even Toller, committed to the enterprise as he was, felt an icy slithering in his gut as he took note of how *small* the unsupported fortress sections looked against the misted infinities all around. Until that point it had seemed to him that the worst thing a man could be called upon to do was to take the long drop to the planetary surface, but he now felt almost privileged in comparison to those who would remain in the weightless zone. Privileged, yet in another way—and the realisation jolted him —oddly cheated.

What is happening to me? he thought, becoming alarmed. He had rarely given himself over to introspection, considering it a waste of time, but recently his emotional reactions to events had been so laden with ambivalence and contradiction that his mind had been obliged to turn inwards. And here was another example. In one instant he had pitied the fortress crews—and in the next he had come close to envying them! Few people knew better than he how illusory was the concept of military glory, therefore he could not have been seduced by his fleeting vision of a new breed of patriots, ultimate heroes, manning their fragile wooden outposts in the lonely reaches of the sky.

What is happening to me? he again demanded of himself. *Why am I no longer satisfied by what satisfied me once? Why, unless I am deranged, do I press forward where any reasonable man would retreat?*

Realisation that he was neglecting his duties prompted Toller to end the self-interrogation and propel himself closer to the first fortress under assembly. The mid-section and one end-section had been successfully aligned and brought together, and now the remaining component was about to be drawn into place. It had been deposited rather a long way from its companions, giving the men who were hauling on the link ropes time to develop a fast and effective rhythm. Clinging to the sides of the mid-section, four of them were working in unison with their free arms. The end-section, which had been sluggish at first, was now moving at a good speed and showed no signs of slowing down as it neared its assigned place. Toller knew it had no weight and therefore could cause no damage by colliding with the rest of the fortress, but on principle he disliked the use of excessive force in any engineering operation. He could foresee the section rebounding and having to be drawn in again.

"Stop hauling—it's coming in too fast," he shouted to the men on the link ropes. "Get ready to grip it and hold it in place."

The men acknowledged his command with waves and made ready to receive the advancing cylinder. Phamarge, who had been overseeing the task, signalled for another two men who were holding on to the short lashing ropes of the mid-section rim to assist their comrades. One of them pulled himself against the leather-covered rim and locked himself in place by clamping his thighs around it.

Toller watched the end-section close in on the waiting man. The wooden structure was losing very little speed and was easily compacting the stout ropes in its path—all of which, Toller thought, was rather strange for an object which was as weightless as a feather. Alarm geysered through his system as he recalled a similar anomaly at the end of Gotlon's first personal flight—the weightless man had delivered a surprisingly powerful impact, almost as though. . . .

"Get off the rim!" Toller bellowed. "Get clear!"

The suited man turned towards him, but made no other movement. There was a frozen instant in which Toller recognised the rough-hewn features of Gnapperl, then the end-section drove against the remainder of the fortress. Gnapperl screamed as his thigh-bone snapped. The entire fortress bucked, dislodging men from its sides, and the end-section—still squandering kinetic energy—slewed a little and partially entered the main structure. Two opposing lengths of rim scissored across Gnapperl's body for a moment, ending his screams, before the fortress sections drifted apart and came to rest.

Toller reflexively triggered his air jet and only succeeded in pushing himself farther away from the scene. He twisted around, pumping more air into the unit, and propelled himself backwards into the confusion of drifting figures. Colliding gently with the mid-section, he grasped a lashing point to steady himself and looked at the injured man. Gnapperl was drifting free of the fortress, arms and legs spread, and there was a long rent across the front of his skysuit. Blood had soaked into the exposed insulation, making the tear resemble a dreadful wound, and bright red globules were floating in a swarm around him, glistening in the sunlight. Toller was left with no doubt that Gnapperl was dead.

"Why didn't the fool get out of the way when you told him?" Umol said, using a rope to draw himself closer to Toller.

"Who's to say?" Toller thought of the dead man's odd moment of paralysis before the impact, and wondered if Gnapperl would have been so slow to react had the warning come from anybody else. It could be that his mistrust of Toller had been responsible for his death, in which case Toller also bore responsibility.

"He was a down-looking brute, anyway," Umol commented. "If any of us had to go, he's the one I would have picked—and at least he taught us something useful."

"What?"

"That something which can crush a man on the ground can crush him up here. It doesn't seem to matter that nothing has any weight. Can you understand it, Toller?"

Toller wrenched his thoughts from morality to physics. "Perhaps being totally weightless affects our bodies. It's something we ought to be careful about in the future."

"Yes, and meanwhile there's a carcase to be disposed of. I suppose we could just leave it be."

"No," Toller said immediately. "We'll take him back to Overland when we go."

Upside down, the six ships had travelled all through the hours of darkness. In addition to the speed imparted by their jets, there had been a slight gain as Overland tightened her gravitational web, but the acceleration had been negligible so early in the descent. And as soon as daylight had returned—with Overland's binary dance swinging her clear of the sun—the engines had been shut down and air resistance had brought the vessels to a halt. The pilots had then used the tiny lateral jets to turn the ships over, an operation conducted in majestic slowness, with the universe and all the stars it contained wheeling at the behest of six ordinary men, and the sun obediently sinking to a new position beneath their feet.

The manoeuvre had been completed without mishap, and now it was time to do things which had never been done before.

Toller was strapped into the pilot's seat, with Tipp Gotlon near to him on the other side of the engine unit. The false deck on which they were sitting was a circular wooden platform, only four good paces across, and beyond its unguarded rim was a yawning emptiness, a drop of more than two thousand miles to the planetary surface. At varying distances the five other sky-ships were suspended in the void against the complex blue-and-silver background of the heavens. Their two-man crews, because they were in the cylindrical shadows of the decks, were only visible where silhouetted against glowing spirals or the splayed radiance of comets. The huge balloons, brilliantly illuminated on their undersides, had the apparent solidity of planets, pear-shaped worlds with meridians marked by load tapes and lines of stitching.

Toller was concerned less with the unearthly ambience than with the demands of his own microcosm. The deck space was occupied by a clutter of equipment and stores, from the pipe runs of the lateral jets to the lockers used for the storage of power crystals, food, water, skysuits and fallbags. Waist-high partitions of woven cane enclosed the primitive toilet and galley. From the latter protruded the lower part of Gnapperl's body, which had been lashed in place to forestall its unnerving tendency to rise up and meander in weightless conditions.

"Well, young Gotlon, this is where we part company," Toller said. "How do you feel about that?"

"Ready when you are, sir." Gotlon gave his centrally divided smile. "As you know, sir, it is my ambition to become a pilot, and I would be honoured if you would allow me to pull the rip line."

"Honoured? Tell me, Gotlon—are you enjoying this?"

"Of course, sir." Gotlon paused while an unusually large meteor burned across the sky below the ship, followed by a sonorous clap of thunder. "Well, perhaps it would be wrong to say I'm enjoying it, but I have no wish to do anything else."

A fair answer, Toller thought, resolving to keep an eye on the youngster's future progress. "All right, pull the line when you're ready."

Without hesitation Gotlon leaned forward, grasped the red line which ran down to the crew stations from the balloon's interior, and tugged hard on it. The line went slack in his hand. There was no perceptible change in the ship's equilibrium or dynamics, but high in the flimsy cathedral dome of the balloon something irrevocable had happened. A large panel had been torn out of the crown, surrendering the ship to the forces of Overland's gravity. From that moment onwards the ship and its crew could do nothing but fall, and yet Toller felt a strange timidity over the next inevitable step.

"I see no point in sitting around here," he said, taking no chances on having his feelings observed. His feet were already tucked inside his fallbag, which was a fleece-lined sack large enough to enclose his entire body. He unfastened his restraints, straightened up, and in the act of doing so noticed his sword, which was still tied by its scabbard belt to a nearby stanchion. For an instant he considered letting it remain. It was an inconvenient and incongruous article to be taken into the confines of the bag, but leaving it behind would have been like abandoning an old friend. He strapped the weapon to his side and looked up in time to see Gotlon—still smiling!—launch himself backwards from the edge of the deck.

Gotlon tumbled away into the sterile blue, sunlight glancing unevenly from the underside of his cocooned form until he came to rest some thirty yards from the ship. He made no attempt to modify his final attitude, and could have been thought lifeless but for the transient feathering of his breath.

Toller looked towards the sister ships and saw that other men, following Gotlon's example, were venturing into the thin air. It had been decided in advance that there would be no synchronis-ation—individuals would jump when they were ready—and suddenly he had a fear of being last, and being seen to be last, which outweighed his reluctance to perform the supremely unnatural act. Toller drew the fallbag up to his chest, pushed hard with his feet and sailed face downwards over the rim of the deck.

Overland slid into view beneath him, and they were face to face like lovers, and she was calling to him from thousands of miles below. Little was visible in the gibbosity where night still reigned, but in the sunlit crescent the equatorial continent could be seen to span the world, pale green powdered with ochres beneath traceries of white cloud, and the great oceans curved away to the mysterious watery poles.

Toller surveyed the entire hemisphere for a short time, chastened and subdued, then drew up his knees to make himself smaller and closed the neck of the fallbag over his head.

I did not expect to sleep.

Who would have thought that a man could sleep during the dizzy plunge from the central blue to the surface of the world?

But it's warm and dark in here, and the hours pass slowly. And as my speed gradually increases and the atmosphere grows thicker, I can feel the bag beginning to rock and sway, and there is a hypnotic quality to the soughing of the air as it rushes by. It is easy to sleep. Almost too easy, in fact. The thought has crossed my mind that some of us may not awaken in time to get out of the bags and deploy our parachutes, but surely that is a ridiculous notion. Only a man with a deep inner urge to end his life could fail to be ready when the time comes.

Sometimes I open the bag and look out to see how my companions are faring, but it is becoming impossible to find them, whether above or below me. We are falling at slightly different rates, and as the hours go by we are being strung out in a long vertical line. It is noteworthy that we are all falling faster than the ships—something which had not been predicted. The false decks, being symmetrically attached to the balloons, are trying to maintain a horizontal attitude even though the balloons have collapsed and are being dragged along in their wakes, thus creating greater air resistance.

As we left the ships behind I noticed the decks oscillating in the air stream, and the last time I picked them out they were like six slow-winking stars. I must relate all this to Zavotle and see if he wants to redesign the attachments so that the decks can fall edge-on. The ships would descend faster that way. The impact with the ground would be worse, but the engine cores are indestructible.

Sometimes I think about the men we left up there in the weightless zone, and have found genuine cause to envy them. They at least have something to do! An abundance of tasks to perform . . . the sealing of the fortresses with mastic . . . the hourly smoke readings to warn of drifting . . . the setting up of the pressurisation bellows . . . the preparation of the first meals . . . the checking of engines and armaments . . . the establishment of watch rotas. . . .

The fallbag rocks gently, and the air whispers persuasively all around.

It is too easy to fall asleep in here. . . .

Chapter 7

"Gold! You have the gall to offer me gold!" Ragg Artoonl, infuriated, slapped the leather bag away with a calloused hand. It fell to the ground and partially opened, allowing a few squares of stamped yellow metal to spill into the wet grass.

"You're just as barmy as everybody says!" Lue Klo dropped to his knees and carefully retrieved his money. "Do you want to sell your section, or do you not?"

"I want to sell it all right—but I want *real* money. Good old-fashioned glass, that's what I want." Artoonl rubbed the thumb of one hand against the palm of the other, mimicking the counting of traditional Kolcorronian woven glass currency notes. "Glass!"

"It all bears the King's likeness," Klo protested.

"I want to *spend* the stuff—not hang it on a wall." Artoonl glowered around the small group of farmers. "Who has real money?"

"I have." Narbane Ellder sidled to the fore, fumbling in his pouch. "I've got two thousand royals here."

"I'll take it! The section is yours, and may you have better luck with it than I did." Artoonl was extending his hand for the money when Bartan Drumme stepped in between the two men and pushed them apart with a force he would have been unable to exert when he first turned to farming.

"What's the matter with you, Ragg Artoonl?" he said. "You can't sell off your land for a fraction of what it's worth."

"He can do as he pleases," the thwarted Ellder cut in, brandishing his wad of coloured squares.

"And I'm surprised at *you*," Bartan said to him, tapping him on the chest with an accusing finger. "Taking advantage of your neighbour when his mind is disturbed. What would Jop say about that? What would he say about this meeting?" Bartan glanced a challenge around the group of men who had come together in a tree-fringed hollow which offered some protection from the weather. A heavy belt of rain was drifting across the area, and the farmers in their sack-like hoods looked sullen and oddly furtive with their hunched shoulders and dripping features.

"There's nothing wrong with my mind." Artoonl stared resentfully at Bartan for a moment, then his face darkened even further as a new thought occurred to him. "This is all *your* fault, anyway. It was *you* who brought us to this place of misery."

"I'm sorry about what happened to your sister," Bartan said. "It was a terrible thing, but you have got to think straight about it and realise it's no reason to give up all you have worked for."

"Who are you to tell me what I can and cannot do?" Artoonl's flushed face expressed the kind of mistrust and hostility Bartan had encountered on first entering the commune. "What do you know about the land anyway, Mister Bead-stringer, Mister Brooch-mender?"

"I know Lue wouldn't be offering to buy your section unless he thought it worth his while. He's taking advantage of you."

"Watch your tongue," Ellder said, stepping closer to Bartan with his stubbled jaw thrust forward. "I grow more than a little weary of you, Mister—" he sought a fresh insult, eyes narrowing under the mental strain, and finally was obliged to copy Artoonl —"Bead-stringer."

Bartan looked around the group of cowled figures, assessing the general mood, and was both shocked and saddened to realise there was a genuine possibility of violence towards him if he remained. It was another indication, contrary to all his own arguments, that the farmers had indeed degenerated since occupying the Haunt. In the year that had passed since his marriage to Sondeweere he had seen their old spirit of camaraderie eroded and replaced by a mean competitiveness, with the largest and most successful families begrudging help to their neighbours. Jop Trinchil's mandate had been totally withdrawn from him, and—coincidentally—the loss of his authority had been accompanied by a spiritual and physical diminution. Shrunken and ill-looking, no longer able to exert a cohesive force on his flock, he was rarely seen outside the boundaries of his own family's section. Bartan had never expected to miss the old Trinchil, with his crassness and bullying ways, but the commune seemed to have lost direction without him.

"I am no longer a bead-stringer," Bartan said stiffly to the rainswept assembly. "More's the pity—because with my finest needle and thread I might have fashioned a slim necklace from all your brains. A *very* slim necklace."

His words drew an angry response from perhaps twenty throats. The sound was formless and blurred, like a conflict of sea waves in a narrow inlet, and yet by a trick of selective perception Bartan was able, or thought he was able, to isolate a single sentence: *The fool would be better employed making a chastity belt.*

"Who said that?" he shouted, almost reaching for the sword he had never worn.

The shadowed archways of several hoods turned towards each other and back to Bartan. "Who said what?" a man asked in tones of gleeful reasonableness.

"Does young Glave Trinchil still lend a hand with your chores?" another said. "If his strength ever fails I'll be willing to take his place—I've been known to plough an excellent furrow in my day."

Bartan came close to running forward and throwing himself at the last speaker, but commonsense and prudence held him in check. The peasants had won again, as they always did, because a dozen cudgels would always overcome one verbal smallsword. The same coarse clichés were ever cherished by them as something entirely original and precious, and thus their ignorance became their armour.

"I hope you will not be too distraught if I withdraw, gentlemen." He paused, hoping the sexual innuendo might have eased some tensions, but it had gone unnoticed. "I have business at the markets."

"I'll travel with you, if that's all right," Orice Shome said, falling in at Bartan's side as he walked away from the group. Shome was an itinerant labourer, one of the few who had recently been hired by members of the commune. He was a slightly wild-eyed young man, with most of one ear missing, but

Bartan had heard no bad reports of him and was prepared to accept his company.

"Join me if you wish," Bartan said, "but doesn't Alrahen expect you to be at work?"

Shome held up a small kitbag. "I'm on the road again. Don't want to stay around here."

"I see." Bartan pulled his oilcloth hood closer around his shoulders and climbed up to the driving seat of his wagon. The warm rain was still coming down hard, but above the western horizon was a band of pale yellow which was growing wider by the minute, and he knew the weather would soon improve. Shome sat on the bench beside him, Bartan twitched the reins and his bluehorn moved off, its rain-slicked haunches rising and descending in a steady rhythm. Inexplicably, Bartan found himself dwelling on the taunts about his wife, and to redirect his thoughts he decided to strike up a conversation with his passenger.

"You weren't with Alrahen for long," he said. "Was he not a good employer?"

"I've had worse. It's the place I don't like. I'm leaving because there's something not right about the place."

"Not another scare-monger!" Bartan gave Shome a critical glance. "You don't look like a man who'd be given over to wild imaginings."

"Imaginings can be a lot worse than anything that comes at you from outside. That's probably why Artoonl's sister killed herself. And I heard that boy of hers didn't just disappear—I heard she slew him and buried the body."

Bartan became angry. "You seem to have heard a lot—for somebody with only one ear."

"There's no need to get touchy," Shome said, fingering the remnant of his ear.

"I'm sorry," Bartan said. "It's just that all this talk of . . . Tell me, where are you bound for next?"

"I'm not sure. Had enough of breaking my back to make other men rich, and that's the truth," Shome replied, staring straight ahead. "Might try to make it as far as Prad. Work is plentiful there—clean, soft work, I mean—because of the war. Trouble is, Prad's so far away. You'd need an. . . ." Shome looked at Bartan with fresh interest. "Aren't you the one who has his own airship?"

"It's laid up," Bartan said, seizing on the mention of the war. "What news have you? Do the invaders still persist?"

"They persist, all right—but always they are repelled."

In Bartan's experience itinerant workers did not identify themselves with national objectives, but there was an unmistakable note of pride in Shome's voice.

"It's a strange war, all the same," Bartan said. "No armies, no battlefields. . . ."

"Don't know about there being no battlefield. I heard the skymen sit astride jet tubes as if they were mounted on bluehorns, and they fly out miles from their fortresses. And there aren't any balloons—no balloons anywhere—nothing to keep you from falling to earth." Shome gave a noisy shudder. "Glad I'm not up there—a man could get himself killed up there."

Bartan nodded. "That's why kings no longer lead their armies into battle."

"Lord Toller doesn't hold with that. You've heard of Lord Toller Maraquine, haven't you?"

Bartan associated the name with the far-off events of the Migration, and was mildly surprised to hear that such an historic figure was still active. "We're not completely cut off from civilisation, you know."

"They say Lord Toller has spent more time up there, fighting the pestilent Landers, than any other man alive." Speaking with patriotic fervour, Shome launched into a series of anecdotes —some of which had to be fanciful—about the heroic exploits of Lord Toller Maraquine in the interplanetary war. At times his voice thickened and shook with emotion, suggesting that he was acting out the tales in his imagination with himself as the central figure, and Bartan's attention began to stray back to the jibes aimed at him by his former friends.

He knew better than to give any credence to the uninspired ritual insults, and yet he could wish that the name of Glave Trinchil had not been used. Glave was one of the few who still came to the farm and helped when there was heavy work to be done, but—the thought slid into Bartan's consciousness like the tip of a poniard—he usually visited when Sondeweere was alone. Bartan thrust the notion away, but into his mind there crept the image of an event he had all but forgotten— Sondeweere and Glave by the side of the Trinchil wagon when they had believed themselves to be unobserved, the moment of intimacy which had taken neither by surprise.

Why am I suddenly doubting my wife? Bartan thought. *What is doing this thing to me? I know that I cannot have been wrong about Sondeweere. And, while conceding that other men have been blinded by love, I know that I am too clever, too world-wise to be duped in that particular manner by a farm girl. Let the bumpkins jeer to their hearts' content—I will never let them influence me in any way.*

The rain was easing off and the well-defined edge of the cloud shield was now directly overhead, creating a feeling that the wagon was emerging into sunlight from the shade of a vast building. A short distance ahead the track on which they were travelling intersected a wider track, where Bartan would have to turn west for New Minnett. Water-filled ruts reflected the clear sky like polished metal rails.

Feeling oddly guilty, Bartan turned to Shome and said, "My apologies for this, but I have decided against attending the markets today. It's a long way for you to go on foot, but. . . ."

"Think nothing of it," Shome said with a fatalistic shrug. "I have already walked halfway around this planet, and I dare say I can manage the rest."

He shouldered his bag, jumped down from the wagon at the intersection and set off towards New Minnett at a good pace, pausing only to wave goodbye. Bartan returned the farewell and directed the bluehorn east towards his own section.

His feeling of guilt increased as he admitted to himself that he was laying a trap for Sondeweere. She would not be expecting him until close to nightfall, and the trip to town had been arranged days in advance, giving her ample time in which to make all her arrangements with Glave. Self-reproach mingled with self-disgust and a curious kind of excitement as he bent his mind to a new kind of problem. If he did espy Glave's bluehorn from afar, tethered by the farmhouse, could he be underhanded enough to halt the noisy wagon and move in silently on foot? And if he were to find the couple in bed—what then? A year's unrelenting toil had clothed Bartan's frame in hard muscle, but he was still a lightweight compared to Glave and had little experience of fighting.

This is terrible, he thought in a crossplay of emotion. *All I want out of life is to find my wife alone, working contentedly in our home. Why take the risk of losing what happiness I have? Why not turn back, catch up on Shome, and go on to the markets as planned? I could sit down with the old crowd and get merry on brown ale and forget all this. . . .*

The landscape ahead of Bartan was becoming obscured by refractive peach-and-silver mists as the fallen rain was lured back into the aerial element by the sun, and in the centre of his field of view there had appeared a wavering dark mote which seemed to change shape every few seconds. As he watched, the mote assumed a definite form, resolving itself into a rider approaching at considerable speed.

Bartan knew, long before proper identification was possible, that the rider was Glave Trinchil, and again there was a clash of emotions—simultaneous relief and disappointment over the fact that a confrontation was ruled out. This far from the farm Glave could claim that he was coming from any one of a number of places, and in all fairness there could be no justification for openly disbelieving him. With that analysis of the situation in mind, Bartan expected Glave to pass him with a casual greeting, and he was taken aback when the younger man began waving to him while still some way off, obviously preparing to stop and talk. Bartan's heart quickened with alarm as he saw that Glave was in a state of agitation. Could there have been an accident at the farm?

"Bartan! Bartan!" Glave reined his bluehorn to a halt beside the wagon. "I'm glad to see you—Sondy said you had gone to town."

"She said that, did she?" Bartan replied coldly, unable to

shape a more appropriate response. "So you've been paying her another of your conveniently timed visits."

The imputation seemed to pass Glave by. His broad, artless face looked troubled, but Bartan could detect no hint of shiftiness or defiance which might have sprung from guilt.

"Go to her without delay," Glave said. "She has need of you."

Bartan swore at himself for having continued nursing his petty suspicions when it was becoming obvious that something serious had happened to Sondeweere. "What's wrong with her?"

"I truly do not know, Bartan. I called at the farm just to be neighbourly, just to see if there was any heavy work to be done. . . ." Even though overwrought, Glave had to direct a satisfied glance at his well-muscled arms. "Sondy told me there was a tree to be uprooted. You know the one—where you want to plant the wirebeans and—"

"Yes, yes! What happened to my wife?"

"Well, I fetched a spade and an axe and set about the roots. It was hot work, in spite of the rain, and I was pleased when I saw Sondy coming down from the house with a pitcher of smallbeer. At least, I think it was smallbeer—I never got to drink any. She wasn't more than a dozen paces away from me when she gave a sort of a gasp and let the pitcher fall and sat down in the grass. She was holding her ankle. I was fearful she had done herself a mischief, so I went to her. She looked up at me, Bartan, and she gave a terrible scream, but the worst thing about it was . . . was. . . ." Glave's voice faded and he stared at Bartan in perplexity, as though wondering who he might be.

"Glave!"

"It was a terrible scream, Bartan, but the worst thing about it was that her mouth was shut. I was looking straight into Sondy's face, and I could hear her screaming, but her mouth was tight shut. It fair made my blood run cold."

Bartan shifted his grip on the reins preparatory to moving off. "What you're saying doesn't make sense. All right, Sondeweere was moaning! Is that all there was to it? *Had* she turned her ankle? What did she say?"

Glave shook his head, slowly and pensively. "She does not say anything."

"She *doesn't* say anything! What way is that to . . . ?" Bartan began to feel a new kind of alarm. "She can still speak, can't she?"

"I don't know, Bartan," Glave said simply. "You should go to her. I stayed as long as I could, but there was nothing I could do. Nothing I could think of. . . ."

His remaining words were lost in the clatter of hooves and equipage as Bartan sent the wagon forward. He goaded the bluehorn up to the best speed that could be achieved on the uneven track, enduring the discomfort of sliding and bouncing on the unpadded seat. The bright mist had now blanked out the horizon and reduced his range of vision so much that he seemed to be travelling at the centre of a bell-shaped dome in whose sides faint pastel colours swirled all the way up to the sun. A short time later the vapours began to boil off, the sky became a milky blue and Bartan saw his own farm in the distance, gleaming, created anew out of rain and mist. By the time he reached it the sky was returning to its normal intense shade of blue and the daytime stars were reappearing.

He brought the wagon to a standstill, jumped down and ran into the house. There was no reply when he called Sondeweere's name, and a rapid search in which he threw himself from room to room established that she had to be out of doors. The first place he could think of looking was by the tree which Glave had mentioned, though it would be odd if she had lingered there so long—unless she had been overtaken by serious illness. Why had the oafish Glave not escorted her back to the house instead of fleeing as if he had seen an apparition?

Bartan left the building, sprinted past the sty which housed his modest stock of pigs, and went to the top of the grassy knoll which blocked the view to the east. He saw Sondeweere at once. She was sitting in the grass near the tree where Glave claimed to have been working, and she was still wearing her pale green oilskin cape. He shouted out to her, but she made no response of any kind. She remained completely motionless as he walked down the gentle slope, and his fears for her increased with every step he took. What manner of illness or disability would induce a person to sit for so long, head bowed, apparently oblivious to everything? Could she be fevered, or semi-conscious, or . . . dead?

When he was about six paces away from his wife he halted, overcome by a strange timidity, and whispered, "Sondeweere, dear one, are you well?"

She raised her head and a pang of relief went through him as he saw that she was smiling. She gazed at him for a few seconds—smile unchanging, no welcome in her eyes—then lowered her head again, obviously studying something on the ground in front of her.

"Don't play games with me, Sondy." Bartan stooped and went closer, and was reaching out to touch Sondeweere's hair when his eyes abruptly focused on what she was watching. Only a hands-breadth away from her crossed ankles were two small multi-legged creatures, seemingly locked in combat. Their articulated, crescent-shaped bodies were longer than a finger and dark brown on top, pale grey on the underside. They were unlike any other crawling thing he had ever seen in that each sprouted a single thick feeler from just below the head. He was already recoiling in disgust when his eyes began to sort out and comprehend the profuse tangle of legs, eye-stalks and antennae. The creatures had bound themselves together by their central feelers and were engaged in copulation, not combat . . . and . . . There was only one head to be seen. The female had eaten off her partner's head, and was gorging herself on the pale ichors oozing from his thorax, and all the while—quite undaunted, rhythm unaltered—his body went on with its ecstatic thrusting and jabbing into her greedy abdomen.

Bartan's reaction was immediate and totally instinctive. He straightened up and smashed his boot down on the writhing obscenity he had witnessed. Sondeweere was on her feet in the same instant, screaming in a way that hurt his brain. Bartan gazed at her, afraid . . . *How can she make a sound like that without opening her mouth?* . . . then caught her as she toppled towards him in a faint.

"Sondeweere! Sondy!" He inexpertly massaged her throat and cheek, trying to restore consciousness, but her head lolled in the crook of his arm and her eyes glimmered white beneath the lids. He gathered up her limp body and began walking back to the house, his mind overloaded with worries and fears.

A short distance along the faint path he saw a movement on the ground, a brown glistening, and knew at once that it was another of the ugly crawlers. The sight added to his forebodings —he had never seen any of the creatures before, nor had he heard them described, but now they were beginning to abound. He altered his stride slightly so that his boot came down squarely on the crawler, crunching it into the soil.

Sondeweere stirred in his arms and, as though emanating from the far end of a mile-long corridor, there came a whispering version of her unnatural scream.

Twice more on the way to the house he encountered one of the nameless creatures, labouring towards him in a seething of many-jointed legs, and each time he pulped it underfoot and each time Sondeweere was affected as before. To Bartan it was unthinkable that there could be any kind of affinity or link between his wife and the crawlers, and yet—in spite of being unconscious—she had definitely flinched as each one of them was dying. And there was the question of the screams. How did she make the sounds without opening her mouth, and why were they so disturbing?

A pressing sense of gloom and a coldness on his spine told Bartan that the sunlit normalcy all around him was a sham, that he was straying into realms beyond his understanding. On reaching the house he carried Sondeweere inside and carefully put her down on her bed. Her brow was cool and her coloration normal, giving the impression that she was merely asleep, but she failed to respond to being shaken or to his urgent repetitions of her name. He eased her out of the oilskin and was removing her sandals when he noticed a speck of dried blood on her right ankle. It came away quite readily on a damp cloth and the skin underneath was unblemished, dispelling the idea that she might have been bitten or stung by one of the creeping horrors. But *something* had happened to Sondeweere, and try as he might he could not rid himself of the notion that the creatures were in some way involved. Could they exude a venom so powerful that merely coming into contact with it was enough to render a person unconscious?

Standing by the bed, staring down at his wife's inert form, Bartan felt his fortitude begin to crumble. *Artoonl was right in what he said to me,* he thought. *I kept quiet about the warnings, and I led everybody to this place—and what has been the upshot? Two suicides, one disappearance which is probably a murder, still births, madness and near-madness, strange sightings and bad dreams, friends turning against friends, malice where once there was goodwill—and now this! Sondeweere has been struck down, and the earth spews out horrors!*

With a considerable effort he wrenched his thinking out of the downward spiral and fought to regain his normal optimism. He, Bartan Drumme, *knew* that ghosts and demons did not exist —and, if there was no such thing as an evil spirit, how could there be an evil place? It was true that there had been a spate of misfortunes since the farmers' arrival in the Basket of Eggs, but runs of bad luck were always cancelled out sooner or later by runs of good. Artoonl was wrong in quitting after investing so much time and effort. What the farmers had to do was stand their ground and wait for things to improve. And Bartan's duty was clear—he had to stay by his wife and do everything in his power to restore her to her old self.

As he settled into his bedside vigil his thoughts were again drawn to the crawling creatures whose appearance had heralded Sondeweere's mysterious affliction. Many curious life forms, some of them highly unprepossessing, had been found on Overland, and it was likely that something so repellent would have been noticed elsewhere. On reflection he had been too quick at destroying the horrors. If he found another crawler he would overcome his revulsion so that he could trap and preserve it for inspection by someone with greater knowledge of such matters.

Bartan raised Sondeweere's limp hand to his lips and was holding it there, willing his own vitality to flow into her body, when he was alerted by a faint scratching sound from another part of the house. He tilted his head and listened intently. The sound was barely audible, but he placed its source at the entrance to the house. He stood up, puzzled, and took the few paces needed to take him out of the bedroom and through the kitchen to the front door. The line of brilliance seeping under the door was uninterrupted, and yet the delicate scratching continued. He opened the door and something which had been clinging to the lintel, something which twisted and squirmed, brushed his face as it fell to the floor.

Bartan gave an involuntary gasp, mouth contorted with shock and loathing, as he leapt back.

The crawler landed upside down with a thud, pale grey underside flashing, then righted itself and began moving into the house with every semblance of purpose. It single thick feeler was extended ahead of it, undulating, questing. Bartan's hoped-for objectivity failed to materialise. He stamped his foot down on the creature, and heard and felt its body burst and flatten—and between his temples there was the sound of Sondeweere's anguish.

He slammed the door shut and pressed his back to it, appalled, remembering times when he had seen human beings—a farmer's wife, little children at play—extend an arm and wave it in a strange, boneless motion which mimed that of a crawler's central feeler.

Chapter 8

After more than a year of near-continuous service in the fortresses Toller had accepted that he would never be able to sleep properly in weightless conditions. The inexplicable sensation of falling which plagued the station crews could be ignored in waking hours, but the dreaming mind had no defences against it. It was common among crew members to spend the entire rest period mumbling and twisting in their sleep-nets, seeing the planetary surface rise up to meet them with ever-increasing speed, and to awaken at the imagined point of impact with shrieks which entered and distorted the dreams of their comrades.

Toller had devised a personal routine which enabled him to deal with the problem. For the sixteen days of each duty period he made no real attempt to sleep, contenting himself with resting and drowsing when not required for active service. When it was time to return to Overland he would curl up inside the fleecy womb of the fallbag and sleep soundly throughout most of the long drop, rocked by its gentle buffeting and comforted by the low gurgling of the slipstream at the neck of the bag. At first he had been puzzled by his ability to sleep well in such unlikely circumstances, then had decided that the knowledge that he really was falling brought about a necessary accord between his intellect and the sensations of the body.

There was only one day left of his current duty spell and the tiredness had built up in him to the extent that within seconds of getting into his net he had lapsed into a bemused state, halfway between sleep and consciousness, in which there was little distinction between the remembered past and the vaguely apprehended present. It was peaceful inside Command Station One, which he had chosen as his living quarters in order to be close to the centre of operations at all times. The only sounds were the bored and scrappy conversation of the two men on watch, and the occasional swishing of the bellows which maintained a tolerable air pressure. Toller had turned his face to the wall of the station and was resting comfortably, something which would not have been possible at the beginning of the war. The walls were now insulated with flock and covered with skins which reduced heat loss and also helped prevent accidental puncturing of the shell.

One night, during one of his earliest duty spells, Toller had become aware of a faint but insistent whistling sound and had tracked it down to a large knot in a section of midship planking. The core of the knot had shrunk and was permitting air to escape. When Toller had tapped it with his knuckle the core had promptly disappeared into the outer void, and as he had occasioned the damage he took it on himself to repair the vent with cork and mastic. He had carried out the chore willingly, knowing that reports of it would be widely circulated, thus reinforcing the message that Lord Toller Maraquine did not set himself above the lowliest conscripts in the Sky Service.

He did such things with an undeniable degree of calculation, but excused himself on the grounds that only one kind of leadership was feasible—and correct—in the unnerving circumstances of the interplanetary war. King Chakkell could force soldiers to venture into the weightless zone on pain of death, but once they were there a commander could only get them to give of their best by showing that he was prepared to share every privation and face every danger.

And the dangers had been plentiful.

It had been fortunate indeed for the defenders that King Rassamarden, going about his unimaginable affairs in the unimaginable environment of the Old World, had not launched his invasion fleet in the shortest possible time. Tens of days had gone by after the positioning of the first two fortresses with no sign of enemy activity, and the grace period had been used—under Ilven Zavotle's direction—to measure the radius of the neck of comparatively dense air at the juncture of the atmospheres. A skyship had been rotated into the plane of the weightless zone and had been driven laterally on jet power for an estimated sixty miles before the pilot had begun to lose consciousness through

136

asphyxiation. He had been in the process of rotating the ship for the return when the balloon had ruptured because of excessive torque from the struts. The pilot had managed to retain his senses long enough to get himself into Overland's gravitational field by means of his personal pneumatic jet, and on the following day had parachuted to the ground within walking distance of Prad. His survival had been a great source of reassurance for rank-and-file members of the Sky Service, but the acquired data had troubled the top echelons of their leadership.

The gateway, as the bridge of breathable air came to be called, had a cross-sectional area of more than ten thousand square miles—and it was apparent that no achievable number of fortresses could bar it to intruders by gunnery alone.

Once again it had been Zavotle, the dogged eroder of problems, who had come up with a solution.

Inspired by the success of the personal flight units, he had proposed the simplest form of fighting craft possible—a jet tube which a man could sit astride as though he were on a bluehorn. Engines taken from ordinary airships would be about the right size, and when powered by pikon and halvell crystals would enable a warrior to range out many miles from his base. Zavotle's preliminary calculations, assuming an effective fighter radius of only twelve miles, showed that the entire area of the gateway could be covered by only twenty-five fortresses.

Drifting in the soft confines of his sleep-net, Toller recalled the look of wonder and gratification on King Chakkell's face as he was given the unexpected good news. There was no doubt that he could have forced through the construction of the hundred fortresses originally envisaged, but the strain on material and human resources would have been severe. Chakkell had been faced by an additional problem in that a large proportion of his subjects were too young to have had any first-hand experience of the terrors of the pterthacosis plague and were not inclined to accept punishing work loads, especially in the cause of a war which seemed so unreal. The concept of the jet fighter craft had therefore been embraced by Chakkell with a boundless enthusiasm which had led to the completion of the first batch in the remarkably short time of five days, thanks to nature having done most of the construction work in advance.

The jet engine was basically the lower part of the trunk of a young brakka tree, complete with the combustion chamber which had powered its pollination discharges. Pikon and halvell crystals were admitted to the chamber under pneumatic pressure, where they combined explosively to produce great quantities of miglign gas which was exhausted through the open end of the tube to drive the engine forward.

To convert the basic engine into an operational craft, it had been given a full-length wooden cowl which made for the easy mounting of equipment. A saddle-type seat had been installed for the pilot, aft of which were pivoting control surfaces. They looked like stubby wings, but in the weightless condition their sole function was to control the direction of flight. The fighter's armament consisted of two small breech-loading cannon, fixed to the sides of the cowl, which could only be aimed by aligning the entire craft with the target.

Toller, hovering between wakefulness and sleep, vividly remembered his first ride on one of the strange looking machines. The bulkiness of his skysuit had been augmented by his personal jet unit and parachute, and it had taken him some time to adapt to the seat and familiarise himself with the controls. Acutely aware of being watched by the skymen in and around Fortress One, he had pumped the pneumatic reservoir to maximum pressure, then had advanced the throttle lever. In spite of his having been modest with the power demand, he had been astonished by the surge of acceleration which had accompanied the roar of the exhaust. It had taken him perhaps three minutes, with an icy slipstream tearing at his face, to get the knack of keeping the fighter from doing a slow spiral as it howled through the sky. He had then shut down the engine, allowed air resistance to bring the craft to a halt and had turned in the saddle, laughing with acceleration rapture, to solicit the applause of his fellow pilots waiting by the fortress.

And the fortress had not been there!

That shock, that exquisite stab of pure panic, had been his introduction to the new physics of the jet fighter. It had taken him many seconds to locate and recognise the fortress as a tiny mote of hard light, almost lost in the silver-speckled blue of the universe, and to realise that he had been travelling at a speed previously undreamt of by man.

The nine fighters of Red Squadron were ranged line abreast, their upper surfaces gleaming in the sunlight. A short distance above them was what had been the first fortress, recently extended by the addition of three new sections to make it a command station. Other fortresses comprising the Inner Defence Group were positioned nearby, but they were insignificant objects, hard to see in the deep blue even though reflectors had been added to increase their visibility. Overland, flanked by the sun, was a fire-edged roof for the universe, and the vastness of Land made a circular floor, blue and green dusted with ochre, scrolled with white.

The other object of significance for the fighter pilots was the target ship. Although it was more than a mile away from them the hugeness of the balloon made it an important feature of the celestial environment, one with the apparent solidity of a third planet. It had been positioned well outside the theoretical plane of weightlessness, in the direction of Land, so that cannon balls fired at it would be drawn down into Land's gravitational field. Of the two fatalities which had occurred thus far in training, one had been that of a young pilot who had been making a high-speed practice run when he had been swept off his machine by a cannon ball which had hit him squarely in the chest. At first it was thought that he had been accidentally shot by another flier, then had come the realisation that the two-inch iron ball had been hanging almost motionless in the air, a deadly residue from an earlier practice firing. To prevent similar incidents, Toller had issued a general order that cannon could only be discharged when angled towards Land.

He was sitting astride his fighter, Red One, watching the target ship through binoculars and waiting for the pilot who had positioned it to return to safety. More than forty days had passed since the arrival of the first two fortresses in the weightless zone, and still there was no sign of a Lander invasion fleet. In some quarters there were rising hopes that King Chakkell's prognosis had been wrong, but Toller and Zavotle refused to be complacent. They had decided to use the strategic leeway to maximum advantage, and to that end were prepared to have a skyship whose balloon was nearing the end of its useful life sacrificed as a target.

The magnified image in Toller's binoculars showed the pilot leaving the skyship's gondola and bestriding a tethered fighter belonging to the as yet incomplete Blue Squadron. The pilot cast off, his craft surged away on a white plume of condensation, and seconds later came the powdery boom of his engine. He swept the fighter into an upward curve and disappeared in the radiant needle-spray of light emanating from the sun.

"Go in without delay," Toller shouted, gesturing to Gol Perobane, pilot of the furthermost left in the line of fighters. Perobane saluted and drove his machine forward, the roar of his exhaust swelling as it engulfed the remaining craft. His fighter swiftly shrank in apparent size, swooping down on the doomed skyship, and as he was flaring out of the curve both of his cannon streamed vapour. Toller, following the action with his binoculars, judged that Perobane had fired at exactly the right moment. He turned his attention to the balloon, expecting to see it quake and deform, and was disappointed when the serene curvatures appeared to be unaffected.

How can he have missed? he thought, giving the signal for the next fighter in line to blast off.

It was not until the fourth machine, flown by Berise Narrinder, had completed its ineffectual attack that he called a halt to the exercise. He blew crystals into his own engine and flew down to the target ship, cutting the power off early so that air resistance would bring him to a halt close to the huge balloon. At short range he was able to discern several holes in the varnished linen envelope, but they were surprisingly small—almost as if the material had partially healed its wounds—and were far short of the catastrophic damage the cannon should have inflicted. The balloon was beginning to show some slight wrinkling and slackness, but Toller attributed it to natural loss of heat as much as to the insignificant punctures. It was apparent to him that the skyship retained the capability of making a safe descent to ground level.

"Does this mean we have to start firing at the gondolas?" said Umol, drifting into position beside him on Red Two. His chest was visibly labouring to deal with the rarefied air.

Toller shook his head. "If we attack the gondolas we expose ourselves to return fire. We must attack from above, staying within the enemy's blind arc, and destroy his balloons with . . . with. . . ." He paused, striving to visualise the weapon his fliers needed, and at that moment a large meteor struck across the sky far below them, briefly illuminating the scene from underneath.

"With something like that," Umol said, pulling down his scarf to unveil a smile.

"That is somewhat beyond our capabilities, but. . . ." Toller paused again to let the meteor's tardy thunderclap roll by them. "But your thoughts fly in the right direction, old friend! Have somebody go back on board the ship and put heat into the balloon. Keep everything as it is until I return."

He placed his foot on the side of Umol's fighter, which had been nuzzling up to his own machine in stray air currents, and pushed hard. The two machines parted with a lazy wallowing action. Toller advanced his throttle lever, using an extreme sensitivity of touch developed since his first flight, and the fighter growled its way forward to pass within a few yards of the target balloon. As soon as he had gained enough speed to render the control surfaces effective he brought the nose up and around, and made a soaring return to the command station.

The weapon he brought back a short time later was a simple iron spike with a bundle of oil-soaked oakum bound to the blunt end. He ignited it by means of a phosphor wick and, whirling the spike to feed the flame, put the fighter into a shallow dive which took it close to the balloon's upper hemisphere. When he hurled the spike it flew down cleanly, with the stability of a dart, and sank its full length into the yielding material of the envelope. The varnished linen caught fire at once, producing a thick brownish smoke, and by the time Toller had come to a halt a sizeable area of the crown was alight. In less than a minute the balloon was beginning to fold in on itself, pulsing and losing symmetry, while the watching pilots shouted their approval. Without convection currents to bear it away, the smoke gathered around the stricken skyship in a strangely localised cloud.

Toller rejoined the group of fighters. The line was uneven, with no two machines parallel to each other or sharing the same up-down orientation, but that was something he had learned to accept. Unless the fighters were on the move there was little the pilots could do to control them, and several of the gifted youngsters—the ones who were already at home with the new form of flying—seemed to get a mischievous pleasure from conducting conversations with him in mutually inverted positions. Toller made no attempt to curb their high spirits—he had already decided that when war came the best fighting pilots would be those who were least shackled by traditional military customs and outlook.

"As we have just seen," he shouted, "fire is a good weapon to use against a balloon, but that was all too easy for me. I was able to go in very close, and at low speed, because there were no defenders on the ship and no enemy ships nearby trying to wing me. The low speed meant that I was able to stay in the ship's blind arc during the whole attack, but in battle things are likely to be very different. Most attacking dives will probably have to be conducted at high speed—which means you will not be able to pull out so quickly and will sink into the defenders' arc of fire. You are going to be very vulnerable at that stage—especially if the Landers have developed instant-fire cannon, like their muskets."

Perobane pulled down his scarf. "But it will only be for a few seconds if we're moving fast." He winked at the nearest pilots. "And I can assure you that I'll be moving *very* fast."

"Yes, but you might be heading straight towards another ship," Toller said, quelling some laughter.

Berise Narrinder signalled that she wanted to speak. "My lord, how about bows and arrows? Fire arrows, I mean. Wouldn't an archer be able to flare out of a dive much earlier and stay out of danger?"

"Yes, but. . . ." Toller paused, realising that his objection had been a reflexive one based on the fact that he personally had never taken to the bow as a weapon. The proposal was sound, especially if the arrows were given fish-hook warheads which would trap them in the balloon material. And even a mediocre airborne archer—as he suspected he was likely to be—should find little difficulty in hitting a target as large as a skyship's balloon.

"But what, my lord?" Berise said, raising herself up on her footrests, encouraged by the other pilots' evident approval for her suggestion.

Toller smiled at her. "But would it be fair to the enemy? Armed with bows and fire arrows we would be able to shoot them out of the sky with the ease of a child bursting soap bubbles. It goes against all my sporting instincts to adopt such a. . . ." His words were drowned out in a general shout of laughter from the line of pilots.

Toller bowed slightly towards Berise then turned away, not begrudging the fliers their moment of jubilation. He was the only member of the company with first-hand experience of warfare, and he knew that—no matter how well things might go for the Overlanders—there were some present whose time for nonchalance, merriment and optimism was drawing to an end, whether they lived or died.

At the midpoint between the two worlds the terms "night" and "littlenight" had lost their meaning. The diurnal cycle was divided into two equal spells of darkness of slightly less than four hours each, while the sun was being occulted by Land or Overland; and two daytime periods of just over eight hours. Toller had given up making any distinction between night and littlenight, foreday and aftday, being content to let time roll by him in an unremarkable sequence mileposted only by the fallbag returns to Overland. Especially when he was off duty, drowsing in his sleep net, there seemed no way to mark the passage of time but for the slow veering of the beams of sunlight from the portholes, and dreamy reprises became as real as life itself. . . .

The sound of an argument slowly drew Toller back to full consciousness.

It was not uncommon to hear members of fortress crews in

disagreement, but on this occasion there was a woman involved and Toller guessed it was Berise. For some reason he could not explain, he was interested in Berise Narrinder. There was no sexual element involved, of that much he was sure, because when Gesalla had made it clear that the intimate side of their marriage was over his capacity for physical passion had abruptly died. The process had been surprisingly quick and painless. He was a man who had no need for sex, who never thought of it or regretted its absence from his life, and yet he was aware of everything that Berise did. Without making any effort, he usually knew when her duty spells corresponded with his, where she was and what she was likely to be doing at any given moment.

He opened his eyes and saw that she was on watch—an obligatory duty for all personnel—tethered close to one of the large fixed binoculars which were permanently aimed at Land. Beside her was the tall angular figure of Imps Carthvodeer, the Inner Defence Group administrator, who normally stayed behind a wicker screen at the far end of the command station, in a cramped room he liked to refer to as his office.

"You can either draw pictures, or you can be on watch," Carthvodeer was saying peevishly. "You can't do two things at once."

"*You* may not be able to do two things at once, but I find it very easy," Berise said, her accentuated eyebrows drawn together.

"That's not what I mean." Carthvodeer's long face showed his frustration over the fact that although fighter pilots had the nominal rank of captain they were effectively senior to all non-combatants. "On watch duty you are supposed to concentrate all your attention on looking out for enemy ships."

"When the enemy ships come—*if* they come—they will be visible for many hours in advance."

"The point is that this is a military installation and has to be run on military lines. You are not being paid to draw pictures." Carthvodeer scowled at the rectangle of stiff paper in Berise's hand. "You don't even show artistic ability."

"How would you know?" Berise said, becoming angry. Farther along the cluttered tunnel of the station the crewman on bellows shift snorted in amusement.

"Why don't you two stop bickering and let a man get some rest?" Toller put in mildly.

Carthvodeer squirmed around in the air to face him. "I'm sorry if I disturbed you, sir. I have to prepare at least a dozen reports and requisitions in time to go down in the next fallbag, and I find it quite impossible to work and listen to the squeak-squeak-squeak of the captain's charcoal at the same time."

Toller was surprised to note that Carthvodeer, a fifty-year-old officer, was pale with emotion over the trivial incident. "You go back into your office and continue with your reports," he said, unfastening his net. "You won't be further distracted."

Carthvodeer, lips quivering, nodded and propelled himself away with poorly co-ordinated movements. Toller launched into a lazy flight which ended when he grasped a handhold close to Berise. Her green eyes triangulated on him in calm defiance.

"You and I are in a privileged position compared to a man like Carthvodeer," he said in a low voice.

"In what respect, my lord?" Of all the fliers in his command she was the only one who continued to address him formally.

"We *wanted* to come here. We leave the murky confines of these wooden boxes every day and fly through the air like eagles. This waiting and waiting is hard on all of us, but consider what it must be like for someone who had no wish to be here in the first place and who has no escape."

"I didn't realise the charcoal was so noisy," Berise said. "I'll find a pencil and work with that—if you have no objection."

"I don't mind at all. As you say, the Landers cannot take us by surprise." Toller craned his neck to see the drawing in Berise's hand. It showed the interior of the station in an atmospheric style, with strong emphasis on the parallel bars of sunlight slanting from the row of portholes. Human figures and machinery were suggested rather than detailed and in a manner Toller thought pleasing, although he was not qualified to judge the picture's merit.

"Why are you doing this?" he said.

She gave him a wry smile. "Old Imps said I was neglecting my duty, but I believe that everybody on Overland has a higher duty. Each of us has to search for and develop his or her artistic gift. I don't know if I can even be an artist, but I'm making the effort. If I fail I'll go on to poetry, music, dance . . . I'll keep searching until I find something I can do, then I'll do it to the best of my ability."

"Why is it a duty?"

"Because of the Migration! You can't do what we did and get away without paying a penalty. We left our racial soul behind on the Old World. Do you know that in all the ships that took part in the Migration there was not *one* painting? No books, no sculptures, no music. We left it all behind us."

"It was hardly a pleasure trip, you know," Toller said. "We were refugees carrying the bare essentials of life."

"We brought jewellery and useless money! Tons of weapons! A race needs an armature of culture to support every other aspect of its being, and we no longer have one. The King left it out of his great plan for a new Kolcorron. We left all that kind of thing behind, and that's why Overland feels so *empty*. It isn't because we are so few, spread out over a whole world—we suffer from spiritual emptiness."

Berise's ideas were strange to Toller, and yet her words seemed to find their mark somewhere far inside him, particularly the references to emptiness. As a young man in Ro-Atabri he had always enjoyed the setting of the sun and the gentle approach of darkness—but of late, even with Gesalla at his side, the once satisfying experience had become oddly flat and disappointing. No matter how beautiful the sunset, there was no longer any pleasure in reviewing the achievements of the day, no anticipation of the morrow. The associated emotion, had he ever acknowledged it, would have been a poignant sadness. Overland's western sky, as it deepened through gold and red to peacock green and blue, had seemed to ring with . . . *emptiness*.

The word had been a curiously apt one to come from a comparative stranger. He had been attributing his feelings to some unrecognised inner malaise, but had he just been offered a better explanation? Could he be an aesthete at heart, troubled by a growing awareness that his people lacked a cultural identity? The answer came quickly as the pragmatic, practical side of his nature reasserted itself.

No, he thought. *The worm which eats out the core of my life is not concerned with poetry and art—and neither am I.*

He half-smiled as he realised how far he had strayed, in an unguarded moment, into realms of fanciful thought, then he saw that Berise was staring at him.

"I wasn't smiling at your ideas," he said.

"No," she replied thoughtfully, her gaze still hunting over his face. "I didn't think you were."

And, of all the scenes which were played and replayed in Toller's memory, the brightest and most clearly incised were those from the day which saw the war's true beginning. . . .

Seventy-three days had passed since the positioning of the first two fortresses. It was not a long period of time by the standards of men and women going about their routine affairs on the surface of Overland, but evolution was swift in the unnatural environment of the central blue.

Toller had completed his daily flying and archery practice, and had felt disinclined to return too quickly to the oppressive confines of the station. His fighter was floating about five hundred yards outside the datum plane, a vantage point from which he could observe the ebb and flow of activity in the Inner Defence Group and the surrounding space. To his left he could see a supply ship crawling up from Prad, its balloon a small brown disk sharply outlined against the convex patterns of Overland; to his right was Command Station One, flaring with sunlight against the indigo of the sky. Close to it were lesser three-section habitats which were used as workshops and stores, and in a loose swarm were the fighters of Red Squadron. Dozens of human figures, moving purposefully, could be seen in perfect detail in spite of being so tiny, mannikins from the hand of a master jeweller.

As always, Toller was impressed by the sheer amount of progress which had been made in the time available, since the first naive scheme to blanket the entire weightless zone with fortresses which would have relied on guns to repel an invasion.

The invention of the fighter craft had been the major step forward, their astonishing speed having rendered obsolete the idea of each fortress being an isolated and self-sufficient entity. They had ceased to be fortresses, and were now assigned specialised roles—dormitory, workshop, store, armoury—in support of the all-important jets.

No matter how clever was the theoretical planner working on the ground, Toller had realised, innovation and development were usually products of practical experience. Even Zavotle, his thinking conditioned by normal gravity, had not foreseen the problems which would be posed by weightless debris and waste matter. The death of young Argitane, the fighter pilot killed by a drifting cannonball, had been a dramatic example, but the pollution of the environment by human wastes had become a matter of increasing concern.

The psychological stress of life in the gateway was augmented by the indignity and sheer unpleasantness of attending to one's bodily functions in zero gravity, and no commander could countenance the prospect of each station being surrounded by a thickening cloud of filth. Carthvodeer had been obliged to set up a collection team—quickly and mercilessly dubbed the Shit Patrol—whose unenviable task it was to trawl all offensive material into large bags. The bags were then towed a few miles down towards Land by a fighter and released to continue their journey under the influence of gravity—a practice which occasioned much ribaldry among the fortress crews.

Another problem, one yet to be resolved, had come with the attempts to establish an outer defensive ring. The original intention had been to place stations on a ring thirty miles across, greatly extending the area of interdiction, but with separations of more than about four miles they had become almost impossible to locate and keep supplied. A second fatality among fighter pilots had occurred when a flier, perhaps with substandard eyesight, had simply become lost while returning from an outer station, and had burned up all her power crystals in vain attempts to locate her base. Deprived of the heat generated by her engine, she had perished of hypothermia, and had been found purely by chance. Since that time the policy had been to concentrate all stations in the central group and rely on the fighters to extend their area of influence as required.

As was the case with all the other fliers, Toller had found that his lung capacity had increased to deal with the rarefied atmosphere, but it was impossible to adapt to the relentless cold of the weightless zone. By the time he had been drifting and meditating for twenty minutes all residual heat had leaked away through the wooden cowling of his engine, and he was beginning to shiver despite the protection of his skysuit. He was pumping up the fighter's pneumatic reservoir, preparatory to returning to the command station, when his attention was drawn to a star which had suddenly increased in luminosity for a second and now was emitting regular pulses of brilliance. No sooner had he deduced that the star was actually a distant station, and that it was sending out a sunwriter message, when he heard the sound of a trumpet, its repeated blasts fast-fading in the thin air. His heart stopped, lay quiescent for a subjective eternity, then began a rhythmic jolting.

They're coming! he thought, sucking in air. *The game begins at last!*

He fed his engine and swooped down towards the command station. As the slipstream began to bite at his eyes he pulled his goggles into place and instinctively searched the area of sky between him and the curving vastness of Land, but was unable to find anything unusual. The slow-moving ships of the enemy armada could be as much as a hundred miles away, visible only in telescopes.

As Toller neared the station the trumpeter, positioned in the newly-added pressure lock, ended the warning call and retreated inside. Fighter pilots, distinguished by the squadron colours on their shoulders, were issuing from the nearby dormitory tube, and swaddled auxiliaries were sailing towards the dart-like machines in their care, propelled by the hissing jets of their personal units.

A mechanic swam to meet Toller with a tethering line, leaving him free to dive straight into the long cylinder of the station. Both doors of the pressure lock had been left open and he found himself suddenly translated from a boundless sunlit universe to a dim microcosm which was fogged with vapours and crowded with human figures and the appurtenances of their continued existence.

Carthvodeer and Commodore Biltid, the operations chief, were hovering by the look-out post, deep in discussion, Biltid, directly appointed by Chakkell, was a stiff-necked and formal individual who was equally embarrassed by his inability to get over the fall-sickness and the ambiguity of his relationship with Toller. The fact that Toller was his superior and yet insisted on riding a jet like an ordinary pilot frequently placed him in dilemmas he found it difficult to resolve.

"Look here, my lord," he said, espying Toller. "The enemy comes in force."

Toller drew himself to the binoculars and looked into the eyepieces. The image which washed into his eyes was of a fiercely brilliant background, blue and green whorled with white, in the centre of which was a meagre sprinkling of black dots, each ringed with prismatic fringes caused by imperfections in the optical system. By narrowing and straining his eyes, Toller found that he could distinguish even smaller specks mingled with the others, and suddenly the scene acquired depth, became vertiginous. He was looking downwards through a vertical cloud of skyships, a cloud which was many miles in depth. It was impossible to say how many ships it contained, but there could not be less than a hundred.

"You are correct," he said, raising his head to look at Biltid. "The enemy comes in force—which is what one would have expected."

Biltid nodded, covered his mouth with a handkerchief, and suddenly the sour smell which usually surrounded him intensified. "I . . . I'm sorry," he said, gulping noisily. "We must make ready."

How astute, Toller thought, then became sorry for a man who had been thrust willy-nilly into an unenviable situation as an instrument of the ruler.

"We retain our two great advantages," he said. "We are in sight of the enemy, but he is not aware of us; and we have the fighter craft—something the enemy cannot have even envisaged at this stage. It is now up to us to press home those advantages while we may."

Biltid nodded even more vigorously. "All fighter craft are in a state of mechanical readiness, and will be fuelled and armed. I propose engaging the enemy with the Red and Blue Squadrons, and holding Green in reserve. That is, if you have no. . . ."

"Those might be good tactics in ground warfare," Toller said, "but remember that we will never again be able to take the Landers by surprise. There is a possibility that we could end this war on the very day it begins if we deal the enemy a sufficiently devastating first blow. In my opinion we should deploy the three squadrons and give all our pilots experience of combat."

"You're right as always, my lord." Biltid finished dabbing his mouth. "Though I'd be happier if we had some means of estimating the enemy's rate of ascent. If they reach the datum plane during the hours of darkness there is a chance of some slipping past us unseen."

"Nothing is to slip past us," Toller snapped, losing his patience. *"Nothing!"*

He moved away from Biltid and Carthvodeer, and went to another porthole where he could have an unobstructed view of Land. The sun was moving towards the Old World and would pass behind its rim in approximately two hours. Toller did some mental calculations and swore as he realised that the timing of the first encounter could be highly unfavourable for the defenders. The two daily periods of darkness had been named Landnight and Overlandnight, depending of which of the planets was occulting the sun, and although they were about equal in length they had important differences.

Landnight, which was coming next, would begin when the sun passed behind Land, but at that stage Overland would still be fully illuminated and the light reflected from it would be strong enough to permit reading. During the following hour that light would steadily weaken as Land's cylindrical shadow slid across Overland, then would come roughly two hours of deepnight, lasting until Overland was again kissed by the sun's rays. Throughout deepnight the heavens would be ablaze with stars, glowing whirlpools and the splayed radiance of comets, but the comparative level of general illumination would be very low —and even a ship's balloon would be hard to detect in the dim reaches of the weightless zone. The problem did not arise to the same extent during Overlandnight because Land was larger than its sister world and could not be completely swallowed by its shadow.

If the enemy ships were a hundred miles away, Toller reckoned, and were already at maximum speed, they could reach the datum plane during deepnight. He contemplated the prospect for a moment, then decided he was being unduly pessimistic. The Lander pilots would be nervous on experiencing the effects of weightlessness for the first time, and would also be apprehensive about the forthcoming inversion manoeuvre. It was entirely reasonable to assume that they would approach the weightless zone slowly and cautiously, and would plan to perform the supremely unnatural act of turning their ships upside down in good light conditions.

Having settled his mind, Toller left the chilling dank fug of the station and devoted the following hour to making a tour of the Inner Defence Group, calling at the other two command stations which were the bases for Blue Squadron and the newly completed Green. Reports from those on watch showed that the invaders were indeed advancing slowly, but the fighter pilots who had turned out prematurely were unable to resume their rest when darkness came. Some of them passed the time in noisy discussion or gambling by candlelight, while others hovered close to their machines, obsessively checking on the fuelling and arming procedures of the mechanics.

Finally a sliver of light appeared at the edge of Overland and rapidly expanded along it to form a slim crescent. As the sunlit area of the planet spread steadily into the gibbous phase, heralding the reappearance of the sun, Toller made repeated visits to the look-out post in Command Station One and peered through the binoculars. The vast disk of Land was bathed in a dim mysterious light, reflected from the sister world, which gave it the semblance of a sphere of translucent wax somehow lighted from within. Although brightening by the minute, the backdrop it provided refused to yield up a discernible image of enemy skyships, and—in spite of himself—Toller began to fantasise about the invaders having sustained a speed which had enabled them to pass through the datum plane under cover of darkness. The partial emergence of the sun flooded the interior of the station with light, and even then there was an instant during which the ships of the Lander armada remained hidden in the fringes of the planet's slow-swinging shadow.

Then, suddenly, they were *there*.

Unexpectedly beautiful, they appeared in Toller's field of view as a swarm of tiny, perfect crescents of brilliance, level upon level of them, exquisite in their crafted uniformity. For a moment he was awe-struck by the achievement the spectacle represented. Given the audacity and courage to cross the interplanetary gulf in frail constructs of cloth and wood, his kind should be able to unite and turn their eyes towards the outer universe instead of squandering their energies in. . . .

"They can't be very far away," Biltid said, looking up from the other pair of binoculars. "Twenty or thirty miles. We haven't much time."

"Time enough," Toller said, recalled to the practical world of the soldier. On an impulse he propelled himself to his sleeping net, unhooked his sword from the wall beside it and strapped the weapon to his waist. He was conscious of how incongruous the sword was in the circumstances, but it had a psychological value to him in the preparation for battle. Going out through the airlock he saw that the other eight pilots of his squadron were already at their machines, and auxiliaries were swimming among them igniting the hooded fire-cups which had been installed forward of the saddles. The same scene was repeated in miniature, some distance away in the boundless blue, as the other two squadrons were made ready.

Some of the Blue and Green machines were already edging towards Command Station One to form a combined force, their paths marked by pulses of white condensation. As the swarm increased in size there were numerous gentle collisions between the fighters, occasioning a good deal of banter among the pilots and angry comments from the mechanics who were in danger of being crushed. As he drifted clear of the station Toller shaded his eyes from the sun with a gloved hand and looked in the direction of Land.

He found that the invaders could now be seen without optical aid, silvery specks at the very limits of vision, and he wished for a means of estimating their range. He had to engage the enemy well below the datum plane so that every ship destroyed would fall back towards Land, but if he went too far down to meet then his fighters' fuel reserves would be depleted. It looked as though the ability to judge distances accurately was going to be even more important in aerial combat than on the ground.

When the three squadrons were assembled Toller got astride Red One and wedged his toes into the fixed stirrups. He unclipped his bow, secured it to his left wrist with the safety loop and checked that the quivers mounted on each side of the cowling had a full complement of arrows. His heart was pounding again, and he was aware of the familiar old excitement, tinged with an inexplicable element of sexuality, which had always preceded a foray into the dangers of combat. While pumping up the pressure reservoir of his fuel feed, he glanced along the straggling, yawing line of fighters. The pilots were androgynous shapes in their skysuits, their faces hidden by scarves and goggles, but he picked out Berise Narrinder immediately and was compelled to issue a final word of caution.

"We have rehearsed our battle plan many times," he called out, "and I know you are all anxious to test your mettle against the enemy. I know, also, that you will conduct yourselves with courage, but beware of becoming *too* courageous. In the fever of battle it is possible to grow reckless, to be lured into taking unnecessary risks. But bear in mind that each of you has the potential to destroy *many* of the enemy's ships, and therefore each of you has a value to our cause which is much greater than you may personally place on your life.

"Today we will smite the invader hard—harder than he can ever have dreamed of—but I will not countenance any losses on our side. Not a single pilot, not a single fighting machine! If you expend all your arrows do not be tempted to attack with your cannon. Retire at once from the battle and console yourself with the knowledge that you will be an even more skilful and more deadly opponent on a future occasion."

Nattahial, the pilot of Blue Three, nodded and vapour wisped through his scarf. "Whatever you wish, sir."

Toller shook his head. "Those are not my wishes—they are my direct *orders*. Any pilot I see behaving like an idiot will have me to answer to afterwards, and I can assure you that will be a more harrowing experience than facing a few scrawny Landers. Is that understood by all?"

Several of the pilots nodded vigorously, perhaps too vigorously, and others chuckled. With few exceptions they were young volunteers from the Air Service. They had been adventure-hungry to begin with, and the boredom of the long wait for this day had turned them into overwound human springs. Toller genuinely wanted them to heed his warnings, but he knew from combat experience that a balance had to be struck between prudence and passion. A warrior with too great a commitment to self-preservation could be even more of a liability than a glory-hunting fool, and the minutes ahead were likely to reveal how many of each were in his command.

"Is it your opinion," he asked, drawing his goggles down into place, "that I have devoted enough time to the making of speeches?"

"Yes!" The loudness of the general assent briefly filled the sky.

"In that case, let us go to war." Toller pulled his scarf up to cover his mouth and nostrils, and put the fighter into a curving dive which centred Land in his field of view. The sun was barely clear of the planet's rim, hurling billions of needles of light against him without creating any warmth. Amid a swelling roar of engine exhausts the other fighters took up their assigned positions, each squadron creating a V-shaped formation.

Slightly behind Toller on the left, leading the Blues, was Maiter Daas, and on his right at the apex of the Green Squadron was Pargo Umol. He wondered what the two middle-aged men—veterans of the old Skyship Experimental Squadron and the Migration—felt as they dropped towards the planet of their birth in circumstances they could never have envisaged. Analysing his own emotions, he was again disturbed to find that he felt youthful, fulfilled, totally alive. Part of him longed to be at home with Gesalla, making amends for all the ways in which he had failed her, and yet within him was the knowledge that, given the impossible opportunity, he would prolong this moment indefinitely. In a magical, irrational universe he would choose to live this way until he died—forever riding out through sprays of cold pure light to face exotic foes and unknown dangers. But in the real universe this phase was likely to be brief, perhaps encompassing only one battle, and when it was all over life would be a thousand times more humdrum than before, with little for him to do other than passively wait for an unremarkable death.

Perhaps, the thought came softly slithering, *it would be better not to survive the war*.

Shocked by where the bout of introspection had taken him, Toller forced his thoughts to bear on the task in hand. The plan was to engage the enemy ten to fifteen miles below the datum plane, but as always he was bedevilled by the impossibility of estimating distance or speed in the featureless oceans of air. When he looked over his shoulder he saw that the twenty-seven fighters had laid down a kind of aerial highway with their condensation trails. It narrowed to a distant point, vaporous white threads gathered into perspective's fist, and already the clustered stations and habitats were hard to see, even though he knew exactly where to look. The condensation would later disperse into invisibility, and when that happened the three squadrons would be in danger of becoming lost.

How far had they descended? Ten miles? Fifteen? Twenty?

Swearing at the sun for capriciously aiding the enemy, Toller screened off the blinding orb with his hand and searched for the ascending fleet. The combined speeds of the two forces had brought them much closer in a short time, and now the array of gleaming crescents could easily be resolved by the naked eye, each a perfect miniature of the fire-cusped planet behind it. They were concentrated in a small area of the sky, like glittering spawn.

This is far enough, Toller told himself. *We wait here*.

He spread both his arms in a prearranged signal and shut down his engine. The absorbent silence of infinity abruptly pervaded the scene as the other pilots closed their throttles in unison. The fighters coasted for some time, gradually becoming uncontrollable as air resistance robbed them of their speed, the V-formations loosening and distorting while they came to rest. Toller knew the appearance of being at a standstill was illusory —the machines had entered Land's gravitational field and were falling, but this close to the datum plane their speed was negligible.

"We will fight here," he called out. "It will profit us to be patient and allow the enemy to come to us, because the longer he takes the farther the sun will move out from behind his ships. Be sure to keep your igniter cups in good trim, and do not allow your hands and limbs to stiffen with the cold. If you think you are becoming too cold you are permitted to make short circular flights to put heat into your machines and warmth into your backsides, but remember that your crystals have to be conserved as much as possible for the battle."

Toller settled into the wait, wishing he had a reliable means of measuring the time. Mechanical clocks were much too large for tactical purposes, and even the traditional military timepiece was of no value in the weightless zone. It consisted of a slim glass tube containing a cane shoot which was marked with black pigment at regular intervals. When a pace-beetle was put into the tube it devoured the shoot from one end, moving at the unchanging rate common to its kind, thus indicating the passage of time with an accuracy which was good enough for commanders in the field. In zero gravity, however, the beetle was found to move erratically, often ceasing to eat altogether. At first it had been thought to be an effect of the extreme cold, but the same unsatisfactory results were obtained when the tube was kept warm, leading to the remarkable conclusion that the mindless bead-sized beetle was disturbed by its lack of weight. Toller had been intrigued by the findings, which in his mind established a link between human beings and the lowliest and most insignificant creatures on the planet. They were all part of the same biological phenomenon, but only humans had the intelligence which enabled them to override the dictates of nature, to impose their will on the organic machinery of their bodies.

Toller could hear the pilots of his squadron conversing as they waited, and he was pleased to note that there was none of the abrupt laughter which often indicated a failure of nerve. In particular he liked the demeanour of Tipp Gotlon, the young rigger he had promoted to pilot status against the counsel of Biltid. Gotlon, who had shown an instinctive grasp of the mechanics of flying, was exchanging occasional quiet words with Berise Narrinder and between times was scanning the sky ahead with shaded eyes. At eighteen he was the youngest of all the pilots, but he looked eminently calm and self-possessed.

As the minutes dragged by Toller gradually became aware of another sound—a low booming which he identified as emanating from the exhaust cones of the approaching fleet. The balloons of the Lander ships were becoming easier to see as the source of illumination moved progressively to the side, and they had greatly increased in apparent size. Umol and Daas were frequently turning their heads in his direction, obviously impatient for the order to attack, but Toller had decided to hold fire until he could pick out some detail of the crown panels and load tapes on the enemy balloons, by which time the foremost of them should be less than a mile below the waiting fighter craft.

The lack of spatial referents helped confuse the eye, but the skyships seemed to be ascending in groups of three and four, with quite a large vertical interval between the echelons. They formed an attenuated and elongated cloud many miles in depth, with those at the bottom of the stack appearing remote and shrunken compared to the leaders. The arrangement was a logical one for considerations of flight safety, especially when flying in darkness, but it was almost the worst possible for the penetration of defended territory. Toller smiled as he saw that the Landers had unwittingly given him an advantage which more than compensated for the unfortunate positioning of the sun.

Yielding to a sudden accession of battlefield humour, he drew his sword and used the incongruous weapon to make the downward stroke of the attack signal.

What followed was not a concerted swoop on the invaders, but a deliberate and systematic process of destruction. In conference with Biltid and his two squadron leaders, Toller had decided that—in the first battle of its kind in all of human history—it would be unwise to have twenty-seven high-speed machines milling and plunging through a comparatively small volume of airspace. Also, for psychological reasons he considered important, he did not want a random pattern of success, with some pilots emerging as heroes claiming multiple kills and others failing to achieve the first blood so vital to their morale.

Accordingly, the response to Toller's signal was that only the ninth pilot in each formation detached his machine and rode down to meet the unsuspecting enemy. The three fighters traced lines of vapour which converged on the uppermost of the Lander echelons, then swung across to the right, each one casting off a splinter of amber light. A few seconds later three of the leading balloons developed penumbras of smoke, became dark flowers with writhing centres of red and orange flame. Toller was surprised by the dramatic speed of their destruction compared with that of the balloon once used for target practice, then realised it was because the Lander ships were rising and creating a slipstream which not only fed the flames but directed them down the sides of the varnished linen envelopes.

Another gift, another good omen, he thought as the second trio of fighters roared away on plumes of condensation. One of them picked off the remaining skyship of the four that had formed the top echelon and curved off to the right, while its companions speared on down to find targets in the next level. Their success was betokened after a brief interval by the blossoming of two more dark flowers.

As the carnage continued, with wave after wave of fighters darting down into the affray, Toller began to speculate on the possibility of the entire Lander fleet being destroyed in a single catastrophic engagement. Due to the great size of a skyship's balloon in comparison to the gondola, an ascent had to be made blindly, with the occupants trusting that the sky directly above contained no hazard. When many ships were travelling together the roar of the burners drowned out all other sounds, therefore the members of any given layer could remain quite unaware of cataclysms above until it was too late to take evasive action. If the fighters were able to work their way down to the bottom of the stack, incinerating the skyships echelon by echelon, none of the enemy would survive to describe to their King how the destruction of his armada had been achieved. Such a total defeat could, indeed, end the interplanetary war on the very day it had begun.

Toller's mind was filled with that heady prospect as he watched the sky being transformed and sullied by conflict. The vapour trails were a complex skein of white tangled around an irregular, granular core of smoke and flame, and as successive fighter groups dived into action it became difficult to impose any sense of order on the scene. The carefully drawn up battle plan was being obscured by frenzied scribblings of condensation.

When it came the turn of the penultimate trio of fighters to set off Toller made a broad curving gesture with his free hand, signifying that they should swing outwards during the descent and intersect the column of skyships below the worst of the chaos. The pilots nodded and roared away on their diverging courses. They were just beginning to swing inwards again when from somewhere in the midst of the havoc came the sound of a powerful explosion.

Toller guessed that a Lander weapon, probably a pikon-halvell bomb, had detonated accidentally—a catastrophic event for the ship carrying it, but one which could benefit the invasion fleet as a whole. The report would have been heard far down the stack, alerting the lower echelons to the fact that all was not well. On hearing it any prudent pilot would use his lateral jets to turn his ship on its side so that he could observe the sky above.

Toller glanced with a new urgency at the other two squadron leaders, Daas and Umol, who were now his only two companions in the serenity of the upper air. "Are we ready?" he shouted.

Daas placed a hand on his lower back. "The longer we sit here the worse my rheumatism gets."

Toller blew crystals into his engine, felt his head being pulled back by acceleration, and watched the battle zone expand to fill his field of view. He had never before been so conscious of the jet fighter's speed. The vapour trails rushing towards him had the semblance of sculpted white marble, and he found it difficult not to flinch as the solid-seeming walls slammed in on him from one side and another, sometimes converging in a promise of certain death. Entire arctic kingdoms had streamed by him before he began to glimpse the wrecks of Lander ships. Their upward momentum had carried them into the flaming tatters of their balloons. He saw soldiers frantically ridding their gondolas of swathes of burning linen and wondered if they understood the futility of their actions. The ruined ships, although apparently locked in place, were already yielding to the gravitational siren call of their parent world, already embarking on the plunge to the rocky surface which waited thousands of miles below.

Toller had expected a considerable gap between the layers of burning ships, and was surprised to find them in a single loose conglomerate, sometimes almost in contact with each other. He realised that the first ships to be attacked had shut down their engines, and those below—still under way—had blundered in among them, vertically compacting the scene of destruction. Floating here and there among the smoke-shrouded leviathans were human figures, some struggling and some quiescent, pathetic debris from the gondola which had been exploded.

Toller barely had time to check that they were not wearing parachutes, then he was through the crowded volume of sky and bearing down on a group of four ships. At the edges of his vision he could see Daas and Umol riding in parallel with him. The Lander pilots must have reacted quickly to the sound of the explosion, because three of the ships were already tilted and he could see rows of faces lining their gondola walls. Far below them other ships, layer upon receding layer, were also turning on their sides.

Toller closed his throttle and allowed the fighter to coast while he snatched an arrow from one of his quivers. The oil-soaked wad at its tip caught fire as soon as he thrust it into the hooded igniter cup. He nocked the arrow and drew the bow, feeling heat from the warhead blowing back on his face, and fired at the balloon of the nearest ship, using the instinctive aiming technique of a mounted hunter. Even at speed and with swiftly changing angles the vast convexity of the balloon was an absurdly easy target. Toller's arrow needled into it and clung like a spiteful mosquito, spreading its venom of fire, and already he was plunging down past the gondola and its doomed occupants. There came a spattering of flat reports and splinters erupted from the wooden engine cowling scant inches from his left knee.

That was quick, he thought, shocked by the speed with which the Landers had brought their muskets into action. *These people know how to fight!*

He steered his machine into a right-hand turn and looked over his shoulder to see two of the other balloons beginning to crumple and wither amid wreaths of black smoke. Daas and Umol, riding on brilliant plumes of condensation, were swinging into wider curves which would bring them into the cluster newly formed by the three squadrons.

As far as Toller could ascertain, all his fliers had survived the first strike and all of them could claim victories, but the nature of the battle was changing and would no longer be so one-sided. The time for calculated and cold-blooded executions had ended, and from now on individual temperament would come into play, with incalculable results. In particular, there could be no more leisurely swoops through the skyships' blind arcs. Not only were the ships far below turning on their sides, they were doing it in such a way that the vulnerable upper hemispheres of their balloons were facing the centre of each group. Toller had no doubt that rim-mounted cannon were already being loaded, and although the Landers had no metals their traditional charges of pebbles and broken stones would be highly effective against the unprotected fighter pilots.

"Strike where you can," he shouted, "but be. . . ."

His words were lost in the roars of multiple exhausts. The air around him became fogged with white as the most impetuous of the young pilots darted away in the direction of the apparently motionless skyships. Cannon began to boom almost immediately.

Too soon, Toller thought, then it came to him that the sheer speed of the fighters could actually be a disadvantage in this kind of aerial warfare. Long after a skyship's cannon had been discharged it would be surrounded by relatively static clouds of rocky fragments, harmless to the slow-moving ships, but potentially deadly to attacking fighter pilots.

Pushing the thought aside, he gunned his machine into a downward curve which took him on a dizzying plunge in parallel with the vertical conflict. In the ensuing minutes the sky became a fantastic jungle, crowded with thickets, ferns and interlocked vines of white condensation, hung with the bulbous fruit of skyships, garlanded with black smoke. The slaughter went on and on in a frenzy incomprehensible to anyone who had never known the bitter passions of battle—and, as Toller had foreseen, the Landers began to draw blood.

He saw Perobane, on Red Nine, make a reckless dive on two ships and pull out of it with such force that his control surfaces were ripped off. The fighter did an abrupt somersault, throwing Perobane clear of it into a course which took him within twenty yards of a gondola. Soldiers on board fired at him with their muskets. The jerking of his body showed that many were finding their mark, but the soldiers—perhaps aware that their balloon was on fire and that they were bound to die—kept on shooting at Perobane in futile revenge until his skysuit was a mass of crimson tatters.

Shortly afterwards, the pilot of Green Four—Chela Dinnitler—made the mistake of slowly coasting past a soldier who was drifting free some distance from a gondola which was wrapped in the blazing material of its envelope. The soldier, who had appeared to be unconscious, stirred into life, calmly levelled his musket and shot Dinnitler in the back. Dinnitler slumped over his controls and the fighter's exhaust spouted vapour. The machine, with the pilot freakishly locked in his seat, went into a twisting descent which carried it through the lower fringes of the battle. It dwindled into the backdrop of Land, passing through a sprinkling of circular white clouds which resembled balls of fluffy wool.

The soldier who had killed Dinnitler was fitting a new pressure sphere to his musket, and—incredibly in view of the death-fall facing him—was laughing as he worked. Toller advanced his throttle and drove straight at the man, intending to ram him, then came the thought that even a fleeting proximity might prove enough to infect him with pterthacosis. He hit the plunger on one of his cannon, shattering power crystal containers in the breech, and held a steady course until detonation occurred. The gun had not been designed for precise marksmanship, but luck was with Toller and the two-inch ball hit the soldier squarely on the head, cartwheeling him away in spirals of blood.

Toller banked the fighter away from the corpse and was about to enter the main battle again when, belatedly, his memory of the odd-looking circular clouds began to trouble him. He flew well clear of the column of turmoil and studied the sky below its base. The clouds were still there and now there were more of them. It took Toller several seconds to realise that he was looking at the exhaust plumes of skyships—seen from "below" their gondolas. Pilots in the lower echelons had inverted their ships and were fleeing the scene of destruction upside down. It was something no commander liked to do, because when the thrust of an engine was augmented by gravity a ship could quickly exceed its design speed and tear itself apart, but for the Landers the risk was an acceptable one in the circumstances.

Toller's first impulse was to reverse his original battle plan and go after the most distant of the enemy ships, but an inner voice sounded a warning. In the heat of combat he had lost track of time, and his fighters had been burning crystals at a prodigious rate all the while. He pumped up the pneumatic reservoir of his fuel feed and knew from the number of strokes required that the amount of solid material within the system had been greatly depleted. Looking up towards where the battle had begun he saw that the earliest condensation trails had faded. The squadron's home base was totally invisible, concealed somewhere in the trackless immensities of the space between the worlds, and finding it could be a lengthy job which would require ample reserves of power.

He ignited one of his remaining arrows and slowly waved it above his head. During the next few minutes the other pilots, recognising the signal, detached themselves from the ferment of smoke and cloud to join him. Most of them were intoxicated with excitement and were loudly exchanging stories of daring and triumph. Legends had been born, Toller knew, and were already acquiring the embellishments which would be further elaborated upon in the taverns of Prad. Berise Narrinder was one of the last to arrive, and there was a cheer when it was seen that she had managed to put a line around Perobane's crippled machine and had it in tow.

When it was apparent that disengagement had been completed, Toller counted the fighters and was disturbed to find there were only twenty-five, including the one Berise had salvaged. He ordered a squadron by squadron check, and there was a lull in the hubbub of talk as it was realised that Green Three, which had been flown by Wans Mokerat, was missing. At some point in the whirling turmoil of the battle Mokerat had met his fate, unobserved by any of his comrades, and had disappeared completely, perhaps engulfed by a burning skyship.

The sobering effect of the discovery was as brief as Toller had expected, with the noise level among the other fliers quickly swelling to what it had been. He knew the youngsters were not heartless by nature—it was simply that, although physically unscathed, they too had become victims of war. *The same thing must have happened to me long ago*, he thought, *but without my understanding. And only recently has it been revealed to me what I am—a fleshly automaton whose essential hollowness renders him incapable of sustaining warmth or joy.*

Directly ahead of him, but a considerable distance away, was the gondola of a ruined skyship. Its occupants had successfully cast adrift all remnants of their burning balloon, which now hovered above and around them in great flakes of grey ash. The gondola and the fighter squadrons remained in fixed relative positions, because all were falling at the same speed.

Again Toller wondered if the Lander soldiers fully understood that their rate of descent, although insensible at this stage, would show an inexorable increase which would guarantee their deaths. Some of the soldiers were still firing their muskets in spite of the fact that the fighters were out of range, and—in one of the flukes which so often occur in seeming defiance of probability—a bullet came slowly tumbling towards Toller and came to rest within arm's length.

He plucked it out of the air and saw that it was a stubby cylinder of brakka wood. He put it away in a pocket, feeling a strange affinity with the alien marksman. *From one dead man to another*, he thought.

"We have done enough for this day," he shouted, raising his gloved hand. "Now let us find our way home!"

Chapter 9

At the sound of the wagon approaching Bartan Drumme stood up and went to the mirror which hung on the kitchen wall. It felt odd for him not to be dressed in work clothes, and even the face which regarded him from the glass seemed unfamiliar. The boyish, humorous look—which had once earned him the farmers' mistrust—was no longer present, and instead there were the hard, sun-darkened features of a man who was no stranger to solitude, sorrow and relentless toil. He smoothed down his black hair, adjusted the collar of his shirt and went to the farmhouse door.

The Phorateres' wagon was drawing to a halt outside, amid much snorting from an elderly bluehorn which was sweating after the journey in the midday sun. Harro and Ennda waved and called a greeting to Bartan. They had actively befriended him since the grim incident at their farm, and it had been at Ennda's insistence that he had agreed to take some hours off and go into New Minnett to relax. He assisted her down from the tall vehicle and, while Harro was leading the bluehorn to the water trough, slowly walked with her to the house.

"What a handsome young toff you look today," she said, a smile erasing the look of tiredness on her face.

"I managed to preserve one good shirt and one pair of trews, but they seem to have shrunk somewhat."

"You have expanded." She halted to give him an appraising look. "It's difficult to realise you are the same baby-face who used to try to dazzle us with his clever city talk."

"I don't talk much at all these days," Bartan said ruefully. "There isn't much point in it."

Ennda gave his arm a sympathetic squeeze. "Has Sondy not improved in any way? How long has it been? Close on two hundred days?"

"Two hundred! I've lost track of the time, but it must be

something like that. Sondy remains as she was, but I'm not giving up hope."

"Good for you! Now, is she still in the bedroom?"

Bartan nodded, ushered Ennda into the house and led the way to the bedroom. He pushed open the door to reveal Sondeweere sitting on the edge of the bed in a full-length white nightdress. She was staring at the opposite wall and remained that way, apparently unaware of the presence of others. Her yellow hair was well brushed, but was unimaginatively arranged in a way which showed that Bartan had done it.

Ennda went into the room, knelt in front of Sondeweere and gathered her unresisting hands into hers. "Hello, Sondy," she said in a gentle but cheerful voice. "How are you today?"

Sondeweere made no response. The beautiful face was untroubled, the eyes unseeing.

Ennda kissed her on the forehead, stood up and returned to Bartan. "All right, young man! You can go off to town and enjoy yourself for a few hours and leave everything to me. Just tell me what has to be done about Sondy's food and the . . . mmm . . . consequences."

"Consequences?" Bartan gazed at Ennda in puzzlement until a look of exasperation made her meaning clear. "Oh! You don't have to do anything. She keeps herself clean, attends to all the basics by herself and eats anything that is prepared for her. It's just that nobody else seems to exist for her. She never speaks. She sits there on the bed all day, staring at the wall, and I don't exist. Perhaps I deserve it. Perhaps it's my punishment for bringing her to this place."

"Now you're being silly." Ennda put her arms around him and he clung to her, immensely comforted by her aura of warmth, femininity and resilience.

"What have we here?" Harro Phoratere boomed jovially, entering the shady kitchen from the sunlight outside. "Is one woman not enough for you, young Bartan?"

"Harro!" Ennda rounded on her husband. "What kind of a thing is that to say?"

"I'm sorry, lad—I wasn't thinking about your Sondy

being. . . ." Harro hesitated, the circular bite-scar glowing whitely against the pink of his cheek. "I'm sorry."

"No need to apologise," Bartan said. "I appreciate your coming here—it's more than generous."

"Nonsense! It's a welcome break for me as well. I intend to spend a very lazy aftday and—I give you fair warning—to consume a quantity of your wine." Harro glanced anxiously at the group of empty demijohns in a corner. "You *do* have some left, I trust."

"You'll find ample supplies in the cellar, Harro. It's the only solace left to me and I take care never to run short."

"I hope you don't drink too much," Ennda said, showing some concern.

Bartan smiled at her. "Only enough to guarantee a night's sleep. It's too quiet here—much too quiet."

Ennda nodded. "I'm sorry you have to bear your burden alone, Bartan, but it's all we can do to manage our own section now that so many of our family have given up and moved north. Did you know that the Wilvers and the Obrigails have gone as well?"

"After all their work! How many families are left now?"

"Five, apart from us."

Bartan shook his head dispiritedly. "If only the pople would wait and. . . ."

"If *you* wait around here much longer it'll be dark before you reach the tavern," Ennda cut in, pushing him towards the front entrance. "Go off and enjoy yourself for a few hours. Go on—*out!*"

With a last glance at his wife, withdrawn to her inaccessible world, Bartan went outside and summoned his bluehorn with a whistle. Within a few minutes he had it saddled and was riding west to New Minnett. He was unable to shake off the feeling that he was doing something shameful, planning to spend half a day free of his crushing burden of work and responsibility, but the fierceness of his hunger for a spell in the undemanding company of amiable topers told him the excursion would be remedial.

The ride through pastoral scenery was refreshing in itself, and on reaching the township he was surprised by his reaction to the sight of unknown people, clusters of buildings in a variety of sizes and styles, and the lofty rigging of sea-going ships at anchor in the river. When he had seen New Minnett for the first time it had seemed a tiny and remote outpost of civilisation—now, after his lengthy incarceration on the farm, it was a veritable metropolis.

He rode straight to the open-fronted building used as a tavern and was gratified to find in it many of the local characters who had welcomed him and his airboat on that far-off first visit. Compared to the harrowing downward trend of life in the Basket, it was as though the townsfolk had been suspended in time, preserved, ready to spring to life at his behest. The reeve, Majin Karrodall, was present—wearing his smallsword—as was the plump Otler, still protesting his sobriety, and a dozen other remembered individuals whose obvious contentment with their lot was a reassurance that life in general was well worth the living.

Bartan happily drank the strong brown ale with them, finding room for pot after pot of it without wearying of the taste. He was appreciative of the way in which the men—including Otler, who was not known for his tact—made no reference to his people's continuing evacuation of the Haunt. As though sympathising with the reasons for his visit they kept the talk on general subjects, much of the time discussing the latest news of the strange war that was being fought in the sky above the far side of the planet. The notion of a new breed of warriors who rode through the heavens on the backs of jet engines, without the support of balloons, seemed to have fired their imaginations. In particular, Bartan was struck by how often the name of Lord Toller Maraquine came up.

"Is it true that this Maraquine slew two kings at the time of the Migration?" he said.

"Of course it's true!" Otler banged his alepot down on the long table. "Why do you think they call him the Kingslayer? I was *there*, my friend! Saw it with my own eyes!"

"Balderdash!" Karrodall shouted amid a general cry of derision.

"Well, perhaps I didn't actually *see* what happened," Otler conceded, "but I saw King Prad's ship fall like a stone." He turned his shoulder to the others and aimed his words at Bartan. "I was a young soldier at the time—Fourth Sorka Regiment —and I was in one of the very first ships to leave Ro-Atabri. I never thought I'd complete the journey, but that is another story."

"One we've heard a thousand times," another man said, nudging his neighbour.

Otler made an obscene gesture at him. "You see, Bartan, Prad's ship got entangled with the one which Toller Maraquine was flying. Chakkell, who was then a prince, and Daseene and their three children were in Toller's ship, and he saved their lives by pushing the two ships apart. It took the strength of ten men, but he did it single-handed, and Prad's ship went down. I saw it plunge past me, and I'll never forget the way Prad was standing there at the rail. Tall and straight he was, unafraid, and his one blind eye was shining like a star.

"His death meant that Prince Leddravohr became King, and three days later—after the landing—Leddravohr and Toller fought a duel which lasted six hours. It ended when Toller struck Leddravohr's head off his shoulders with a single blow!"

"He must have been quite a man," Bartan said drily, trying to separate fact from fiction.

"Strength of ten! And what do you mean by must have *been* quite a man? None of those striplings up there can keep pace with him to this day. Do you know that in the first battle against the Landers, after all his fire arrows had been expended, he started cutting their balloons into shreds with his white sword? The selfsame sword with which he overcame Karkarand— Karkarand, mark you!—with only one blow. I tell you, Bartan, we owe that man everything. If I were twenty years younger, and didn't have this bad knee, I'd be up there with him at this very minute."

Reeve Karrodall guffawed into his beer. "I thought you said they had no need of gasbags at the midpoint."

"Very droll," Otler muttered. "Very droll indeed."

The following hours slipped by pleasantly and quickly for Bartan, and it was with some surprise that he noticed the sun's rays slanting redly into the tavern at a shallow angle. "Gentlemen," he said, getting to his feet, "I have stayed longer than it was my intention to do. I must leave you now."

"Have but one more," Karrodall said.

"I'm sorry, but I am obliged to leave. Friends are attending to the farm for me, and I have already done them a discourtesy."

Karrodall stood and took Bartan's hand. "I heard about your wife's misfortune, and I'm sorry," he whispered. "Would you not consider taking her away from that baneful place?"

"The place is just a place," Bartan said lightly, determined not to be offended at this late stage of the gathering, "and I won't surrender it. Good-bye, Majin."

"Good luck, son!"

Bartan saluted the rest of the company and walked out to where his bluehorn was tethered. The alcoholic warmth in his stomach and the pleasant optimistic tingle in his brain, important allies in the day-to-day battle of life, were at their height. He felt privileged to be alive, a beautiful feeling which in the past had suffused his existence, but which of late could only be recaptured near the bottom of a demijohn of black wine. He hoisted himself into the saddle and nudged the bluehorn forward, delegating to the intelligent creature the task of getting him home.

As the sky gradually deepened in colour the daytime stars became more prominent, and the spirals and braids of misty light began to emerge from the background. There were more major comets than usual. Bartan counted eight of them, their tails fanning right across the dome of the heavens, creating alternate bands of silver and dark blue among which meteors darted like fireflies. In his mellow speculative mood he wondered if men would ever solve the mystery of the sky's largest features. The stars were thought to be distant suns; the single green point of brilliance was known to be a third planet, Farland; and the nature of meteors was well understood because sometimes they crashed to the ground, leaving craters of various sizes. But what was the vast whirlpool of radiance which spanned the entire night sky for part of the year? Why did the heavenly population contain so many similar but smaller spirals, sometimes overlapping each other, ranging in shape from circles through ellipses to glowing spindles which concealed their structure until examined by telescope?

The train of thought caused Bartan to pay more attention than usual to the luminous arches of the sky, and thus it was that he noticed an entirely new phenomenon which might otherwise have escaped him. Due east, roughly in the direction of his farm, he saw a tiny and oddly-formed patch of light a short distance above the horizon. It was like a four-pointed star with in-curved sides, the kind of geometrical shape created at the middle of four touching circles, and each point appeared to be emitting a faint spray of prismatic colour. The object was too small to yield much detail without a glass, but its centre seemed to be teeming with multi-hued specks of brilliance. Intrigued, Bartan watched the eerily beautiful apparition sink swiftly downwards and pass out of sight behind the crest of the nearest drumlin.

Shaking his head in wonderment, Bartan urged his bluehorn forward to the high ground, greatly extending his range of vision, but the object was nowhere to be seen. What had it *been*? Meteors falling to earth sometimes blossomed into vivid colour, but they were accompanied by violent thunderclaps, whereas the phenomenon he had just witnessed had been characterised by silence and the smoothness of its movement. He tentatively reached the conclusion that the object had been much larger than he had supposed, dwarfed by distance, mysteriously sailing through space far beyond Overland's atmosphere.

With his mind fuelled for further musings about the wonders of the universe, Bartan continued on his way. Almost an hour later he caught the first glimpse of the yellow lights of his own farmhouse and felt a fresh pang of guilt over having detained the Phorateres until after darkness. The fact that Sondeweere and he had only one bed made it difficult for him to invite them to stay until morning, unless Harro and he were to spend the night sleeping on the floor. It seemed a poor reward for their kindness to him, especially as neighbourly acts had become so rare in the Basket. Wondering how he was going to excuse himself, he increased the bluehorn's speed to a trot, trusting it to maintain a sure footing on the star-silvered ground.

He was about a mile from the house when his surroundings

were suddenly drenched in a varicoloured light so intense that his eyes reflexively clamped themselves shut.

The bluehorn reared up, barking in terror, and Bartan clung to it, quaking in expectation of the cataclysmic explosion which instinct told him had to accompany such a flash of brilliance. There was no explosion—only a ringing, reverberating silence during which he felt his clothing ripple and flap although there was no rush of air. He opened his eyes as the bluehorn dropped its forefeet to the ground. He found himself to be virtually blinded by after-images of trees and shrubs, orange and green silhouettes which seemed permanently printed on his retinas.

"Steady, old girl, steady," he breathed, patting the animal's neck. He blinked hard, knuckled his eyes and looked all about him in search of clues as to the origins of the bewildering, frightening and wildly unnatural event. The dark landscape had regained its eternal quietude. The sleeping world was trying to reassure him that things were as they had always been, but Bartan—prey to crawling apprehensions—knew better.

He urged the bluehorn forward as fast as he dared and in a few minutes was approaching the farmhouse. The very fact that Harro and Ennda were not outside and scanning the skies was a subtle indication that things were seriously amiss. Or was it? Perhaps he had been caught up in an essentially local disturbance of nature—after all, there were those who claimed that lightning sprang out of the ground, entirely contrary to the popular belief that it struck downwards from the heavens. He rode into the yard, dismounted and went to the farmhouse door. When he opened it the scene before him was a tableau of commonplace domesticity—Ennda doing her embroidery work on a sun hat, Harro in the act of tilting a demijohn to pour himself a cup of wine.

Bartan sighed with relief and then hesitated, his uneasiness returning, as he realised that the couple were indeed like part of a tableau. They were unmoving, rigid as statues. The only hint of animation in their features was a false one, due to the flickering of the lanterns in the draught from the open door.

"Harro? Ennda?" Bartan advanced uncertainly into the kitchen. "I . . . I'm sorry I'm so late."

Ennda's needle began to move on the instant, and wine gurgled into Harro's cup. "Don't fret yourself, Bartan," Ennda said. "The sun has hardly set, and. . . ." She looked through the doorway into the blackness beyond and began to frown. "That's strange! How did it . . . ?" Her words were lost in a dulled splintering of glass as the demijohn Harro had been holding crashed on the stone floor. Tentacles of dark wine raced outwards from the shattered vessel.

"Curses!" Harro grabbed at his right shoulder and massaged it. "My arm hurts! My arm is so tired that it . . . *hurts*!" He looked down at the floor and his eyes grew round in self-reproach. "I'm sorry, lad—I don't know what. . . ."

"It doesn't matter," Bartan cut in. "What about the light? What do you think it was?"

"The light?"

"The blinding light. The *light*, for pity's sake! What do you think caused it?"

Harro glanced at his wife. "We didn't see any lights. Did you by any chance fall and knock your head?"

"I'm not drunk." Bartan was staring at the couple in perplexity when his gaze was drawn to the bedroom door. It was partially open, allowing a strip of light to slant across the bed, and from what he could see of it the bed appeared to be empty. He strode across the kitchen and pushed the bedroom door fully open. Sondeweere was not in the small square room beyond.

"Where is Sondy?" he said quietly.

"*What?*" Harro and Ennda leapt to their feet and came to his side, their faces registering astonishment.

"Where is Sondy?" Bartan repeated. "Did you let her go outside alone?"

"Of course not! She's in there!" Ennda thrust her way past him and halted, confounded by the room's patent emptiness and lack of hiding places.

"You must have been asleep," Bartan said. "She must have gone out past you when you were asleep."

"I wasn't asleep. This is imposs—" Ennda paused and pressed a hand to her forehead. "There's no point in our standing around here arguing. We have to go out and find her."

"Take the lights." Bartan picked up a tubular lantern and hurried outside. Even after they had checked the lavatory hut and found it empty he was still only mildly concerned. Although Sondeweere had never strayed like this before, there were no predatory wild animals in the area, no cliffs or crevasses to threaten her safety. Her absence might even be a good omen, a sign that she was at last beginning to emerge from the shadow which had dimmed her mind and occulted her personality for so long.

It was not until they had been searching and calling her name for more than an hour that a different kind of premonition began to exercise its sway. Firstly, there had been the terrifying manifestation, the unbearable cascade of light; secondly, his wife had mysteriously vanished—and there had to be a connection between the two events. The Haunt—it had been naive and futile to rechristen it the Basket of Eggs—was going about its malign activities again, and Sondeweere had become its latest victim. He had been given ample opportunity to take her away from the place of evil, but in his stubbornness and intellectual arrogance he had continued to expose her to dangers that no man understood. And *this* was the inevitable outcome. . . .

"This blundering about in the darkness will gain us little," Harro Phoratere said, tiredness and reason combining in his voice. "We should repair to the house and conserve our strength till daybreak. What do you say?"

"I think you're right," Bartan said dully.

The farmhouse had grown cold by the time they reached it, and while Bartan was preparing a fire in the hearth Harro busied himself by fetching a full demijohn from the cellar and pouring three cups of black wine. But, far from comforting Bartan, the cosy firelit ambience served only to remind him that he had no right to be enjoying the luxury while his wife was wandering somewhere in the night. At best she was cold and lost; at worst. . . .

"How could a thing like this happen?" he said. "If I had known a thing like this could happen I would never have left her side."

"I suppose I could have fallen asleep," Harro said. "The wine. . . ."

"But Ennda was with you."

Ennda, who had apparently been on the verge of sleep, turned on Bartan immediately, her face twisted with fury. "What are you trying to say, city boy? Are you hinting that I killed your young whore? Do you think I ate her face off? Is *that* what you are saying? But where is the blood? Do you see any blood on my person? Or on this?" She gripped the neck of her blue blouse with both hands and ripped it downwards, partially exposing her breasts.

Bartan was aghast. "Ennda! *Please!* I had no thought of. . . ."

She silenced him by springing out of her chair and dashing her cup into the fireplace. "I keep the dream at bay! It can't devour me any more, and that's the truth!"

Harro stood up and embraced his wife, drawing her tortured face against his shoulder. She leaned into him, sobbing and trembling violently. The wine she had thrown hissed and sputtered in the fire.

"I. . . ." Bartan stood up and set his drink aside. "I didn't know the dream persisted."

"This happens sometimes," Harro said, his eyes contrite, miserable and haunted. "It would be best if I took her home."

"Home?" Ennda, the manic energy having been drained from her, spoke like a child. "Yes, Harro, please take me home . . . away from this terrible land . . . back east to Ro-Amass. I can't live this way any longer. Let's go back to our *real* home, where we were happy."

"Perhaps you're right," Harro murmured, patting her on the back. "We'll talk about it in the morning."

Ennda turned her head and looked at Bartan with a tremulous smile. "And what have I done to you, Bartan? You're a good boy, and Sondy is a good girl. I didn't mean anything I said."

"I know that," Bartan said uncomfortably. "There is no need for you to leave."

Harro shook his head. "No, lad, we'll go now, but I'll come back in the morning with extra hands. If Sondy hasn't shown up by that time we'll soon find her. You'll see."

"Thanks, Harro." Bartan went outside with the couple and helped them harness their bluehorn to the wagon. Throughout the task he was unable to prevent himself from scanning his dimly seen surroundings, hoping to pick out a drifting patch of white which would betoken Sondeweere's safe return.

His vigilance went unrewarded.

Unknown to Bartan, he was entering the blackest phase of his life, one in which—over a period of several days—he would come to accept that his dumb, tranced wife had departed his world for ever.

Chapter 10

There was nothing unusual about the fact that the enemy was coming out of the sun, but what surprised Toller was the size of the attack wave. It contained at least sixty ships laid out in a protective grid pattern.

His hope that the punishment inflicted on the first invasion fleet would have been enough to end the war had been unjustified, but subsequent attacks had been on a smaller scale. Many of them had seemed like suicide missions whose purpose was to test Overland's defences in new ways. The second force had tried to get through the weightless zone at night, but they had been betrayed by the sound of their exhausts, and had been forced to retreat with heavy casualties. Others had been equipped with varieties of ultra-powerful cannon, the recoil of which had destabilised and destroyed their own ships. And on two occasions the Landers had even deployed jet fighters of their own, launching them from the sides of gondolas. At first the enemy pilots had tried engaging the machines of the three squadrons in direct aerial combat, but they had been hopeless novices compared to Toller's skilled fliers and had been slaughtered, almost to a man. In a second experiment, they had attempted to make high-speed sorties into the Inner Defence Group, evidently with the intention of ramming the stations, but again had been driven off and destroyed.

With the passage of time it had become apparent to Toller that the establishment of a permanent base in the weightless zone had given the defenders an overwhelming advantage. It was a matter for surprise that King Rassamarden had not reached the same conclusion and abandoned the unequal struggle. The only explanation Toller could think of was contained in Colonel Gartasian's report of his meeting with the Lander scouting group. Gartasian had stated that they were overweeningly arrogant, proud and unamenable to reason. Perhaps the New

Men of Land, their ruler included, were belated victims of pterthacosis in ways they did not even comprehend, destined to drown in their own irrational venom.

The only noticeable step they had taken towards self-preservation was that they had begun to wear parachutes, and thus could survive the destruction of their ships. It was impossible to say if they had invented the parachute independently, or if they had copied it after finding the body of Dinnitler, the pilot whose machine had made the runaway plunge towards Land. There was also a theory that they had arrived at the design of their own fighters by piecing together the wreckage of Dinnitler's jet.

But Toller's mind was occupied with more immediate conjectures—did the appearance of a large fleet at this stage of the war betoken nothing more than a massive venting of self-destructive passion on the part of the Landers?

Or was it a sign of confidence in a new type of weapon?

Toller mulled the question over as he rode down against the sunlight at the apex of Red Squadron's formation. The sloping glass screen, a recent modification to the fighter's design, was protecting him from the worst of the icy slipstream. A furlong away on either side he could see the Blues and Greens scoring their own white trails through the spangled heavens, and the old guilt-tinged excitement began to course through him.

Far below, outlined against the great painted curvature of Land, some of the enemy fleet were already turning on their sides. The Landers no longer sailed blindly into ambush. They had developed a method of observing the sky above, probably using look-outs at the end of long tethers, and at the first sign of the fighters' condensation trails rolled their ships into varying attitudes for mutual defence. For that reason the three squadrons now went into action separately, and the style of combat had become individualistic and opportunist. Spectacular individual victories and equally spectacular deaths had ensued; legends had proliferated.

What is going to happen this time? Toller thought, his pulse quickening. *Is there a soldier down there whose destiny it is to end my life?*

As the array of skyships expanded across the view the fighters broke away from their formations and began to weave a basket of vapour trails around their quarry. Toller was aware of Berise Narrinder curving away to his left. There came a spattering of fire from long-range muskets, but it seemed sporadic in comparison to the usual fierce volleying, and Toller's premonition about a radical new weapon returned to him in force. He shut down his engine and waited for the fighter to coast to a halt so that he could study the skyships better. Several of the other fighters were already darting through the grid in high-speed attack runs, and he could see the orange flecks of their arrows, though as yet no balloons were on fire.

Toller reached for his binoculars, but his gauntlets and the bow tied to his left wrist made him clumsy, and it was with still unaided vision that he saw some of the enemy gondolas become surrounded with brownish specks, as though the crews were hurling dozens of missiles towards their attackers. But the specks were fluttering and beginning to move of their own volition.

Birds!

Still untangling the strap of his binoculars, Toller had a moment to let his mind race ahead to the question of what kind of bird the Landers would have chosen to send against human opponents. The answer came immediately—the Rettser eagle. Found in the Rettser mountains in the north of Kolcorron, the eagle had a wingspan exceeding two yards, a speed which defied accurate measurement, and the ability to gut a deer—or a man—almost in the blink of an eye. In the past they had not been trained for hunting or warfare, even against ptertha, because of their unpredictability—but the New Men had shown themselves to have little regard for their own lives when bent on the destruction of an enemy.

Toller's first look through the glasses confirmed his fears, and a chill went through him as he waited to see what havoc the great birds, natural masters of the aerial element, would wreak among his pilots. The pattern of vapour trails abruptly changed as the pilots closest to the skyships perceived the new threat and took evasive action. Seconds dragged by, then it dawned on Toller that the battle situation was remaining strangely static. He had expected the eagles, with their incredibly fast reflexes, to begin their unstoppable attacks on the instant of sighting the human fliers—but they were remaining in the vicinity of the ships from which they had been launched.

The magnified image in the binoculars revealed a curious spectacle.

The eagles were vigorously beating their wings, but instead of being propelled forward by the action were spinning head over tail in tight circles, making little or no progress through the air. It was as though they were being held in place by some invisible agency. The more frantically they flapped their wings the faster they revolved without changing position.

Toller was so bemused by the phenomenon that more drawn-out seconds passed before he began to appreciate that in weightless conditions the eagles would never be able to fly. In the absence of gravity the equations of winged flight were no longer valid. The dominant force acting on the birds was the upward thrust from their wings, and without weight to counterbalance it they were thrown into continuous backward rolls. An intelligent creature might have responded by altering its wing movement to something akin to a swimmer's stroke, but the eagles—prisoners of reflex—could only go on and on with their futile expenditure of energy.

"Bad luck, Landers," Toller murmured, feeding his engine. "And now you have to pay for your mistake!"

In the ensuing minutes he saw balloon after balloon set alight, apparently without loss among his own fliers. Now that the Landers fought from stationary positions their balloons burned less readily, lacking a flow of air to feed the blaze, and sometimes the flames extinguished themselves long before the entire envelope was consumed, though without making any difference to a ship's eventual fate.

On this occasion the battle was given a touch of the bizarre by the presence of the gyrating eagles. Their terrified shrieking formed a continuous background to the roar of fighter jets, the patter of muskets and occasional blasts from cannon. Most of them kept on spinning, mindlessly squandering their strength, but Toller noticed that some had become quiescent and were drifting with their heads tucked under their wings as though asleep. A few were inert with wings only partially furled, giving every indication of being dead, perhaps overcome by sheer panic.

Immensely gratified by the turn of events, Toller pulled clear of the white-swaddled tumult to search for a likely target and saw a pilot of his own squadron closing in on him. It was Berise Narrinder, and she was rapidly opening and closing her right hand, signalling that she wanted to talk. Puzzled, he closed his throttle and allowed the fighter to coast to a halt. Berise did likewise and the two craft drifted together, gently yawing as their control surfaces became more and more ineffective.

"What is it?" Toller said. "Do you want to bring one of the birds back for dinner?"

Berise shook her head impatiently and pulled her scarf down below her chin. "There's a ship far down below the battle zone. I'd like you to have a look at it."

He looked in the direction she was indicating, but was unable to find the ship. "It has to be an observer," he said. "The pilot was told to remain well out of trouble and return to base with a report."

"My glasses tell me it is not an ordinary ship," Berise said. "Look carefully, my lord. Use your binoculars. Look where that line of cloud crosses the Gulf of Tronom."

Toller did as instructed, and this time was able to pick out the tiny outline of a skyship. It was on its side relative to him, reinforcing his opinion that its function was to observe the outcome of the battle. He wondered if it had yet become apparent to those on board that all was far from well with their fellows.

"I see nothing unusual about it," he said. "Why are you interested?"

"What about the markings on the gondola? Can't you see the blue and grey stripes?"

After further study of the miniature shape Toller lowered his binoculars. "Your young eyes are obviously better than mine." He paused, a coolness on the nape of his neck, as the full import of Berise's words reached him. "Blue and grey were always the colours of the royal ships—but would Rassamarden have retained them?"

"Why not? They might mean something to him."

Toller nodded thoughtfully. "In spite of his declarations of contempt he seems to covet everything the old kings had. But would any ruler be foolhardy enough to venture so close to a battle?"

"I've been told that Leddravohr often *led* his troops—and he wasn't a New Man," Berise said through featherings of vapour. "And what about the eagles? If they had done what was required of them things would probably have gone very badly for us. Rassamarden may have expected to witness a famous victory."

"Your mind is as sharp as your eyes, captain." Toller gave her an approving smile.

"Compliments are all very well, my lord—but I have a more apt reward in mind."

"Assuming it *is* a royal ship, you want the honour of destroying it."

Berise met his gaze squarely, eyebrows drawn together. "I believe I have that right—I am the one who saw it."

"Your feelings are understandable—and I sympathise with them—but you must consider my position. If Rassamarden is on board that ship all else should be subordinated to the task of slaying him, thus bringing this war to an end. In all conscience, it is my duty to attack the ship with every fighter at my disposal."

"But you don't *know* that Rassamarden is there," Berise said, shifting her argument with a casual speed which reminded Toller of his wife's similar ability. "Surely it would be wrong of you to divert your forces from the main battle to pursue a single ship, especially one which in any case cannot hope to escape us."

Toller gave an exaggerated sigh. "May I at least accompany you and witness the exploit?"

"Thank you, my lord," Berise said warmly, and for once without the hint of challenge she always insinuated into the title. She immediately reached for the throttle of her red-striped machine.

"Not so fast!" Toller protested, pausing as the exhaust of a jet slewing wide of the battle made communication momentarily impossible. "First I want you to seek out Umol and Daas and bring them to me, and I will tell them what we are about. They must keep an eye on our progress. If we fail to return, they must attack that ship in force—on *no* account can the ship be permitted to withdraw with any of its crew or passengers still alive."

Berise tilted her head and frowned, her face a beautiful mask in the upflung light of the sun. "We are two fighters against one skyship—how can you doubt our success?"

"Because of the parachutes," Toller said. "When a skyship carries common soldiers it is enough for us to destroy the balloon. It matters little to us if they survive the drop and come back for more of the same medicine another day. But in this case the ship is of no importance—it would be less than pointless to burn the balloon, but allow Rassamarden to return safely to his pestilent kingdom. In this *crucial* case the balloon is not our target, nor even the gondola.

"We have to kill Rassamarden himself, and I don't need to tell you that will be a far more hazardous business than merely spiking a balloon at long range. Do you still claim the honour?"

Berise's expression was unaltered. "I am still the one who saw the ship."

A few minutes later Toller was riding down towards the distant ship, with Berise holding a parallel course, and it was then that he began to have doubts about allowing her to accompany him. The fighter pilots shared a special bond, a spirit of comradeship which surpassed anything he had previously known in ordinary military service, and she had skilfully made use of it to influence his decision. It was perhaps all right for him, half in love with death, to undertake such a dangerous mission—but what about his responsibility towards all those he commanded?

The dilemma was intensified by the fact that if he were to send Berise back to comparative safety she would jump to the conclusion that his motives were selfish, that he wanted the glory of killing Rassamarden all to himself. Most of the other fighter pilots would side with her, their impulse-governed natures allowing no options, and he dreaded the prospect of losing their esteem. Could that be the obvious nub of a childishly simple problem? Was he prepared to waste a young woman's life rather than forfeit the flattering regard of a handful of young bucks?

The only reasonable and honourable answer had to be: *No!*

Toller looked at Berise, preparing himself for an ordeal, then he was overwhelmed by a rush of unexpected emotion. It was a blend of affection and respect, triggered by the sight of her diminutive figure astride the streamlined bulk of the jet fighter and outlined against silver whirlpools in a dark blue infinity. It came to him that she was both courageous and intelligent, that she had certainly been ahead of him in every one of his ponderous deliberations, and that she was fully qualified to choose her own destiny. As though sensing his interest she gave him an enquiring glance, her features all but hidden by her scarf and goggles. Toller gave her a salute, which she returned, then he concentrated his thoughts on the forthcoming skirmish.

He and Berise were on a straight line between the main battle and the lone skyship. His hope had been that their condensation trails would remain unnoticed against the tangled confusion of smoke and sun-glowing vapour above, but the evidence was that keen-eyed lookouts had already spotted them. Musketeers were diving out from the gondola, tumbling to the ends of their lines, forming a sparse circle from which they could direct fire at a fighter going for the balloon's vulnerable upper surface. Their chances of disabling a pilot were not great, but the problem in this particular instance was that Berise was required to go in on a level with the musketeers in order to attack the gondola itself, and in previous encounters the Landers had proved themselves to be excellent marksmen.

A few furlongs away from the ship Toller gave the talk signal and shut down his engine, and when Berise drifted to a halt beside him he said, "Before taking any unnecessary risks, have a closer look at the gondola. Find me some evidence that Rassamarden really is on board."

Berise raised her binoculars to her eyes, was quiet for a moment and then—unexpectedly—began to laugh. "I glimpsed a crown! A glass crown! Is that what King Prad and all the others wore? Did they really walk about with ridiculous ornaments like that on their heads?"

"On certain occasions," Toller said, wondering why he had begun to feel offended. "If what you saw was the Bytran diadem it is composed principally of diamonds, and is worth—" He broke off, suffused by a savage gladness. "The fool! The puffed-up, vainglorious *fool*! His fondness for that little glass hat has cost him his life for certain! How many cannon shells have you?"

"The full six."

"Good! I'll take the balloon, but from the side rather than above, so that I'll be visible from the gondola. All eyes will be upon me when I loose my arrow—and that's the moment for your attack. Perhaps fate will let you burst their crystal stores on the first pass. Are you ready?"

Berise nodded. Toller made sure his pneumatic reservoir was at maximum pressure, then blew crystals into his engine and the responsive machine surged towards the skyship. He flew a little slower than he would normally have done and swept outwards into a curve which would take him past the balloon on a descending diagonal. Berise was on a steeper downward course, using her engine in short bursts which left an intermittent trail of white.

As the blue-and-grey gondola expanded in his vision Toller saw a milling of figures among the wicker partitions. He counted eight soldiers at the ends of radial lines, all with a hunched foreshortening of their upper bodies which told him they were aiming their muskets in his direction.

That's what I want, he thought, removing his right glove. *That's just what I want*.

He took an arrow from a quiver, ignited the tip and nocked it on to his bowstring. He gunned his engine, bracing himself against the acceleration, and dived on the balloon. The howl from the exhaust obliterated all musket reports, but he saw their toadstool billows of white. As the monstrous shape of the balloon swelled to become a curved brown wall blotting out much of the universe, he rolled the fighter to put the solidity of the engine between him and most of the enemy marksmen. Land and Overland obediently slid into new positions in the firmament.

Toller drew the bow and fired in a single practised movement, and in the same movement heard the double blast of Berise's cannon. His arrow streaked into the balloon, its line of flight vectored into an arc by his own speed. Something flicked his left leg and tufts of cottony insulation whirled away in the fighter's slipstream. He crouched low on the rounded back of the machine and burned his way out towards the stars. At a safe distance he shut down the engine and pulled into a turn which gave him a view of the battle scene.

Berise was completing a similar manoeuvre above him and to his right. Fire was spreading on one side of the Lander balloon, but although he was certain Berise's aim had been good, the gondola appeared to be undamaged. There was no way of telling what injury, if any, the iron balls passing through it had inflicted on those inside.

Berise was busy clearing the breeches of her cannon and inserting fresh shells. When she had finished she raised a hand and Toller went for the balloon again, trying to draw as much fire as possible in order to give her a second clear run. He successfully put an orange-streaming dart into the now misshapen giant and again sought out Berise in the empty sky beyond. Instead of pausing she reloaded during a sweeping turn and drove in beneath him at speed, coming up from beneath the Lander gondola.

The tethered soldiers were turning their muskets towards her as she fired both cannon. The gondola shuddered as the shot ploughed into the planking of the deck, but it remained structurally intact, and soldiers on board kept on firing through the black smoke which was gathering around the stricken craft.

Toller, who had been praying for a crystal explosion, coasted to a halt. There was a possibility that Rassamarden had been hit, but a man was a small target within the volume of a gondola, and in this instance he *had* to be able to claim a certain kill. Nothing else could be acceptable under the circumstances. He looked around for Berise and saw her swooping down on him in a nimbus of brilliant vapour. As she drew near he tapped his chest and pointed at the skyship, signifying that he intended to mount his own attack. She pulled down her scarf and shouted something he failed to hear above the growl of her engine. Her face was savage, almost unrecognisable. He barely had time to note that her windscreen was spidered with white lines, then she had given her engine full throttle and was dwindling into the distance —heading straight for the skyship amid an appalling blast of sound.

Toller gave an involuntary cry of protest as the fighter streaked towards the gondola and it became obvious that Berise had no intention of changing course. Barely two seconds before impact she leapt off the machine. It sledged through the wall of the gondola and struck the centrally mounted engine, driving the entire structure forward in a tumbling movement which wrapped large pieces of the still-burning balloon around it. An acceleration strut broke free and flailed off to one side while tethered soldiers were snatched into the turmoil by coiling ropes. A moment later there came a series of whooshing explosions —typical of the pikon-halvell reaction—followed by a great billowing of greenish flame. Toller knew at once that nobody aboard the gondola could possibly have escaped death.

Berise, having kicked herself into a trajectory only slightly different from that of her fighter, had disappeared into the opaque seethings of smoke, becoming lost to Toller's view. Cold with apprehension, senses overloaded, he fed his engine and flew in a semi-circle around the slow-spinning chaos, reaching the dark blue serenity beyond. At first there was no sign of Berise, then he saw a twinkling white mote which was changing position against the background of stars and silver spirals. His glasses showed that it was Berise, perhaps a mile distant and still receding, still using up the energy imparted to her by the fighter's speed.

He went after her, dreading the prospect of finding a mutilated body, adjusting his speed and direction as he drew near. The fighter had begun to wallow as it closed in on Berise, and he had to raise himself on the footrest in order to grip her arm and pull her towards him. He knew immediately that she was alive and well because she expertly took command of their relative motion, guiding herself in such a way that she ended up astride of him, face to face, arms around his neck.

He saw the manic ecstasy on her face, felt the quivering

tension of her body despite the bulkiness of her skysuit, and in that moment there was nothing they could do but kiss. Berise's lips were cold, even her tongue was cold, but Toller—the man who had forsworn sexual passion for ever—was unable to stop his groin lifting up against her again and again. She clamped her legs around him and rode him eagerly for the duration of the kiss, then used both hands to push his face away from hers.

"Was I good, Toller?" she breathed. "Was that the best thing you ever saw?"

"Yes, yes, but you're lucky to be alive."

"I know, I *know*!" She laughed and returned to the kiss and they drifted that way for a long time, lost among the stars and luminous swirls of their private universe.

For the most part it was quiet on board the skyship. Toller had carried out the inversion manoeuvre some two hundred miles below the weightless zone, and now the ship was gently falling towards Overland. During the next few days little would be required other than periodic injections of hot gas to give the huge balloon a positive internal pressure which would keep it from falling in on itself. The bitterness of the aerial element was mitigated to some extent by a crystal-powered heater and the fact that it was now standard practice for gondolas to be lined with vellum to prevent the ingress of chill air through chinks in the walls and deck.

It was, however, still very cold within the circumscribed space of the gondola, and when Berise removed her blouse her nipples gathered into brown peaks. Toller, who was already naked and ensconced in layers of eiderdown, extended an inviting hand to her, but she held back for the moment. She was kneeling beside him, gripping one of the transverse lines which were a vital safety feature in the virtual absence of gravity.

"Are you sure about this?" she said. "You haven't been at all discreet." She was referring to Toller having announced his intention of presenting her to the King, and —instead of returning to Overland by fallbag and parachute—commandeering a skyship for just the two of them.

"Are you delaying in this way to give me the opportunity to

change my mind?" He smiled and glanced at the globes of her breasts, which were buoyantly beautiful in a way which would have been impossible in normal gravity. "Or is it to prevent me changing my mind?"

Berise placed a forearm across her breasts. "I'm thinking of the Lady Gesalla. It is almost certain that she will be informed, by somebody, and I have no wish for you to look on me afterwards with cold eyes."

"The Lady Gesalla and I live in different worlds," Toller said. "We both do what it is in us to do."

"In that case. . . ." Berise squirmed her cold little body into the quilts beside him, making him gasp with the touch of her cold fingers.

In the days and nights that followed, while the meteors flickered all around, Toller rediscovered vital aspects of his being, learned the extent to which his life had become arid and deficient in recent years. The experience was unbearably sweet and unbearably bitter at the same time, because an inner voice informed him that he was committing a form of self-murder—a spiritual suicide—while the meteors flickered all around.

PART III

Silent Invasions

Chapter 11

By the time Sondeweere had been away for eighty days Bartan Drumme had developed a new pattern of living.

Each morning he went out and made some attempt to cultivate the nearer portions of his farm—that was a duty he could not ignore—but his real preoccupation was with his hoard of glass and ceramic demijohns, the source of his sustenance and comfort. The production and consumption of wine claimed most of his waking hours. He had learned to dispose of such niceties as using fresh yeast and of waiting for the wine to clear, the latter being an exercise in pointless aesthetics which had no effect on a beverage's alcohol content.

As soon as a jar of wine had ceased working he siphoned it off the dregs and poured in a new batch of juice expressed from fruit or berries, restarting the fermentation with the sludge of the old yeast. The yeast quickly became contaminated with wild strains, yielding wines which were marred by sourness and off-flavours, but the method had the overriding virtue of being *fast*.

Efficiency of production was all that mattered to Bartan. He frequently became ill and was racked by diarrhoea caused by drinking his murky potions, but that seemed a small price to pay for the ability to escape his guilt and to sleep the long night through. The bargain was enhanced by the fact that he had little need of solid food, the bubble-ringed glasses providing most of the nourishment he required to get through the weary succession of days.

Now that even the Phoratere family had left the Basket he had no companionship from other farmers, but he had given up riding into New Minnett to spend time in the tavern. The journey had begun to seem tedious and lacking in purpose when he had all he could drink at home, and in any case he could detect a new lack of warmth in his reception. Reeve Karrodall had counselled him about his drinking and personal appearance, and subsequently had become a much less congenial person with whom to while away the hours.

He was returning from the fields one day, just before sunset, when he noticed a flurry of movement ahead of him in the dust of the path. Closer inspection revealed that it was a crawler, the first he had seen in a long time. The glistening brown creature was labouring along the path in the direction of the house, with occasional flashes of pallid grey from its underside as it clambered over pebbles.

Bartan stared at it for a moment, his mouth twitching in revulsion, then looked around for a large stone. He found one which required two hands to lift, and dashed it down on the crawler. With his gaze averted in case he glimpsed the sickening result of his handiwork, he stepped over the stone and continued on his way. There were many varieties of small life forms to be found in the soil of Overland, most of them repugnant to his eye, but he usually left them alone to go about their business in peace. The sole exception was the crawler, which he had a compulsion to destroy on sight.

The house and outbuildings were bathed in a mellow red-gold light as he drew near, and he felt the familiar sinking of his spirits at the prospect of spending the night there alone. This was the worst time of the day, when he was met by silence in the house in place of Sondeweere's laughter, and the darkening dome of the sky seemed to reverberate with emptiness. The whole world felt empty at sunset. He passed the pigsty, which was also silent because he had turned the animals out into the wild to fend for themselves, and crossed the yard to the house. On opening the front door he paused, his heart beginning to pound as he realised the place *felt* different.

"Sondy!" he called out, giving way to an irrational impulse. He darted through the kitchen and flung open the bedroom door. The room beyond was empty, with no change in the squalor he had allowed to overwhelm it. Downcast and feeling like a fool, he nevertheless returned to the front entrance and scanned the surroundings. Everything was as usual in the sad coppery light, the only sign of movement coming from the blue-horn which was grazing near the orchard.

Bartan sighed, shaking his head over the bout of idiocy. He had a throbbing pain in his temples, legacy of the wine he had drunk in the afternoon, and he felt parched. He selected a full demijohn from the array in the corner, picked up a cup and returned outside to the bench by the door. The wine tasted less palatable than usual, but he drank the first two cupfuls greedily, pouring them down like water in order to win the blessed muzziness which dulled intellect and emotion. He had a feeling he was going to need it more than ever in the hours to come.

As darkness gathered and the heavens began to throng with their nightly display, he picked out Farland—the only green-tinted object in the firmament—and allowed his gaze to dwell on it. He still retained all his scepticism for religion, but of late had begun to understand the comforts it could offer. Assuming that Sondeweere was dead, it would be so good to believe, or even half-believe, that she had merely taken the High Path to the outer world and was beginning a new existence there. A simple reincarnation without continuance of memory or personality, which was what the Alternist religion postulated, was in many ways indistinguishable from straightforward death—but it offered *something*. It offered the hope that he had not totally destroyed a wonderful human life with his stubbornness and arrogance, that in the eternity which lay ahead he and Son-deweere would meet again, perhaps many times, and that he would be able to make amends to her in some way. The fact that they would not consciously recognise each other, and yet might respond as soul mates, unaccountably drawn to each other, made the whole concept romantically beautiful and poignant . . .

Tears flooded Bartan's eyes, expanding the image of Farland into consecutive rings filled with radial prismatic needles. He gulped down more wine to ease the choking pain in his throat.

Let me know that you are up there, Sondy, he pleaded in his thoughts, surrendering to the fantasy. *If only you could grant me a sign that you still exist, I too would begin to live again.*

He continued drinking as Farland drifted down the sky. Now

and again he lost consciousness through exhaustion and increasing intoxication, but when he opened his eyes the green planet was always centred in his field of vision, sometimes as a swirling luminous bubble, at others in the semblance of a circular chalcedonic gem, slowly rotating, striking a languorous green fire from a thousand facets. It seemed to grow bigger, and bigger, finally to develop a mobile core which displayed a creamy luminance, a core which by imperceptible stages evolved into the likeness of a woman's face.

Bartan, Sondeweere said, not in an ordinary voice, but an inversion of sound in which one kind of silence was imposed on another. *Poor Bartan, I have been aware of your pain, and I am glad that I have at last succeeded in reaching you. You must desist from blaming yourself, and punishing yourself, and thus squandering your one-and-only life. You have no reason to reproach yourself on my account.*

"But I brought you to this place," Bartan mumbled, unastonished, playing the game of dreams. "I am responsible for your death."

If I were dead I would be unable to speak to you.

Bartan replied in his fuddled obstinacy. "The crime remains. I deprived you of a life—the one we should have shared—and you were so lovely, so sweet, so good. . . ."

You must remember me as I actually was, Bartan. Do not fuel your self-pity by imagining that I was anything but a very ordinary woman.

"So good, so pure. . . ."

Bartan! It may help you if I make you aware that I was never faithful to you. Glave Trinchil was only one of the men from whom I took my pleasures. There were many of them—including my Uncle Jop. . . .

"That isn't true! I have dreamed foul lies into your mouth." On another level of Bartan's drugged consciousness there came the first stirrings of comprehension and wonder: *This is not a dream! This is really happening!*

That is so, Bartan. The non-voice, the modulations of silence, somehow conveyed wisdom and kindliness. *This is really happening, but it will not happen again—so mark well what I am saying. I am not dead! You must stop torturing yourself and dissipating your one-and-only life. Put the past behind you and go on to other things. Above all, forget about me. Goodbye, Bartan. . . .*

The sound of his cup splintering on the ground brought Bartan to his feet. He stood there in the star-shot darkness, swaying and shivering, staring at Farland, which was now just above the western horizon. It registered as a point of pure green light without fringes or optical adornments—but for the first time he saw it as another planet, a *world*, a real place which was as large as Land or Overland, a seat of life.

"Sondy!" he called out, running a few futile paces forward. *"Sondy!"*

Farland continued its slow descent to the rim of the world.

Bartan went back into the house, fetched another cup and returned to his bench. He filled the cup and drank from it in small, regular, relentless sips as the enigmatic mote of brilliance gradually extinguished itself, winking on the horizon. When it had vanished from sight he found that his mind had acquired a strange and precarious clarity, an ability—which had to fade soon—to deal with unearthly concepts. Momentous judgments and decisions had to be made quickly, before a vinous tide swept him into lasting unconsciousness.

"I still repudiate all religious belief," he announced to the darkness, calling on the act of speaking aloud to help imprint his thinking on the coming days and years.

"In doing so I am being totally logical. How do I know I'm being totally logical? Because the Alternists preach that only the soul, the spiritual *essence*, ventures along the High Path. It is an article of faith that there is no continuance of memory—otherwise every man, woman and child would be burdened beyond endurance with recollections of previous existences. It is obvious that Sondeweere remembers me and every circumstance of our lives—therefore she cannot be an Alternist reincarnation.

"As well as that, there are no known instances of those who have passed on communicating with those who remain. And Sondeweere herself referred to my one-and-only life, which . . .

which does not really prove anything . . . but if we all have only one life, and she *spoke* to me, that proves her life has not ended. . . .

"Sondeweere is physically alive somewhere!"

Bartan shivered and took a longer drink, blurrily elated and overwhelmed at the same time. His momentous discovery had brought many questions in its wake, questions of a kind he was not accustomed to dealing with. Why was he persuaded that Sondeweere was on Farland and not, as was much more likely, in another part of his own world? Was it that the apparition had been so intimately associated with the image of the green planet, or had the strange voiceless message from her been layered with meanings not contained in the bare words? And if she were on Farland—how had she been transported? And why? Was it something to do with the inexplicable lights he had seen on the night of her disappearance? And, granting the other suppositions, what had given her the miraculous ability to speak to him across thousands of miles of space?

And—most pressing of all—now that he had been vouchsafed the new knowledge, what was he going to do with it? What action was he going to take?

Bartan grinned, staring glassily into the darkness. The last question had been the only one to which he could easily supply an answer.

It was obvious that he had to go to Farland and bring Sondeweere home!

"Your wife was abducted!" Reeve Majin Karrodall's cry of astonishment was followed by an attentive silence among the tavern's other customers.

Bartan nodded. "That's what I said."

Karrodall moved closer to him, hand dropping to the hilt of his smallsword. "Do you know who did it? Do you know where she is?"

"I don't know who was responsible, but I know where she is," Bartan said. "My wife is living on Farland."

Some of those nearby emitted gleeful sniggers and the group around him began to increase in size. Karrodall gave them an impatient glance, his red face deepening in colour, before he narrowed his eyes at Bartan.

"Did you say Farland? Are you talking about Farland . . . in the sky?"

"I am indeed talking about the planet Farland," Bartan said solemnly. He reached for the alepot which had been set out for him, overbalanced and had to grasp the table for a moment of support.

"You'd better sit down before you fall down." Karrodall waited until Bartan lowered himself on to a bench. "Bartan, is this more of Trinchil's teachings? Are you trying to say your wife has died and travelled the High Path?"

"I'm saying she is alive. On Farland." Bartan drank deeply from the alepot. "Is that so hard to understand?"

Karrodall straddled the bench. "What's hard to understand is why you let yourself into a condition which so ill becomes you. You look terrible, you stink—and not only of bad wine—and now you are so soused that your talk is that of a madman. I have told you this before, Bartan, but you must quit the Haunt before it is too late."

"I have already done so," Bartan said, wiping froth from his lips with the back of a hand. "I'll never set foot there again."

"At least that is *one* sensible decision on your part. Where will you go?"

"Have I not said?" Bartan surveyed the ring of gleefully incredulous faces. "Why, I'm going to Farland to rescue my wife."

There was an outbreak of laughter which the reeve's authority could no longer hold in check. More men crowded around Bartan, while others hurried away to spread the word of the unexpected sport which was to be had at the tavern. Somebody slid a fresh tankard into place in front of Bartan.

The plump, limping figure of Otler approached the group, shouldered his way in and said, "But, my friend, how do you *know* that your wife has taken up residence on Farland?"

"She told me three nights ago. She spoke to me."

Otler nudged the man beside him. "The woman looked as

though she had a healthy set of bellows, but they must have been better than we knew. What do you say, Alsorn?"

The remark disturbed Bartan's alcoholic composure. He grabbed Otler's shirt and tried to pull him down on to the bench, but the reeve thrust them apart and swung a warning finger between the two men.

"All I meant," Otler complained, tucking his shirt back into his breeches, "was that Farland is a long way off." He brightened up as a witticism occurred to him. "I mean, that's what Farland means, isn't it? *Far*-land!"

"Being in your company is an education in itself," Bartan said. "Sondeweere appeared to me in a vision. She spoke to me in a vision."

Again there was a burst of merriment, and Bartan—stupefied though he was—recognised that he had only succeeded in making himself a figure of fun.

"Gentlemen," he said, rising unsteadily to his feet. "I have tarried here too long, and soon I must depart for the noble city of Prad. I have spent the past two days repairing and refurbishing my wagon—therefore the journey should not be overly prolonged—but nevertheless I will have need of money along the way for the purchase of food and perhaps just a little wine or brandy." He nodded in acknowledgment of an ironic cheer.

"My airboat is on the wagon outside—it needs only a new gasbag—and in addition I have brought some good furniture and tools. Who will give me a hundred royals for the lot?"

Some of the listeners moved away to inspect what was undoubtedly a bargain, but others were more interested in prolonging the entertainment. "You haven't told us how you propose to reach Farland," a hollow-cheeked merchant said. "Will you shoot yourself out of a cannon?"

"I have as yet little idea how to make the flight, and that is why I must begin my journey by going to Prad. There is one man there who knows more about journeying through the sky than any other, and I shall seek him out."

"What is his name?"

"Maraquine," Bartan said. "Sky Marshal Lord Toller Maraquine."

"I'm sure he'll be very glad to see you," Otler said, nodding in mock-approval. "His lordship and you will make a fine pair."

"Enough of this!" Karrodall gripped Bartan's arm and forcibly drew him away from the group. "Bartan, it grieves me to see you thus, with all your drunken babbling about Farland and visions . . . and now this talk of trying to approach the Kingslayer. You can't be serious about that."

"Why not?" Striving to look dignified, Bartan prised the reeve's fingers off his arm. "Now that the war is ending Lord Toller will have no further use for his fortresses in the sky. When he hears my proposal to fly one of them to Farland—bearing the flag of Kolcorron, mark you—he will doubtless be pleased to give me his patronage."

"I am sorry for you," Karrodall remarked sadly. "I am truly sorry for you."

As he travelled to the east Bartan kept an eye on the horizon ahead, and eventually was rewarded with his first sight of Land in a long time.

In the beginning the sister world appeared as a curving sliver of pale light atop the distant mountains, then as the journey progressed it gradually rose higher to become a glowing dome. The nights grew noticeably longer as Land encroached upon more and more of the sun's path. As the planet continued its upward drift, to show a semi-circle and more, the outlines of the continents and oceans became clearly visible, evocations of lost histories.

Eventually there came the time when Land's lower edge lifted clear of the horizon, creating a narrow gap through which the rising sun could pour mingling rays of multi-coloured fire. The diurnal pattern of light and darkness, familiar to born Kolcorronians, was beginning to re-establish itself, although at this stage foreday was extremely brief. For Bartan—journeying alone in dusty landscapes—the occasion was a significant one, worth commemorating with extra measures of brandy.

He knew that when foreday and aftday reached a balance he would be close to the city of Prad, and from that moment onwards his future would be in the hands of a stranger.

Chapter 12

A great deal of thought and effort had been put into making the garden look as though it had been established for centuries. Some of the statues had been deliberately chipped to give them semblance of antiquity, and the walls and stone benches were artificially weathered with corrosive fluids. The flowers and shrubs had either been grown from seeds brought from Land, or were native varieties which closely resembled those of the Old World.

In a way Toller Maraquine sympathised with the intent—he could imagine that being in the garden would help counter-balance the aching emptiness of the sunset hour—but he had to wonder at the psychology involved. King Chakkell's personal achievements since arriving on Overland would guarantee him a place in history, but somehow that was not enough to satisfy him. He obviously craved all that his predecessors had enjoyed—not only power itself, but the trappings and emblems of power. Identical motivation had just brought about the death of the King of the New Men, reinforcing Toller's belief that he would never be able to comprehend the mentality of those who needed to rule others.

"I am well pleased with the outcome," King Chakkell said, stroking his paunch as he walked, as though having enjoyed a banquet. "The expense of it all was proving a great drain on our resources, but now—with Rassamarden dead—I can rid myself of all those floating fortresses. We will drop them on Land and, with any luck, kill a few more of the diseased upstarts."

"I don't think that would be a good idea," Toller said impulsively.

"What is wrong with it? They have to fall somewhere—and surely better on them than on us."

"I say the defences should be maintained." Toller knew he would be called upon to marshal logical arguments, but was having difficulty in concentrating his thoughts on impersonal matters such as the strategies of war. He and Berise had landed their skyship only hours earlier—and now it was necessary for him to speak to his wife.

Chakkell spread his arms, halting their progress through the garden. "What do you say, Zavotle?"

Ilven Zavotle, who had a hand pressed into his stomach, looked blank. "I beg your pardon, Majesty—what was the question?"

Chakkell scowled at him. "What's the matter with you these days? You seem more preoccupied with your gut than with anything I have to say. Are you ill?"

"It's just a touch of the bile, Majesty," Zavotle said. "It may be that the food from the royal kitchen is too rich for my blood."

"In that case your stomach has reason to be grateful to me—I propose to dismantle the aerial defence screen and drop the fortresses on Land. What do you say to that?"

"It would advertise our lack of defences to the enemy."

"What does it matter if they lack the means or the will to attack?"

"Rassamarden's successor could be just as ambitious," Toller said. "The Landers may yet send another fleet."

"After the total destruction of the last one?"

Toller could see that the King was becoming impatient, but he did not want to yield. "In my opinion we should retain all the fighters, plus enough stations to support them and their pilots." To his surprise Chakkell gave a hearty laugh.

"I see your game!" Chakkell said jovially, slapping him on the shoulder. "You still haven't grown up, Maraquine. You always have to have a new plaything. The fighters are your toys and the weightless zone is your playground, and you want *me* to go on footing the bill. Isn't that it?"

"Certainly not, Majesty." Toller made no attempt to hide the fact that he was offended. Gesalla had often spoken to him in a similar vein, and he . . . *Gesalla! I have betrayed our love, and now I must confess to you. If only I can win your forgiveness I swear to you that I will never again. . . .*

"Mind you," Chakkell went on, "I have a certain sympathy with your viewpoint now that I have met your little playmate."

"Majesty, if you are referring to Skycaptain Narrinder I. . . ."

"Come now, Maraquine! Don't try to tell me you haven't bedded that little beauty." Chakkell was enjoying himself, eagerly resuming the private game now that he had discovered an unexpected area of vulnerability in his opponent. "It's obvious, man! It's written all over your face! What do you say, Zavotle?"

Thoughtfully massaging his stomach, Zavotle said, "It seems to me that if we burned the command stations and fortresses, the ashes could fall anywhere without harming us or betraying information to the enemy."

"That's an excellent thought, Zavotle—and I thank you for it—but you have not addressed the subject."

"I dare not, Majesty," Zavotle said humorously. "To do so I would either have to disagree with a King or insult a nobleman who has a reputation for reacting violently in such instances."

Toller gave him an amiable nod. "What you're saying is that a man's private life should be his own."

"*Private* life?" Chakkell shook his brown-domed head in amusement. "Toller Maraquine, my old adversary, my old friend, my old court jester—you cannot row upstream and downstream at the same time. Messengers in fallbags preceded your arrival in Prad by days, and the news of your honeymoon flight with the delectable Skycaptain Narrinder has travelled far and wide.

"She has become a national heroine, and you—once *again* —have become a national hero. In the taverns your union has already been blessed with a million beery libations. My subjects, most of whom appear to be romantic dolts, seem to see you as a couple chosen for each other by destiny, but none of them is faced with the unenviable task of explaining that to the Lady Gesalla. As for myself, I almost think I would rather go against Karkarand."

Toller gave the King a formal bow, preparatory to taking his leave. "As I said, Majesty, a man's private life should be his own."

Riding south on the highway which connected Prad to the town of Heevern, Toller reached a crest and—for the first time in well over a year—saw his own home.

Still several miles away to the south-west, the grey stone building was rendered white by the aftday sun, making it sharply visible among the green horizontals of the landscape. Within himself Toller tried to manufacture a surge of gladness and of affection for the place, and when it failed to materialise his feelings of self-reproach grew more intense.

I'm a lucky man, he told himself, determined to impose will on emotion. *My beautiful solewife is enshrined in that house, and—if she forgives the sin I have committed against her—it will be my privilege to be her loving companion for the rest of our days. Even if she cannot absolve me at once, I will eventually win her over by being what she wants me to be, by being the Toller Maraquine I know I ought to be, and which I genuinely crave to be—and we will enjoy the twilight years together. That is what I want. That is what I WANT!*

From Toller's elevated viewpoint he could see intermittent traces of the road which joined his house to the north-south highway, and his attention was caught by a blurry white speck which betokened a single rider heading towards the main road. The stubby telescope which had served him since boyhood hinted at a bluehorn with distinctive creamy forelegs, and Toller knew at once that the rider was his son. This time there was no need to contrive gladness. He had missed Cassyll a great deal, primarily because of the ties of blood, but also because of the satisfaction he had found when they were working together.

In the unnatural circumstances of the aerial war he had somehow almost managed to forget about the projects he and Cassyll had been engaged on, but much remained for them to do—more than enough to occupy any man's days. It was absolutely vital that the felling of brakka trees should be brought to a halt for ever—otherwise the ptertha would again become invincible enemies—and the key to the future lay in the development of metals. King Chakkell's reluctance to face up to the problem made it all the more imperative for Toller to rejoin his son and resume their work together.

Toller increased his speed towards the juncture of the two roads, anticipating the moment in which Cassyll would notice and recognise him. The intersection was the one where the unhappy incident with Oaslit Spennel had begun, but he pushed the memories aside as he and Cassyll steadily grew closer together on their converging paths. When they were less than a furlong apart and nothing had happened Toller began to suspect that his son was riding with his eyes closed, trusting the bluehorn to find its own way, probably to the ironworks.

"Rouse yourself, sleepyhead!" he shouted. "What manner of welcome is this?"

Cassyll looked towards him, with no sign of surprise, turned his head away and continued riding at unchanged speed. He reached the road junction first and, to Toller's bewilderment, turned south. Toller called out Cassyll's name and galloped after him. He overtook his son's bluehorn and brought it to a halt by grasping the reins.

"What's the matter with you, son?" he said. "Were you asleep?"

Cassyll's grey eyes were cool. "I was wide awake, father."

"Then what. . . ?" Toller studied the fine-featured oval face—previewing the forthcoming meeting with Gesalla—and any joy that was within him died. "So that's the way of it."

"So that's the way of what?"

"Don't fence with words, Cassyll—no matter what you think of me you should at least speak forthrightly, as I am doing with you. Now, what troubles you? Is it to do with the woman?"

"I. . . ." Cassyll pressed the knuckles of his fist to his lips. "Where is she, anyway? Has she, perhaps, transferred her attentions to the King?"

Toller repressed a surge of anger. "I don't know what you have heard—but Berise Narrinder is a fine woman."

"As harlots go, that is," Cassyll sneered.

Toller had actually begun the back-handed slap when he realised what was happening and checked the movement. Appalled, he lowered his gaze and stared at his hand as though it were a third party which had attempted to intrude on a private discussion. His bluehorn nuzzled against Cassyll's, making soft snuffling sounds.

"I'm sorry," Toller said. "My temper is . . . Are you on your way to the works?"

"Yes. I go there most days."

"I'll join you later, but first I must speak to your mother."

"As you wish, father." Cassyll's face was carefully expressionless. "May I go now?"

"I won't detain you any further," Toller said, struggling against a sense of despair. He watched his son ride off to the south, then resumed his own journey. Somehow it had not occurred to him to take Cassyll's feelings into account, and now he feared that their relationship had been damaged beyond repair. Perhaps the boy would relent with the passage of time, but for the present Toller's main hope lay with Gesalla. If he could win her forgiveness quickly his son might be favourably influenced.

The crescent of sunlight was broadening on the great disk of Land, poised overhead, reminding Toller that aftday was well advanced. He increased the bluehorn's pace. Here and there in the surrounding fields farmers were at work, and they paused to salute him as he rode by. He was popular with the tenants, largely because he charged rents that were little more than nominal, and he found himself wishing that all human relationships could be so easily regulated. The King had joked about facing up to Gesalla, but Toller could remember times when he had genuinely been more apprehensive on the eve of a battle than he was at this moment, preparing to run the gauntlet of his wife's reproach, scorn and anger. Loved ones had an intangible armoury—words, silences, expressions, gestures— which could inflict deeper wounds than swords or spears.

By the time Toller reached the walled precinct at the front of the house his mouth was dry, and it was all he could do to prevent himself from trembling.

The bluehorn was one borrowed from the royal stables, and therefore Toller had to dismount and open the gate by hand. He led the animal inside and while it was ambling to the stone drinking trough he surveyed the familiar enclosure, with its ornamental shrubs and well-tended flower beds. Gesalla liked to look after it personally, and her skilled touch was evident everywhere he looked—a reminder that he would be with her in a matter of seconds.

He heard the front door opening and turned to see his wife standing in the archway. She was wearing an ankle-length gown of dark blue and had bound her hair up in such a manner that its stripe of silver made a natural coronet. Her beauty was as complete and as daunting as Toller had ever known it to be, and when he saw that she was smiling the weight of his guilt became insupportable, turning his own smile into a nerveless grimace, rooting him to the spot. She came to him and kissed him on the lips, briefly but warmly, then stepped back to examine him from head to foot.

"You're not hurt," she said. "I was so afraid for you, Toller . . . it all sounded so impossibly dangerous . . . but now I see you're not hurt and I can breathe again."

"Gesalla. . . ." He took both her hands. "I must talk to you."

"Of course you must—and you're probably hungry and thirsty. Come into the house and I'll prepare a meal." She tugged at his hands, but he refused to move.

"It might be best if I stayed out here," he said.

"Why?"

"After you hear what I have to say I may not be welcome in the house."

Gesalla eyed him speculatively, then led the way to a stone bench. When he had sat down she straddled the bench and moved close to him so that he was partly within the triangle formed by her thighs. The intimacy both thrilled and embarrassed him.

"And now, my lord," she said lightly, "what terrible confessions have you to make?"

"I. . . ." Toller lowered his head. "I've been with another woman."

"What of it?" Gesalla said in a calm voice, expression unchanged.

Toller was taken aback. "I don't think you under . . . When I said I'd been with another woman I meant I'd been in bed with her."

Gesalla laughed. "I know what you meant, Toller—I'm not stupid."

"But. . . ." Toller, knowing he had never been able to predict his wife's reactions, became wary. "Aren't you angry?"

"Are you planning to bring the woman here and put her in my place?"

"You know I'd never do a thing like that."

"Yes, I do know that, Toller. You are a good-hearted man, and nobody is more aware of that than I, after the years we have had together." Gesalla smiled and gently placed one of her hands on his. "So I have no reason to be angry with you, or to reproach you in any way."

"But this is wrong!" Toller burst out, his bafflement increasing. "You were never like this before. How can you remain so placid, knowing the way I have wronged you?"

"I repeat—you have not wronged me."

"Has the world suddenly been stood on its head?" Toller demanded. "Are you saying that it is perfectly acceptable and seemly for a man to betray his solewife, the woman he loves?"

Gesalla smiled again and her eyes deepened with compassion. "Poor Toller! You still don't understand any of this, do you? You still don't know why for years you have been like an eagle pent up in a cage; why you seize every possible opportunity to put your life at risk. It's all an impenetrable mystery to you, isn't it?"

"You make me angry, Gesalla. Please do not address me as though I were a child."

"But that's the entire point—you are a child. You have never ceased to be a child."

"I grow weary of people telling me that. Perhaps I should come back on another day when, if fortune smiles, I will find you less disposed towards talking in riddles." Toller half-rose to his feet, but Gesalla drew him back on to the bench.

"A moment ago you spoke of betraying the woman you love," she said in the softest, kindest tones he had ever heard, "and there lies the source of all your heartache. You see, Toller. . . ." Gesalla paused, and for the first time since their meeting her composure seemed less than perfect.

"Go on."

"You see, Toller—you no longer love me."

"That's a lie!"

"It's the truth, Toller. I have always understood that the long-lasting embers of love are of more importance than the brief bright flame which marks the beginning. If you also understood that, and accepted it, you might go on being happy with me—but that was never the way with you. Not in anything. Look at all your other love affairs—with the army, with skyships, with metals. You always have some impossible idealistic goal in mind, and when it proves illusory you have to find another to put in its place."

Toller was hearing things he had no wish to hear, and the hated worm of disenchantment at the centre of his being was beginning to stir. "Gesalla," he said, making himself sound reasonable, "aren't you allowing yourself to be carried away with words? How could I have a love affair with metals?"

"For you it was easy! You couldn't simply discover a new material and plan to experiment with it—you had to lead a crusade. You were going to end the felling of brakka for ever; you were going to initiate a glorious new era in history; you were going to be the saviour of humanity. It was just beginning to dawn on you that Chakkell and his like would never change their ways when the Lander ship arrived.

"That saved you, Toller—provided you with yet another shining goal—but only for a short while. The war ended too soon for you. And now you are back in the ordinary, humdrum world . . . and you are getting old . . . and, worst of all, there is no great new challenge ahead of you. The only prospect is of living quietly, on this estate or somewhere else, until you die a commonplace death—just as every commonplace mortal has done since time began.

"Can you face that prospect, Toller?" Gesalla locked solemn eyes with his. "Because if you cannot, I would prefer that we lived separately. I want to spend my remaining years in peace

—and there was precious little of that for me in watching you search for ways to end your life."

The worm was eating hungrily now, and within Toller a dark void was spreading. "There must be some comfort for you in possessing so much knowledge and wisdom, in having such mastery over your feelings."

"The old sarcasm, Toller?" Gesalla tightened her warm grip on his hand. "You do me an injustice if you think I have not wept bitterly over you. It was on the night I stayed with you at the palace that I finally saw through to the heart of this matter. I became angry with you for being what you could not help being, and for a time I hated you—and I shed my tears. But that was in the past. Now my concern is with the future."

"Have we a future?"

"*I* have a future—I have decided that much—and the time has come when you must make your own choice. I know I have caused you great pain this day, but it was unavoidable. I am going back into the house now. I want you to remain out here until you have reached that decision, and when you have done so you must either join me or ride away. I make only one stipulation—that the decision be final and irrevocable. Do not come into the house unless you know in your heart that I can make you content until your last days, and that you can do the same for me. There can be no compromise, Toller—nothing less will suffice."

Gesalla rose weightlessly to her feet and looked down at him. "Will you give me your word?"

"You have my word," Toller said numbly, racked by fears that this was the last time he would ever see his solewife's face. He watched her go into the house. She closed the door without glancing back at him, and when she was lost to his view he stood up and began aimlessly pacing the precinct. The shadow of the west wall was spreading its domain, deepening the colours of the flowers it engulfed, bringing a hint of coolness to the air.

Toller looked up at Land, which was steadily growing brighter, and in an instant traced the course of his life, from his birthplace on that distant world to the quiet enclosure where he now stood. Everything that had ever happened to him seemed to have led directly to this moment. In retrospect his life appeared as a single, clear-cut highway which he had followed without conscious effort—but now, abruptly, the road had divided. A momentous decision had to be made, and he had just learned that he was ill-equipped for the making of *real* decisions.

Toller half-smiled as he recalled that only minutes earlier he had regarded his dalliance with Berise Narrinder as something of importance. Gesalla—far ahead of him, as usual—had known better. He had reached the fork in the road, and had to go one way or the other. *One way or the other!*

As he wandered the precinct the sun continued its descent to the horizon and the daytime stars became more numerous. Once the transparent globe of a ptertha sailed overhead on a breeze which could not be detected within the vine-clad walls. It was not until silver whirlpools were beginning to show themselves in the eastern blue that Toller abruptly ceased his pacing, stilled by an accession of self-knowledge, by an understanding of why he was taking so long to choose the future course of his life.

There was no decision point before him! There was no dilemma!

The issue had been decided for him, even as Gesalla was putting it into words. He could never make her content, because he was a hollow man who could never again make himself content—and the subsequent delay had been caused by his craven inability to face the truth.

The truth is that I am halfway to being dead, he told himself, *and all that remains for me is to find a suitable way to finish what I have begun.*

He gave a quavering sigh, went to the bluehorn and led it to the precinct gate. He took the animal outside, and while closing the gate looked for the last time at the drowsing house. Gesalla was not at any of the darkening windows. Toller got into the saddle and put the bluehorn into a slow-swaying walk on the gravel road to the east. The workers had departed the fields and the world seemed empty.

"What comes next?" he said to the universe at large, his words swiftly fading into the sadness of the surrounding twilight. "Please, what do I do next?"

There was a tiny focus of movement on the road far ahead of him, almost at the limits of vision. In a normal frame of mind Toller might have used his telescope to gain advance information about the approaching traveller, but on this occasion the effort seemed too great. He allowed the natural progression of events to do the work for him at its own measured pace.

In a short time he was able to discern a wagon driven by a solitary figure, and within another few minutes he could see that both the wagon and its occupant were in a sorry state. The vehicle had lost much of its siding and its wheels were wobbling visibly on worn axles. Its driver was a bearded young man, so caked with dust that he resembled a clay statue.

Toller guided his bluehorn to the side of the road to give the stranger room to pass, and was surprised when the wagon drew to a halt beside him. Its driver peered at him through red-rimmed eyes, and even before he spoke it was apparent that he was very drunk.

"Pardon me, sir," he said in slurred tones, "do I have the honour of addressing Lord Toller Maraquine?"

"Yes," Toller replied. "Why do you ask?"

The bearded man swayed for a moment, then unexpectedly produced a smile which in spite of his filthy and dishevelled condition had a boyish charm. "My name is Bartan Drumme, my lord, and I come to you with a unique proposition—one I am certain you will find of great interest."

"I very much doubt that," Toller said coldly, preparing to move on.

"But, my lord! It was my understanding that as Chief of Aerial Defence you concerned yourself with all matters pertaining to the upper reaches of the sky."

Toller shook his head. "All that is over and done with."

"I'm sorry to hear it, my lord." Drumme picked up a bottle and drew the cork, then paused and gave Toller a sombre stare. "This means I shall have to seek an audience with the King."

In spite of all that was pressing on his mind, Toller had to chuckle. "Doubtless he will be fascinated by what you have to say."

"No doubt at all," Drumme agreed, comfortable in his intoxication. "Any ruler in history would have been intrigued by the idea of planting his flag on the world we call Farland."

Chapter 13

The Bluebird Inn in Prad was named after a prominent hostelry in old Ro-Atabri, and it was the ambition of its landlord to win a comparable reputation for decorum. As a consequence, he had been visibly disturbed when Toller had walked into his premises with the disreputable figure of Bartan Drumme in tow. It had been obvious that in his mind the honour of accommodating the heroic aristocrat scarcely compensated for the presence of his smelly and bedraggled companion. He had, however, been persuaded to provide two bedchambers and to set up in one of them a large bath filled with hot water. Bartan was now soaking in the bath, and except for his head the only part of him visible above the soap-greyed water was the hand which was clutching a beaker of brandy.

Toller took a sip from the drink Bartan had given him and grimaced as the crude spirit burned his throat. "Do you think you should be drinking this concoction all the time?"

"Of course not," Bartan said. "I should be drinking *good* brandy all the time, but this is all I can afford. It has cost me my last penny to get here, my lord."

"I told you not to address me as lord." Toller raised his drink to his lips, smelled it and emptied the ceramic beaker into the bath.

"There was no need to waste it," Bartan complained. "Besides, how would *you* like that sort of stuff swilling around your private parts?"

"It may do them good—I think it was intended for external application," Toller said. "I'll have our host serve us with something less poisonous in a little while, but in the meantime I have to go back to the part of your story which sticks in my craw."

"Yes?"

"You claim that your wife is alive on Farland, not as a spirit or

217

a reincarnation—but in the flesh as you knew her. How can you believe that?"

"I can't explain. Her words conveyed more than words—and that was what I got from them."

Toller tugged thoughtfully at his lower lip. "I'm not conceited enough to think I know all there is to know about this strange existence of ours. I concede that there are many mysteries, most of which we may never penetrate, but this does not sit easy with me. It still binds."

Bartan stirred in the bath, slopping water over the side. "I have been a convinced materialist all my life. I *still* scorn those simpletons who cling to a belief in the supernatural, in spite of all I went through in the Basket—but although I am at a loss to explain it, this is something I *know*. There were strange lights that night. Sondeweere did something beyond my understanding, and now she lives on Farland."

"You say she appeared to you in a vision, spoke to you from Farland. I find it difficult to imagine anything more supernatural than that."

"Perhaps we use the word in different ways. My wife did speak to me—therefore it was a natural occurrence. It only appears to smack of the supernatural because of elements beyond our comprehension."

Toller noted that Bartan spoke with impressive fluency in spite of his intoxication. He stood up and walked around the lamplit room, then returned to his chair. Bartan was contentedly sipping his brandy, not looking at all insane.

"Ilven Zavotle is going to be here soon, provided the messenger has found him all right," Toller said. "And I warn you that he is going to laugh at your story."

"There is no need for him to believe it," Bartan replied. "The part about my wife is of concern to me alone, and I related it only to show that I have personal reasons for wanting to voyage to Farland. I could not expect others to undertake such a journey on my account, whatever my reasons. But it is my hope that the King will wish to succeed where Rassamarden failed—by extending his domain to another world—and that, as originator of the scheme, I will be granted a place on the expedition if it becomes a reality. All I ask of your friend Zavotle is that he devise a means of making the journey possible."

"You don't ask much."

"I ask more than you will ever know," Bartan said, a brooding expression appearing on his young-old face. "I am responsible for what happened to my wife, you see. Losing her was bad enough, but carrying the burden of guilt. . . ."

"I'm sorry," Toller said. "Is that why you drink?"

Bartan tilted his head as he considered the question. "It's probably the reason I started drinking, but after a while I found that I simply prefer being drunk to being sober. It makes the world a pleasanter place to live in."

"And on the night you had the vision? Were you. . . ?"

"Drunk? Of course I was drunk!" Bartan gulped some more brandy as if to reinforce his statement. "But that has no bearing on what happened that night. Please, my lord. . . ."

"Toller."

Bartan nodded. "Please, Toller, feel free to regard me as insane or deluded on that particular point—it is irrelevant, after all—but I beg you to take me seriously on the question of the expedition to Farland. I *must* go. I am an experienced airship pilot, and if necessary I will even stop drinking."

"That would be necessary, but—much though I am intrigued by the idea of flying to Farland—I can't speak seriously about it, to the King or anybody else, until I hear what Zavotle has to say. I will meet him downstairs and take a private parlour where we can have some refreshment and discuss the matter in comfort." Toller stood up and set his empty beaker aside. "Join us when you have completed your toilet."

Bartan signalled his assent by raising his drink in a salute and taking a generous swallow. Shaking his head, Toller let himself out of the room and went along a shadowy corridor to the stair. Bartan Drumme was a highly disturbed young man, not to say a madman, but when he had first spoken of a mission to Farland something deep within Toller had responded immediately and with a passion akin to that of a traveller who had just glimpsed his destination after an arduous journey lasting many years. A yearning had been born in him, accompanied by a powerful surge of excitement which he had repressed for fear of disappointment.

Wild, extravagant and preposterous though the idea of flying to Farland was, Chakkell could be in favour of it for the reasons Bartan had suggested—but only if Ilven Zavotle considered the mission feasible. Zavotle had won the King's confidence in anything to do with the technicalities of interplanetary flight, so if the little man with the clenched ears considered Farland to be unreachable then Toller Maraquine would indeed have to accept the prospect of becoming a commonplace mortal awaiting a commonplace death. And that could not be allowed to happen.

I'm behaving exactly as Gesalla says I behave, he thought, pausing on the stair. *But, at this stage of our lives, what would be the point in my trying to do anything else?*

He completed the descent to the inn's crowded entrance hall and saw Zavotle, clad in civilian clothes, making enquiries of a porter. He called out a greeting and within a few minutes he and Zavotle were installed in a small room with a flagon of good wine on the table between them. Lamps were burning steadily in the wall niches, adding a bluish haze to the air, and by their light Toller noticed that Zavotle was looking tired and introspective. Instead of being obviously premature, the whiteness of his hair was now making him look old, although he was some years younger than Toller.

"What ails you, old friend?" Toller said. "Is your stomach still misbehaving?"

"I get indigestion even when I haven't eaten." Zavotle gave him a wan smile. "It hardly seems fair."

"Here's something to take your mind off it," Toller said, pouring out two glasses of green wine. "You recall the talk we had with the King this morning? Our disagreement about what should be done with the defence stations?"

"Yes."

"Well, only this aftday I met a young man called Bartan Drumme who put forward an intriguing thought. He is permanently soused and quite mad—you'll see that for yourself in a short time—but his idea has a certain appeal to it. He suggests taking one or more of the stations to Farland."

Toller had kept his tones light and almost casual, but he was watching Zavotle's reactions closely and felt a pang of alarm as he saw his lips twitch with amusement.

"Did you say your new friend is *quite* mad? I'd say he's a raving lunatic!" Zavotle smirked into his wine.

"But don't you think it just might . . . ?" Toller hesitated, realising he would have to deliver himself into his friend's hands, come what may. "Ilven, I *need* Farland. It is the only thing left for me."

Zavotle eyed him speculatively for a moment.

"Gesalla and I have parted for ever," Toller replied to the unspoken question. "It is all finished between us."

"I see." Zavotle closed his eyes and delicately massaged the lids with the tips of a finger and thumb. "A lot would depend on Farland's position," he said slowly.

"Thank you, thank you," Toller said, overwhelmed with gratitude. "If there is anything I can do to repay you, you have but to name it."

"There is something I expect in repayment—and I do not have to name it. Not to you, anyway."

It was Toller's turn to try reading his friend's face. "The flight is bound to be dangerous, Ilven—why do you want to risk your life?"

"For a time I thought my digestion was too weak, then I discovered it is too strong." Zavotle patted his stomach. "*I* am being digested, and the incestuous banquet cannot be prolonged indefinitely. So you see, Toller, I need Farland as much as you do, perhaps even more. For myself, it would suffice to plan a one-way journey, but I suspect that the other members of the crew would not take kindly to such an arrangement, and therefore I will have to tax my brain and make provision for their safe return. The problem will provide an excellent distraction for an hour or two, and I thank you for that."

"I. . . ." Toller glanced around the room, blinking as his tears surrounded the wall lights with spiky haloes. "I'm so sorry, Ilven. I was too wrapped up in my own worries even to consider that you might be. . . ."

Zavotle smiled and impulsively caught his hand. "Toller, do

you remember how it was on the skyship proving flight all those years ago? We flew into the unknown together, and were glad to do so. Let us now put our personal sorrows aside and be thankful that ahead of us—just when we need them—are an even greater proving flight and an even greater unknown to explore."

Toller nodded, gazing at Zavotle in affection. "So you think the flight is possible?"

"I'd say it might be done. Farland is many millions of miles away, and it is moving—we mustn't forget that it moves—but with plenty of the green and purple at our disposal we could overtake it."

"How many millions of miles are we talking about?"

Zavotle sighed. "I wish that *somebody* had brought science texts from Land, Toller—we have lost most of our store of knowledge, and nobody has had time to start rebuilding it. I have to go by memory, but I believe that Farland is twelve million miles from us at the nearest approach, and forty-two million when it's at the opposite side of the sun. Naturally, we would have to wait for it to come near."

"Twelve million," Toller breathed. "How can we think of flying a distance like that?"

"We can't! Remember that Farland moves. The ship would have to travel at an angle to meet it, so we have to think about flying perhaps eighteen million miles, perhaps twenty million, perhaps more."

"But the speeds! Is it possible?"

"This is no time to be faint-hearted." Zavotle took a pencil and a scrap of paper from his pouch and began to scribble figures. "Let us say that, because of our human frailties, the outward journey must be completed in not more than . . . um . . . a hundred days. That obliges us to cover perhaps 180,000 miles each day, which gives us a speed of . . . a mere 7,500 miles an hour."

"Now I *know* you are toying with me," Toller said. "If you considered the journey impossible you should have said so at the outset."

Zavotle raised both hands, palms outward, in a placatory gesture. "Calm yourself, old friend—I am not being frivolous.

You have to remember that it is the retarding of the air, which increases according to the square of the speed, which holds our airships to a snail's pace and even limits the performance of your beloved jet fighters. But on the voyage to Farland the ship would be travelling in almost a vacuum, and would also be away from Overland's gravity, so it would be possible for it to build up quite an astonishing speed.

"Interestingly, though, air resistance could also *aid* the inter-planetary traveller. If it weren't for the necessity of returning we could plunge the ship into Farland's atmosphere, jump clear of it when the speed had been reduced to an acceptable level, and descend to the surface by parachute.

"Yes, it's the necessity of coming back which forms the main stumbling block. That is the nub of the problem."

"What can be done?"

Zavotle sipped his wine. "It seems to me that we need . . . that we need a ship which can divide itself into two separate parts."

"Are you serious?"

"Absolutely! I visualise a command station as the basic vessel. Let's call it a voidship . . . no, a *space*ship . . . to distinguish the type from an ordinary skyship. Something the size of a command station is necessary to accommodate the large stores of power crystals and all other supplies needed for the voyage. That ship, the spaceship, would fly from the weightless zone to Farland —but it could never make a landing. It would have to be halted just outside the radius of Farland's gravity, and it would have to hang there, stationary, until it was time for the return journey to Overland."

"This is like having wedges driven into one's brain," Toller complained, struggling to assimilate the shockingly new ideas. "Do you see the spaceship dispatching something like a lifeboat to the planetary surface?"

"Lifeboat? That's the general idea, but it would have to be a fully fledged skyship, complete with a balloon and its own power unit."

"But how could it be carried?"

"That's what I was getting at when I said the spaceship would have to be able to divide itself into two parts. Say the spaceship is made up of four or five cylindrical sections, just as a command station is now—the entire front section would have to be detached and converted back into a skyship for the descent. There would have to be an extra partition, and a sealable door, and. . . ." Zavotle shuddered with pleasurable excitement and half-rose from his seat. "I need proper drawing materials, Toller—my mind is on fire."

"I'll have them brought for you," Toller said, motioning for Zavotle to sit down again, "but first tell me more about this dividing of the spaceship. Could it be done in the void? Would there not be a great risk of losing all the ship's air?"

"It would certainly be safer to do it within Farland's atmosphere, and easier as well—that's something I need to ponder over. It may be, if we are lucky, that the atmosphere is so deep that it extends beyond the radius of Farland's gravity, in which case the operation would be relatively straightforward. The spaceship would simply be hanging there in the high air. We could detach the skyship, inflate the balloon and connect the acceleration struts—all in a fairly routine manner. It is something which should be practised in our own weightless zone before the expedition starts.

"On the other hand, if the spaceship has to wait *outside* the atmosphere, the best course might be for it to descend briefly to a level where the air is breathable, and only then cast the skyship section adrift. The skyship would of course be falling while its balloon was being inflated, but—as we know from experience —the fall would be so gradual that there would be ample time to do all that was necessary. There is much to think about. . . ."

"Including air," Toller said. "I presume the plan would be to use firesalt?"

"Yes. We know it puts life back into dead air, but we don't know how much would be needed to keep a man alive during a long voyage. Experiments will have to be done—because the quantity of salt we'll have to transport could be the principal factor in deciding the size of the crew."

Zavotle paused and gave Toller a wistful look. "It's a pity Lain isn't with us—we have need of him."

"I'll fetch the drawing materials." As Toller was leaving the room his memory conjured up a vivid image of his brother, the gifted mathematician who had been killed by a ptertha on the eve of the Migration. Lain had possessed an impressive ability to unveil nature's hidden machinations and predict their outcome, and yet even he had been seriously in error concerning some of the scientific discoveries made on the first flight from Land to the weightless zone. The mental image of him was a reminder of just how presumptuous and reckless was the plan to fly through millions of miles of space to a totally unknown world.

A man could very easily die attempting a journey like that, Toller told himself, and almost smiled as he took the thought one step further. *But nobody would ever be able to say it had been a commonplace death. . . .*

"I'm trying to decide what irks me most about this Farland business," King Chakkell said, gazing unhappily at Toller and Zavotle. "I don't know if it's the fact that I'm being manipulated . . . or if it's the sheer lack of subtlety with which the manipulation is being conducted."

Toller put on an expression of concern. "Majesty, it dismays me to hear that I'm suspected of having an ulterior motive. My sole ambition is to plant the flag of. . . ."

"Enough, Maraquine! I'm not a simpleton." Chakkell smoothed a strand of hair across his gleaming brown scalp. "You prate about planting flags as though they were capable of taking root unaided and producing some manner of desirable crop. What yield would I get from Farland? A meagre one, I'd say."

"The harvest of history," Toller said, already beginning to plan the Farland project in detail. Chakkell's display of peevishness was a sure indication that he was about to give his consent for the construction and provisioning of the spaceship. In spite of his show of doubt and indifference, the King had been seduced by the idea of laying claim to the outer planet.

Chakkell snorted. "The harvest of history will not be gathered in unless the ship successfully completes both legs of the voyage. I am by no means convinced that it will be able to do so."

"The ship will be designed to cope with any exigency, Majesty," Toller said. "I have no desire to commit suicide."

"Haven't you? There are times when I wonder about you, Maraquine." Chakkell stood up and paced around the small room. It was the same apartment in which he had consulted Toller about the aerial defence of Overland immediately after his reprieve. The circular table and six chairs took up most of the floor space, leaving the King a narrow margin through which to guide his paunchy figure. On reaching the chair in which he had been seated, Chakkell leaned on the back of it and frowned at Toller.

"And what about the money?" he said. "You never trouble yourself with such mundane concerns, do you?"

"One ship, Majesty—and a crew of not more than six."

"The size of the actual crew is a flea-bite, and well you know it. This scheme of yours is bound to cost me a fortune in development and in keeping support stations operational in the weightless zone."

"But if it opens the way to a new world. . . ."

"Don't start playing the same tune all over again, Maraquine," Chakkell interrupted. "I'm going to let you proceed with your wild enterprise—I suppose you are entitled to some indulgence on account of your services during the war—but I make one provision, and that is that Zavotle does not accompany you. I cannot afford to lose his services."

"I regret to say this, Majesty," Zavotle put in before Toller could speak, "but you will shortly be deprived of my services come what may, expedition or no expedition."

Chakkell narrowed his eyes at Zavotle and scrutinised him as though suspecting deviousness. "Zavotle," he finally said, "are you going to die?"

"Yes, Majesty."

Chakkell looked embarrassed rather than concerned. "I would have had it otherwise."

"Thank you, Majesty."

"I must attend to other matters now," Chakkell said brusquely, moving towards the door, "but, under the circumstances, I will not object to your going to Farland."

"I'm most grateful, Majesty."

Chakkell paused in the doorway and gave Toller a look

of peculiar intensity. "The game has almost run its course, eh, Maraquine?" He moved away into the corridor before Toller could frame a reply, and a quietness descended on the room.

"I'll tell you something, Ilven," Toller said in a low voice. "We have made the King afraid. Did you notice how he twisted everything around so that it appears he is granting us a favour by permitting the expedition to go ahead? But the real reason is that he *wants* his standard to fly on Farland. A guaranteed place in history is a poor kind of immortality, but all kings seem to crave it—and we remind Chakkell of just how futile such ambitions are."

"You speak strangely, Toller," Zavotle said, his gaze hunting over Toller's face. "I won't return from Farland—but surely you will."

"Put your mind at ease, old friend," Toller replied, smiling. "I'll return from Farland, or die in the attempt."

Toller had not been certain that his son would agree to meet him, and it was with a profound sense of gladness that he saw a lone rider appear on the skyline on the road that led south to Heevern. He had chosen the meeting place partly because the nearness of a gold-veined spire of rock and a pool made it easy to specify, but also because it was on the northern side of the final ridge on the way to his house. Had he ridden an extra mile to the crest, Toller would have been able to view his former home in the distance. The knowledge that Gesalla was within the familiar walls would have caused him fresh pain, but that was not the reason he had held back. It was simply that he had taken a vow to separate the courses of their lives for ever, and in a way which was important to him, although he could not rationally justify it, going within sight of the house would have been a breach of his word.

He dismounted from his bluehorn and left the beast to graze while he watched the other rider approach. As before, he was able to identify Cassyll from afar by the distinctive creamy colour of his mount's forelegs. Cassyll rode towards him at moderate speed and reined his bluehorn to a halt at a distance of about ten paces. He remained in the saddle, studying Toller with pensive grey eyes.

"It would be better if you got down," Toller said mildly. "It would make it easier for us to talk."

"Have we anything to talk about?"

"If we haven't there was little point in your riding out here to meet me." Toller gave his son a wry smile. "Come on—neither your honour nor your principles will be compromised if we talk face-to-face."

Cassyll shrugged and swung himself down from his bluehorn, a movement he accomplished with athletic grace. With his oval face and pronounced widow's peak of glossy black, he owed much of his appearance to his mother, but Toller observed a sinewy strength in his spare figure.

"You look well," Toller said.

Cassyll glanced down at himself and his clothing—rough-spun shirt and trews which would not have looked out of place on a common labourer. "I do my share of work at the foundry and factories, and some of it is heavy."

"I know." Toller was heartened by the civility of Cassyll's response and decided to go straight to the points he had to make. "Cassyll, the Farland expedition leaves in a few days from now. I have faith in Ilven Zavotle's designs and calculations, but only a fool would refuse to acknowledge that many unknown dangers lie ahead of us. I may not return from the voyage, and it would ease my mind greatly if we settled some matters concerning the future for you and your mother."

Cassyll showed no emotion. "You will return, as always."

"I intend to, but nevertheless I want you to give me your word on certain matters before we part this day. One of them is to do with the fact that the King has confirmed my title as being hereditary—and I want you to accept it if I am declared dead."

"I don't want the title," Cassyll said. "I have no interest in such vanities."

Toller nodded. "I know that, and I respect you for it, but the title represents power as well as privilege—power you can use to safeguard your mother's position in the world, power you can put to good use in worthwhile endeavours. I don't need to remind you how important it is for metals to replace brakka wood in our society—so vow to me you will not reject the title."

Cassyll looked impatient. "All this is premature. You will live to be a hundred, if not more."

"Your vow, Cassyll!"

"I swear that I will accept the title on that far-off day when it eventually falls my due."

"Thank you," Toller said earnestly. "Now, the management of the estate. If at all possible I want you to perpetuate the system of peppercorn rents for our tenants. I take it that the revenues from the mines, foundries and metal works are still increasing and will be ample for the family requirements."

"Family?" Cassyll gave a half-smile to show that he considered the word inappropriate. "My mother and I are financially secure."

Toller allowed the tacit challenge to pass and spent more time on practicalities connected with the estate and its industrial associations, but all the while he was aware that he was delaying the moment when he would have to admit his most important motive in arranging the meeting with his son. At last, after a tense silence had developed and looked like continuing indefinitely, he accepted that it was necessary for him to speak out.

"Cassyll," he said, "I met my father for the first time only a few minutes before he died by his own hand. There was so much . . . *waste* in both our lives, but we were united before the end. I . . . I don't want to leave you without putting things right between us. Can you forgive me for the wrongs I have done you and your mother?"

"Wrongs?" Cassyll spoke lightly, affecting puzzlement. He stooped and picked up a pebble which was heavily banded with gold, examined it briefly and hurled it into the nearby pool. The image of Land mirrored on the water broke up into jostling curved fragments.

"What wrongs do you speak of, father?"

Toller could not be put off. "I have neglected you both because I can never be content with what I have. It's as simple as that. My indictment takes but a few words—none of them fancy or abstruse."

229

"I never felt neglected, because I believed you would love us both for ever," Cassyll said slowly. "Now my mother is alone."

"She has you."

"She is *alone*."

"No more than I am," Toller said, "but there is no remedy. Your mother understands that better than I. If you could learn to understand you might also learn to forgive."

Cassyll suddenly looked younger than his twenty-two years. "You're asking me to understand that love dies?"

"It *can* die, or it can refuse to die; or a man or a woman can change, or a man or a woman can remain changeless; and when a person does not change with time the effect—from the viewpoint of a person who *is* changing—is as if the unchanging person is actually the one who is undergoing the greatest change. . . ." Toller broke off and stared helplessly at his son. "How can I know what I'm asking you to understand when I don't understand it myself?"

"Father. . . ." Cassyll moved a step closer to Toller. "I see so much pain inside you. I hadn't realised. . . ."

Toller tried to check the tears which had begun to blur his vision. "I welcome the pain. There is not enough of it for my needs."

"Father, don't. . . ."

Toller opened his arms to his son and they embraced, and for the fleeting period of the embrace he could almost remember what it had been like to be a whole man.

"Put the ship on its side," Toller ordered, his breath rolling whitely in the chill air.

Bartan Drumme, who was at the controls because he took every possible opportunity to practise skyship handling techniques, nodded and began firing short bursts on a lateral jet. As the thrust gradually overcame the inertia of the gondola, Overland slid up the sky and the great disk of Land emerged from behind the brown curvature of the balloon. Bartan halted the ship's rotation by means of the opposing jet, stabilising it in the new attitude, with an entire world on view on either side of the gondola. The sun was close to Land's eastern rim, illuminating a slim crescent of the planet and leaving the rest of it in comparative darkness.

Against the dim background of Land, the waiting spaceship, now less than a mile away, was visible as a tiny bar of light. It was attended by several lesser motes, representing the few habitats and stores which King Chakkell had permitted to remain in the weightless zone to service the newly completed vessel. The group was an undistinguished feature of the crowded heavens, almost unnoticeable, but the sight of it caused a stealthy quickening of Toller's pulse.

Sixty days had passed since he had received the royal assent for the expedition to Farland, and now he was finding it hard to accept that the hour of departure was at hand. Trying to dispel a slight sense of unreality, he raised his binoculars and studied the spaceship.

There had been one major amendment to the design which Zavotle had sketched out during their meeting in the Bluebird Inn. The foremost of the ship's five sections had originally been designated as the detachable module, but the arrangement had posed too many problems in connection with obtaining a view ahead of the vessel. After some unsatisfactory experiments with mirrors it had been decided to use the aft section as the landing module. Its engine would power the flight to Farland, and when the section was separated from the mother craft a second engine would be exposed, ready for the return to Overland.

Toller lowered the binoculars and glanced around the other members of the crew, all of them swaddled in their quilted suits, all of them deep in their own thoughts. Apart from Zavotle and Bartan, there was Berise Narrinder, Tipp Gotlon and another ex-fighter pilot, a soft-spoken young man called Dakan Wraker. Toller had been surprised by the large number of volunteers for the expedition, and he had selected Wraker because of his imperturbable nature and wide range of mechanical skills.

The conversation among the crew members had been lively in the preceding hour, but now, suddenly, the magnitude of what lay ahead seemed to have impressed itself on them, stilling their tongues.

"Spare me the long faces," Toller said, grimly jovial. "Why, we might find Farland so much to our liking that none of us will ever want to return!"

Chapter 14

As commander of the spaceship, Toller would have liked to have been at the controls when the *Kolcorron* burned its way out of the weightless zone at the beginning of the voyage to Farland.

During training sessions, however, it had become apparent that he was the least talented of the crew when it came to the new style of flying. The ship's length was five times its diameter, and keeping it in a stable attitude while under way required precise and delicate use of the lateral jets, an ability to detect and correct yawing movements almost before they had begun. Gotlon, Wraker and Berise seemed to do it without effort, using infrequent split-second blasts on the jets to keep the crosshairs of the steering telescope centred on a target star. Zavotle and Bartan Drumme were competent, though more heavy handed; but Toller—much to his annoyance—was prone to make overcorrections which involved him in series of minor adjustments, bringing grins to the faces of the other fliers.

He had therefore given Tipp Gotlon, the youngest of the crew, the responsibility for taking the ship out of the twin planets' atmosphere.

Gotlon was strapped into a seat near the centre of the circular topmost deck. He was looking into the prismatic eyepiece of the low-powered telescope which was aimed vertically through a port in the ship's nose. His hands were on the control levers, from which rods ran down through the various decks to the main engine and the lateral thrusters. The fierceness of his gaptoothed grin showed that he was keyed up, anxiously waiting for the order to begin the flight.

Toller glanced around the nose section, which in addition to accommodating the pilot's station was also intended as living and sleeping quarters. Zavotle, Berise and Bartan were floating near the perimeter in various attitudes, keeping themselves in place by gripping handrails. It was quite dim in the compartment, the only illumination coming from a porthole on the sunward side, but Toller could see the others' faces well enough to know that they shared his mood.

The flight would possibly last two hundred days—a dauntingly long period of boredom, deprivation and discomfort—and, regardless of how dedicated a person might be, it was only natural to experience qualms at such a moment. Things would be easier after the main engine had begun to fire, finally committing everybody to the venture, but until that psychological first step had been taken he and the crew were bound to be racked by doubt and apprehension.

Growing impatient, Toller drew himself to the ladder well and looked down into the ship. The cylindrical space was punctuated by narrow rays of sunlight from portholes which created confusing patterns of brightness and shadow in the internal bracing and among the bins which housed the supplies of food and water, firesalt and power crystals. There was a movement far down in the strange netherworld and Wraker, who had been checking the fuel hoppers and pneumatic feed system, appeared at the bottom of the ladder. He came up it at speed, agile in spite of his bulky suit, and nodded as he saw Toller waiting for him.

"The power unit is in readiness," he said quietly.

"And we are likewise," Toller replied, turning to meet Gotlon's attentive eyes. "Take us away from here."

Gotlon advanced the throttle without hesitation. The engine sounded at the rear of the ship, its roar muted by distance and the intervening partitions, and the crew members gradually floated downwards to take up standing positions on the deck. Toller looked out of the nearest porthole just in time to see the cluster of store sections and habitats slide away behind the ship. Some heavily muffled auxiliary workers were hanging in the air near the structures, all of them vigorously waving their farewells.

"This is quite touching," Toller said. "We're being given a rousing send-off."

Zavotle sniffed to show his scepticism. "They are merely expressing heartfelt relief at our departure. Now, at last, they can quit the weightless zone and return to their families—which is what we would be doing if we had any sense."

"You forget one thing," Bartan Drumme said, smiling.

"Which is . . . ?"

"I *am* returning to my family." Bartan's boyish smile widened. "I get the best of both worlds, so to speak—because my wife is waiting for me on Farland."

"Son, it is my considered opinion that *you* should be the captain of this ship," Zavotle said solemnly. "A man needs to be crazy to set out on a journey such as this—and you are the craziest of us all."

The *Kolcorron* had been under way for a little more than an hour when Toller began to feel uneasy.

He visited every compartment of the ship, checking that all was as it should be, but in spite of his being unable to find anything wrong, his sense of disquiet remained. Unable to attribute it to any definite cause, he chose not to confide in Zavotle or any of the others—as commander he had to provide resolute leadership, not undermine the crew's morale with vague apprehensions. In contrast to his own mood, the others seemed to be relaxing and growing more confident, as was evidenced by the sprightliness of the conversation on the top deck.

Finding the talk distracting, Toller went back down the ladder and, feeling oddly furtive, positioned himself at a midships porthole, in a narrow space between two storage lockers. It was the sort of thing he had sometimes done in childhood when he needed to shut off the outside world, and in the contrived solitude he tried to pinpoint the source of his forebodings.

Could it be the fact that the sky had unaccountably turned black? Or could it be a deep-seated worry, an instinctive emotional protest, over the idea of building up to a speed of thousands of miles an hour? The main engine had been firing almost continuously since the start of the voyage, and therefore —according to Zavotle—the ship's speed already had to be far in excess of anything in man's previous experience. At first there had been a clearly audible rush of air against the hull, but as the sky darkened that sound had gradually faded away. Sunlight slanting in through the porthole made it difficult for Toller to perceive the outside universe clearly, but the eternal calm seemed to reign as always, yielding no evidence that the ship was hurtling through space at many hundreds of miles an hour.

Could *that* fact be related to his unease? Was some part of his mind troubled by the discrepancy between what he observed to be happening and what he knew to be happening?

Toller considered the notion briefly and pushed it aside—he had never been unduly sensitive, and travelling in space was not going to alter his basic nature. If he was going to be nervous it was more likely to be over some practical matter, such as having positioned himself so close to a porthole. The planking of the *Kolcorron*'s hull was reinforced with extra steel hoops on the outside and layers of tar and canvas on the inside, imparting great strength to the ship's structure as a whole, but there were areas of vulnerability around the portholes and hatches. On one early test flight a porthole had blown out and a mechanic's eardrums had been ruptured, even though the accident had not occurred in true vacuum.

A brief hissing sound from the upper deck indicated that somebody had mixed a measure of firesalt and water to renew the air's life-giving properties. Perhaps a minute later its distinctive odour—reminiscent of seaweed—reached Toller's nostrils, mingling with the smell of tar which seemed to have been growing stronger.

He sniffed the air, realising that the tarry smell was indeed more noticeable, and his sense of alarm suddenly intensified itself. On impulse he removed one of his gauntlets and touched the black surface of the hull beside him. It felt warm. The degree of heat was far short of what would have been needed to soften the tar, less than his skin temperature, but it was strikingly in contrast with the chill he had expected. The discovery burst open a gateway in his mind, and all at once he knew exactly what had occasioned all his vague forebodings. . . .

His entire body felt uncomfortably warm!

The quilted skysuit had been designed to keep the fierce cold of the weightless zone at bay, and had been barely adequate for its purpose, but now it was proving so efficient that he was on the verge of breaking into a sweat.

This can't be right! We can't be falling into the sun!

Toller was striving to bring his thoughts under control when the sound of the engine died away and in the same moment he heard Zavotle calling his name from the upper part of the ship. Finding that he was again completely without weight, Toller dived through the air to the ladder and went up it hand over hand. He drew himself on to the top deck by means of a rail and faced the rest of the crew, all of whom, with the exception of Gotlon, were clinging to their sleeping nets.

"Something strange is happening," Zavotle said. "The ship grows warm."

"I have noticed." Toller looked at Gotlon, who was regarding him from the pilot's seat. "Are we on course?"

Gotlon nodded vigorously. "Sir, we are exactly on course and have been since the outset. I swear to you that Gola has not departed the crosshairs for as much as one second." Gola was a figure in Kolcorronian myth who appeared before lost mariners and led them to safe havens, and the name had been given to the guide star selected for the first part of the outward journey.

Toller addressed himself to Zavotle. "Couldn't we nevertheless be moving sideways? Falling towards the sun, but with the prow of the ship pointed at Gola?"

"Why should we fall? And even if we were falling it's too soon for extra warmth to manifest itself on that account."

"If you look aft you'll see that we are still in the same relationship with Overland and Land," Berise added. "We are on course."

"This is something for my flight log," Zavotle said, almost to himself. "We have to take it that space is warm. It isn't surprising, really, because in space there is eternal sunshine. But the sun also shines in the weightless zone—and there a terrible coldness reigns. It's yet another mystery, Toller."

"Mystery or no mystery," Toller replied, deciding to act in a positive manner to offset the uncertainty which had been engendered by the first brush with the unexpected, "it means we can divest ourselves of these cursed suits, and that's something for which to be thankful. We can at least enjoy a little comfort."

By the third day of the flight a shipboard routine had become well established, much to Toller's satisfaction. He was aware of the dangers of monotony and boredom which could lie ahead, but those were predictable human problems and he felt capable of dealing with them. It was when nature itself became capricious, giving the lie to man's most cherished beliefs, that he began to feel like a babe wandering in a dangerous forest.

Since the initial, and now welcome, discovery that space was comfortably warm, the nearest thing to a revelation to come along had been the observation—first reported by Wraker —that there were no meteors in the interplanetary void. To Toller's surprise, Ilven Zavotle had seized on the observation, apparently in the belief that it possessed some significance, and had made it the subject of another long entry in his log.

The little man's illness seemed to be progressing according to his expectations. Although he uttered no complaints he was visibly thinner, and spent much of his time with both fists pressed into his stomach. He had also, which was quite out of character with the old Zavotle, become short-tempered and acidulous with the younger crew members, particularly Bartan Drumme. The others, while convinced that Bartan was subject to spells of insanity, were tolerant in the matter whereas Zavotle frequently made him a target for ridicule. Bartan accepted the abuse with equanimity, secure in his fortress of delusion, but on several occasions Berise had been stung into taking his part and her relationship with Zavotle had become strained.

Toller was loath to interfere, knowing that his old friend was being driven by a demon worse than his own, and he was trusting that Berise would not let the situation get out of hand. His own relationship with her—ever since their five days in the exclusive universe of the sinking skyship—was warm, comforting and totally dispassionate. They had found each other at a special time, a unique time during which their needs had been perfectly complementary, a time which would never come again, and now they were shaping their own separate courses into the future, without obligations or regrets. It had not even occurred to him to object when she had claimed a place with the expedition. He knew that she understood the dangers, that her reasons had to be at least as valid as his own.

Human interactions apart, Toller foresaw that food and drink—whether being ingested or eliminated—were likely to make the greatest demands on the crew's powers of endurance. There could be no fire for cooking, so the diet consisted of strictly apportioned cold servings of dried and salted meat and fish, desiccated fruit, nuts and biscuits, washed down with water and one tot of brandy per day.

The fact that the main engine was being fired almost continuously, thus imparting some weight to everything, made the toilet procedures less onerous than in zero gravity conditions, but the experience remained one which called for reserves of stoicism. In the midships lavatory there was a complicated tubular exhaust with one-way valves—the only point at which the hull could be breached in space. Unavoidably, a small quantity of air was lost each time the device was operated, but the volume of gas generated by the firesalt was enough to compensate.

It had originally been envisaged that all six of the crew would take equal turns in the pilot's seat, but the plan was soon modified by practical considerations. Berise, Gotlon and Wraker were able to hold Gola on the crosshairs with ease, and Bartan was rapidly acquiring the same facility—but for Toller and Zavotle the task became even more irksome and tiring. Bowing to expediency, Toller rearranged the duty schedules to let the four young people keep the ship on its interception course with Farland, while he and Zavotle had more time to dispose of as they saw fit. Zavotle was able to occupy himself with astronomical studies and prolonged entries in his leather-bound log, but for Toller the extra hours were burdensome.

At times he thought about his wife and son, wondering what they were doing, and at others he gazed moodily through portholes at a frozen, unchanging panoply of stars, silver whirlpools and comets. In those periods the ship seemed to be permanently locked in place, and try as he might Toller was unable to accept that it was achieving the kind of speed necessary for the interplanetary crossing.

"Are you ready?" Bartan said to Berise. When she nodded he shut down the engine, floated himself out of the pilot's seat and held the straps for Berise while she took his place.

"Thank you," she said, giving him a cordial smile. He nodded politely, impersonally, made his way to the ladder and went down it, leaving Berise to share the top deck with Toller and Zavotle. Gotlon and Wraker were busy loading the fuel hoppers in the tail section.

"I think someone is developing a soft spot for young Bartan," Toller commented, addressing himself to nobody in particular.

Zavotle sniffed loudly. "If that is the case, then that someone is only wasting her time. Our Mister Drumme reserves all his affections for spirits of one kind or another—bottled or disembodied."

"I don't care what you say." Berise paused, hands resting lightly on the controls. "He must have loved his wife very much. If I died or disappeared soon after being married I'd like my husband to fly to another world in search of me. I think it's very romantic."

"You're nearly as mad as he is," Zavotle told her. "I hope we're not all going to be afflicted by some mental contagion, a pterthacosis of the mind. What do you say, Toller?"

"Bartan does his job—perhaps we should leave it at that?"

"Yes." Zavotle gazed through the porthole beside him for a few seconds, his expression becoming enigmatic. "Perhaps he does his job much better than I do mine."

Toller's interest was aroused not only by what the other man had said, but by something in his inflexion. "Is there something wrong?"

Zavotle nodded. "I selected a guide star which was supposed to put us on an interception course with Farland. Had I done the calculations properly, and chosen the guide star well, we should see it and Farland gradually drawing closer together ahead of us."

"Well?"

"We are only five days into the flight, but already it is apparent that Farland and Gola are moving apart. I have put off telling you because I was hoping—foolishly, I suppose—that the situation would change, or that I would be able to devise an explanation. Neither of those things has come to pass, so I must consider myself to have failed to discharge my duties."

"But it isn't all that serious, is it?" Toller said. "Surely, all we have to do is aim closer to Farland. We are not under any threat."

"Only the threat posed by incompetence." Zavotle produced a rueful smile. "You see, Toller, *nothing* is working out as I expected. Farland seems too bright, and also its image in the telescope is too large. I would swear it is twice as big as when we started out. Perhaps optical instruments work differently in the void. I don't know—I can't explain it."

"It could mean that we have completed half the journey," Berise said.

"I didn't ask for your opinion," Zavotle replied tartly. "You speak of matters far beyond your understanding."

Berise's eyebrows drew together. "I understand that when something appears to double in size the distance to it has been halved. It seems quite simple to my mind."

"To the simple mind everything appears simple."

"Let's have no bickering," Toller said. "What we need. . . ."

"But the idiotic woman is suggesting that we have travelled nine or ten million miles in only five days," Zavotle protested, kneading his stomach. "Two million miles in a day! That is a speed of more than eighty thousand miles an hour—which is impossible. The true speed. . . ."

The true speed of your ship is now in excess of one hundred thousand miles an hour, said the golden-haired woman who had shimmered into existence near the side of the compartment.

Chapter 15

Toller stared at the woman, knowing without being told that she was Bartan Drumme's wife, and his inner model of the universe and all its ways flowed and was changed for ever. He felt cold and weak, but somehow unafraid. Berise and Zavotle had not moved, and although they were looking in different directions he knew they were seeing exactly what he was seeing. The woman was beautiful, and she was wearing a simple white dress, and she glowed like a candle in the dimness of the ship's interior. She spoke in anger shaded with concern.

At first I could not believe it when I sensed Bartan drawing nearer, and then I searched and found that it was true! You set out across space without even understanding the effects of continuous acceleration! How could you fail to realise that you were heading for certain death?

"Sondy!" Bartan had returned to the upper deck and was clinging to a handhold near the head of the ladder. "I am coming to bring you home."

You are a fool, Bartan. All of you are reckless fools. You, Ilven Zavotle, you who drew up the plans for the voyage—how did you expect to land on this world?

Zavotle spoke like a man in a trance. "We planned to slow our ship down by plunging it into Farland's atmosphere."

And that would have been the end of you! At the speed you would have attained on reaching Farland the friction with the atmosphere would have produced so much heat that your ship would have become a meteor. And even if by some miracle you had landed safely—had you simply assumed that the air would be breathable?

"Air? Air is air."

How little you know! And you, Toller Maraquine, you who style yourself leader of this ill-conceived expedition—do you accept full responsibility for the lives of those you command?

"I do," Toller said steadily. A part of his mind was telling him that he and the others ought to be cringing with fear or reeling with astonishment, anything but calmly answering questions put to them by an apparition, but it was in the nature of the mental communion that all normal human reactions were prorogued. He now understood Bartan's previous assertion that, by definition, anything which *happens* cannot be supernatural.

In that case, Sondeweere continued, *if you retain any vestiges of a conscience, you will immediately abandon this wildest of ventures. I will give you the instructions and guidance necessary to effect a safe return to Overland.*

"I cannot agree to that proposal," Toller said. "While it is true that I boast the title of commander of this extraordinary mission, its members have their individual and separate reasons for wanting to set foot on Farland. My authority is rooted in the common will to proceed, and were I to propose turning back my voice would become only one among many."

A slippery answer, Toller Maraquine. The vision regarded him with blue-seething eyes. *Does it mean that you are prepared to lead your crew to their deaths?*

"I see no need for that? If it is within your power to guide us safely to Overland you must be able to do the same with regard to Farland."

How little you understand! How little you know of the dangers that await you here! The silent words were now tinged with impatience. *Many years ago you found Overland to be un-inhabited, and now—blindly—you presume that Farland is the same. Has it not occurred to you that this world is peopled, that it has its own civilisation? Did you think I had an entire planet to myself?*

"I had given the matter no thought," Toller said. "Until this minute I believed that Bartan was mad, and that you did not exist anywhere."

I see now that I should never have reached out to you, Bartan. It was a mistake I would not have made had my development been complete, but I must bear the responsibility for the jeopardy in which you and your companions have been placed. I beg you,

Bartan—do not add to my remorse. You must persuade your friends to return to Overland.

"I love you, Sondy—and nothing will keep me from your side."

But what you contemplate is sheer folly! You cannot hope to rescue me with a force of only six.

"Rescue!" Bartan's voice became sharper. "Are you being held captive?"

There is nothing that anyone can do. I am content here. Turn back, Bartan!

In spite of the curious mood that had been induced in him, the casual and dreamy acceptance of the miraculous, Toller was aware of a growing clamour deep within himself as he listened to the exchange between Sondeweere and Bartan. Revelation was piling on revelation, and with each there came a host of questions which cried out for answers. What were the people of Farland like? Had they landed on Overland by stealth and physically abducted Bartan's wife? If so, what had been their motive? And, above all, how had an unremarkable woman living on a remote farm acquired the awesome ability to project her image and thoughts across millions of miles of space?

Seeking enlightenment, Toller tried to study Sondeweere's face and discovered that it was impossible to focus on any single aspect of her. The vision he had seemed to exist *behind* his eyes, and it was a composite of many images which continually shifted and merged, making it impossible to scrutinise any one in particular. She was standing a few paces away from him, and at the same time she was so close that he could distinguish the individual down hairs on her skin, and at the same time she was so far away that she had the semblance of a bright star which pulsed in harmony with the silent rhythms of her speech. . . .

By refusing to turn back you place me in an impossible situation. The only way I can save you from certain death in space is by leading you to an equally certain death here on Farland.

"We are responsible for our own lives," Toller said, knowing that he had the full support of his crew. "And we are not easy to kill."

Sondeweere came to the ship many times in the days that followed her first visitation, and for the most part her concern was with discarding its stupendous velocity and altering the course.

After he had recovered from the shock of learning the vessel's true speed, Zavotle became absorbed by the mechanics of the operation. It had not simply been a matter of turning the ship over to reverse the direction of its thrust—numerous course corrections had to be carried out by tilting the ship and firing the engine at an angle to the line of flight. There was no means of looking directly aft, therefore Farland could not be seen and the crew had to take it on trust that they were steadily drawing nearer to their destination.

Zavotle found much to write about in his log, and was particularly intrigued when his spectral tutor explained to him what had been wrong with the plan to halt the ship outside the reach of Farland's gravity. The radius of a planet's gravity can be regarded as infinite, Sondeweere told him, and therefore the ship had to be placed in orbit, a condition in which it falls forever *around* the planet, in exactly the same manner as the planets circle their parent sun.

Toller tried to take an interest in the difficult concept, but found that his normal thought processes were inhibited by the essential strangeness of the situation. There had been too many revelations, and too many mysteries had been uncovered—all of them turning on the central enigma of Sondeweere herself.

He would have expected Bartan Drumme to be more taxed by that enigma than any other member of the company, but the youngster seemed too bemused by the prospect of being reunited with his wife to think much about what had so drastically interfered with the course of her existence. Allowances had to be made, Toller decided, for the fact that Bartan had spent a long time in an alcoholic twilight of the mind, living with the knowledge that his wife had somehow been transported to Farland and had communicated with him from that distant world.

Also, Bartan was drinking heavily again. With the realisation that the ship was vastly overstocked with all supplies, including brandy, Toller had given permission for the crew to drink freely—seemingly a small enough concession in the circumstances. It had soon become evident to him that Bartan was abusing the privilege, but he had lacked the will to issue a corrective. Matters of shipboard discipline, in which he would normally have been very strict, now seemed irrelevant and trivial in a universe where the impossible had become probable, and the bizarre had become commonplace.

Three days into the deceleration phase he found himself gazing through the forward porthole—which now faced aft—at the twin points of light which were Land and Overland, the worlds which had encompassed his entire life and which he had left far behind. They seemed more distant than the stars, and yet—from what he had learned—there was a human connection between Overland and Farland. What could it be? *What could it be?*

Toller's frustration was increased by the fact that, no matter how insistent were the questions hammering in his mind, each time Sondeweere established communication he was overcome by the same mood of passivity and acceptance, and she was gone before the questions could be put to her. It was as if, for reasons of her own, she had used her strange powers to smother his spirit of enquiry. If that were the case, a new mystery had been added to a surfeit of mysteries, and it all seemed so . . . *unfair*.

He glanced around the upper deck, wondering if the rest of the crew shared his frustration. Wraker was in the pilot's seat, holding the crosshairs on the current guide star, and the others were drowsing in their sleeping nets, seemingly unperturbed by their vulnerability, their total ignorance of what lay ahead.

"This is not the way things should be," Toller whispered to himself. "We are entitled to more consideration than this."

I have to agree with you, Sondeweere said, hovering before him, warping space around her to create strange geometries which defied perspective.

I confess that I have done my utmost to erect a barrier around your minds, but my concern was with your collective safety. You see, telepathy—direct mind-to-mind communication—is largely

an interactive process. You have enemies here on Farland, power-
ful enemies, and I had to be certain that I could prevent the
symbonites from becoming aware of your approach to the planet.
That much I have been able to achieve, but it would still be best if
you would agree to turn back.

"We cannot turn back," Bartan Drumme said, forestalling
Toller's response.

"Bartan speaks for all of us," Toller added. "We are prepared
to face any foe, to die if need be, but by the same token we are
entitled to be apprised of the terms of the conflict. What are
symbonites, and why are they hostile to us?"

There was a brief pause during which Sondeweere's multi-
dimensional image underwent several shifts and changes in
luminosity, then she began to unfold a tale. . . .

The symbons had been drifting in space for untold thousands of
years before blind chance brought them into an unremarkable
planetary system. It consisted of a small sun which had a retinue of
only three worlds, two of them forming a closely matched binary.
Under the influence of the sun's gravity the tenuous cloud of
spores—many of them linked by gossamer-like threads—sank
inwards over a period of centuries.

Almost all of them continued the slow descent to the heart of the
system, where they were destroyed in the sun's nuclear furnace,
but a few were lucky in that they were captured by the outermost
planet.

There they settled in the soil, were nourished by the rain, and
entered the receptive phase of their existence. They were doubly
lucky in that all of them eventually came into physical contact with
members of the planet's dominant species—a race of intelligent
bipeds who had recently discovered the use of metals. They
entered their hosts' bodies and multiplied and spread through
them, showing a special affinity for the nervous system, and
produced composite beings in which some of the characteristics of
both species were enhanced to a great degree.

The symbonites were stronger and vastly more intelligent than
the unmodified bipeds. They also had telepathic powers with
which they sought each other out and formed a group of super-

beings who easily dominated the indigenous species. The relationship was an amicable and peaceful one, bringing to an end the natives' tribal squabbling.

It could even have been thought of as beneficial to the host race, except that the bipeds were cheated of the right to follow their own evolutionary course.

There followed two centuries during which the symbonites flourished. The offspring of a coupling between a symbonite and an ordinary native was always another symbonite, and with that overwhelming genetic advantage the superbeings inexorably increased their numbers. They developed their own culture, secure in the knowledge that in time they would entirely supersede the native population.

But millions of miles away, on one of the pair of inner worlds, a new development was taking place.

As the original cloud of symbon spores was drifting towards the sun, two of its members had been intercepted by one of the twin worlds. After they had floated down to the lowest levels of the atmosphere their link had been broken by wind forces, but they had entered the soil close to each other in a fertile region of the planet.

A symbon has no powers of selection. It has to merge into the first living creature with which it comes into contact, and one of the spores was quickly absorbed by one of the planet's lowest life forms—a myriapod which combined some characteristics of scorpion and mantis.

The crawling creature reproduced itself, giving rise to a breed of super-myriapods. They had no brains as such, being controlled by groups of ganglia, so they could not become telepathic in the full sense of the word, but they had the ability to broadcast dim proto-feelings and images from their nervous systems.

They also perpetuated themselves on a downward evolutionary curve, gradually losing their special chracteristics, because as organisms they were far too primitive to form a viable symbiotic partnership.

In the case of that symbon spore, nature's blind gamble had not paid off. The breed of super-myriapods was destined to revert to type within a few centuries, and their existence would pass

*unnoticed by the world at large—except for one relatively un-
important instance. The sub-telepathic emanations of their
descendants caused disturbing mental effects among humans who
chanced to settle in their locality.*

*In the case of the second symbon spore, however, the outcome
was vastly different. . . .*

"Sondy!" It was Bartan Drumme who broke the spell cast by the
cool overview of the reaches of time and space, and his anguish
was apparent. "Please don't say it! That can't be what happened
to you."

*That is what happened to me, Bartan. I came in contact with the
second spore—and now I too am a symbonite.*

There was an awed silence on the upper deck of the ship, then
Bartan spoke again, his voice quiet and strained. "Does it mean
I've lost you, Sondy? Are you dead to me? Are you now one
of . . . them?"

*No! My appearance has not changed, and in my heart I am as
much a human being as ever, but . . . how can I explain it? . . .
raised to a power. I tried to persuade you to turn back, but having
failed I can reveal that I long to escape from this cold, rainy world
and live among my own kind again.*

"You're still my wife?"

*Yes, Bartan, but it is futile to dream of such things. I am
a prisoner here, and it would be suicidal for you and your
companions to try to alter that fact.*

Bartan gave a tremulous laugh. "Your words have given me
the strength of a thousand, Sondy—and I'm coming to take you
home."

The odds against you are too great.

"There are things we must know," Toller put in, driven to
speak in spite of the awareness that he was intruding. "If you are
not allied to these . . . symbonites—why have you joined them
in Farland? And how was it done?"

*Once the spore had entered my system I was destined to become
a symbonite, but the more advanced the host is in evolutionary
terms the longer the process takes. I spent more than a year in a
semi-comatose condition while the inner metamorphosis was*

taking place, and during that time my telepathic ability was not under control. At a certain stage the symbonites of Farland became aware of me, and they understood at once what was happening.

They are not a belligerent or acquisitive race—violent conquest is not their way—but they divined enough about human nature to fear the rise of human-based symbonites on Overland. They built a spaceship—one which operates on principles I could never explain to you—and flew to Overland.

They spirited me away from the midst of my people, anxious to do so before I could bear children. The action was necessary in their eyes because my children's children would also have been symbonites, and in time there would have been an entire planet populated with them. Springing from a higher evolutionary base, they would have been much superior to the symbonites of Farland. Although transmogrified, it is almost certain that they would have retained the human taste for exploration and expansion—and inevitably they would have set foot on Farland. So, here I am, and here they are determined I will stay.

"It would have been less trouble to kill you," Zavotle said, expressing a thought which had occurred to more than one of the *Kolcorron's* crew.

Yes, and that is precisely the kind of thinking which prompted the symbonites to abduct me. They are not a murderous race, so they were content to isolate me from my kind and wait for me to die of natural causes. However, they made the mistake of under-estimating my telepathic potency. They did not allow for my being able to contact Bartan in an effort to assuage his grief.

And I in turn did not expect this terrible outcome—otherwise I would have remained silent. Sondeweere's indefinable face, simultaneously close and remote, expressed regret. *I must bear the responsibility for whatever befalls you.*

"But why should we come to any harm?" Berise Narrinder said, speaking to Sondeweere for the first time. "If your captors are as timorous as you say, they will be unable to stand in our way."

Readiness to kill is no yardstick of courage. Although the symbonites abhor the taking of life, they will do so if they adjudge it necessary—but they are not the ones with whom you will have to contend. The native Farlanders are the instruments of the symbonites . . . and they are numerous . . . and they are untroubled by any scruples over the shedding of blood.

"Nor are we when the cause is just," Toller said. "Will the symbonites become aware of us before we land?"

Probably not. No mind—telepathic or otherwise—can continue to function unless it protects itself from the spherical bombardment of information. I became aware of you mainly because of the special relationship with Bartan.

"Are you permitted freedom of movement?"

Yes—I roam the planet at will.

"In that case," Toller said, still dully astonished at his ability to commune with a mental apparition, "surely it is within your power to guide our skyship to some remote and lonely spot—at night, if need be—where we could meet you and take you on board our craft. A few seconds should suffice—it is not even necessary for the ship to touch down—and then we could be on our way back to Overland."

The extent of your presumption amazes me, Toller Maraquine. Do you dare to imagine that your analysis of the possibilities, carried out on the spur of the moment, is superior to mine?

"All I'm. . . ."

Do not trouble yourself to answer. Instead, let me put another question to you—for the last time, is it totally inconceivable that you can be persuaded to turn back?

"We go on."

If that is the way of it, Sondeweere's image was retreating as she spoke, *we will meet under your terms. But I guarantee that all of you will come to rue the day you left Overland.*

Chapter 16

The *Kolcorron* completed two orbits of the planet at a height of more than three thousand miles, hurtling through the tenuous outer fringes of the atmosphere. And then, after Sondeweere was satisfied that she had taken all variables into account, she gave instructions for a series of firings of the main engine, the effect of which was to kill the ship's orbital speed.

The *Kolcorron* began to drop vertically towards the surface of Farland.

At first the rate of fall was negligible, but as the hours went by the speed built up and those on board began to hear a burbling rush of air against the planking of the hull. Tipp Gotlon was at the controls. Under Sondeweere's seemingly omniscient guidance, he brought the ship into a vertical attitude, tail down, and fired a long blast on the engine which not only checked the descent but produced a small upward velocity. At that stage the ship was surrounded by air which, although still rarefied, was capable of supporting human life for a reasonable period. The ship's upward movement would soon be halted and reversed by Farland's gravity, but for the time being the exterior working conditions resembled those of Overland's weightless zone—and the task of deploying the skyship began.

Before going outside, Toller went to the top deck for a final word with Gotlon, ascending the ladder with some difficulty because of his skysuit and the added encumbrances of the parachute and personal propulsion unit. A single ray of sunlight from a porthole was slanting across the compartment, casting a lemon-coloured glow over the pilot's face, upon which was an expression of moody discontent.

"Sir," he said on seeing Toller, "how is Zavotle coping with the outside work?"

"Zavotle is coping very well," Toller replied, aware of what was in Gotlon's mind. He had been disappointed on being told that he was to remain with the ship, and had argued that only the able-bodied members of the crew should take part in what promised to be an arduous and dangerous rescue mission. Toller had countered by saying that the role of the *Kolcorron* was of paramount importance to the whole project, therefore logic demanded that the best pilot should be left in control of the vessel. The tribute to his flying skills had mollified Gotlon only a little.

"The work I am given could as easily be done by a sick man," he said, returning to his original argument.

Toller shook his head. "Son, Ilven Zavotle is not merely a *sick* man. He would not thank me for telling you this, but there is little time remaining to him, and I think it is in his heart to be buried on Farland."

Gotlon looked uncomfortable. "I hadn't realised. So that's why he has been so crabbed of late."

"Yes. And if he were to be left here alone on the ship, and chanced to die, what would become of the rest of us?"

"I didn't say goodbye to him. I was resentful."

"He won't be concerned about that. The best thing you can do for Zavotle is to make sure that his logbook is returned safely to Overland. There is much in there that will be invaluable to future space travellers, including all that he has learned from Sondeweere, and I am charging you with the personal responsibility for ensuring that it is delivered into King Chakkell's hands."

"I'll do my utmost to. . . ." Gotlon paused and looked at Toller with eyes which had become strangely aware. "Sir, the mission . . . Are you in any doubt about the outcome?"

"No doubt at all," Toller said, smiling. He gripped Gotlon's shoulder for a second, then drew himself back to the ladder and went down it, controlling his bulk with difficulty in the confined space because of the weightless conditions.

When he got outside the ship, into the boundless sky, movement became effortless. The others were already at work, separating the skyship section from the main body of the *Kolcorron*, and Farland was an enormous, mind-stunning convex backdrop to their activities.

A white polar cap was visible on the planet, which had more

cloud than Land or Overland, giving it a reflective power which enveloped the floating figures in a storm of brilliance. The sky in the lower half of the sphere of visibility had returned to the dark blue coloration with which Toller was familiar, but above him it shaded into a near-blackness in which the stars and spirals shone with unusual clarity.

He took a deep breath as he relished every aspect of the unearthly scene, feeling privileged, savouring the fact that he had been born into unique circumstances which had directed his life to this unparalleled moment.

Ahead of him was a new experience, a new world to ravish his senses, a new enemy to conquer; within him was the kind of fevered joy he had first known when riding down on Red One to engage a Lander fleet.

But there was something else there—an undertow of panic and despair. The worm at the core of his life had chosen that very instant to resume its coiling and uncoiling, reminding him that after Farland there was nowhere else to go. *Perhaps*, the now familiar thought came stealing, *my grave is down there on that alien globe. And perhaps that is where I want it to be.* . . .

"We need those muscles of yours, Toller," Zavotle called out.

Toller jetted down to the aft section of the ship. The criss-cross ropes which bound the section to the main hull had already been slackened off the lashing pins, but the mastic was exerting an obstinate cohesive force which preserved the unity of the structure. Toller helped drive in wedges, work which was irksomely difficult because of the need to cling to the ship with one hand and contain the reaction of the hammer within his own frame. Levers were quite useless for the same reason, and in the end separation was only achieved by the group working their toes and fingers into the partial gap at one side and using their combined muscle power to rip the skyship clear of the mother craft.

It tilted away, wallowing gently, exposing the exhaust cone of the engine which would take the main ship back to Overland. Dakan Wraker had disconnected the control extensions in advance, and his task now was to rejoin the various rods to both engines and to check that they were functioning properly.

"We should have had jacks," Zavotle commented, his face pale and gleaming with sweat. "And have you noticed that it isn't cold here? We're farther from the sun and yet the air is warmer than in our own weightless zone. Nature delights in confounding us, Toller."

"There's no time to fret about it now." Toller flew to the skyship and took part in pushing it sideways, clear of the *Kolcorron*, with the combined thrust of five personal jets. The crew then began drawing the folded balloon out of the gondola, straightening it out and connecting the load lines. The acceleration struts, which had been sectionised to fit into the ship, were tricky to assemble, but the routine had been practised before the start of the voyage and was completed in good time. Wraker finished his work on the mother ship and within a few minutes of returning to the gondola had fettled its engine in readiness for inflation of the balloon. The operation was facilitated by the fact that the whole assemblage was slowly falling, creating a drift of unheated air into the balloon and helping prepare it for the influx of hot gas.

Toller, as the most experienced skyship pilot, took the responsibility for starting the engine in the burner mode and inflating the balloon with no heat damage to the lower panels. As soon as the insubstantial giant, with all its geometrical traceries, had been conjured into being above the gondola he turned the pilot's seat over to Berise and went to the side.

The *Kolcorron* was now falling slightly faster than the skyship, its varnished timbers gradually slipping downwards past those who watched from the gondola's rail. Gotlon appeared at the open midsection door and waved briefly before closing it and sealing the ship.

A minute later the main engine began to roar. The spaceship stopped sinking, hovered for a fleeting moment and started to climb. Its engine seemed to grow louder as it moved above the skyship and Toller felt the hot miglign gas blasting out of the exhaust, disturbing the equilibrium of the balloon and gondola. He watched the larger ship until it passed out of sight behind the curving horizon of the balloon, and suddenly he felt in awe of Gotlon, an ordinary young man who nevertheless had the courage to fly off into the void alone, trusting a woman he had never met to guide him into orbit with ethereal commands.

Not for the first time, it came to Toller just how foolhardy he had been in setting out to cross interplanetary space with scarcely an inkling of the dangers ahead. Such hubris surely merited disaster. For himself and Zavotle the ordained penalty was perhaps acceptable, but he had to do all that was in his power to ensure that his youthful companions were not drawn into the maelstrom of his own destiny.

The same thought was to recur to him many times during the six days that it took to descend to the surface of Farland.

Associating with the young fighter pilots, especially Berise, had shown him how much they resented any attempt at what they saw as wet nursing. He had to respect their feelings, but was in a dilemma because he knew their outlook was tinged with overconfidence, the unconsciously arrogant belief that they could triumph over any adversary, survive any danger. The exhilaration of riding jet fighters through the central blue had persuaded them that recklessness was a viable philosophy of life.

His own career hardly gave him the right to take a different standpoint, but he was haunted by the knowledge that from the start he had been woefully unfit to lead an expedition to Farland. Even Zavotle had not understood that in space a moving ship can continue at the same speed for ever with its engine shut down, and that the effects of any extra thrusts were cumulative. They would all have died on entering Farland's atmosphere had it not been for Sondeweere's intervention—and she had been right to condemn him for another crass oversight. He had not even considered the idea that Farland might be populated with ordinary beings, let alone talented super-creatures with powers far beyond his understanding. Sondeweere had assured him that landing on the planet would mean death for the astronauts, and as the descent continued he found it harder and harder to erect barriers of disbelief against her prediction.

Another contributor to his disquiet was Sondeweere herself. Her telepathic visitations had been no surprise to Bartan; Berise and Wraker seemed to have accommodated her in their systems of belief without much difficulty—but Toller had spent too many years as a materialist and sceptic not to feel his inner universe quake every time he thought of her.

The story about the symbon spores had been truly astonishing, but at least he could comprehend every part of it, and with comprehension came acceptance. The notion of direct mind-to-mind contact was in a different category, however.

Even though he had seen the curiously elusive image of her and had listened to her silent voice, something within him rebelled each time he recalled the experience.

It smacked too much of mysticism. If there really were other levels of reality, not accessible to his five ordinary senses, who was to say—to choose but one example—that religious beliefs about the transmigration of souls were unfounded? Where was one to draw the line? Sondeweere's private message for him was that his conviction that he understood the nature of reality, give or take a few minor areas of uncertainty, was and always had been a ludicrous conceit—and that was hard to swallow at his time of life.

Unsettling through Sondeweere's manifestations were, he had little respite from them. She appeared to the crew many times during the descent, especially in the final stages, giving instructions to slow their downward speed, to hover, and once even to ascend for an hour. Her objective was to guide them down through wind layers and weather systems, which were more evident than on Overland, to a landing site she had chosen.

At one stage she correctly warned them of a region of intense cold, many miles in depth, in which the temperature was even lower than that of the weightless zone although the air above and below was relatively warm. In reply to Zavotle's question she spoke of the atmosphere reflecting away some of the sun's heat and of convection currents carrying more of it down to sea level, resulting in a cold layer.

The very fact that Sondeweere knew of such things, she who until recently had been an unlettered agricultural worker, added to Toller's general misgivings. It substantiated her claim to have been sublimated into a superwoman, a genius beyond the ken of genius, and made him feel apprehensive about meeting her face

257

to face. What would a goddess think of ordinary human beings? Would she look on them in much the same manner as they had regarded the gibbons which abounded in the Sorka province of old Kolcorron?

He would have expected Bartan Drumme to show some degree of concern over the same issue, but the youngster gave no sign of it. When not sleeping or taking his turn at the controls, he spent his time talking to Berise and Wraker, quite often swigging from one of the skins of brandy he had included in his kit. Berise had brought drawing materials and she devoted hours to sketching the others and making maps of the approaching planet, the latter mainly for the benefit of Zavotle. For his part, the little man appeared to be deteriorating at an increasing rate. He lay on his palliasse, forearms pressed against his stomach, and rarely became animated except when in communion with Sondeweere. Given the opportunity he would have questioned her for hours, but her visitations were always brief and her instructions terse, as though many other matters competed for her attention.

Unexpectedly, Toller got the most companionship from the crew member he knew least—Dakan Wraker. Although he had been born after the Migration, the soft-spoken man with the crinkly hair and humorous grey eyes had an intense interest in the history of the Old World. While helping Toller to grease and clean the muskets and five steel swords which had been brought on the mission, he encouraged him to talk for long periods about daily life in Ro-Atabri, Kolcorron's former capital city, and the practical arrangements by which it had spread its influence through an entire hemisphere. It transpired that he had ambitions to write a book which would help preserve the nation's identity.

"So we have an artist and a writer on one ship," Toller said. "You and Berise should form a partnership."

"I'd love to form *any* kind of partnership with Berise," Wraker replied in a low voice, "but I think she has her sights set on another."

Toller frowned. "You mean Bartan? But he's soon to be reunited with his wife."

"An ill-matched couple, don't you think? Perhaps Berise sees no future in the union."

In Wraker's comments Toller recognised an echo of his own thoughts, so it seemed that the only one who was not in doubt about the prospects for Bartan's strange marriage was Bartan himself. Mildly drunk for most of the time, Bartan appeared to live in a state of euphoria, supported by his monomania, buoyed up by the belief that when he met Sondeweere again all would be as it was before. Toller was at a loss to explain how the young man continued to nourish such naive expectations—but could any of the company claim to be displaying greater foresight?

Toller had noticed that even when Sondeweere used a word he had never heard before he nevertheless understood its meaning. It was as though the words themselves were merely convenient carriers, each one freighted with multitudinous layers of meaning and complementary concepts. When mind spoke to mind there were no misunderstandings or areas of vagueness.

No man who listened to Sondeweere's silent voice could doubt anything she said—and she had predicted that the rescue mission would end in tragedy.

It was dark when the skyship drifted down towards the plain —the kind of darkness Toller had previously known only during the hours of deepnight. While the ship still had some altitude there had been soft glimmerings of light visible here and there in the mysterious black landscape, indicative of scattered towns or villages. But this close to touchdown the only luminance came from the sky, and even the Great Spiral could do little more than add fugitive hints of silver to the mist which patchily shrouded the ground.

The air was seeded with moisture, and to Toller—equatorial dweller from a sun-scoured world—it seemed dauntingly cold, with a strange ability to draw the heat out of his body. He and the others had shed the cumbersome skysuits hours earlier, and now they were shivering and rubbing their goose-pimpled arms in an effort to keep warm. The air was also laden with the smell of vegetation, a dank essence of *greenness* more powerful and pervasive than anything Toller had ever known, and which told him more forcibly than his other senses that he was close to the surface of an alien planet.

As he stood at the gondola's rail he felt keyed-up, exhilarated, entranced—and also regretful that there was to be no opportunity to roam across Farland on foot in daytime and sample its wonders with his own eyes. If Sondeweere met the ship according to plan—and he had little doubt that she would—they would be able to take her on board within seconds. It would not even be necessary for the gondola's legs to make contact with Farland's soil before they headed skywards again under cover of night. By morning they would be out of sight of anybody on the ground, well on their way to a rendezvous with the *Kolcorron*.

Not for the first time, the thought caused Toller to frown in puzzlement. There seemed to be a wide divergence between the actual course of events and Sondeweere's confident forecast of a disastrous end to the venture. Everything seemed to be going too well. Had she simply been doing her best to keep the would-be rescuers out of *possible* dangers, or were there other factors in the situation which Toller had not considered and which she had chosen not to divulge? The extra element of mystery, the hint of lurking perils, worked on him like some potent drug, stepping up his heart rate and increasing his brooding sense of anticipation. He scanned the darkness below, wondering if the enigmatic symbonites could have intercepted and silenced Sondeweere, if the projected landing site could be thronged with waiting soldiers.

Wraker was now firing frequent short bursts into the balloon, reducing the speed of descent to a crawl, and as the ground came nearer Toller's eyes began to play malicious tricks on him. The darkness was no longer homogenous, but was composed of thousands of crawling, squirming shapes, all of them with the potential to be what he least wanted them to be. They ran beneath the drifting ship, silently and effortlessly keeping pace with it, their upraised arms imploring him to come within range and be cut and clubbed and hewn and hacked into anonymous fragments of flesh and bone.

It seemed a long, long time before the encompassing gloom relented and yielded up something unambiguous—a tremulous mote of pale grey which gradually lightened in tone and resolved itself into the figure of a woman dressed in white. . . .

Chapter 17

"Sondy!" Bartan Drumme called, leaning far over the rail beside Toller. "Sondy, I'm here!"

"Bartan!" The woman was walking quickly to keep abreast of the ship. "I see you, Bartan!"

There was no awesome, mind-numbing telepathic contact —just a woman's voice charged with understandable human excitement—and the sound of it overwhelmed Toller with wonder. For the moment all cognisance of symbonite super-beings was gone, and he could think of nothing but the strangeness of this meeting. Here was a woman who had been born on his home world and had lived an ordinary life there before being transported to another planet in bizarre circumstances. Every dictate of reason said that she should then have vanished forever from human ken, but her grief-crazed, drink-sodden husband had inspired a voyage across millions of miles of space, and—against all the odds—they had reached her. That woman, whose voice trembled with natural emotion, was only a few yards away from him in the alien darkness—and Toller spellbound by the reality of her.

The sound of the gondola's exhaust cone and legs swishing through vegetation snapped him back into a universe of practicalities. Bartan had climbed over the gondola's side and was perched on the outer ledge, reaching towards his wife with one hand. She caught hold of it and within a second was standing beside him. Toller helped her roll herself over the rail, marvelling as he did so at the simple bodily contact. Bartan came inboard again with a single lithe movement and clutched Sondeweere to him. Toller, Berise and Zavotle were spontaneously drawn to them, and arms were lapped upon arms in a gratifying multiple embrace. It ended when the gondola's legs glanced against the ground, sending a shudder up through the deck.

"Take us aloft," Toller said to Wraker, who at once began firing a long burst which was to revitalise the gigantic entity of the balloon waiting patiently above them.

"Yes, *yes!*" Sondeweere divorced herself from the cluster of bodies and stepped towards Wraker, her right hand extended in a gesture of greeting. He responded by raising his free hand, but the expected clasp did not take place.

Sondeweere reached past him and—before anybody watching could react—caught the red line connected to the balloon's rip panel and jerked it downwards with irresistible force.

There was no immediate reaction in the cramped microcosm of the gondola, but Toller knew that the balloon had been *killed*. Far above him a large trapezium of linen had been torn out of the balloon's crown, and the envelope would already be starting to wrinkle and sag as the hot gas which sustained it was vented into the atmosphere. The ship was now committed to setting down on Farland—possibly for ever.

"Sondy! What have you done?" Bartan's anguished cry was heard clearly through the general clamour of shocked protest. He lurched towards Sondeweere with both arms outstretched, as though belatedly trying to prevent her making an injudicious move. She fended him off and went quickly to an empty section of the gondola. *Sondeweere has gone*, Toller thought. *The symbonite superwoman is now among us.*

"There was good reason for what I did," she said in a firm, clear voice. "If you will listen to me for. . . ."

Her words were lost as the gondola struck the ground and tilted to a steep angle, hurling bodies and loose equipment against one wall, before dropping back to the horizontal.

"Get the struts off," Toller shouted, jolted out of his reverie. "The balloon is coming down around us."

He tugged the quick-release knots which were securing a strut to the corner nearest him and pushed the slim support away from the rail, hoping to prevent it taking the weight of the subsiding envelope. The gondola was being inundated with choking hot miglign gas which was belching down out of the balloon's mouth. A sound of splintering told Toller that at least one of the other struts had already been overloaded.

He climbed over the side, peripherally aware of others doing the same, and leaped down to the ground. He ran a short distance through what felt like ordinary grass and turned to view the collapse of the balloon. The vast shape was still tall enough to blot out part of the sky, but it had lost all symmetry. Distorted, writhing like a leviathan in its death throes, it sank downwards at increasing speed. The slight breeze deposited most of it downwind of the gondola where it lay flapping in the grass, raised into shifting humps here and there by gas that was trapped within.

A brief period of silence followed, then the crew members turned and closed in on Sondeweere. There was no hint of threat in their demeanour, nor even of resentment, but the courses of their lives had been profoundly altered by a single unexpected action on her part and they sought some kind of reassurance. Toller could see them well enough in spite of the darkness to note that he was the only one wearing his sword. Obeying old instincts, he dropped his hand to the hilt of the weapon and looked all about him, trying to penetrate the folds of alien night.

"There are no Farlanders within many miles," Sondeweere said, addressing herself directly to him. "I have not betrayed you."

"May I be so bold as to enquire what you *have* done?" he replied, falling back on sarcasm. "You will appreciate that we have a certain interest in the matter."

"We need to know," Bartan added in a quavering voice which indicated that he, perhaps more than anybody else, had been devastated by the turn of events.

Sondeweere was wearing a belted white tunic and she drew it closer around her throat before she spoke. "I invite you to consider two facts which are of paramount importance. The first is that the symbonites of this world are aware of my exact whereabouts at all times. They know precisely where I am at this moment, but their suspicions are not aroused and they will take no action because—fortunately for all of us—I am of a restless disposition and it is my habit to travel far and wide at irregular hours.

"The second fact," Sondeweere went on, speaking with a calm fluency, "is that the symbonites brought me here in a ship which can make the interplanetary crossing in only a few minutes."

"Minutes!" Zavotle said. "Only a few minutes?"

"The journey could have been completed in a few seconds, or even fractions of a second, but for short distances it is more convenient to proceed at a moderate speed. My point is that if I had gone aloft in the skyship the symbonites would very quickly have realised what was happening and would have intercepted us with their own ship. As I have already told you, they are not homicidal by instinct, but they will *never* permit me to return to my home world. They would have forced the skyship down, and in doing so would have killed everyone on board."

"Is their weaponry so much superior to ours?" Toller said, trying to visualise the aerial encounter.

"The symbonite ship carries no weapons as such, but in flight it is surrounded by a field—call it an aura—which is inimical to life. The underlying concept cannot be explained to you, but be assured that a meeting with the symbonite ship would have resulted in all our deaths. Whether the symbonites wanted it that way or not—we would have died."

A silence descended on the group of fliers while each assimilated Sondeweere's message. The breeze suddenly freshened, spanging the mute figures with chilling drops of rain which easily penetrated their light shirts and breeches, and clouds slid across the stars like prison doors closing. *Farland exults*, Toller thought, trying to repress a shiver.

Berise was the first to speak, and when she did so her voice carried an unmistakable note of anger. "It seems to me that you were somewhat high-handed in tampering with our ship," she said to Sondeweere. "Had you told us the full story when you came on board, we could have dropped you off again and returned to Overland unmolested."

"But would you have done so?" Sondeweere gave them a wan smile. "Would any of you have chosen to be so . . . logical?"

"I can't speak for the others, but *I* certainly would," Berise said, and all at once Toller intuited that the challenge to Sondeweere had less to do with the ship and the outcome of the expedition than with rivalry for Bartan's affections. He found time, in spite of the extremeness of their plight, to be once again awed by the female mind and to become slightly afraid of Berise. She was another Gesalla. Now that he thought of it, all women seemed to be Gesallas to one extent or another, and a man was no match for them in their chosen arena.

"The skyship has not been harmed beyond repair," Sondeweere pointed out. "I purposely brought you to a remote area where you are unlikely to be discovered by Farlanders, so there is ample time for the work to be carried out."

Then what was the point of collapsing the balloon? Toller thought. *The woman has more to tell us. . . .*

Bartan took a step towards Sondeweere. "The others may leave if they wish—I will stay here with you."

"No, Bartan! Have you forgotten why I was brought here in the first place? The symbonites would slay me rather than permit me to associate with a functional male of my own race."

Toller, with his soldier's interest in tactics, was locked into the problem he had set himself. *The reason Sondeweere collapsed the balloon had to be that she intended the ship never to fly again. In which case. . . .*

"There is an alternative course open to all of you," Sondeweere said. "I will describe it for you, but you must make the decision for yourselves. If you decide against it, I will help repair your ship and will undertake to guide you back to Overland, while I remain here. If you decide in favour of it, you must be apprised of all the dangers and. . . ."

"We decide in favour," Toller cut in. "How far is the symbonite spaceship from here? And how well is it guarded?"

Sondeweere turned to face him. "I am surprised by you, Toller Maraquine."

"There is no need," Toller said. "I am not a clever man, but I have learned that there are some issues which—no matter how wise and learned the disputants—can be settled in only one way. It is a way I understand."

"The killing way."

"The way of justifiable force, of blocking an enemy sword with a sword of my own."

"Say no more, Toller—I am in no position to make moral

judgments. It was my idea to take the ship, because it offers my only hope of escape from this drear and unfulfilled existence, but there are many dangers."

"We are prepared to face danger," Toller said. He glanced around his companions, associating them with the statement.

"But why should any of you be prepared to risk death on my behalf?"

"We all had our own good reasons for taking part in this expedition."

Sondeweere moved closer to Toller, all the while gazing into his face, and for the first time since their meeting he sensed she was employing her extraordinary powers of mind.

"Yours was not a good reason," she said sadly.

"How long must we stand around in this freezing quagmire?" he demanded, stamping his feet on the squelching ground. "We are likely to die of the ague unless we stir our bones. How far from here is the ship?"

"A good ninety miles." Sondeweere spoke with a new brisk-ness, apparently having accepted that an irrevocable decision had been reached. "But I have a transporter which can take us there."

"A wagon?"

"A kind of wagon."

"Good—this is no country for a forced march." Relieved at having been spared any further deliberation, Toller ran with the others to the gondola for the unloading of weapons and food supplies. He took one of the five muskets for his own use, but without much enthusiasm. The net of pressure spheres which accompanied it was likely to be an encumbrance in close combat, and the time it took to lock on a new sphere before each shot detracted seriously from the weapon's efficacy.

"Look what I have found." Zavotle, who was shivering violently, extended an unsteady hand in which he was holding a brakka shaft around which was rolled the blue-and-grey flag of Kolcorron.

Toller took it and hurled it into the ground like a spear. "That's our obligation to Chakkell taken care of—from now on we go about our own business."

He descended from the gondola and was placing his supplies with the others when it occurred to him that Sondeweere was no longer with the company. He scanned the darkness and in that instant heard a strange sound, one which was made up of other sounds—the hissing of a giant snake, the snorting of a bluehorn, the creaking and rattling of a wagon. A moment later he discerned the squarish outline of a vehicle which was slowly approaching the ship. Curious as to what kind of draught animal was responsible for such a cacophony, he went forward to meet Sondeweere, and halted—confounded—as it became apparent that the lurching vehicle was moving under its own power.

The rear of it resembled a traditional wagon covered with canvas supported on stretchers, but in front was a fat cylinder from which ascended a tube belching white vapours into the murky air. Sondeweere was visible as a pale blur behind the glass screen of a cabin-like structure which formed the forepart of the vehicle's main body. It drew to a halt on wide, black-rimmed wheels, the noise from it decreased to a ruminative snuffling and Sondeweere leapt down from the cabin.

"The wagon propels itself by harnessing the power of steam," she said, forestalling a barrage of questions. "I sometimes use it as a caravan when I'm travelling long distances, and it is well suited for our purposes."

The journey across that region of Farland was one of the most singular Toller had ever undertaken.

Part of the strangeness sprang from the unique governing circumstances and the ambience. In spite of the protection offered by the transporter's canvas top, the five astronauts were oppressed by a clammy coldness unlike anything in their previous experience. Dawn came, not as a fountaining of golden light and heat as on Overland, but as a stealthy change in the colour of the environment, from black to a leaden grey. Even the air within the vehicle became tinged with grey, a mix of exhaled breath and dank mist seeping in from outside which seemed to curdle around the passengers and chill their blood. Only Sondeweere, clad in substantial tunic and trews, was unaffected by the penetrating cold.

Toller and the others parted the canvas frequently, hungry for the sight of an alien world and its inhabitants, but found little to inspire wonder in the glimpses of blue-green grasslands swept by curtains of rain and fog. Toller noted that the road on which they were travelling was paved and well maintained, much superior to anything on Overland. As it gradually widened they got their first glimpse of Farlander dwellings.

The buildings drew some comment, not because they were exotic in any way but because of their sheer ordinariness. Had it not been for the steeply pitched roofs the unadorned single-storey cottages could have blended in with the local architecture almost anywhere on the twin worlds. There was no sign of their inhabitants so early in the morning, and Toller thought it entirely reasonable that they should choose to remain abed for as long as possible, rather than venture out in such an inhospitable clime.

"It isn't always as cold and gloomy as this," Sondeweere explained at one stage, speaking from her isolated position at the vehicle's tiller. "We are in the mid-latitudes of the northern hemisphere, and you happen to have arrived in the middle of winter."

Toller was familiar with the concept of seasons, thanks to his upbringing in one of the philosophy families of old Kolcorron, but it was new to the younger members of the group, mentally conditioned by living on a world whose equator was exactly in the plane of its orbit around the sun. At first the idea that Farland was tilted was quite difficult for them to grasp, and then as it began to take hold they questioned Sondeweere extensively, intrigued by the thought of days and nights which constantly varied in length, and the consequences thereof. For her part, Sondeweere seemed pleased to be able to put aside the symbon component of her identity for a while, and to react naturally as a human among humans.

Listening to the intercourse, Toller was occasionally overcome by a sense of unreality. He had to keep reminding himself that Sondeweere had undergone an incredible metamorphosis, that the group was on its way to do battle with alien beings for the possession of a ship which had been wrought out of miracles and magic. And, above all, that every member of the group could easily die in the hours that lay ahead. The young warriors appeared to have dismissed that thought, supremely confident—as he had once been—that death could not touch them.

Stay that way as long as you can, he advised them mentally, aware that the nerve-thrumming exhilaration which had always sustained him on the eve of battle was totally absent. Was it the reaction of a sun-dweller to this bleak and mist-shrouded world whose clammy coldness penetrated him to the marrow? Or were premonitions at work? Was the capacity for any kind of pleasure being withdrawn from him in preparation for the final disillusionment?

During one of his periodic inspections of the dreary landscape his attention was caught by the sight of a distant building which, as at last befitted an alien world, was unlike any he had seen before. Nested in a narrow valley, it was little more than a silhouette of near-black among dark greys, but it was huge in comparison to the Farlander houses and had numerous chimneys which plumed smoke into the sullen sky.

"An iron foundry which supplies factories throughout this region," Sondeweere explained in response to his query. "On Overland the various operations would be carried out in the open air, but here—because of the climate—it is necessary to have an enclosure. The native Farlanders would doubtless have produced similar structures in due time, but the symbonites have artificially accelerated the process of industrialisation. It is one of their crimes against nature in general and against the people of this world in particular."

But you too are a symbonite, Toller thought. *How can you criticise the activities of your own kind?*

The question, far-reaching though he sensed it to be, was at once displaced by others, less philosophical in nature, which had begun to swarm in his mind. Previously, far out of his intellectual depth, he had conjured a simplistic vision of superbeings effortlessly taking control of a primitive world—but now it was dawning on him that the symbonites had been in a situation similar to that of a platoon of well-armed Kolcorronian soldiers facing a thousand Gethan tribesmen. In a straight and simple conflict, no matter how superior their weaponry, they were bound to be overwhelmed—therefore other strategies had been called for.

"Tell me," he said to Sondeweere, "have the Farlanders never offered any resistance to the invaders?"

"They are unaware of any intrusion," she replied, eyes fixed on the dull-gleaming road ahead, "and who could possibly make them aware? You were quite unable to accept anything that Bartan told you about me—so just imagine how you would have reacted had he told you that King Chakkell and Queen Daseene and their children, plus all the aristocrats in the land and *their* children, were alien conquerors in human guise! Would you have believed him and tried to lead a rebellion? Or would you have dismissed him as a raving lunatic?"

"But you speak of the ruling classes. You told us that the symbon spores descended on this world at random, and that they had no choice as regards their hosts."

"Yes, but can't you see that symbonites in any society would quickly infiltrate and dominate the power structure?" Sondeweere went on to outline her view of the developments on Farland over the previous three centuries. In the beginning was the gulf of incomprehension which exists between the masses and the rulers in any primitive society. As far as the indigenous Farlanders were concerned, their lords and masters—already mysterious and god-like—gradually became more innovative, more inventive. They introduced new ideas, such as steam engines for heavy work, and with each step forward their position became more unassailable.

They were forcing the pace of industrial development, but with a sure hand and with patience. Having started with perhaps as few as six symbonite individuals, they well understood the need to proceed with caution, but as decade followed decade they laid down the foundations for a symbonite culture which was destined to dominate an entire world. They mingled freely with the native population, but also had retreats in which no Farlander ever set foot, secret places where they carried out research work and experimented with scientific ideas which might have excited alarm had they been made public. It was in one of those protected enclaves that the symbonite spaceship had been designed and built.

As Sondeweere was speaking Toller began to piece together from stray references a picture of her own lonely existence on the unprepossessing planet. The native Farlanders saw her as a grotesque caricature of a normal being, a freak which for some inscrutable reason was under the protection and patronage of their masters. They tolerated her presence among them, but made no attempts to communicate.

To the self-interested symbonites she was a mild encumbrance, a threat which had been neutralised. At first they had tried to establish a rapport with Sondeweere, but in return she had displayed all the traits which had led them to forestall the emergence of human-based symbonites—resentment, contempt, hatred and implacable hostility among them—and since then they had been content to keep her under continual telepathic surveillance. They learned what they could from her, stole what they could from her mind, and waited for her to die. Time was on their side. They were a new race and as such potentially immortal; she was an individual—vulnerable and impermanent. . . .

"There's one! More than one!" The exclamations came from Wraker, who had raised the canvas cover to look outside, triggering a general rush to do the same.

"Remember, they must not see us," Toller said as he created a narrow gap between the material and the transporter's wooden siding. He peered out and saw they were passing through a village which to his eyes was remarkable in that it was so unremarkable. It seemed that craftsmen everywhere—masons, carpenters, smiths—came up with universal practical solutions to universal practical problems. The village, like the isolated houses seen earlier, might have been anywhere in the temperate zones of Land, but its inhabitants were a different matter.

They resembled humans, but were considerably shorter, and with quite different bodily proportions. Their hooded and layered garments, obviously designed to turn away rain, did not disguise the fact that their spines arched forward almost as semi-circles, predisposing them to waddle with out-thrust bellies and faces tilted upwards. Their legs were short and stubby, but not as truncated as their arms, which angled outwards from the shoulder and ended where the human elbow might have been placed. Massive hands, which seemed to have only five fingers, clenched and unclenched as they walked. It was difficult to see much of their faces, but they seemed pale and hairless, the features all but lost in folds of fat.

"Elegant little fellows," Bartan commented. "Is that the enemy?"

"Do not be complacent," Sondeweere said over her shoulder. "They are strong, and they seem to have little fear of pain or injury. They are also fanatical in their obedience to authority."

Toller saw that the Farlanders, possibly on their way to jobs, were regarding the passing transporter with interest, buried eyes emitting flickers of amber and white. "Have they noticed you?"

"Possibly, but such curiosity as their dull minds can muster is probably directed towards the vehicle—motorised transporters are still quite rare. I am privileged in a way."

"How well organised and equipped is their army?"

"The Farlanders do not have an army in your sense of the word, Toller Maraquine. A world state has been in existence for over a hundred years and internecine conflict has been outmoded, thanks to the symbonites, but there is an immense body of citizenry with a title I can best translate as the Public Force. They single-mindedly execute any task assigned to them—flood control, forest clearance, the building of new roads. . . ."

"So they are not trained fighters?"

"What they lack in individual skills they make up for in numbers," Sondeweere said. "And I repeat—they are very strong in spite of their lack of stature."

Zavotle aroused himself from a contemplation of inner pain. "They are not like us, and yet . . . How can I put it? They have more points of similarity than of difference."

"Our sun is close to the centre of a galaxy, where the stars are very close together. It is possible that all the habitable worlds in this region of space were seeded with life aeons ago, perhaps more than once. An interstellar traveller might find humans or their cousins on many planets."

273

"What is a galaxy?" Zavotle said, initiating a long question-and-answer session in which Toller, Wraker and Berise participated, eager for the gifts of knowledge which Sondeweere had acquired both from the symbonites and her own powers of deduction, enhanced beyond the understanding of ordinary men and women. For Toller, the realisation that each of the hundreds of misty whirlpools visible in the night sky was a conglomeration of perhaps a hundred thousand million suns came as a blend of mind-stretching delight and poignant regrets. He was simultaneously uplifted by the scope of the new vision, and depressed by two other factors—his personal inadequacy when confronted by the scale of the cosmos, and sorrow over the fact that his long-dead brother, Lain, had been denied his rightful place at the intellectual banquet.

As the transporter continued its hissing and puffing way through a thickening chain of villages, it gradually came to Toller's notice that Bartan Drumme was the only member of the company to have excluded himself from the precious communion with Sondeweere. He looked uncharacteristically morose and apathetic, not even bothering to change his position to evade a persistent dripping of rain from a leak overhead, and—while drinking very little—was protectively nursing a skin of brandy he had brought from the skyship. Toller wondered if he was downcast at the prospect of going into battle, or if it was beginning to sink into him that the woman he had married and the omniscient, awesomely gifted being they had met on Farland were two quite different people, and that any future relationship between them could not resemble that of the past.

". . . not like the burning of fuel, as in a furnace," Sondeweere was saying. "Atoms of the lightest gas present within a sun combine to form a heavier gas. The process yields great amounts of energy and that is what makes a sun shine. I'm sorry I cannot give you a clearer explanation at this time—it would take too long to expound the underlying principles and concepts."

"Could you explain it in your silent voices?" Toller said. "As you did when we were still in the void."

Sondeweere glanced back at him. "That would help,

undoubtedly, but I dare not enter into any telepathic communication. I told you that the symbonites are aware of me at all times, and the closer I get to their ship the more I will become a focus of their attention, because it is the one place in all the land which is forbidden to me. Were they to pick up the slightest wisp of telepathic activity their interest in my movements would at once be translated into direct action—and that is something which will happen soon enough."

"They should have destroyed the ship," Berise commented, traces of sourness still in her voice.

"Perhaps—but they have no way of knowing how many symbon spores may remain on Overland waiting to create more human symbonites." Sondeweere cast Berise a smile which perhaps hinted that her preoccupations were far removed from personal rivalries. "Also, the ship was not built without considerable sacrifice on their part."

"The sacrifices may not all be on one side."

"I know," Sondeweere said simply. "I told you that at the outset."

Chapter 18

The transporter made an abrupt turn to the left and within minutes its comparatively smooth movement had given way to a bumpy and lurching progress which drew creaks from the chassis. Toller raised himself and looked out in front, past Sondeweere's white-clad figure, and saw they had left the road and were now heading across open grassland. The horizon seen through rain-spattered glass was almost flat and the terrain was quite featureless except for a scattering of squatly conical trees.

"How far now?" he said.

"Not far—about twelve miles," Sondeweere replied. "This will be uncomfortable for you, but we must proceed with all possible speed from here on. Until now the symbonites had no real cause for alarm, because the highway leads to many destinations, but on this course there is only. . . ." She broke off with a sharp intake of breath and her grip on the tiller failed momentarily, allowing the vehicle to pull to one side. Those beside Toller sat up straighter, hands straying towards weapons.

"Is anything wrong?" he said, half-knowing what had happened.

"We are discovered. The alarm has gone out—and sooner than I had expected." Her voice betrayed no anxiety, but she advanced a lever and the sound from the engine increased. The protests from the chassis grew louder as the vehicle gained speed.

Toller felt a stirring of the old squalid excitement. "Can you tell us anything about what lies ahead? Fortifications? Weapons?"

"Very little, I'm afraid—intelligence of that nature is hard to gather." Sondeweere went on to say that, to the best of her knowledge, the symbonite ship was kept in an ancient meteorite crater which served as a natural revetment. She believed it was further protected by a high fence along the crater's rim. There would be armed guards, whose numbers she could not predict, and their weapons were likely to be swords, and perhaps pikes.

"No bows? No spears?"

"The native physique does not readily lend itself to the use of the bow or any kind of throwing weapon."

"How about firearms?"

"There are no brakka trees on this world, and the Farlanders' knowledge of chemistry is not yet sufficiently advanced for them to have invented artificial explosives."

"This sounds quite encouraging," Wraker put in, nudging Toller. "The defences seem to be disproportionately light."

"In the normal scheme of things there would have been no need to defend the ship against anything but troublesome wild animals," Sondeweere said. "There would have been no point in my trying to get near it alone—and no logical person could have anticipated the arrival of a ship from Overland before another four or five centuries had elapsed." She smiled and a note of warmth crept into her voice. "In the symbonites' eminently reasonable view of the universe people like you five simply do not exist."

Wraker grinned in return. "They'll learn about us soon enough—to their cost."

Toller frowned. "We must not allow ourselves to become too confident. How long will it take the symbonites to call up reinforcements?"

"I don't know," Sondeweere said. "There are large-scale road works to the north of the site, but I cannot say how close they are."

"But you knew *our* exact position when we were many thousands of miles away in the void."

"There is a natural and very powerful empathy between us because we come from the same human stock. The Farlanders' minds are all but closed to me."

"I see," Toller said. "Obviously we cannot decide our tactics in advance, but I have one final question . . . about the ship itself."

"Will I be able to fly it? The answer is yes.'

"In spite of never having seen it?"

"Again, this cannot be explained to you, not even by telepathic means—and I am deeply sorry about that—but the ship is not governed by mechanical controls. For a person who comprehends all the operating principles it will do exactly as it is bidden; without that necessary understanding it will not move a single inch."

Toller fell silent, chastened by the reminder that Sondeweere, in spite of her perfectly normal appearance and demeanour, was in actuality an enigmatic superbeing. The fact that he and the others could communicate with her on what felt like equal terms had to be almost entirely due to skilled indulgence on her part—as a venerable philosopher contrives to amuse a two-year-old child.

He glanced at Bartan, freshly made aware of the young man's unprecedented situation, and saw that he was staring fixedly at the back of Sondeweere's head, his expression broody and almost sullen. Becoming conscious of Toller's scrutiny, Bartan mustered a wry smile and raised the skin of brandy to his lips. Toller reached out to prevent him drinking, saw the beginnings of defiance on the young man's face and reflexively turned his hand palm upwards. *I'm growing soft*, he thought as he accepted the skin and took a sizeable drink from it, *but perhaps not before my time.*

"How about you, Sondy?" Bartan said as though issuing a challenge. "Would you like a warming drop of brandy?"

"No. The warmth is spurious, and I find the taste unpleasant."

"I thought you might," Bartan said, and now an aggrieved and surly note was plain in his voice. "What do you subsist on these days? Nectar and dew? When we return to the farm you will be able to have your fill of those, but I trust you won't object if I go on preferring stronger potions."

Sondeweere gave him a single pleading glance. "Bartan, you have the right to force the issue—even though some of what I have to say to you would be best said in private—but we. . . ."

"I have nothing to hide from my friends, Sondy. Proceed! Explain to all of us that it would be unseemly for a princess to bed down with a peasant."

"Bartan, please do not cause yourself needless pain."

Sondeweere was speaking loudly to overcome the sounds of the transporter at speed, but there was a concerned tenderness in her voice. "Even though I have changed a great deal, I would still have been a wife to you, but it can never be . . . because. . . ."

"Because of what?"

"Because I have a higher duty to the entire human population of Overland. I refuse to deprive my own people of their evolutionary heritage by founding a dynasty of symbonites which would dominate the ordinary humans and eventually drive them into extinction."

Bartan looked stunned, obviously having heard something totally outside his expectations, but he was still nimble enough of mind to respond quickly. "But there is no need for us to have children. There are ways . . . maidenfriend is only one of them . . . I never wanted to be burdened with noisy offspring anyway."

Sondeweere managed to laugh. "You cannot lie to me, Bartan. I know how much you want children, *true* descendants— not alien hybrids. If you have the great good fortune to return to Overland alive, your only chance of happiness will lie in settling down with a normal young woman who will bear you normal children. That, believe me, is a future worth looking forward to and fighting for."

"It is also a future I reject," Bartan said.

"The decision is not in your hands, Bartan." Sondeweere paused as the transporter hit a rough patch of ground and the thunder of it made conversation impossible. "Have you forgotten about the symbonites of this world? If we do succeed in stealing their ship and getting back to Overland with it, they will build another and go after me. They will take no chances on my surviving, possibly with child. It is my belief that the second ship will have weapons, terrible weapons, and the symbonites will be prepared to use them."

"But. . . ." Bartan drew his fingers across his wrinkled brow. "This is terrible, Sondy. What will you *do*?"

"Assuming I survive the next hour, there is only one course open to me," Sondeweere said. "I will take the ship and fly off into the galaxy, perhaps into many galaxies, beyond the reach of this world's symbonites. It will be a solitary existence, but it will have its compensations. There is much to see before I die."

"I'll go with. . . ." Bartan began the sentence impulsively, then halted, and a tormented look appeared in his eyes. "I could never do that, Sondy. I would die of fear. You have already left me behind."

Toller knew that he had been listening to Sondeweere's normal voice, but her words rang through him—with multiple resonances of meaning—almost as if she had been speaking telepathically. There were echoes of dreams he had never dared to dream, of a vision he had once glimpsed—while riding a jet down through needle-sprays of sunlight—of being able to go on and on until he died, gorging his eyes and mind and soul with images of things he had never seen before, of new worlds, new suns, new galaxies, always something new, new, *new*. It was a prospect the architect of the universe might have designed especially for him; it flooded the dark void at the core of his being with hard light, joyous light; and he had to make the claim, no matter how slight the chances of winning. . . .

"I would go with you," he murmured. "Please take me with you."

Sondeweere half-turned towards him, her mind-force swinging through him like the beam of a lighthouse, and he waited numbly for her answer.

"Toller Maraquine, I told you that your reason for coming to Farland was not a good one," she said, "but your reason for wanting to leave it has its own kind of merit. I make no promises—for all of us may die within minutes—but if you succeed in taking the symbonite ship the universe is yours."

"Thank you." Toller's voice was a painful croak, and he had to blink back his tears. "Thank you!"

The wall of the crater was low, not much differentiated from the surrounding terrain, never lifting itself above the horizon. A general paucity of illumination coupled with the blurring effect of the rain meant that the transporter was less than a mile from the site before Toller was able to pick out any evidence that it was defended.

As Sondeweere had predicted, there was a tall fence around the rim—barely visible as a hazy grey ellipse—and in it was a darkish knot suggestive of an entrance. His telescope was virtually useless because of the jouncing of the transporter, but its slewing images told him that at least two other mechanised vehicles had been parked across the gateway. Farlanders appeared as moving specks of blackness milling in the general vicinity.

"We must avoid the gate and break through the fence," he said to Sondeweere, putting the telescope away. "Can you make the wagon go faster?"

"Yes, but there is the risk of breaking an axle on this kind of ground."

"Use your best judgment—but remember that if we don't go through the fence we don't go anywhere."

Toller turned to the others and knew at once that they had experienced a loss of confidence, something he had seen happen many times in the irreducible few minutes before a battle. Bartan's face was almost luminous in its pallor, and even Berise and Wraker—proficient in the abstract art of long-range killing—had a look of glum uncertainty about them. Only Zavotle, busy checking his musket, seemed to be unperturbed.

"Don't try to plan anything ahead," Toller told them. "Believe me, you can trust your sword arm to do all the thinking that will be necessary. Now, get those covers out of the way." Within seconds the coarse material screening the truck bed from the outside world had been pulled down and cast off behind the dangerously swaying vehicle. Cold rain swirled in around the lightly clad figures.

"There's something else to bear in mind." Toller glanced at the teeming heavens and gave an exaggerated grimace of distaste. "*Anything* is better than living in this accursed place and slowly turning into a fish."

The laughter his remark drew was louder than it deserved, but Toller had long since learned that subtlety was out of place in battlefield humour, and he was satisfied that vital psychological bridges between him and the crew were being maintained. He drew his sword and positioned himself behind Sondeweere, looking forward over the top of the driving cabin.

The transporter was starting up the incline towards the rim of the crater, and now he could see that the fence was made of spear-like metal uprights railed to stout posts. He considered urging Sondeweere to strive for more speed and momentum, then remembered that her understanding of the mechanics of the operation far surpassed his own. The smokestack ahead of him spouted orange sparks as the heavy vehicle clanked its way to the top of the slope. Far to his left Toller saw Farlanders running, and beyond them he glimpsed a complex greyish lesion in the landscape which indicated road works barely a mile away.

"Hold on!" he shouted and gripped the cabin roof as the transporter sledged into the fence.

The entire section was torn from its supports and fell inwards, the sound of the impact merging into an appalling mechanical clamour from the engine and a hissing explosion. Hot vapours fanned out around the boiler, momentarily whiting out the entire scene, then the vehicle was rolling down into a circular depression at the centre of which was the symbonite ship. It was sitting on an area of masonry ringed by what was meant to be a moat or a wide drainage ditch.

Toller had tried to visualise the ship's appearance in advance, but he was unprepared for the sight of a nearly featureless metal sphere supported by three flaring legs which ended in circular pads. The sphere was a good ten yards in diameter and had a ring of what seemed to be portholes on the upper half, but there was no sign of an entrance.

In the instant of eyeing the strange ship which embodied his future Toller became aware of brown-clad Farlanders, who had chanced to be near the breach in the fence, running towards the transporter from the right. Although the vehicle was now on a downward slope it was rapidly losing speed, amid a continued metallic thrashing, and the Farlanders were easily intersecting its course. They looked like circus grotesques as they bounded along on stocky legs, cowls thrown back to reveal hairless skulls.

Toller's stomach gave an icy spasm as he saw they were not carrying weapons.

"Stay back!" he cried involuntarily as the two reached the side of the transporter, but one of them sprang and gripped its siding while the other leaped on to the running board of the cabin, reaching for Sondeweere with a powerful hand. Toller split his unprotected skull with a downward sword-stroke which went deep into the head, and he fell away without a sound, radially spurting blood.

The other, trying to raise himself over the siding, took Wraker's sword through the throat. He sank down again, but his fingers remained in view, obstinately clinging to the wooden edge. Wraker and Berise both hacked at his fingers, severing most of them, before he dropped to the ground. He lay where he fell, but to Toller's amazement the one with the cloven skull was on his feet. The alien took several steps in the grassy wake of the transporter, arms outspread, before sinking to his knees and pitching forward.

So hard to kill, Toller thought. *These little people could bring down giants*. . . .

The transporter clanked and shuddered to a halt, wreathed in smoke and mist. Toller glanced towards the gateway on the crater's rim and saw that other Farlanders were coming through it and beginning to head down the long slope in groups of two or three. Occasional dull flashes told him they were armed. He took a musket, straddled his way over the side of the transporter, and jumped down to the ground as part of a general abandonment of the vehicle.

Sondeweere flitted ahead of the others, unencumbered by weapons, and sped across a simple wooden bridge. Toller and the others followed her, feeling the boards quiver beneath their feet. As Sondeweere neared the ship a rectangular section opened in its side, gliding outwards on elbowed hinges. Toller slid to a halt, raising his musket.

"Don't shoot!" Sondeweere called out to him. "I opened the door. A ladder will now descend, or . . . or. . . ." An uncharacteristic note of indecision had crept into her voice.

Toller, following the upwards direction of her gaze, noticed empty metal brackets below the doorway, and for the moment his soldier's mind was abreast of hers in comprehending that the ship was normally entered by means of a fixed ladder. Someone had taken the simple and pragmatic precaution of removing it, and as a result entry was denied to genius and fool alike. The lower edge of the doorway was at least twelve feet above ground level, on the out-curving lower half of the sphere, and to an individual of typical Farlander stature its elevation would have created a formidable barrier indeed. But for humans. . . .

"Bring the wagon across the bridge," Zavotle shouted. "We can climb on it."

"It cannot be moved," Sondeweere replied. "And the bridge is too light, anyway."

"We can reach the door," Toller said, laying his weapons on the paving. "Sondeweere, it is logical that you should go first. You will stand on my shoulders. Come!"

He looked briefly towards the advancing Farlanders, then made a gesture which took in Zavotle, Wraker and Berise. "Go forward and defend the bridge! Use the muskets as much as possible. Take mine as well and persuade the wretched pygmies that they would be better to keep their distance. And see if the timbers of the bridge can be torn up."

They ran to the bridge, unhitching their nets of pressure spheres, inside which minute measures of pikon and halvell had already been combined. Toller positioned himself beneath the ship's doorway and extended his hands to Sondeweere, who came to him immediately. He put his hands around her waist and lifted her to his shoulders, a process which she aided with a kind of scrambling movement of her feet. She straightened up, standing on him, and became steady as she got her hands on to the sill of the doorway.

Concurrently, the first groups of Farlanders racing down the slope were coming within musket range and the defenders were opening fire. The first volley of shots appeared to bring down only one of the attackers, but the musket reports—magnified by the natural amphitheatre—threw them into disarray. They slid and skidded into each other in their efforts to check the downward rush.

Toller turned away from the scene to get his hands under Sondeweere's feet and as he was straightening his arms to propel her into the ship's doorway he was acutely aware of a nerve-thrumming pause before the muskets could be fired again. The delay, caused by the need to unscrew each expended sphere and replace it, was the main reason he had scant regard for firearms.

By the time Sondeweere was safely into the ship it was beginning to dawn on the Farlanders that, no matter how terrifying the psychological impact of the unfamiliar weapons, the actual casualties inflicted by them had been light. They were surging forward again, short swords in hand. A fresh volley of shots, this time at shorter range, knocked over at least three more of the aliens, but failed to check their general advance.

"Find a rope," Toller shouted up to Sondeweere.

"Rope? The ship has no need of ropes."

"Then find *something*!" Toller turned towards the bridge in time to see a knot of Farlanders press across it.

Ilven Zavotle, fighting his own war against a private enemy, ran to meet them with a musket in his left hand and sword in his right. He fired the musket at point blank range through a Farlander's out-thrust belly and almost at once was lost in a flailing confusion of arms and swords. Toller sobbed aloud as he saw that his oldest friend, the patient eroder of problems, was being hacked to death.

Within seconds there came a fresh round of musket fire and this time, on the narrow front of the bridge, the effect on the Farlanders was considerable. They fell back, leaving their dead and convulsing wounded, but retreated no farther than the opposite bank, where one who seemed to be a commander began to harangue them in the staccato alien tongue. Facing them across the bloodied bridge, the three remaining Over-landers were feverishly recharging their guns.

Toller ran towards his companions, at the same time glancing back at the ship. Sondeweere was visible in the dark rectangle of the doorway, helplessly watching the fighting.

I'll be with you soon, he vowed inwardly, repulsing a new enemy, an enemy of the mind which could wreak even greater havoc than an external foe by implanting the idea that defeat was inevitable. Nearing the bridge from the side, he confirmed his first impression that it was simply an arrangement of thick timbers resting on a masonry shelf on each side of the moat.

"Berise," he shouted, "take the muskets and try to use all of them. Bartan and Dakan, help me with these boards!"

He knelt beside the bridge, got his hands under the nearest timber and used all the power of his back and thighs to stand up with it. Bartan and Wraker lent a hand, and together they turned the massive waterlogged timber and hurled it down into the moat. There was a shout from the Farlanders and a fresh surge on to the remaining five boards. Berise fired four muskets in rapid succession, during which time Toller and his helpers, working with panic-boosted strength, lifted and disposed of four more timbers, sending bodies—living and dead—down into the brown water. Toller did not look at the curious white-and-crimson thing which had been Zavotle.

He picked up his sword as desperate Farlanders streamed on to the last timber. Wraker, already facing them, caught the leading alien with a lateral blow to the neck which cart-wheeled him into the moat. Berise shot the next Farlander in the throat, propelling him back against the one behind. They both swayed and began to fall sideways, but in the instant of parting company with the bridge the uninjured one hurled his sword. The short heavy weapon flew with freakish accuracy and buried itself almost to the hilt in Wraker's stomach. He emitted a terrible bubbling belch, but stood his ground.

Toller pounced past him, dropping to his knees, and grasped the last timber. It was slimed with algae and the extra weight of the Farlanders moving on to it defeated even his vein-corded muscles. He was vaguely aware of another musket shot and of Bartan taking up a protective stance over him. He pushed the timber to one side, this time aided by its slippery surface, and got it almost off the shelf. Two Farlanders reached him as he was making the final effort which sent the timber tilting down and away, and he heard the impact of blows just above him as Bartan engaged the aliens. The tip of a sword sliced through Toller's right ear as he threw himself back and scrambled to his feet.

One of the Farlanders had disappeared with the timber, but

the other had leapt on to the paving and his arms were circling as he strove to regain his balance. Wraker, still on his feet in spite of being transfixed, disposed of him by driving the point of his sword into the alien's face, sending him backwards over the edge.

Bartan, looking pale and introspective, was standing close by, clutching a wound in his left shoulder. Blood was flowing copiously through his fingers. Berise was on her knees, her diminutive figure bowed over the muskets, fingers flying as she changed pressure spheres.

Toller looked beyond the milling group of Farlanders on the far side of the moat and saw a much greater force of them pouring through the gateway on the crater's rim. The action at the bridge had bought the defenders some time, but a miserly amount, a period which could conveniently be measured in seconds—and they were going to be at their most vulnerable while trying to enter the ship.

Toller turned his attention to Wraker, wondering if the soft-spoken young pilot understood that he was dying, that his history book would never be written. Bloodstains were spreading swiftly in his rain-soaked clothing, from around the protruding handle of the Farlander sword, and he was becoming unsteady on his feet, but he managed to speak clearly.

"Toller, why are you wasting valuable time?" he said. "Go while the going is good. I'm sorry I am unable to join you—but I have some unfinished business with our unprepossessing little friends."

He turned at once and sank to his knees at the edge of the moat, placing his sword in readiness on the masonry beside him. Berise stood up, carried three loaded and charged muskets to Wraker and laid them with his sword. He looked around as if to say something to her, his eyes seeking hers, but she had already retrieved the fourth musket and had run to Bartan. She pushed Bartan, rousing him from his bemused state, and they both ran towards the waiting ship.

Toller hesitated. He saw two Farlanders leap out from the other side of the moat, their short legs pedalling the air as they strove for maximum distance. Even if the aliens were inept swimmers they would soon be able to make use of the strewn timbers of the bridge to cross the water barrier—all the more reason to abandon Wraker, who was already doomed, and get on board the spacecraft. Still unable to shake off the feeling that he was betraying a comrade, Toller turned and ran to where Berise and Bartan were waiting for him below the huge, enigmatic sphere.

"There aren't any ropes," Sondeweere cried from the darkness of the doorway overhead. "What can you do?"

"As before," Toller replied. "I can lift Berise and Bartan."

"But what about *you*? How will you get in?"

Battle fever inflamed Toller's mind as he heard Wraker fire a musket. "Lower a sword belt—I'll be able to reach." He sheathed his sword and extended his hands to Berise. "Come!"

She shook her head. "Bartan is hurt and he needs help even to reach your shoulders. He must go first."

"Very well," Toller said, reaching for Bartan, who was swaying drunkenly. Bartan made as if to evade him, but there came the sound of another musket shot and Toller's forbearance deserted him. Growling with rage and frustration, he encircled Bartan's thighs with his arms and hoisted him upwards. Berise joined in, steadying Bartan and getting a shoulder beneath one of his feet, and from above Sondeweere lent her own strength to pull the protesting man over the rim of the doorway.

The entire operation had been completed in a few seconds, but in that sliver of time Toller had heard two more musket shots. He glanced towards the moat and saw that Wraker had his sword in hand and was chopping downwards at Farlanders who must have been threatening him from the angled timbers of the bridge. Toller's heartbeat became a series of dull internal explosions as he realised that his precious store of hard-won seconds was spilling away at a prodigious rate.

Berise had slung her musket on her back and was reaching out to him. He caught her by the waist and raised her to his shoulders in one movement. Even then she was not tall enough to reach the sill of the doorway, and she swayed precariously for a moment before Sondeweere and Bartan reached down, found her hands and drew her up into the ship.

During that moment Wraker was snatched out of sight, down to join Zavotle in the pit of death, and the white-gleaming heads of four Farlanders appeared above the moat's nearer edge. They threw weapons in front of them and began to squirm up on to the pavement. The slope beyond them was now massed with Farlander reinforcements, swarming like a field of brown insects.

Toller looked up into the mysterious interior of the ship, which now seemed as remote as the stars to which it was to carry him, and after a subjective lifetime saw Bartan's leather belt being reached to him. It had been re-buckled to form a loop, and the three inside the doorway each had a hand on it.

Two Farlanders, more agile than their fellows, were on their feet and running, swords at the ready.

Toller estimated the time left to him and knew he could expect only one chance to reach safety. Sondeweere's voice rang in his head: *Hurry, Toller, hurry!* He tensed himself—aware of the snorting approach of the Farlanders, hearing the slap of their feet—then sprang upwards and caught the belt with his right hand. The sudden manifestation of his weight on the belt was too much for those above, dragging them downwards and away from whatever purchase they had on the inside of the hull. Berise, lightest of the three, was pulled halfway through the opening and would have fallen had she not released the belt and grabbed the rim of the doorway.

Toller let go in the same instant.

He had his sword half-drawn when he hit the ground between the two Farlanders, but there was little he could do to compensate for the terrible disadvantage of his position. He turned the withdrawal of the weapon from its sheath into a cross-stroke which deflected a thrust from the alien in front, and at the same time leaped sideways to evade danger from behind—but he was slowed by his recovery from the drop.

The delay was only a fraction of a second, but it felt like an age in the fevered entropy of close combat. Toller grunted as the Farlander blade stabbed upwards into his lower back. He spun around, his sword singing in a horizontal sweep which caught his attacker on the side of the neck and all but decapitated him. The alien went down in pulsing gouts of crimson.

Toller continued his spin to face the other one, but the truncated warrior was backing away, knowing that time was on his side—at least ten of his fellows were racing across the paving stones and would be around Toller in the space of a few heartbeats. A smile of triumph appeared on the alien's fat-enfolded face, but almost at once it was transformed into an expression of blank astonishment as Berise—who was directly above him—fired a shot into the top of his head. He sat down abruptly in a vertical fountain of blood.

"Grab the musket, Toller!" Bartan shouted from the ship's entrance. "We can still bring you in!"

But Toller knew it was too late.

The bounding Farlanders were almost upon him, and even if he could be supported by the down-reaching musket his undefended body would be run through a dozen or more times while he tried to pull himself upwards. Experiencing a peculiar reticence, a desire to prevent his friends witnessing what had to come next, he retreated out of their sight towards the centre of the spherical hull.

But, although there was little pain from the wound in his back, his legs were weak and strangely difficult to control. He halted with the lowest point of the metal curvature almost brushing his head, and tried to make a final stand which would cost the enemy dearly, but his legs failed him and he went down under a concerted onslaught.

Sondeweere, he called as the grey light was blocked out by dripping brown forms and alien blades began to find their marks, *don't allow the pygmies to have the satisfaction. Please fly the ship . . . for me. . . .*

We love you, Toller, she said inside his head. *Goodbye.*

Unexpectedly, in the seconds remaining to him—before his body was sheared into atoms by a conflict of natural and artificial geometries—Toller achieved a final triumph.

He found he was genuinely sorry to die.

And there was gladness in the discovery.

The full measure of his humanity was restored to him by the

realisation that it was far worse for a man to live when he would rather die, than to die when he would rather live.

And there's another consolation, he thought as the ultimate deepnight closed around him. *Nobody could ever say mine had been a commonplace dea—*

Chapter 19

Bartan and Berise kept looking back over their shoulders as they walked, and they were almost two furlongs from the ship when it abruptly disappeared.

In one second it was there—a dull grey sphere perched on the crest of a low hill; and in the next second there was a complex of globes of radiance, expanding and contracting through each other. There was no sound, but even the foreday sun was dimmed in comparison to the fierce light which washed out of the spectacle. It rose vertically into the sky, gaining speed, changing shape. For a moment Bartan saw a four-pointed star with in-curved sides, each point emitting a spray of prismatic colour. There was a core which seethed with multi-hued specks of brilliance, but even as he was trying to focus his eyes on it the beautiful star was dwindling out of sight, swinging clear of the great disk of Land before finally vanishing into the blue.

The emotional turmoil within Bartan intensified into an ache which swamped the pain from his wounded shoulder. Less than an hour earlier he had been on rain-swept Farland, watching his friends die one by one—Zavotle, Wraker, and finally Toller Maraquine. Somehow, even in those last terrible seconds, Bartan had not expected the big man to die. He had seemed unkillable, an imperturbable giant destined to go on fighting his wars for ever. It was not until he had asked Sondeweere to take him with her into the bleakness of infinity—an unthinkable prospect which withered Bartan's soul—that he had realised Toller was more than just a gladiator. Now it was too late to get to know him, too late even to offer his thanks for the gift of life.

In addition to his grief over Toller, Bartan had been forced to accept that his wife could no longer be his wife, that she had become another kind of a giant, an intellectual colossus with whom he was unfit to share the man-woman relationship. He

knew that Sondeweere had not yet flown off into the galaxy
—she would spend some days guiding Tipp Gotlon safely home
—but in a way she was already more remote from him than the
faintest stars. His personal Gola had winked out of existence,
leaving him with no direction to his life.

"I don't think we need to walk any farther," Berise said. "It
looks as though we will have transport into the city."

Bartan shaded his eyes and looked towards Prad, the outskirts
of which were about two miles away. He was peering through a
shifting screen of after-images, but was able to discern dust
clouds being thrown up by wagons and riders on a winding road.
Some agricultural workers, no doubt drawn by the spectacle of
the symbonite ship, were approaching at a run through nearby
fields.

"I'm glad we have plenty of witnesses," Berise went on,
"otherwise the King would have difficulty in swallowing all we
have to report to him."

"Witnesses," Bartan said humbly. "Yes, witnesses."

Berise looked closely into his face. "I don't think you could go
much farther, anyway. You'd better sit down and let me check
that bandage."

"I'll be all right—I still have some of my excellent cure-all."
Bartan untied the skin of brandy from his belt and was pulling
out the stopper when he felt Berise's restraining hand on his
own.

"You don't really need that kind of medicine, do you?" she
said.

"What's it got to do with. . . ?" He paused, blinking
down into Berise's face, noting that her expression was one
of concern more than anger. "No, I don't actually *need* the
drink."

"Then throw it away."

"*What?*"

"Throw it away, Bartan."

It came to him that it had been a long time since anybody had shown concern about what he did, but it was with
some reluctance that he let the leather container fall to the
ground.

"Anyway, it was nearly empty," he muttered. "Why are you smiling?"

"For no reason." Berise's smile grew wider. "For no reason at all."

Here is an excerpt from Marching Through Georgia *by S.M. Stirling, published in May 1988 by Baen Books:*

MARCHING THROUGH

GEORGIA

S.M. STIRLING

ARCHONA TO OAKENWALD
PLANTATION OCTOBER, 1941

The airdrop on Sicily had earned Eric von Shraken-burg a number of things: a long scar on one thigh, certain memories, and a field-promotion to Centuri-on's rank. When the 1st Airborne Chiliarchy was pulled back into reserve after the fall of Milan, the promotion was confirmed; a rare honor for a man barely twenty-four. With it came fourteen-day leave passes to run from October 1st, 1941, and unlike most of his comrades, he had not disappeared into the pleasure quarter of Alexandria. The new move-ment orders had already been cut: Draka Forces Base Mosul, Province of Mesopotamia. Paratroopers were cutting-edge assault troops; obviously, the High Command did not expect the *de facto* truce with Hitler to last. And that would be a more serious matter than overrunning an Italy taken by surprise and abandoned by its Axis allies. It was well for a man to visit the earth that bore him before he died. He would spend his leave in Oakenwald, the von Shrakenberg plantation, now that the quarrel with his father had been patched up. After a fashion.

Travel space was scarce, as mobilization built toward its climax, but even in the Draka army it helped to be the son of an *Arch-Strategos*, a staff general. A place was found on a transport-dirigible heading south with a priority cargo of machine-parts; two days nonstop to the high plateau of southern Africa. He spent the last half-hour in the control gallery, for the view; they were coming in to Archona from the north, and it was a side of the capital free citizens seldom saw, unless business took them there. For a citizen, Archona was the marble-and-tile public buildings and low-rise office blocks, parks and broad avenues, the University campus, and pleasant, leafy suburbs with the gardens for which the city was famed.

Beyond the basin that held the freemen's city lay the world of the industrial combines, hectare upon hectare, eating ever deeper into the bush country of the middleveld. A spiderweb of roads, rail-sidings, monorails, landing platforms for freight airships. The sky was falling into night, but there was no sleep below, only an unrestfulness full of the light of arc-lamps and the bellowing flares of the blast furnaces; factory-windows carpeted the low hills, shifts working round the clock. Only the serf-compounds were dark, the flesh-and-blood robots of the State exhausted on their pallets, a brief escape from a lockstep existence spent in that wilderness of metal and concrete.

Eric watched it with a fascination tinged with horror as the crew guided the great bulk of the lighter-than-air ship in, until light-spots danced before his eyes. And remembered.

In the center of Archona, where the Avenue of Triumph met the Way of the Armies, there was a square with a victory monument. A hundred summers had turned the bronze green and faded the marble plinth. About it were gardens of unearthly loveliness, where children played between the flower-banks. The statue showed a group of Draka soldiers on horseback; their weapons were the Ferguson rifle-muskets and double-barreled dragoon pistols of the eighteenth century. Their leader stood dismounted, reins in one hand, bush-knife in the other. A black warrior knelt before him, and the Draka's boot rested on the man's neck.

Below, in letters of gold, were words: *To the Victors*. That was *their* monument; northern Archona was a monument to the vanquished, and so were the other industrial cities that stretched north a thousand kilometers to Katanga; so were mines and plantations and ranches from the Cape to Shensi.

Eric slept the night in transit quarters; he got the bed, but there were two other officers on the floor, for lack of space. He would not have minded that, or even their insistence on making love, if the sexual athletics had not been so noisy . . . In the morning the transport clerk was apologetic; also harried. Private autocars were up on blocks for the duration, mostly; in the end, all she could offer was a van taking two Janissaries south to pick up recruits from the plantations. Eric shrugged indifferently, to the clerk's surprise. The city-bred might be prickly in their insistence on the privileges of the master caste, but a von Shrakenberg was raised to ignore such trivia. Also . . . he remembered the rows of Janissary dead outside Palermo, where they had broken the enemy lines to relieve the encircled paratroops.

The roadvan turned out to be a big, six-wheeled Kellerman steamer twenty years old, a round-edged metal box with running boards chest-high and wheels taller than he. It had been requisitioned from the Transportation Directorate, and still had eyebolts in the floor for the leg shackles of the work gangs. The Janissaries rose from their kitbags as Eric approached, flicking away cigarettes and giving him a respectful but unservile salute; the driver in her grimy coverall of unbleached cotton bowed low, hands before eyes.

"Carry on," Eric said, returning the salute. The serf soldiers were big men, as tall as he, their snug

uniforms of dove-grey and silver making his plain
Citizen Force walking-out blacks seem almost drab.
Both were in their late thirties and Master Sergeants, the highest rank subject-race personnel could
aspire to. They were much alike—hard-faced and
thick-muscled; unarmed, here within the Police Zone,
but carrying steel-tipped swagger sticks in white-
gloved hands. One was ebony black, the other green-
eyed and tanned olive, and might have passed for a
freeman save for the shaven skull and serf identity-
number tattooed on his neck.

The Draka climbed the short, fixed ladder and
swung into the seat beside the driver. While the
woman fired the van's boiler, he propped his Priority
pass inside the slanted windscreen that ran to their
knees; that ought to save them delay at the inevitable Security Directorate roadblocks. The vehicle pulled
out of the loading bay with the smooth silence of
steam power, into the crowded streets; he brought
out a book of poetry, Rimbaud, and lost himself in
the fire-bright imagery.

When he looked up in midmorning they were
south of the city. Crossing the Whiteridge and the
scatter of mining and manufacturing settlements along
it, past the huge, man-made heaps of spoilage from
the gold mines. Some were still rawly yellow with
the cyanide compounds used to extract the precious
metal; others were in every stage of reclamation,
down to forested mounds that might have been natural. This ground had yielded more gold in its century
and a half than all the rest of the earth in all the
years of humankind; four thousand meters beneath
the road, men still clawed at rock hot enough to raise
blisters on naked skin. Then they were past, into the
farmlands of the high plateau.

He rolled down the window, breathing deeply.
The Draka took pains to keep industry from fouling
the air or water too badly; masters had to breathe
and drink too, after all. Still, it was a relief to smell
the goddess breath of spring overtaking the carrion

stink of industrial-age war. The four-lane asphalt surface of the road stretched dead straight to meet the horizon that lay around them like a bowl; waist-high fields of young corn flicked by, each giving an instant's glimpse down long, leafy tunnels floored with brown, plowed earth. Air that smelled of dust and heat and green poured in, and the sea of corn shimmered as the leaves rippled.

They spent noon at a roadside waystation that was glad to see him; Eric was not surprised, remembering how sparse passenger traffic had been. Most of the vehicles had been *drags*—heavy haulers pulling articulated cargo trucks—or plantation vans heading to the rail stations with produce; once there had been a long convoy of wheeled personnel carriers taking Janissary infantry toward the training camps in the mountains to the east. He strolled, stretching his legs and idly watching the herds of cattle and eland grazing in the fields about; listened to the silence and the rustling of leaves in the eucalyptus trees that framed the low pleasant buildings of colored brick with their round stained-glass windows; sat in the empty courtyard and ate a satisfying luncheon of fried grits, sausage and eggs—not forgetting to have food and beer sent out to the van . . .

The manager had time on her hands, and was inclined to be maternal. It was not until he had sat and listened politely to her rambling description of a son and daughter who were with the 5th Armored in Tashkent that he suspected that he was procrastinating; his own mother had died only a few years after his birth, and he did not generally tolerate attempts at coddling. Not until he found himself seriously considering her offer of an hour upstairs with the pretty but bedraggled serving-wench was he sure of it. He excused himself, looked in the back window of the van, saw that one of the Janissary NCO's had the driver bent over a bench and was preparing to mount. Eric rapped on the glass with impatient disgust, and the soldier released her to scurry, whimpering, back to the driver's seat, zipping her overall with shaking fingers.

It would be no easier to meet his father again if he delayed arrival until nightfall. Restlessly, he reopened the book; anticpation warred with . . . yes, fear: he had been afraid at that last interview with his father. Karl von Shrakenberg was not a man to be taken lightly.

The quiet sobbing of the driver as she wrestled with the wheel cut across his thoughts. Irritated, he found a handkerchief and handed it across to her, then pulled the peaked cap down over his eyes and turned a shoulder as he settled back and pretended to sleep. *Useless gesture*, he thought with self-contempt. A serf without a protector was a victim, and there were five hundred million more like this one. The system ground on, they were the meat, and the fact that he was tied on top of the machine did not mean he could remake it. And there were worse places than this—much worse: in a mine, or the newly taken Italian territories he had helped to conquer, to the drumroll beat of the Security Directorate's execution squads, liquidation rosters, destructive-labor camps.

Shut up, he thought. *Shut up, wench, I've troubles of my own!*

It was still light when they turned in under the tall stone arch of the gates, the six wheels of the Kellerman crunching on the smooth, crushed rock, beneath the sign that read: "Oakenwald Plantation, est. 1788. K. von Shrakenberg, Landholder." But the sun was sinking behind them. Ahead, the jagged crags of the Maluti Mountains were outlined in the Prussian blue of shadow and sandstone gold. This valley was higher than the plateau plains west of the Caledon River; rocky, flat-topped hills reared out of the rolling fields. The narrow plantation road was lined with oaks, huge branches meeting twenty meters over their heads; the lower slopes of the hills were planted to the king-trees as well.

Beyond were the hedged fields, divided by rows of Lombardy poplar: wheat and barley still green with a hint of gold as they began to head out, contour-ploughed cornfields, pastures dotted with white-fleeced sheep, spring lambs, horses, yellow-coated cattle. The fieldworkers were heading in, hoes and tools slanted over their shoulders, mules hanging their heads as they wearily trudged back toward the stables. A few paused to look up in curiosity as the vehicle passed; Eric could hear the low, rhythmic song of a work team as they walked homeward, a sad sweet memory from childhood.

Despite himself he smiled, glancing about. It had been, by the White Christ and almighty Thor, two years now since his last visit. "You can't go home again," he said softly to himself. "The problem is, you can't ever really leave it, either." Memory turned in on itself, and the past colored the present; he could remember his first pony, and his father's hands lifting him into the saddle, how his fingers smelled of tobacco and leather and strong soap. And the first time he had been invited into his father's study to talk with the adults after a dinner party. Ruefully, he smiled as he remembered holding the brandy snifter in an authoritative pose anyone but himself must have recognized as copied from Pa's . . . And yet it was all tinged with sorrow and anger; impossible to forget, hurtful to remember, a turning and itching in his mind.

He looked downslope; beyond that screen of pines was a stock dam where the children of the house had gone swimming sometimes, gods alone knew why, except that they were *supposed* to use the pool up by the manor. There, one memorable day, he had knocked Frikkie Thyssen flat for sneering at his poetry. The memory brought a grin; it had been the sort of epic you'd expect a twelve-year-old in love with Chapman's Homer to do, but that little bastard

Thyssen wouldn't have known if it had been a work of genius . . . And over there in the cherry orchard he had lost his virginity under a harvest moon one week after his thirteenth birthday, to a giggling field wench twice his age and weight . . .

And then there had been Tyansha, the Circassian girl. Pa had given her to him on his fourteenth birthday. The dealer had called her something more pronounceable, but that was the name she had taught him, along with her mother tongue. She had been . . . perhaps four years older than he; nobody had been keeping records in eastern Turkey during those years of blood and chaos. There were vague memories of a father, she had said, and a veiled woman who held her close, then lay in a ditch by a burning house and did not move. Then the bayonets of the Janissaries were herding her and a mob of terrified children into trucks. Thirst, darkness, hunger; then the training creche. Learning reading and writing, the soft blurred Draka dialect of English; household duties, dancing, the arts of pleasing. Friends, who vanished one by one into the world beyond the walls. And him.

Her eyes had been what he had noticed first— huge, a deep pale blue, like a wild thing seen in the forest. Dark-red hair falling to her waist, past a smooth, pale, high-cheeked face. She had worn a silver-link collar that emphasized the slender neck and the serf-number tattooed on it, and a wrapped white sheath-dress to show off her long legs and high, small breasts. Hands linked before her, she had stood between his smiling father and the impassive dealer, who slapped her riding-crop against one boot, anxious to be gone.

"Well, boy, does she please?" Pa had asked. Eric remembered a wordless stutter until his voice broke humiliatingly in a squeak; his elder brother John had roared laughter and slapped him on the back, urging him forward as he led her from the room by the hand. Hers had been small and cool; his own hands

and feet felt enormous, clumsy; he was hideously aware of a pimple beside his nose.

She had been afraid—not showing it much, but he could tell. He had not touched her; not then, or in the month that followed. Not even at the first shyly beautiful smile . . .

Gods, but I was callow, Eric thought in sadly affectionate embarrassment. They had talked; rather, he had, while she replied in tense, polite monosyllables, until she began to shed the fear. He had showed her things—his battle prints, his butterfly collection—that had disgusted her—and the secret place in the pine grove, where he came to dream the vast vague glories of youth . . . A month, before she crept in beside him one night. A friend, one of the overseer's sons, had asked casually to borrow her; he had beaten the older boy bloody. Not wildly, in the manner of puppy fights, but with the *pankration* disciplines, in a cold ferocity that ended only when he was pulled off.

There had been little constraint between them, in private. She even came to use his first name without the "master," eventually. He had allowed her his books, and she had devoured them with a hunger that astonished him; so did her questions, sometimes disconcertingly sharp. Making love with a lover was . . . different. Better; she had been more knowledgeable than he, if less experienced, and they had learned together. Once in a haystack, he remembered; prickly, it had made him sneeze. Afterward they had lain holding hands, and he had shown her the southern sky's constellations.

She died in childbirth three years later, bearing his daughter. The child had lived, but that was small consolation. That had been the last time he wept in public; the first time since his mother had died when he was ten. And it had also been the last time his father had beaten him; for weakness. Casual fornication aside, it was well enough for a boy to have a serf-girl of his own. Even for him to care for her, since it helped keep him from the temptations that all-male boarding schools were prone to. But the public tears allowable for blood-kin were unseemly for a concubine.

Eric had caught the thong of the riding crop in one hand and jerked it free. *"Hit me again, and I'll kill you,"* he had said, in a tone flat as gunmetal. Had seen his father's face change as the scales of parental blindness fell away, and the elder von Shrakenberg realized that he was facing a very dangerous man, not a boy. And that it is not well to taunt an unbearable grief.

He shook his head and looked out again at the familiar fields; it was a sadness in itself, that time healed. Grief faded into nostalgia, and it was a sickness to try and hold it. That mood stayed with him as they swung into the steep drive and through the gardens below Oakenwald's Great House. The manor had been built into the slope of a hill—for defense, in the early days—and it still gave a memorable view. The rocky slope had been terraced for lawns, flowerbanks, ornamental trees and fountains; forest grew over the steepening slope behind, and then a great table of rock reared two hundred meters into the darkening sky.

The manor itself was ashlar blocks of honey-colored local sandstone, a central three-story block fronted with white marble columns and topped with a low-pitched roof of rose tile; there were lower wings to each side—arched colonnades supporting second-story balconies. There was a crowd waiting beneath the pillars, and a parked grey-painted staff car with a *strategos'* red-and-black checkerboard pennant fixed to one bumper; the tall figure of his father stood amidst the household, leaning on his cane. Eric took a deep breath and opened the door of the van, pitching his baggage to the ground and jumping down to the surface of the drive.

Air washed over him cool and clean, smelling of roses and falling water, dusty crushed rock and hot metal from the van; bread was baking somewhere, and there was woodsmoke from the chimneys. The globe lights came on over the main doors, and he saw who awaited: his father, of course; his younger sister Johanna in undress uniform; the overseers, and some of the house servants behind . . .

He waved, then turned back to the van for a moment, pulling a half-empty bottle out of his kit and leaning in for a parting salute to the Janissaries.

They looked up, and their faces lit with surprised gratitude as he tossed the long-necked glass bulb; it was Oakenwald Kijaffa, cherry brandy in the same sense that Dom Perignon was sparkling wine, and beyond the pockets of most freemen.

"T'anks be to yaz, Centurion, sar," the black said, his teeth shining white. "Sergeants Miller and Assad at yar s'rvice, sar."

"For Palermo," he said, and turned his head to the driver. She raised a face streaked with the tracks of dried tears from where it had rested on the wheel, glancing back apprehensively at the soldiers. "Back, and take the turning to the left, half a kilometer to the Quarters. Ask for the headman; he'll put you all up."

A young houseboy had run forward to take Eric's baggage; he craned his head to see into the long cabin of the van after making his bow, his face an O of surprise at the bright Janissary uniforms. And he kept glancing back as he bore the valise and bag away. Eric paused to take a few parcels out of it, reflecting that they probably had another volunteer there. Then he was striding up the broad black-stone steps, the hard soles of his high boots clattering. The servants bowed like a rippling field, and there were genuine smiles of welcome. Eric had always been popular with the staff, as such things went.

He clicked heels and saluted. His father returned it, and they stood for a wordless moment eye to eye; they were of a height. Alike in color and cast of face as well; the resemblance was stronger now that pain had graven lines in the younger man's face to match his sire's.

"Recovered from your wound, I see." The strategos paused, searching for words. "I read the report. You were a credit to the service and the family, Eric."

"Thank you, sir," he replied neutrally, fighting down an irrational surge of anger. *I didn't want the Academy,* a part of him thought savagely. *The first von Shrakenberg in seven generations not to, and a would-be artist to boot. Does that make me an incompetent, or a coward?*

And that was unjust. Pa had not really been surprised that he had the makings of a good officer; he had too much confidence in the von Shrakenberg blood for that. *What was it that makes me draw back?* he thought. Alone, he could wish so strongly to be at peace with his father again. Those grey eyes, more accustomed to cold mastery, shared his own baffled hurt; he could see it. But together . . . they fought, or coexisted with an icy politeness that was worse.

Or *usually* worse. Two years ago he had sent Tyansha's daughter out of the country. To America, where there was a Quaker group that specialized in helping the tiny trickle of escaped serfs who managed to flee; they must have been surprised to receive a tow-haired girlchild from an aristocrat of the Domination, together with an annuity to pay for her upkeep and education. Not that he had been fond of the girl; he had handed her to the women of the servant's quarters, and as she grew her looks were an intolerable reminder. But she was Tyansha's . . . It had required a good deal of money, and several illegalities.

To Arch-Strategos Karl von Shrakenberg, that had been a matter touching on honor, and on the interests of the Race and the nation. His father had threatened to abandon him to the Security Directorate; that could have meant a one-way trip to a cold cellar with instruments of metal, a trip that ended with a pistol-bullet in the back of the head. Eric suspected that if his brother John had still been alive to carry on the family name, it might have come to that. As it was, he had been forbidden the house, until service in Italy had changed the general's mind.

I saved my daugh . . . a little girl, he thought. *For that, I was a criminal and will always be watched. But by helping to destroy a city and killing hundreds who've never done me harm, I'm a hero and all is forgiven.* Tyansha had once told him that she had given up expecting sense from the world long ago; more and more, he saw her point.

He forced his mind back to the older man's words. "And the Janissaries won't have any problems in the Quarters?"

"Not unless someone's foolish enough to provoke them. They're Master Sergeants, steady types; the Headman will find them beds and a couple of willing girls."

There was another awkward pause, and the strategos turned to go. "Well. I'll see you when we dine, then."

Johanna had been waiting impatiently, but in this household the proprieties were observed. As Eric turned to face her she straightened and threw a crackling salute, then winked broadly and pointed her thumb upward at the collar of her uniform jacket.

He returned the salute and followed her digit. "Well, well! *Pilot Officer* Johanna von Shrakenberg, now!" He spread his arms and she gave him a swift fierce hug. She was four years younger than he; on her the bony family looks and the regulations that cropped her fair hair close produced an effect halfway between elegance and adolescent homeliness.

"That was quick—fighters? And what's this I hear about Tom? You two are still an 'item'?" With a stage magician's gesture he produced a flat package.

"They're turning us out quick, these days—cutting out nonessentials like sleep. Yes, fighters: Eagles, interceptors." The wrapping crumpled under strong, tanned fingers. "And no, Tom and I aren't an item; we're *engaged*." She paused to roll her eyes. "Wouldn't you know it, guess where his lochos's been sent? *Xian!* Shensi, to watch the Japanese!"

The package opened. Within were twin eardrops, cabochon-cut rubies the size of a thumbnail, set in chased silver. Johanna whistled and held them up to the light as Eric shook hands with the overseers, inquired after their children in the Forces, handed out minor gifts among the house servants and hugged old Nanny Sukie, the family child-nurse. Arms linked, Eric and Johanna strolled into the house.

"Loot?" she inquired, holding up the jewels. "Sort of Draka-looking . . ."

"*Made* from loot," he said affectionately. It was a rare Draka who doubted the morality of conquest. To deny that the property of the vanquished was proper booty would go beyond eccentricity to madness. "You think I'm buying rubies like that on a Centurion's pay? They're from an Italian bishop's crozier—he won't be needing it in the labor camp, after all." The man had smiled under the gun muzzles, actually, and signed a cross in the air as they prodded him away. Eric pushed the memory aside. "I had the setting done up in Alexandria . . .

To order any Baen Book by mail, send the cover price to: Baen Books, Dept. BB, 260 Fifth Avenue, New York, N.Y. 10001.

A CHOICE OF DESTINIES: "Melissa Scott [is] one of science fiction's most talented newcomers. . . . The greatest delight of all is finding out how she managed to write a historical novel that could legitimately have spaceships on the cover . . . a marvelous gift for any fan."—*Baltimore Sun*   65563-9 • 320 pp. • $2.95

THE GAME BEYOND: "An exciting interstellar empire novel with a great deal of political intrigue and colorful interplanetary travel."—*Locus*

55918-4 • 352 pp. • $2.95

MAGIC AND *COMPUTERS* DON'T MIX!

RICK COOK

Or . . . do they? That's what Walter "Wiz" Zumwalt is wondering. Just a short time ago, he was a master hacker in a Silicon Valley office, a very ordinary fellow in a very mundane world. But magic spells, it seems, are a lot like computer programs: they're both formulas, recipes for getting things done. Unfortunately, just like those computer programs, they can be full of bugs. Now, thanks to a *particularly* buggy spell, Wiz has been transported to a world of magic—and incredible peril. The wizard who summoned him is dead, Wiz has fallen for a red-headed witch who despises him, and no one—not the elves, not the dwarves, not even the dragons—can figure out why he's here, or what to do with him. Worse· the sorcerers of the deadly Black League, rulers of an entire continent, want Wiz dead—and he doesn't even know why! Wiz had better figure out the rules of this strange new world—and fast—or he's not going to live to see Silicon Valley again.

Here's a refreshing tale from an exciting new writer. It's also a rarity: a well drawn fantasy told with all the rigorous logic of hard science fiction.

February 1989 • 69803-6 • 320 pages • $3.50

Available at bookstores everywhere, or you can send the cover price to Baen Books, Dept. WZ, 260 Fifth Ave., New York, NY 10001